C000246752

THE R
CALLER

BY RICHARD LAWS

First published 2021 by Five Furlongs

© Richard Laws 2021
ISBN 978-1-9164600-7-2 (Paperback)

Cover photography © Sarah Shears

My sincere thanks for their help and advice:
Sarah Shears, Patricia Grant, Linda Cronk, Claire Dickens, Bob Ledger, and Mike Dunn.

One

'Anything *said* in this room, *stays* in this room,' the consultant stated. This undue emphasis was further strengthened when he fixed his client with an earnest stare.

He had built his reputation, and therefore his ability to charge exorbitant fees, by specializing in the treatment of business executives and other high achievers. The man sitting nervously on the other side of the consultant's desk fitted this profile, but was of special interest for other, even more lucrative reasons.

The consultant produced a well-practised, carefully crafted empathetic expression, ensuring there was no suggestion of pity - and it did the trick. His potential new client gave him a faint smile in return.

'I don't know whether I have that much to say,' shrugged the man, turning his head to regard the cityscape scene afforded by the huge floor to ceiling window dominating one side of the seventh floor consulting room.

The consultant remained silent, his gentle gaze not leaving the man. Presently his client started to speak, just as he had intended. When, twenty minutes later, the man had run out of words, the consultant placed his pen and pad to one side, pursed his lips and decided he could risk cutting to the bone.

'Do you feel anger toward those you hold responsible?'

'Yes.'

'Would you ever act upon these… violent urges?'

The man eyed the consultant pensively before breaking off to stare through the window once more. He finally ceased scanning the city rooftops and met the consultant's gaze, holding his attention with a ferocity that the consultant found… promising.

He's trying to determine whether he can trust me, thought the consultant, but after allowing the silence to linger a few more seconds, realised he was losing him. Curling his top lip into a grimace, the man had started to push himself up from his seat. The consultant held up both palms.

'Believe me, it will get easier… with my help.'

The soles of the man's highly polished shoes met the carpet and he stood, muttered an excuse, and strode toward the door.

'Will I see you again?' the consultant called after him, careful not to sound overly concerned.

The man took two more steps, slowed, finally coming to a halt. He spun around and found the consultant standing facing him.

'I need to... I have to rid myself of this horrible, debilitating sense of...'

The man's voice trailed off, and the consultant took a gamble. 'Betrayal?'

The man's eyes had been darting around the carpet. Now he cocked his head and studied the consultant.

'You believe you can... ?'

He wanted to say, 'Help me?' but the words seemed to stick in his throat. They were too bland, too weak.

'It takes work... but yes, I can.'

The man stared at the consultant for a moment, making a fist and unconsciously grinding his fingers into his palm as he silently debated whether to believe him. Sucking in a lungful of air through his nose and blowing it out over his teeth, he spun around and placed his hand on the doorknob.

'My secretary will be in touch,' the consultant called after him, as the man took a step into the waiting room.

The man half turned and muttered a positive reply that made the consultant's eyes sparkle.

A minute later the consultant's new client had descended the numerous flights of stairs, preferring to avoid the lift. He stepped onto the pavement, paused to breathe in the London street air, and was soon dodging around clumps of evening shoppers.

There was a crooked smile on the consultant's lips as he watched his client head for the nearest underground station. Leaving the window, he allowed his smile to grow as he tapped his phone, held it to his ear, and waited for his call to connect.

Without preamble he stated, 'This is the call you've been waiting for. I've found a candidate for you. In fact, he's perfect... and you won't believe what he does for a living.'

There was a short pause during which the consultant cast his eye over the group of nine framed certificates hanging on the wall behind his desk. Each glassy oblong had his name displayed boldly on the certificate within.

'Are you sure?'

'I'm positive. He's a compulsive obsessive with violent tendencies.'

Again, the line fell silent for a few seconds. The consultant

3

waited.

'When do I introduce my man?' asked the voice.

'Give me a month and I'll have him ready for you.'

There were no pleasantries. The phone went dead. The consultant dropped his phone into his pocket and stepped forward to straighten one of his certificates. He smirked at the irony. The frame he was adjusting held his accreditation to practise with victims of gambling addiction.

By the time he'd stepped back to ensure his group of achievements was aesthetically pleasing to him once more, he was grinning. He'd hit the jackpot. He'd found someone who really, truly, hated Michael Gray.

Two

EIGHTEEN MONTHS LATER

First to rise to his feet and point a questioning finger upwards was a twelve-year-old boy. He peered beyond the white plastic railings in front of him, over the racetrack and gazed higher and higher, up into the three-tiered grandstand on the opposite side of the racecourse. It was rapidly filling with race-goers ahead of the fifth race on the card, but it wasn't the crowd which aroused his curiosity, or the huge letters announcing 'Ripon Races – Yorkshire's Garden Racecourse' emblazoned upon the bottom tier. Instead, he was drawn to the woman. He was fascinated by her unsmiling face and how it hung ghostlike in the small window at the summit of the grandstand.

The boy screwed his face up against the sun. It had been beating down relentlessly on this cloudless July Saturday afternoon and so he shaded his freckled nose with a small left palm. The window was definitely open and the lady seemed to be assessing the roof of the grandstand, first looking down at the pitched tiles, then all around her, hands gripping both sides of the window frame. She dipped back inside again, the window becoming an inky black square once more, but the boy waited, idly wondering how *he* could get to look out of the highest window on the racecourse, just like the lady. But then she was back, sitting on the window ledge pulling a rucksack over her shoulders. Then, without warning she grasped the top corners of the window and catapulted her feet, legs and thighs out of the black void. A set of dark stockings splayed ungainly onto the grey roof tiles.

She stayed there for a few seconds, seated on the window ledge, holding onto the frame. She tried to flatten her feet to the angle of the roof, as if contemplating whether to stand up. Her feet didn't reach more than a quarter of the way to the bottom row of tiles and for a moment she scrabbled around, trying to determine whether the tiles could take her weight.

Tugging on the trouser pocket of the man standing beside him and still watching the lady, the boy called out, 'Dad. There's a lady on the roof.'

The man continued to examine a folded copy of The Racing Post intently and mumbled a placatory, 'Mmm... yes.'

Frowning at his father, the boy's hands went back to shading his eyes and he squinted skywards again. With more urgency and discontent in his eyes, he looked up at his father and pointed again to the top tier of the grandstand. 'Dad!' he insisted.

'Not now, son,' replied his father softly, checking his wristwatch, 'The race is about to start. In fact, it should have been off by now.'

The boy's father looked up from his newspaper and cast a glance to his left, straight down the undulating green racetrack to the five furlong start. He sighed, unable to determine whether the runners were loaded into the starting stalls or not.

'The course commentary should have started by now,' he told his son with mild irritation, screwing his head over his shoulder to glimpse the huge public video screen behind them. He grumpily noted the last racehorse of the twelve runners being led into its starting stall.

'The commentator can't be concentrating,' he muttered, and looked down to where the boy stood. Then he followed the direction of his son's raised arm and pointed finger, gasping as a woman in a white blouse and knee-length skirt thrust herself out of a window one-hundred and twenty feet above the ground. She slid uncontrollably on her back, hands slapping and heeled shoes scraping, down fifteen feet of sharply inclined tiles, coming to an uneasy stop halfway down the grandstand roof.

One by one, racegoers on the inside of the racecourse took note of the drama being played out on the roof of the grandstand. Hands shaded eyes, then went to mouths, and soon there was a forest of fingers pointing upwards from the centre of the racecourse. In the grandstand enclosure, race watchers situated close to the racetrack rails were now looking back toward the stands and upwards. Some shouted, others covered their eyes and looked away. A few started to film the scene with their mobile phones. The figure was about to stand up, on the very edge of the roof.

People started to leave the stands. The grassed area near the rails, along with the concreted bookmaker area quickly became over-run with people shoulder to shoulder, gawping up at the figure on the tiles. Curious course officials joined the crowd and immediately started to whisper agitatedly into walkie-talkies. Boorish men with pint glasses gripped in tight young fists flooded out of the bars beneath the stands, a few shouting drunkenly at the woman. She could be seen clearly now: a smartly dressed young lady with a fixed, determined look on her face. A slurred, drink-fuelled shout of 'Jump!' went up from one of the melee of newcomers and was greeted with a cacophony of angry rebukes from all corners of the racecourse.

Down at the five furlong start the last racehorse was installed and a shout of 'Jockeys!' went up from the starter. The stalls clanged opened and twelve three-year-old thoroughbreds with a dozen brightly coloured riders urging their mounts forward, jumped from their berths and jostled for a tactically superior position. The horses accelerated up to an evenly paced gallop and the field edged over towards the rail closest to the stands side, settling into a tightly packed unit.

The lady on the roof moved crab-like, inching sideways, each movement gambling with her continued connection with each grey, lichen encrusted roof tile. Beneath her, a further six rows of tiles separated her from the guttering and over a hundred foot plunge to the concrete concourse below. The figure seemed oblivious to the people massing below her. She stared fixedly to her right-hand-side and what appeared to be her objective, the nearest hip of the roof, five yards away.

Without commentary, the sound of approaching hooves prompted a few race-goers to switch their attention to the large public television screen in the middle of the course, unaware of the young lady's rooftop antics. They saw four young handicappers hit the two furlong pole together and, with whips raised, the riders entered the last four hundred yards of their race with little to split them.

The lady on the roof had the crowd in her thrall, but was still oblivious to the drama she was providing. She continued her sideways crawl. Her right foot slipped and she dropped half a foot suddenly. Three-thousand watchers below took an intake of breath in unison. The lady looked down, for the first time appreciating the spectacle she was creating. She was motionless, knees bent, feet and back flat to the roof, fingers wide on tiles that were warm to her touch.

The crowd gasped again when the lady suddenly jerked her head up and to the right. A man's head, bald and forehead creased, emerged from the black oblong of the window, turned sharply towards her, and said something which couldn't be heard. He looked beyond the woman, took in the crowd, and quickly recoiled into the blackness.

The lady immediately started to move, quicker, more urgent than before. She was definitely heading for the edge of the roof. Pushing upwards with her hands, the lady precariously rose to her feet, though still crouching, and started to make significantly faster progress across the tiles.

It only took two steps for her to falter. Her left foot slipped, she tried to compensate and lost grip. The crowds below saw a crack of light appear beneath her foot and she fell with an audible crunch onto the roof. Scrabbling unsuccessfully to find a hold, the lady gathered speed, rolling onto her side, fingers unable to grip, as she reached the guttering which marked the edge of the precipice. People rushed from the potential impact zone, screams, fretful hands covered eyes, and children were commanded to turn away.

When her left foot hit the fifty-year-old cast-iron guttering it wrenched away from its fixings and shattered, sending foot-long shards of rusty old metal, dirt and moss raining down on the bottom steps of the grandstand below. But her right foot found a solid hold, deep in the semi-circular cut out. The woman squirmed, her left leg waving out over the sheer drop, eliciting another horrified gasp from her audience below. She leaned back now, the side of her body touching the tiles once more, then retrieved her left leg, hooking it back up and into the gutter. She shot a look up to the window again and then peered down at the crowd, her face once again determined. With one foot in the gutter and the other knee on the tiles she rose to a kneeling position then crawled along the iron frame towards the corner of the roof.

A line of four horses reached the furlong pole, jockeys thrusting their hands into the necks of their mounts, asking for the extra effort which would mean the difference between winning or losing. The squawk of the commentary would now reach them, and the tension in the crowd would burst forth in shouts of encouragement. But this time there was no sound from the stands, no reverberation of an excited voice over the public address system.

Several thousand watchers shaded their eyes and wiped sweat from their foreheads as the female figure edged closer to the corner of the grandstand. Eyes widened as the lady reached her goal then slowly, balancing with arms held wide, she rose uncertainly to a standing position. Wiping the blackness from her hands down the sides of her oatmeal skirt and sucking in three deep breaths, she took one last glance to her left, at the upturned faces and the dozen horses and riders racing towards the finishing post. She offered the crowd below a quick, tight smile… and jumped off the side of the grandstand.

Three

Converting to a sand-based All-Weather surface meant Newcastle racecourse increased its number of race meetings, which was absolutely fine as far as Joe Lawlor was concerned. Living on the North-East coast made working at Gosforth Park a relatively easy day for him, and this Saturday afternoon had worked out to be easier than most, with a small, racing-savvy weekend crowd, fine weather and all the races going off on time. There had also been a few competitive heats which had given him the opportunity to enlarge the excitement in his commentaries and stir the racing public's enthusiasm, probably the greatest enjoyment he got from his day's work.

Seated in his commentary position at the highest point in the stands, Joe took a sip from his can of Vimto and contemplated the eight runners in the last race on the card. Straddled around his neck were a pair of headphones with a moveable mouthpiece, and binoculars lay on the table in front of him, the essential tools of his trade. A laptop was open close by, unused at present, a racecard lying across the keyboard and beside it a mobile phone switched to silent mode. These three items were superfluous to requirements. As Joe would explain to those who showed an interest, as long as he had the ability to see and speak, he was golden. His memory took care of the rest.

Joe leaned back in the hard wooden chair supplied by the racecourse and adjusted his cushion, a constant companion that travelled to every racecourse with him. Most of the racecourses in the North of England were over a century old, and some of the viewing boxes for race-callers were equally antiquated. He sat upright, almost rigid, ensuring both his feet were flat to the floor, and his back supported. Comfort, and a lack of distractions was paramount when you were commentating on a race. There were other considerations of course: in winter you must deal with the cold, in summer the heat, but a comfortable seat for the duration of the race meeting was the top priority.

The commentary itself was Joe's primary concern; the tenor of his voice at each stage of the contest, his reaction to events before, during, and after the runners had passed the winning post. Those few, well chosen words that could communicate where the action was coming from, and how the race was changing, elevated his job from a simple monologue of linear happenings, into an art-form.

Joe, much to the chagrin of almost everyone around him, had dissected the many attributes of race calling, through forensic analysis of each phrase, tone and inflection he used during a race. He added new phrases to his race-calling lexicon on a regular basis, seeking to avoid repetition. He'd achieved notoriety after being attributed with the first use of the phrase 'on a canyon charge' to describe a horse picking up with purpose and coming between two horses to challenge. Those words were now widely in use among race commentators.

Trainers, jockeys, and his colleagues in the media, referred to him as the 'consummate race-caller' when his name came up in conversation. Privately, Joe was aware he was also referenced as a bore by a number of the same people. He shrugged this off easily; he'd learnt early in his career that his pursuit of linguistic excellence wasn't a topic many in racing were drawn to. The fact he didn't gamble also left his racing colleagues somewhat bewildered.

Aged thirty-two, Joe hadn't changed that much since leaving Newcastle University nine years previously. He still weighed the same, ate the same food, and for all he knew, probably looked the same; he wasn't the sort to take photos. He certainly had a similar haircut: an easy to manage short cut at the sides and a little longer on top to allow him to comb his thick dark brown hair quickly into order every morning. He was a tad above six foot three, had a flat stomach and a moderation of muscle to go with it, dressed unfashionably, but neatly, and most women seemed to like his green eyes and quiet, easy-going nature. Girlfriends came along sporadically. He was most notably described by one as 'a quietly intelligent beanpole with eyes you could go boating in'. This had struck him as a little odd, and perhaps she had meant it that way, as she quietly disappeared off the scene a few weeks into their relationship, just like the handful before her.

Career progression wasn't something which bothered Joe either. As long as he earned enough to pay his mortgage each month on his two bedroom ex-miners cottage up in Seaton Delaval, run his car, and have enough left over for a holiday in the sun once a year, he was content. He'd been tipped for national TV at one stage in his twenties, but his lack of enthusiasm for climbing corporate ladders had consigned him to minor racetracks in recent years. He did some little pieces of voice work on adverts, and managed to get the odd one-liners in TV dramas filmed in the North East. He was happy enough with that, and had no wish to be the star of the show, or tied completely to either racing, or acting.

The floorboards creaked under Joe's feet, which signaled that someone else was making their way up the steps of the entirely wooden built commentary position. It literally was a commentary 'box', a structure added to the top of the grandstand which provided an excellent view of the entire racecourse, but afforded a 1960's level of accommodation. It was a shed with a view.

A female voice called from out of sight, 'Joe... You up... there?'

Joe recognised Erin's call, one of the racecourse technical assistants.

'Hello, Erin, I'm still here.'

The door to the box opened and Erin's doughy young face poked inside. He'd anticipated she would be smiling, as it seemed this was her default setting. Instead, she wore a rare, worried look.

'Why haven't you got your headphones on? Turn to the racing channel!' she demanded, immediately bending over, holding her sides with both hands and taking a deep, lung-filling gulp of air.

'Been... running... up the stands... to get to you. It's Billie... you need to see this,' she choked out between further intakes of breath.

Joe frowned at the young woman, just out of university and full of eagerness. He doubted anything warranted a dead run up the four levels of the Newcastle stands in twenty-five degrees of heat, but he did as she instructed and powered up his laptop and started his racing television channel app.

The image consolidated and there stood Micky Goodham, one of the channel's racetrack correspondents. Joe's lip curled slightly on sight of him. He couldn't help it. He couldn't stand the man. As far as Joe was concerned Micky Goodham personified everything that was wrong with the racing media. Micky was framed holding a large microphone and was doing a piece to camera with the Ripon parade ring behind him.

'.. and with the disruption this event has caused, the last race at Ripon today has been abandoned,' Micky reported stoically to the camera.

This wasn't normal for Micky. He usually had a spark of boyish rebellion in his eyes and revelled in exaggeration and hyperbole. There could only be two reasons for this, either the news he was reporting was so serious he was suppressing his standard method of delivery, or the news was of so much interest there was a chance the major news networks had picked up the feed. Joe watched with renewed interest.

Micky continued, 'We've never seen anything like this on a UK racecourse, and of course in this day and age every tense second was caught on video by racegoers around the track. I've already viewed a couple of the videos uploaded to the internet and they are truly shocking. I wouldn't be surprised if we discover Billie...'

And there he is, thought Joe with distaste. There's the real Micky, with his brand of shallow sensationalism bubbling uncontrollably to the surface. He had no idea why the network employed him.

The camera stayed on Micky, but the voice of anchorman Sam Croft interrupted his flow mid-sentence from the studio.

'Of course we all know Wilhelmina, or Billie, as she prefers to be known as in the press room, as she is a well respected colleague in the racing media. Given we don't know the full circumstances, or even her current state of health, we won't be introducing any conjecture to this discussion. Tell us, Micky, have the racecourse issued a statement yet?'

Micky's eyes flicked dangerously off-camera for a moment, but he swallowed down whatever resentment he was feeling for having been interrupted and instead produced a sheet of paper. 'Indeed they have, Sammy,' responded Micky whilst apparently finding his place on the page. But Joe recognised this retort for what it was; a childish rebuke to Sam Croft, who was known to no one, save his wife, as 'Sammy'.

Micky went on to read the entire statement made by the Clerk of the course at Ripon which described how a woman had exited a window at the top of the grandstand for reasons unknown during the fifth race on the card. She had then fallen on the tiles before reportedly jumping off the roof. Given the distress caused, the final race of the day...

'Joe... Joe?' Erin persisted, tugging the arm of his shirt.

Still transfixed by the report, Joe spun round and looked uncomprehendingly into the young woman's wide, concerned face.

'Are you okay? I thought she was... I mean Billie *is* your friend isn't she...?' her query trailed off as she saw how ashen Joe appeared. He was facing her head on, but was certainly not looking at her.

'Yes,' he managed, with eyes unfocussed, 'She…' he stopped and stared directly back at his laptop.

'I need to see the videos. This isn't right,' he stated firmly.

Erin nodded, with tears welling. She blinked them away once Joe turned back to his table.

Closing the racing channel feed on the laptop, Joe switched to a browser and after typing a quick search found various videos from Ripon racecourse, all posted in the last twenty minutes. He chose the first he came to, entitled, 'Woman jumps off Ripon grandstand.'

He adjusted the laptop screen so both he and Erin could get a better view, the video being of low quality and also shot in portrait, rather than landscape. Erin pulled up a second wooden chair and the two of them nervously hunkered down at the table.

They quickly gave up on this first video as it jerked all over and only showed a distant figure at a very acute angle, barely recognisable as Billie. The person behind the camera seemed to be more concerned with the reactions in the crowd rather than what was going on eighty feet above. The second was much better, taken from a position over on the inside of the racecourse and in landscape mode. They watched it through. Joe immediately recognised the window of the commentator's box at the top of the grandstand. Erin, fingers in her mouth, squealed when Billie slid to the bottom of the tiles and again when she jumped. Joe was silent throughout and when fixing eyes with Erin after the video had finished, realised his young co-worker was softly weeping.

'Wait!' he exclaimed positively and replayed the last ten seconds again.

'There! She was at the edge, the bottom corner of the top roof. I'm sure there's a…'

'Joe, look!' Erin barked, desperately pointing out through the window of his caller's box and towards the racetrack. The runners for the last race on the Newcastle card were cantering past their position and down the straight towards the mile start.

Joe checked his watch, cursed under his breath and sat back down in his chair, pulling on his headphones and adjusting the microphone. As soon as the gear was clamped to his ears, he was assaulted by the irate tones of his production manager demanding to know where he had been for the last five minutes.

Billie was a colleague and... yes, a good friend. He didn't have a preponderance of the latter. For a split second Joe considered the situation. He had every right to drop everything and walk out right now after tearing a strip off his production manager for being such an uncaring arse. But Joe didn't, and he never would. For Joe, following through and delivering on a commitment, either work related or personal, meant everything.

Joe turned to Erin, gave her a hopeful smile, and squeezed her hand in his. Then he went back to work for the last fifteen minutes of his day. He provided the racecourse preamble up until the 5-10pm off time, then switched to the course and the racing channel network hook-up and provided another consummately professional and accurate race commentary before handing over to the channel studio and signing off for the day. Apart from the Newcastle racegoers receiving a slightly shortened build-up to the final race of the day, no one would have known it was anything other than business as usual.

Once he'd completed his last race comments and signed out of production he went back to his laptop and switched on his mobile phone. It made a buzzing noise almost immediately; a voice message. Still flicking through the plethora of videos from Ripon now popping up on the streaming website, he picked up his phone, expecting to see a message from a production manager. Instead, Billie Davenport's name shone back at him. He checked the time of the call and blew out a long exhalation of relief; the message had been left *after* her leap from the roof of the grandstand.

Swiping the 'listen now' option, he waited impatiently for voicemail to connect and was then met with Billie's slightly elevated voice, sounding like she was out of breath.

'Hi Joe, its Billie,' she started quickly, almost shouting. There was a long pause and for a moment Joe's heart dropped, imagining this was the total extent of the message. The sound of a car travelling at speed in the background came and went. Then Billie's voice returned.

'Joe, I'm sorry to ask, but I need your help. I know you'll be calling the last from Newcastle, but I'd be really grateful if you could act quickly once you get this message.'

Again, she paused. This time Joe could hear the sound of her taking deep breaths. Her message restarted again, her voice on a steadier note.

'I know this is going to sound strange... I could do with

15

meeting up with you to discuss a few things. Do you remember that racehorse Saxon Crypt? We watched him race about a month ago at Ripon? I've got a theory about his pedigree. I'd *really* like your thoughts on it… as soon as possible. That's *Saxon Crypt*.'

Was there a small degree of despair in the last few words? Joe was still contemplating this when the standard network menu started speaking, signalling the message had finished.

He hurriedly saved the message, collected his belongings and was down into the foyer of the main entrance a couple of minutes later, his saddlebag looped over his shoulder and his mind still engrossed in Billie's message. Heading straight for the heavy oak doors of the exit, he hardly noticed the two men falling into stride with him, one at either side. They both wore light coloured suits and summer trilbies.

'Now then, Joe. Everything okay?'

This pleasant, but slightly concerned query broke Joe's train of thought and brought him to a halt. He'd recognised the voice and was greeted with questioning looks from both men.

Simon Weller and Neil Tuton were racing regulars around the northern racing circuit and Joe regularly spent time in their company, either between races or more often than not, to share a drink and animated discussions with them after racing. Although his friendship with the two of them rarely extended beyond spending time together on racecourses, Joe counted the two retired businessmen among his most genuine and entertaining of friends.

'Oh gosh! sorry, Simon. I was miles away,' Joe managed, although he was aware he'd sounded flustered.

'No need to apologise. Come on, what's up?' asked Neil, the smaller of the two well turned out retirees.

Joe hesitated. He was keen to reply honestly, but also aware Billie's cry for help had been both urgent and worryingly cryptic.

'I've a friend in trouble,' he said in a serious tone.

Neil and Simon returned blank expressions and Joe immediately felt a pang of guilt for not explaining further.

'That's okay, we understand,' Neil said, quickly meeting Simon's eyes to confirm. Simon nodded and both men forced a smile to relate their understanding of the situation.

'Go on,' Simon urged, 'Get yourself gone,' he said, tilting his head toward the exit.

The two men watched relief spread across their friend's face and tipping their summer trilbies, ushered him on his way.

'Are you calling the races tomorrow at Pontefract?' Neil called after him. When Joe indicated he was, Simon responded with a shouted, 'We'll see you there!'

Crossing the standing traffic on the road outside the racecourse, Joe walked swiftly over to the car park reserved for staff. As soon as his car was ready Joe punched 'Ripon Cathedral' into its satellite navigation system and by exiting via an alternative back road route out of Gosforth Park, by five-thirty he was on the motorway, travelling south.

Four

For the first time in her life, Billie Davenport had broken a bone. At least that's what it felt like. She sat with her back to the external wall of the Cathedral, enjoying the coolness of the stone sinking through her thin cotton blouse. The trickles of sweat running down her neck to her shoulder blades were the result of her mile and a half run through fields and country paths. This made her uncomfortably sticky, but the throbbing pain from her collarbone provided an overture of pain which made all the complaints from her ribs, and various other muscles, fade into the background.

Billie probed the left-hand side of her collarbone with careful, sensitive fingers, moving down the pronounced hardness until the pain increased to a point where she began to feel dizzy and her sight blurred. She took a few breaths, keeping her head steady and when her vision stopped smudging all the trees and grass together she started at her shoulder and worked the other way. She reflected that, as self-diagnosis went prodding an index finger at the part of your body in extreme pain was definitely less desirable than someone else looking on your behalf. On her own, with no money, no transport and a dead phone, meant she had no other option. However, there appeared to be no obvious breaks or bones poking through the skin, which she took as a good sign, despite the ripples of pain working down the left-hand side of her upper torso. She reasoned she'd probably cracked her collarbone and perhaps done the same to a rib or two. The lack of a major injury was a relief, given she would be unable to attend an emergency room any time soon.

The alcove she had chosen to creep into at the back of the cathedral cast a shadow which was lengthening by the minute. Shielded by this wedge of darkness, the few people who walked past were unaware of the twenty-four year old sitting head down, black hair obscuring most of her face, silently hugging her legs to her chest. She remained like this until the evening breeze dried her forehead and her heart had stopped banging angrily up into her throat. The shadow in her refuge grew longer still and the warmth of the day mellowed into a humid evening, the sun dialing down its ferocity with every minute that passed.

The number of people ambling around the cathedral grounds to view the wonderful seventh century architecture dropped markedly. The odd individual who passed had places to go and wheeled away down the narrow path without looking skyward as the tourists did. They certainly didn't examine the dark recesses at the foot of the two-hundred foot high columns for cowering racing reporters.

The sun was turning a deep red and approaching the horizon when Billie heard a rich, almost golden voice softly calling her name. Raising her head, she opened her eyes and looked up to find an earnest man with wavy brown hair and lazy green eyes peering anxiously at her from the cathedral footpath. When he strode purposefully across the grass, stopped, bent down, and pushed a lock of his hair from his eyes, Billie was filled with relief.

'Joe! Yes, it's me,' she said quickly, levering herself away from her shaded corner. A number of her muscles complained at the sudden movement and she fought off stiffness for a few moments, rubbing her thigh vigorously before bending down to retrieve a small rucksack. Then she picked her way over the grass verge and around a standing stone that lay between her and her rescuer, stepping gingerly around the large block of sandstone.

'Am I pleased to see you!' she murmured, grabbing Joe's arm and half hugging it to the side of her body that wasn't aching. Joe responded with an easy smile, relieved Billie had taken command of the introduction, something he'd been worrying about for the last fifteen minutes of the journey. He hoped his concerned expression hadn't betrayed him.

'It's not a problem. Your message was a bit cryptic, but not completely indecipherable,' he answered lightly, 'I'm just relieved that you're okay. I wasn't too sure what to expect, after all, you're officially a missing person at the moment.'

Billie, still holding Joe's arm, pushed her face into his shoulder, the warmth of skin through his shirt making her feel far more protected.

'That's the way it's got to stay as well,' she replied quietly, 'I'll explain everything Joe, but we… well, I need to get out of Ripon before they find me.'

Joe let this settle on him. He had far too many questions for her. However, it seemed he must wait. Instead, he put his arm tentatively around the girl and when she moved in closer to him, he took confidence from this and tightened his grip on her. She was speaking clearly and strongly, but he sensed a need to be stronger than her, mentally as well as physically, if only for the time being.

He started to walk the two of them down the cathedral path 'Okay, questions later then. I'm parked in the main street, so let's get you home.'

'Yesss. About that...'

'You're not going home?' asked Joe, looking down at Billie, still buried in his shoulder.

She stopped walking and met his gaze full on for the first time since his arrival. 'Look, I know this is really weird, but please trust me. I know you'll have a hundred questions, I would too, and I've been thinking about the answers ever since I left you that voicemail. I'm just glad you brought me to the crypt here that day racing was abandoned at Ripon, otherwise I'd never have known where to run to...'

She looked away, not finished, trying to find the right words for the situation. Joe remained silent and waited.

Her eyes locked with his again. 'You're the only person I could trust... who they don't... But right now I really need to get away from here and *make sure Taz is okay*,' she pleaded. A sense of desperate urgency rose spirit-like from the girl, enveloping Joe, spiking a compulsion to protect her. Being a work colleague the subject of their private lives hadn't really come up before, but if he remembered correctly, Billie and her boyfriend lived together in Durham.

Joe maintained eye contact with Billie and couldn't help being entranced by the warm glow he was experiencing. He was regularly asked to step up and solve someone else's problem; he did it regularly at work. If he believed in the person, or the cause, he rarely said no. Could he work fourteen days straight in August to cover for summer holidays? Of course... Might he remain after racing to make an unpaid voice-over trailer? Sure... Could he ferry two cameramen and some equipment with him up to Ayr racecourse tomorrow morning? No problem... He was reliable, solid, and implacable when it came to seeing his commitments through. Did some people take advantage of him? Well, yes... There had been occasions when his predilection for being reliable and flexible was abused, but surely, this wasn't one of those times.

Even with her hair tousled, foundation rubbed away, and the smell of dried sweat wafting up from her, plus all those unanswered questions, Joe was incapable of refusing. Billie was a beautiful girl, intelligent and humorous. He imagined her hazel-coloured eyes and wonderfully symmetrical white-toothed smile had broken the hearts, if not the nerve, of many potential suitors. Of course, he would never be one of them. Quite apart from the fact she was ten years younger than him, she was way out of his league.

In Joe's experience, attractive women were either soul-crushingly shallow, and so of no interest to him, or good looking and intelligent, a combination which seemed to render him utterly invisible to them. He had been delighted to find a call for help from Billie waiting on his phone. The rush of pleasure he'd experienced when listening to her voicemail had resulted in him laughing inwardly at his reaction, knowing full well she'd chosen to call him as a result of his reliability, rather than any romantic reason.

Theirs was a platonic relationship, borne out of their shared love for horseracing and a sense of humour. At present, Billie worked as a race spotlight and comments author in the pressroom, but Joe was under no illusions; Billie was exactly the right material for working in front of the camera. Her employers were already preparing her for television and Joe was convinced it was a medium within which she was destined to excel.

'Okay, but once we get going, do I get to ask as many questions as I like?' queried Joe slightly mischievously with one eyebrow raised.

'Yes, and I even promise to answer you,' she retorted wryly. 'So please, *get a move on!*'

'Come on then,' responded Joe sharply, 'I've parked my car around the corner. It's only a two hundred yard walk at most.'

They walked another half a dozen paces down the cathedral path, Joe's arm taking more and more of the girl's weight. It soon became obvious that Billie was in too much pain to be moving anywhere quickly, or quietly, for that matter. She was groaning with each step; her stride becoming shorter, her body heavy under Joe's arm. It appeared her two-hour long wait for him had allowed her adrenaline to ebb and she was now feeling the full effects of her afternoon's exertions.

'Look, there's a bench over there,' Joe nodded in the direction of an old, crumbling oblong of stone shaded by a bushy tree. A chest high hedge ran behind it, providing an effective shield from the road that encircled the cathedral grounds. On second look, Joe thought the 'bench' may well be a tombstone. Regardless of its original purpose, it was clearly being used as a resting point by cathedral visitors and any inscription on its surface had been lost to the elements many years ago.

Billie grimaced then moaned an, 'Okay,' under her breath, begrudgingly accepting the change of direction across the cathedral's ancient graveyard.

'I'll leave you there, get my car, bring it round and stop behind this hedge,' said Joe, indicating the end of the privet hedge and the road beyond, 'You'll only need to walk a few yards. Then I can lift you into my car.'

The two of them shuffled slowly over to the ancient seat and Joe carefully supported his friend until she was sitting unaided. Despite looking uncomfortable and holding one hand to her ribs, Billie smiled weakly and pulled Joe down by the cuff of his shirt to sit beside her. He carefully placed an arm around the girl once more and squeezed her palm with his free hand. She nodded and gratefully leaned back into his shoulder.

Joe watched the girl's eyes flick violently in their sockets for a moment, as if disconnecting for a split second. He immediately felt his own heart jump, and thump louder.

'I need to get you to a doctor. I'll go get the car,' he informed her, making to stand. There was a sudden tightness in her grip on his hand and he immediately settled back into the bench. Billie's eyes plead for attention with an intensity that was hard to ignore, and Joe had no intention of denying her.

'You have to listen,' she began. 'Before you get the car... you need to understand... why I called you.'

She looked into Joe's face and saw her own worry reflected in his tight lips and pained expression. She'd made the right decision to get him involved. He had such an attractive mind and was so genuine and reliable, but also so aloof and, well, like so many men who had been on their own for a little too long, set in his ways. She reflected ruefully that these attributes also combined to make him the perfect recruit to help her.

'You know I've been investigating betting exchange algorithms recently?'

Joe nodded. In between writing her daily race analysis for publication onto various racing websites, Billie obsessively analysed the online betting markets, but particularly the so-called betting exchanges, where punters can bet to win, but also lay horses to lose. She was a techno-junkie and an adept writer of programming code.

Joe had seen this first-hand, as he'd watched one of her bet analysis apps working for himself. Not for the first time, he reflected that Billie's talents already outstripped many of her colleagues and she deserved to be in front of a television audience.

'Well… I found something a bit weird about a month ago in the matching of bets on one of the main betting exchanges. I didn't pay any attention to it at first, but I noticed it was repeated a few weeks later, but only in certain races.'

She took a few seconds to re-arrange her posture into a less painful position, then grimaced when her searching fingers found bruising. Joe winced as she continued to finger various tender parts of her side which clearly didn't want to be poked, resulting in several sharp in-takes of breath. Finally, after a further leveling lungful of the evening air she continued.

'So about ten days ago I wrote a short post to my blog detailing what I'd found and possible reasons for what I was seeing in the data. It was pretty innocuous, dry, un-exciting stuff.'

Joe was an infrequent reader of Billie's blog as it tended to concentrate on betting patterns, a topic that held little interest for him. So he remained silent and waited.

Billie suddenly appeared downcast, 'Then the whole world went crazy,' she added quietly.

'It started with a really strange email exchange I had with someone who called himself flutter#1, suggesting I look harder at my data. It continued for two days, with flutter#1 prompting me, no… really they were *guiding me* down the right avenues.'

Billie took a pained breath and continued, 'So four days ago I posted another blog on the subject. Within hours I got a message from the company who host the blogging website telling me I had infringed their rules and I was being immediately banned and my account deleted – and that was it! – three years worth of my blogs disappeared. I emailed and called them to complain but no-one would re-instate it or give me a straight answer as to why I was being treated this way, it was so frustrating.'

Billie's eyes were now blazing and her cheeks flushed. She took a few shallow breaths and swallowed before resuming her story.

'Flutter#1 emailed me direct within a few hours of my blog being deleted. The email had an attachment and *very* specific instructions, insisting I install an old, out-of-date operating system.

The attachment contained an app and when I installed and ran it, well it was… incredible. I couldn't believe what I was seeing. I've hardly slept the last few nights… I'd been sent an app that was the work of a hacker… the hacking code granted me access into the computer systems of the biggest betting exchange in Europe… Fairbet!'

Billie extracted her head from the crook of Joe's shoulder and locked eyes with him. '…a backdoor into Fairbet!' she whispered, making no effort to restrain the awe in her voice.

'It helped confirm what I'd seen in my data, but not only that, the hacking code was allowing me to…'

She paused, tentatively placing a hand to her forehead and slowly massaging her temples with thumb and middle finger, her palm hiding her face.

'I could cheat,' she said, dropping her hand from her face to reveal eyes suddenly bright with excitement, '…I could cheat other punters on Fairbet.'

Joe's mouth opened and closed, but before he could conjure a response Billie was into the next slice of her story.

'I've been working in a daze for the last two days, trying to work out what to do. Then today, after the first race, I got a call from Taz that scared me.'

Billie closed her eyes and screwed her face up, trying to ensure she related the call succinctly and clearly. Joe remained silent.

'A man had phoned. Taz said he sounded older than us… forties or fifties. He mentioned my name, and said I was to hand over the device holding the Fairbet hacking code. That meant… he wanted my laptop.'

Joe was about to start asking questions, however Billie wouldn't allow him, plunging on between short intakes of breath.

'That's when it got really scary. Taz said there was a man parked outside our house in Durham. He was leaning against a car and he had a hammer in his hand… he was sort of toying with it menacingly.'

Joe felt Billie shiver and gave her a little squeeze intended to comfort her.

'I was all set to leave the racecourse when a text message arrived from an anonymous number telling me to get out, like, straight away. It freaked me out *completely*. They even described the two men who would be coming to see me… I didn't know whether to believe it or not. I was so stunned, I just sat there in the pressroom, reading and re-reading the message. Then at quarter to four, only ten minutes after the text had landed, the door of the press room opened and…'

Billie stopped talking and grimaced, holding onto her ribs and then started to issue short, sharp breaths, as if the act of breathing was bringing her discomfort. Her face drained of its colour once again, becoming contorted as the pain increased. She brought it under control by bending forward on the bench, taking some of her weight onto her side and leaning with more purpose into Joe's body.

'Your ribs and collar bone…' Joe started as the girl turned her face into his chest and moaned, 'You did that jumping from roof to roof?' He sensed a nodding head beneath his chin, but she didn't answer.

During his drive up the motorway he had been contemplating her strange message and what he'd seen of her videoed jump from the grandstand. Joe had surmised that Billie had jumped from the top tier which held the commentary box, onto the narrow flat area about five yards below. From there, she'd have done the same sort of leap to land on the smaller stand, again with a flat roof, and then found her way down from there. Looking up into the Ripon grandstand from ground level the perspective made the main stand appear to have a single roof, but that wasn't the case. There were flat areas between each of the three levels. Billie had simply jumped down the levels. To everyone looking up from the ground, her first jump would have appeared to have been a desperate leap off the top of the grandstand. You could never have known the flat areas existed, unless you had access to the commentary box.

Joe held Billie gingerly, the two of them huddling together like a pair of entangled teenagers on their secluded cathedral bench. The girl seemed to be fragile all of a sudden. Joe decided she definitely needed to see a doctor whether Billie liked it or not. She was probably just battered and bruised, but he couldn't take the chance there wasn't something more serious wrong with her. The difficulty with her breathing was his main worry. But Joe did have a question he needed to ask before they moved. He gently pushed the girl's head away from his chest and asked her 'What made you go out the window?'

'I was stupid. I should have given them my laptop. They

knocked on the pressroom door and I went out into the corridor to speak with them. An older bald chap and a younger one with short hair demanded all my data, my laptop and any written records referring to my last few posts. If I didn't give up my blog, and the work I'd done on the website, they would hurt me... They were *very* clear on that point.'

Billie looked hard at Joe and read nothing but concern in his face. This is why I called you, she thought. No judgment, only genuine, unquestioning trust. And if he promises something, Joe always delivers.

'But someone is stealing money from Fairbet customers, so I said I was going to get my laptop... and ran. The only door out of there led to the commentator's booth.'

She turned her face up to Joe's, giving him a meaningful stare, 'I wanted to find out how deep this deception went... but now I've brought you and Taz...'

Billie's grip on Joe tightened. He felt the ripple of unnecessary fatty flesh above his hip being dug into with sharp fingernails. His hand found hers and gently started to release her fingers. She apologised but Joe shushed it away.

'You're going to be fine, and so is Taz, but it's important I get you some medical attention.'

He gave Billie's shoulder a squeeze. Making sure she was aware he was going to move, he carefully got up and then bobbed down in front of her, leaving her sitting alone on the stone bench, one arm protecting her ribs, the other extended and being cupped by his hands.

Adopting a stern expression, Joe looked directly into the young woman's scared eyes.

'I'm going to bring the car to you. We'll find a doctor to look at your ribs and collar bone. I think they're badly bruised, or at worst cracked. Then we'll go find Taz.'

Disregarding her immediate objections to his suggestion he added, 'We can tell a doctor anything, especially if it's not your local GP. You need pain relief, now. Right, I'm off to get the car. Stay right here, I'll only be two minutes.'

She nodded her agreement and it occurred to him that the transfer of information to him had lifted her spirits; information which must have been weighing her down.

'Take my rucksack,' Billie insisted as Joe got up to leave,

'It's got my laptop inside. Take it with you. I've left the laptop logged in, look for the ghost…'

Billie winced, digging her hand into her abdomen. Her face contorted into a rictus of pain and she soon doubled up, giving an involuntary groan. Joe placed what he hoped was a reassuring hand on the girl's shoulder and contemplated whether it wouldn't simply be easier to call an ambulance. The girl blew out several constricted, quick breaths and waved him away.

'Go,' she insisted, 'Go get the car.'

Joe surveyed her dark eyes once more and sensed Billie was indeed safe enough to leave. Her pain burned in her eyes; however, he was buoyed by the fact she was a good deal calmer than a few moments before. Squeezing her hand once more he told her, 'Don't worry, we can fix this. I'll make sure both you and Taz come out of this okay.'

'Promise?'

Joe smiled, 'Of course. I promise.'

He scooped up her rucksack, turned, took a few seconds to get his bearings, before striding off down the small winding path that had brought him to her ten minutes earlier. A moment later he looked over his shoulder to check the stone bench and found Billie still sitting where he'd left her. She was hunched over, hugging herself and staring at her feet.

Slipping the rucksack over one shoulder Joe started to jog, skirting around the rear of the cathedral, taking care to move between the ancient tombstones. He slowed for a moment when he passed a young woman bent over a large fallen headstone, apparently reading the inscription. She didn't even look up as he skipped past. Once on the main stone slab path, it was a straight run to where his car was parked.

On his arrival at the cathedral he had found an empty parking spot off the road in a set of spaces intended for the Dean and other church officials. He'd surmised it wouldn't hurt anyone to leave his car in this private space for a few minutes. As he slowed down at the end of the path, marked by the small, single-story cathedral hall, Joe began patting his jacket pockets in an attempt to locate his car keys.

He clicked his key-fob, threw the rucksack into the passenger seat, and slid into his car. Whilst turning the engine over, Joe noticed a pale faced man watching him from the shadows of the hall building. He held a small pad and was writing something in it.

Upon being stared at by Joe, the man bowed his head and shuffled into the shadows.

'Great,' Joe thought, 'I've been spotted by the local parking mafia with nothing else to do at this time on a Saturday night but take down my car's registration.'

Once he'd gunned the engine of his sensible, eight-year-old Volvo estate, the shadowy figure popped the pad in his jacket pocket and strode off in the direction of the cathedral.

Joe had been through Ripon plenty of times, and to the cathedral crypt itself, so he knew he needed to drive round in a semi-circle in order to pick up Billie. The cathedral was bounded by an almost circular road peppered with several junctions running away from the church grounds. He'd be with Billie within a minute.

The moment he set off, his phone started to vibrate from within his inside pocket. Ignoring its insistent chirping he concentrated on picking his way around the cathedral's perimeter. Once the buzzing ceased it restarted almost immediately. Grumbling, Joe reached out and tapped the answer icon on his car's bluetooth.

'Mr Lawlor,' a gruff male voice stated curtly.

Joe waited for more, but when nothing was forthcoming he asked, 'Who is this, I'm a little busy?'

'Joe,' the man continued, as if Joe's query had confirmed who was speaking, 'I understand you have a rucksack in your possession.'

There was no upward inflection at the end of this statement, it wasn't a question; the man *knew*.

'I need you to stop your car *now*. Take the rucksack and place it over the wall, into the cathedral grounds, and then leave the area.'

Joe stared at the unknown caller number blinking on his car's display, slowed his speed, looking around his mirrors and through each window in turn. Was this man watching him?

'Mr Lawlor, I need you to stop your vehicle and do as I say,' insisted the man's voice.

'Or what?' asked Joe, still moving his car forward. Despite his wish to be swift, Joe had made slow progress down the ancient lane but he'd finally reached the small junction only fifty yards from Billie.

'Miss Davenport will draw you into a very dangerous situation…'

'Tell me who you are,' Joe shouted over the man's words.

A couple of seconds of silence filled the car.

'Yeah, I thought so,' Joe interjected, killing the call.

A ripple of fear worked its way up from his stomach. What had he done? For a fevered second or two Joe allowed his mind to rip through several possible scenarios resulting from his rash response to the caller, but he soon cast them away and cleared his head. Besides, it was too late now, he'd promised Billie.

Looking to his left he could see the hedge and imagined Billie sitting behind the privet hedge on her stone plinth. With a quick glance up the lane to his right he engaged the clutch and moved away, dimly aware that a text message had just pinged onto his phone. Late-evening, there wasn't anything else on the road and he expected he could leave his car parked in the road, help Billie in and head straight off, she'd only need to walk a few yards. He half hoped she might have moved to the hedge and be waiting to jump straight into the passenger seat. Straining his head to the left he allowed the car to creep forward in second gear as he tried to judge how far down the hedge Billie's stone seat would be. He wound down his window, peered up, and shouted her name.

Confirmation of Billie's location was almost immediate. Joe caught a flash of something large, looping over the hedge. Billie's body slammed into Joe's windscreen with a limb-shattering thump, her head and elbows smashing through the toughened glass with enough force to poke raggedly at the dashboard. For a split second Billie's dull, unseeing eyes stared coldly into Joe's terrified face before he stamped the brake flat to the floor. Splinters of glass rained onto the front seats and the forward momentum scraped Billie's face up the windscreen. Joe was pushed forward, his nose almost touching the smudged blood and spots of flesh hanging from the jagged glass. The Volvo ground to a halt. Billie's body responded by shifting down the car, ripping flesh from her arms as she rolled off the front bonnet and slapped lifelessly onto the asphalt.

Nothing moved. Joe didn't move. He analysed. He processed. He processed the view out of his passenger side door window and it seemed to him it took too many precious seconds for him to understand what had just happened. His head was singing and he realised he was still gripping the steering wheel tight with both hands. They were covered in a mixture of splattered blood and minute silvery glass fragments which flickered in the light as he relaxed his grip. Heart beating thickly in his throat, he pushed his driver's door open and got out.

Having watched Billie's body being tossed unnaturally down the bonnet, spiraling with a mix of arms and legs before disappearing beyond the nose of the car, he steeled himself before rounding the front of his car. He winced, biting his bottom lip at the sight of Billie lying face down, both arms and legs at contorted, unnatural angles.

Joe knelt beside her bloodied face with closed eyes, bruises already starting to colour and winced once more when he saw the gooey mess on the side of her head from which a steady flow of rich, dark red blood oozed. He instinctively dug out a folded cloth hankie from his trouser pocket, balling it up and pushing it gently to the side of Billie's head. Then he applied a little more pressure, as much as he dared, in an attempt to stem the free flow of her blood.

Someone else entered the scene. They said something and bent down, placing a female hand on the girl's wrist. Joe continued to hold his position, staring down at Billie's face, tears starting to well in his eyes. He quickly blinked them away and instructed himself to concentrate, to think, to make a difference in this situation. Then Joe was aware of another person standing behind him and of more people approaching. The sounds of the street suddenly rushed at him and while maintaining a steady hand he looked up and examined the knot of people who now stood around himself, Billie, and the young woman kneeling at her side.

Trying to commit the faces to memory, Joe maintained the pressure to Billie's head. The small crescent of faces looked down, displaying every emotion from concern, anger, and awe to disgust. He counted eight onlookers, plus the girl still knelt down, her head bowed, concentrating on Billie. She ran hands down Billie's arms and legs. More people stood a little way off, arms crossed, debating with neighbours, not daring to come closer for fear of too much involvement.

The girl looked up, young, vibrant, and earnest. She told Joe 'She's alive. Broken bones and a head injury, but you have to leave. Now!'

Joe frowned, regarding the girl's face properly for the first time, then looked her up and down. A teenager, wearing canvas jeans, trainers, and a sleeveless cloth jacket peppered with a multitude of pockets. She was small, thick set, and possessed boyish good looks that weren't helped by a rash of untidy hair in three garish colours. Her look of rebellion was finished off with a small diamond nose stud. He returned her an uncomprehending stare.

'Seriously!' she barked urgently, 'They are just on the other side of the hedge. I've just watched them throw her onto your car. You have to go... Now!'

This outburst had a few of the onlookers elbowing each other and a couple of typically gossipy conversations broke out. Phrases such as 'drunk driver', 'given no chance', and 'hit and run' started to be sprinkled into the chatter around him.

The girl sprang to a standing position, grunted in frustration and pushing through the ribbon of onlookers, stalked off to the passenger door of Joe's car. She flung it open and dipping in for a few seconds, reappearing with Billie's rucksack.

'Come on!' she shouted over to Joe, not without a touch of petulance, and set off at a run across the road, pulling the rucksack onto her back.

Breaking his gaze with the teenage girl, Joe looked down and drank in Billie's battered body. He remembered his promise to her: 'I'll make sure both you and Taz come out of this okay...'

Billie had thought it important enough to attempt to run from whoever did this to her. And she'd not given them what they wanted. He'd be no use to her, or Taz, being questioned by police... besides, this other girl clearly knew something and she'd witnessed someone attacking Billie. He glanced down the street again; the girl's outline was receding quickly.

Joe took another look down at Billie. Torn between what was right, and what needed to be put right, Joe Lawlor stepped out of his comfort zone.

His decision made, he reached out and pulled at the first hand which came close. A middle-aged woman frowned when he tugged at her, but she quickly crouched down. Joe pushed her hand into place against his hankie on Billie's head and commanded her to continue to hold it firmly until the ambulance crew arrived.

Now the sound of sirens came and a general movement as uniformed figures converged in the distance. Standing, Joe turned in the direction of the girl and froze when he spied two men inside his car. A stumpy, bald headed man in a suit appeared to be rifling through his glove compartment; a second man was kneeling on the back seat, rummaging in the footwell. They were so intent on their search neither looked up to see Joe gaping at them.

The girl had to be at least fifty yards away now, head down, rucksack bouncing on her back. Joe glanced the other way and discovered police and ambulance vehicles picking their way around a short line of stationary cars. There were questions fired at him from one or two of the circle of watchers, which he didn't register. The girl was about to disappear from view as she approached a corner. She slowed and turned to walk backwards, waving encouragingly for him to join her. Joe looked down at Billie's inert body, considered his promise, and fought the urge to remain with her. As ambulance staff pushed the onlookers aside he shouted a curt message to a couple of bystanders and set off running after the girl.

Five

'I'm telling you, Davenport's gone.'

'She can't have,' the voice countered.

'Look,' Anthony Gerard blurted through gritted teeth, 'I've gone inside and right around the cathedral grounds, she's not here.'

Taking a white handkerchief from the back pocket of his jeans, he wiped away a thin layer of sweat that had burst onto his forehead since he'd begun navigating around the medieval building. The sun was low yet the humidity ensured his shirt was sticking irritatingly to his back. His reply had resulted in an extended silence from his caller. Gerard waited patiently, amused at the level of contemplation from his boss. In Gerard's opinion his boss over-thought everything.

The shriek of an ambulance siren behind the cathedral immediately hardened Gerard's eyes. He muted the call and set off at a brisk walk. When, a minute later, he returned the mobile phone to his ear, his caller was asking whether he was still there.

'I'm here,' he cut across the increasingly excitable shouting.

'What's going on, Gerard?'

'I'm too late.'

'She's not...?'

Go on, say it, Gerard thought. Dead. It's just a word. Amateurs could never face saying it. He waited patiently once again, the conversational void with his caller continuing to lengthen. Standing in the graveyard he could look down on the knot of people huddled around the girl lying in the road. He took a few photos and then extended his attention to the car, and then further up the narrow road to where it was bisected by a four-way junction.

'No, I don't think so,' he reported quietly, 'Not yet,' and set off through the ancient headstones to inspect the car at closer quarters, his phone still clamped to his ear.

'Good. That's good,' replied the voice, 'And does she...'

'I'm looking now. I'll report back,' said Gerard flatly, summarily killing the call.

He approached a newly clipped privet hedge and peered over and onto the roof of the Volvo.

The back of a shiny bald head emerged from the passenger seat, standing to face the way the car had travelled. He was no more than two yards from Gerard, thankfully facing away from him. It was a dome of skin and skull he recognised. He shrank down behind the hedge, listening intently; where 'Ronnie' went, 'Jack' and 'Reggie' wouldn't be far away. Only a few phrases drifted over but they were enough to confirm what he'd already guessed. They'd been too slow to get to the car after the… accident. Although he seriously doubted it was a pure accident. It was unfortunate he hadn't got to Davenport first.

It appeared girl's possessions had already been lifted, perhaps by the driver of the car, or possibly a passerby. Maybe they'd never been in the car in the first place? He cursed under his breath when considering those minutes he'd spent in fruitless searching. But you had to give Davenport some credit. She'd given Ronnie the slip from a locked room at the races and protected her secret, even though it had cost her… her consciousness, and possibly a lot more.

A few seconds later Gerard was picking his way across the churchyard at speed, swerving around headstones and dipping under low hanging branches. The half-heard conversation Ronnie and Jack had shared replayed through his mind as he broke cover from one tree to the next. Jack had said, 'It was that punk'. Gerard came to a shambling halt under a yew, retrieved his phone, and in the darkness gifted by the ancient tree he examined his photos of the accident scene. There was no one he would describe as a 'punk' standing around the girl's body. He flicked through the half dozen images again and stopped at a photo of the smashed car and the road beyond. Gerard's eyes widened once he found the indistinct figure in the distance, running on the road. He carefully squeezed his fingers apart on the small screen to make the figure larger. It was definitely a man running away from the car. He was dressed in a suit. Gerard frowned. The punk reference was still puzzling him.

His concentration was broken by the sound of car wheels screeching and the roar of an engine accelerating. After only a moment's thought Gerard set off at a dead run in the direction of the squealing tyres. Fifteen seconds later, he came to a panting stop under a large sycamore tree in the corner of the cathedral grounds just in time to watch the rear end of a silver Mercedes disappearing at speed. He swore out loud before setting off at a dead run in the opposite direction, attempting to pull the keys to his Land Rover out of his jeans as he dodged between gravestones.

Six

Joe was gaining on her when the girl slipped around the corner into St. Mary Gate and out of view. It had been a while since he'd last run flat out and his suit and sensible black shoes weren't aiding his progress. He tried to run harder, afraid he might lose her, but only succeeded in losing his balance and came up on the corner with arms flailing. A vintage red mini with a white strip down its bonnet poked its nose out of the junction and he tottered to an unflattering stop. The passenger door swung open and the girl peered up at him from the driver's seat and raised one eyebrow, simultaneously tapping an index finger to her wrist.

The compact little car completed a slick u-turn at the junction and whipped away from the cathedral grounds, flashing past triangular warnings of elderly people crossing and roaring through an ancient single lane, tree-covered route which still boasted the odd cobbled area in places. Still sweating from his hundred yard dash, Joe's left hand felt greasy as he gripped the hard plastic door handle, while his right was leaving a wet smudge on the dashboard as he braced himself against what he was convinced was an impending high speed collision. He checked for a second time that his seat belt was correctly fastened.

Shouting over the engine noise of the thirty-year-old mini, he cried, 'Take it easy for crying out loud!' whilst still staring ahead, boggle-eyed.

'What, and let them catch up?' the girl replied.

Joe stole a look across at the girl and his heart sank when he realised she was grinning. She looked insanely happy, her face hardly able to contain her glee in racing the little car through tiny walled lanes and tall terraces of houses with parked cars strewn on both sides. Joe swallowed hard and slammed his eyes shut as she pointed the mini into an impossibly tight gap between a ten-foot high brick wall and a fifteenth century public house that inexplicably poked out into the footpath enough to reduce the road to its absolute minimum. His right foot shot out; an involuntary reaction as he tried to stamp on his own imaginary brake. The girl glanced across to him and guffawed.

'Behind us,' she told him as they bounced along, running a set of traffic lights. They flew past a supermarkets and a fire station and the girl ran another red light, slewing the car across the junction to miss a cyclist.

'Look behind us!' she insisted.

Joe tried the tiny chrome-plated mirrors, but they were at the wrong angle. Then he took a breath and screwed his head round. A large, silver Mercedes, probably executive class, was navigating the last set of lights. Its grill rose slightly as it accelerated once it was through the danger area.

'They've been following us since we ran,' the girl shouted. 'We need to lose them.'

'If you keep driving at this speed, it won't be long before we crash and die, so being caught looks a decent option at present,' Joe cried over the sound of the mini's exhaust scraping on the road as they bounced over a small rise.

The girl scowled but said nothing, maintaining her concentration on thrashing through the gears and hitting the apex of the next bend in the road. After passing another pub, areas of lush green grass started to appear on both sides; they were reaching the edge of the city. The road stretched out straight for a quarter of a mile and thankfully there were no cars coming from the opposite direction. The mini switched to the right-hand side of the road and opened up.

'I can't outrun them, they're gaining,' she reported angrily.

The road now bore left and Joe felt relief as the brakes were applied and the speed fell below fifty. The Mercedes drew up closer to the back of the mini and the girl slowed further.

Joe took a long look over his shoulder. The two men who had been rooting through his car stared back at him through a tinted windscreen, but it was definitely them. An older bald man and a younger man, no more than ten yards away. She was right, they couldn't outrun them.

'I wasn't serious about getting caught you know!' Joe exclaimed as the car continued to slow.

'I'm thinking!' the girl shouted back, all signs of mirth gone from her face and voice.

He hadn't noticed until now. Hanging from the rear view mirror was a small cardboard cutout scented tree and it was at this moment that Joe got a waft of pine that triggered a memory. They were coming to a major junction and Joe instantly recognised the road layout. For a split second his mind was filled with a girl, her small car, a picnic in long grass, and... a rejection.

'Slow right down,' he ordered. 'You have to get the timing right. When I say go, you head straight across the junction, alright?'

'No, you old fool!' the girl retorted angrily, starting to squirrel across the road to stop the following car from coming around them.

'Old?' Joe demanded.

'Really?' the girl replied with a roll of her eyes, 'That's what you homed in on, the old bit?'

'Just do as I say, when I say it!' Joe hissed. Even before he'd completed his sentence he wondered who was saying the words. This wasn't him at all. Nonetheless, he received no rebuke from the driver's seat and so steeled himself.

The mini was now crawling toward the junction and Joe was checking the Mercedes out and the oncoming traffic from the intersecting main road.

'Come on! Now surely?' the girl demanded.

'No, wait, wait...' he held his hand up as if starting a race, '...Go now!'

The girl gunned the engine and the little red mini leapt across the junction in front of a line of oncoming traffic. Angry honks of incredulous rage came from both directions but the mini made it to the other side of the junction unscathed. Behind them the Mercedes was being subjected to far more horn play as it tried unsuccessfully to edge out into the oncoming traffic.

'Cool!' remarked the girl and it was Joe's turn to grin.

'But we're going down a dead end...' she added as they accelerated up a thin, leafy, single-track lane.

'Maybe for them, but not for us,' Joe promised.

The track soon came to an end, finishing in a compact, round car park which served a small leisure complex. As the girl had indicated, there was nowhere to run now.

'Over there,' Joe said calmly, just as the girl started to curse under her breath, 'We should just about get through.'

A line of concrete posts ran across the back of the car park, with a large field of rough grass on the other side. Right in the corner, one of the posts was missing, and there was perhaps just enough room for a small car to nip through. The girl giggled once more, a crazy big smile bending her face in a delightful way as she lined up her charge.

There was a faint scraping noise as grass rubbed against the sills. The girl grumbled something as her driver's door wing mirror flicked inwards as the tiny mini squeezed through the gap between the concrete posts. Once through, they bounced away over the undulating meadow. Joe craned his neck to peer out of the back window. The silver Mercedes had just entered the car park and he watched as the large vehicle headed for the gap in the posts, then slowed, as if in contemplation.

'Down to the bottom of the field and through the hedge,' he commanded, switching his attention to the view ahead. A second later there was a bang and Joe looked back over his shoulder once more.

The Mercedes had decided to have a go, and to Joe's delight had failed wonderfully. He could see a crumpled wing, a burst front tyre and a concrete post still standing resolutely upright, albeit a little wonkier than before.

Joe guided the girl through a gap in the bottom hedge and they joined another empty field of grass. This one had been grazed down and progress over it was far easier.

'Go left and follow the hedge until you reach a piece of tarmac and there will be a three bar gate. I'll get out and let you through.'

'Good going race caller!' the girl chuckled in a surprisingly hearty voice, 'You're not as boring as your profile suggests.'

Joe rubbed a hand down his face before he caught up with the importance of the girl's reference.

'How do you know what I do?' he asked, genuinely surprised, and also a little impressed with the girl's knowledge.

'I googled you as soon as I saw you with Night Nurse in the cemetery. Come on, we've time to talk later. Open that gate and let's get as far away from here as we can.'

A few minutes later they pulled into a small roadside coffee shop and the girl switched the ignition off, having parked the mini out of sight of the road, hidden behind an articulated lorry.

'You sure about this?' the girl asked, 'Shouldn't we just get going up the motorway?'

'Which is exactly where they will assume we'll head,' Joe retorted, 'This way, they'll hopefully put distance between us. Besides, we need to talk. The two of us have just committed a crime together and I don't even know your name.'

'What crime's that then?'

'Leaving the scene of an accident.'

'That was no accident. I watched them hit her and then throw her over the hedge onto your car!' the girl replied bitterly. Joe watched her shudder at the memory and suggested they get a hot drink. He thought she could do with one. He was starting to bottom out too, now the adrenaline from the accident and their pursuit through Ripon was leaving his system.

The coffee shop was more of a greasy spoon, but was clean and cheerful enough. Their young waitress was working on her own and didn't seem to mind the fact they had walked in only ten minutes before closing time at eight o'clock. There was only one other customer, presumably the driver of the lorry behind which they'd parked the mini. He had his head down, attacking an all-day breakfast with gusto. They chose a table away from the window but facing the roadside, sat Billie's rucksack on a spare chair and took seats opposite each other, nursing their drinks and failing to make eye contact. The girl had produced a laptop of her own from under her driver's seat and added it to the rucksack's contents, pointing out she would never be parted from her computer, and leaving anything of value in her ancient mini was, 'a burglary waiting to happen.'

'Night Nurse,' Joe said in a quiet voice, 'That's Billie's blogging username isn't it?'

The girl nodded and clicked an artificial sweetner into her coffee from a lipstick sized plastic device she'd found in one of her many jacket pockets. From another she removed a packet of chewing gum branded as 'Glee' and popped a small block in her mouth.

'I read her post a few days ago,' she said, sipping her coffee from two hands, both elbows on the table, legs crossed. She took several chews on her gum between sips.

It was the first time Joe had been able to look solidly at the girl for more than a few seconds since the accident. Small, but certainly not petite, a round, happy face which crinkled easily into a smile was tinged with red at the centre of her cheeks and topped off by expressive brown eyebrows. Her features were offset with large hazel eyes and primarily brown hair, apart from a few strands of red and pink which brushed her forehead, all cut to a single length of around three inches. He reflected that it was probably the hair which delivered the boyish looks, however she was certainly no slave to fashion. A white t-shirt with some sort of musical design on it, partially covered by her pocket-ridden cloth jacket and her canvas trousers gave off an aura of teenage rebellion.

Joe considered his own attire, which consisted of his work suit, white shirt, dark tie and patent leather shoes. It slowly dawned on him that for the first time in his life a woman in his company might be mistaken for his daughter. This revelation produced an involuntary shudder.

'Are you okay?' the girl asked with a modicum of concern in her eyes.

'Sure, yes. Just a bit cool in here I guess,' he lied. She eyed him suspiciously; it had to be twenty-five degrees in the café. She decided there and then: he was a really bad liar. That was a plus.

Not wishing to dwell on this subject he quickly added, 'You read Billie's blog, but that doesn't explain how you came to be hanging around Ripon cathedral…'

'For your clandestine meeting!' she finished for him, giggling and producing such a joyous smile, Joe couldn't help joining her. It had only been an hour ago he had been sitting with Billie on the stone bench. However, the memory of her lying unconscious in front of his car soon served to wipe the smile from his lips.

The girl must have joined his line of thought as her expression also turned serious.

'I'm Sparky247,' she announced in a whisper, as if this one revelation would explain her entire life story to him, 'And I do like your green eyes!'

Her face lit up across the plastic table, enjoying the impact her teenage cheekiness had on the man in his early thirties. Joe placed both elbows on the table and cupped his face in his hands, rubbing them up and down his cheeks before tiredly leaning his head on his left hand.

'Hello, my name is Joe Lawlor; I'm a race commentator, part-time actor, and voice over artist. I also write for a couple of horse racing publications,' he told her in a purposefully monotone voice, 'I was asked by Billie to meet and help her out, that's why I was at the cathedral, so tell me, who are you and *why were you there*?'

The girl bit her lip. 'Hello, my name is Sparky,' she started in a worryingly accurate impression of Joe's voice, 'I read Night Nurse's blog posts and realised it was potentially hot stuff. A day after her last, most important blog was posted, her profile was deleted from the website. Twenty-four hours later she is on social media jumping off the roof of a racecourse grandstand.'

She abruptly dropped the impression, continuing in a lower register, 'I googled the racecourse satellite images and realised she'd been trying to get away from someone, probably those Mercedes men. The videos on YouTube backed this up. I jumped in my car and got to the racecourse intending to pick her up and er... *rescue* her I guess. I was touring around the racecourse car park when I came across two men brazenly breaking into a car, and one of them looked just like the bald-headed chap on the YouTube videos. I assumed it had to be Night Nurse's car, so I waited and watched. One of them made a call and they both jumped into that Mercedes that tried to catch us. I followed them into Ripon, but they ended up at a school.'

Joe couldn't help smiling, 'They went to the wrong cathedral. They went to Ripon Cathedral School, I guess it's an easy mistake to make!'

'Yeah, they must be pretty dumb,' Sparky smiled back, 'I saw the school sign and realised their error, so headed straight for the cathedral. I pitched up and found you outside in the churchyard talking with her.'

'So how did you know it was me?'

Sparky slowly shook her head and adopted a '*really?*' expression. Joe thought for a moment.

'You knew Billie worked for the racing channel, and the website has all the presenters listed, doesn't it, so I guess my ugly mug is on there too?'

The girl responded by nodding her head slowly up and down, brows high on her forehead. He gave her a wry smile to indicate he accepted her digital prowess.

Sparky leaned forward and shot a glance toward the girl at the counter. She was busy wiping various pieces of kitchen equipment down with a damp cloth. To Joe's mind she seemed disinterested in them and more involved with the mobile phone she held in her other hand.

'Don't worry, she's texting a boyfriend,' Joe said, waving a wrist in the waitress's direction, 'Tell me about Billie's blog.'

Sparky dipped into one of her multitude of pockets, and popped another block of chewing gum into her mouth. She ground the chewing gum for a few seconds, then started to explain.

'Billie found some anomalies in the Fairbet betting data stream. She was collecting betting data to match volumes and time lines,' Sparky whispered, 'It looked like nothing too remarkable at first, it was when you looked at the data in detail and analysed the timings you could see the problem.'

Joe was acquainted with the online betting exchanges, but couldn't claim to completely understand them. He knew you could either bet on a horse to win, or lay a horse to lose, basically allowing anyone to become the bookie, but he'd never actually used them. However, he understood there were many punters using so-called 'betting bots' to automatically place wagers when certain pre-set circumstances were reached, for example to guarantee a profit by backing, then laying the same horse. It sounded plausible that Billie had used a self-coded betting bot to collate betting data.

'She posted something contentious on her blog?' queried Joe.

'Yep!'

'So come on, what was it? What was so important?'

She drew closer to him and lowered her voice further, 'It looks like someone has hacked the Fairbet website and is placing a time delay into some of the in-play markets.'

Sparky watched Joe's features quickly flit from idle curiosity, into shock. He went very still and gazed into the middle distance. It was as if she could see the gears in his mind turning over.

'I see,' he managed after half a minute of silence through which Sparky sipped at her coffee, chewed her gum, and didn't take her eyes off him.

Another twenty seconds ticked by while Joe once again went off into the realms of thought. Suddenly he snapped back and locked eyes with the girl.

'Sorry, this is a bit off subject. What happened when I left Billie in the graveyard?'

Doing her level best to remain patient, she swallowed a frustrated sigh.

'Just what I said, the bald-headed guy and his ugly mate turned up. They argued with her, shouting about her computer or something. Baldy punched her and she just went limp, like straight away! The ugly one called someone on his phone and a minute later they picked her up, waited until you came along and… well, you know the rest.'

'So you don't know Billie?'

'I know her as Night Nurse, her username on the betting forum. I guess you could describe us as online pals. We've traded email suggestions on data analysis and some bits of coding, but I'd never met her. Once I read that blog about the hacking code I knew she'd stumbled on something pretty big. That was only a day ago. When the Ripon racecourse videos started to appear, I knew who she was and couldn't help myself, I had to help. To be honest, I felt a bit responsible.'

Sparky pushed back from the table, 'I thought it would be fun, you know, to help her escape,' she added miserably.

'I want to check with the hospital to find out if she's okay,' Joe said, fishing out his mobile phone from his suit pocket. There was a single text message showing on his alerts, the one that had arrived just after the call to threaten him before Billie was thrown onto his car.

Joe tapped the view icon and read the message: 'Go to police and u + Davenport's family r dead.'

Across the table Sparky's eyes grew wide, 'Is that switched on?' she asked nervously.

'Yes?'

'Give it here,' she demanded fiercely with an outstretched hand, 'Come on, our freedom and good health could depend on it,' she added, irritated with Joe's initial reluctance to part with his device.

'Don't you know anything about technology?' she admonished whilst jemmying the back off the phone and removing the battery and SIM card, 'If they have friends in the right places, those Mercedes men will know exactly where we are!'

A cold sweat broke out down the back of Joe's neck. She was right of course. The police would be able to track his phone. He cursed his inability to think like a criminal, and marvelled at how Sparky seemed totally in tune with law breaking. The girl went to another pocket in her jacket and produced a replacement SIM, locking it in place. Within another twenty seconds the phone was back in his hand and working once more.

'They won't be able to track you now, but we still better get going just in case they've got around to tracking the old SIM,' Sparky said, getting up from the table and downing the last of her coffee in one gulp.

'You carry extra SIM's around with you for this express purpose?' Joe asked incredulously.

'Yeah, I always carry a couple. The one you've got is an

untraceable 'pay as you go' SIM I bought in Sunderland about two years ago. It's got plenty of data on it but only an hour of talk time. Go on, check the BBC and the Yorkshire Post websites and see if the accident has been reported.'

Joe fiddled with the screen and brought up his BBC app. He was relieved when he wasn't headlining the home page, but conducted various other searches and found nothing. He looked up and found Sparky doing something similar.

'Twenty-four tweets mentioning a crash beside the Cathedral, two reference a hit and run, plus a man running off afterwards. Oh, and the Racing Post have a short piece on what happened at Ripon,' she reported, 'Hold up, let's see what the hospital says.'

She tapped her phone a few more times and a minute later she was explaining to someone she was Billie's sister. She hung up with a glum expression.

'Well?' Joe prompted.

'She was alive when she arrived at Harrogate District Hospital but she's currently being assessed, so there's no update yet. The nurse said to ring back tomorrow morning.'

The two of them fell silent for a minute before Sparky reminded him they really needed to move, even if they didn't know where they should head, just in case his phone had been monitored.

'We better use the washrooms too. We don't know when we'll next get a chance,' she added, and again Joe found himself wondering whether Sparky was a survivalist.

'The Mercedes men may know who you are too,' Joe pointed out, pausing slightly to note that he was aping Sparky's nickname for their pursuers, 'Those two will be able to check your registration and find out where you live.'

'Only if they can get access to the DVLA database.'

'You reckon men who are happy to force a women to flee over rooftops, punch her unconscious, throw her body onto the windscreen of a car and then try and chase us down on public roads at high speed, just to retrieve her laptop, will let a little thing like accessing a database get in their way?'

Sparky bit her lip, 'You could have a point, that database isn't too difficult to crack. I had a boyfriend who once …' she stopped speaking once she caught Joe's exasperated expression.

Before they left the café, they'd bought a few snacks and bottles of water. With little idea when they'd next enjoy a solid meal,

Joe amused himself with the thought that he was missing his usual microwave curry, it being a Saturday night. Instead, he would be sharing bottled water and a packet of Frazzles in a mini, with a teenage girl he'd known for less than an hour.

Joe met up with his partner in crime at the door to the café. Sparky was engrossed in a small television sitting on a grimy plinth high up in the corner of the room and silently indicated for him to listen when he approached. Joe immediately recognised it was a news report.

'They've already mentioned your name twice,' Sparky whispered, slanting a look at the girl behind the counter. A ticker scrolled along the bottom of the small screen stating, 'Ripon hit and run: man wanted for questioning.'

Joe became entranced for a few seconds, fascinated to hear his own name being broadcast. He soon lost focus; he'd promised Billie to make sure her boyfriend was safe. That was the imperative. There was something of value on Billie's laptop, but it wasn't as valuable as Taz's life.

'Come on, we need to get going,' he said, cutting across a reporter's description of the scenes at Ripon earlier in the day.

As they were making their way out of the café car park, Joe turned and inspected his travelling partner. She wore an angelic expression, which made him curl his lip into a grimace. Sparky glanced over, took note of Joe's apprehension, and sighed loudly.

'What now?' she demanded.

'Nothing,' he answered lamely, 'It can wait.'

He had questions for this young woman, but they weren't of great importance just at the moment.

She pulled out onto the moderately busy country 'A' road and accelerated toward the motorway, Joe insisting she slow down so as not to draw attention to themselves.

'We need to head to Durham, across country if possible. I'm pretty sure we'll have the police, or our friends in the Mercedes after us if we use the motorway.'

Sparky nodded her agreement and inspected her phone that she had clipped into a mount on her dashboard, 'We can do that,' she said, tapping at a navigation app.

They rushed through a number of country lanes for the next few minutes without sharing any words, the first time they'd been silent in each other's company since they'd met. Both of them were turning over their situation and their immediate goal; finding Taz before anyone else did. Finally, Sparky broke through the sound of the engine noise.

'It will be interesting if those idiots chasing us find out who owns this car,' Sparky commented after a short silence.

'Oh God, tell me this is your car!' Joe exclaimed, his mind filling with the consequences of being wanted by the police *and* being driven around in a stolen car.

'It's not quite my car,' she admitted, 'It's my mother's.'

Joe relaxed a little. At least the ownership was within the same family.

'So you're insured to drive it?'

'Oh yes, that's not the problem.'

'Okay, what's the problem?'

'It's my father,' Sparky stated theatrically, as if staging a big reveal of a magic trick.

Bemused by the lack of relevance, Joe stared across at his driver blankly. This revelation meant nothing to him.

'My father is Michael Gray,' Sparky continued with an expectant air.

Still unable to determine any link to their current predicament, Joe watched as the girl in the driver's seat slowly shook her head.

'You're kidding me? You've never heard of Michael Gray, the founder and chief executive officer of the biggest betting exchange in the country? I thought you worked in racing?

'I'm not in the least bit interested in bookmakers,' Joe replied apologetically, 'The craft of delivering a commentary is what drew me to racing.'

'At least… up until a few hours ago,' he modified.

'Well, you'll be interested in *this* bookmaker. The betting exchange Billie's hacking code was able to infiltrate is called Fairbet, and my dad is the CEO.'

Seven

Jeremy Tottering-Smythe inspected his features in the washroom mirror. He patted his chin, stroking it between finger and thumb to detect further evidence of rolls of flab forming and realised his five o'clock shadow had arrived. That signalled it was late evening and he should have been home hours ago. Given it was Saturday evening, he shouldn't even be in the building. Tottering-Smythe stepped back from the wash basin, ran a fingertip across his eyebrow, and asked himself where he'd gone wrong.

A short and exciting career as a jump jockey after Cambridge, followed by ten years in the city, then taking over the family distillery business for the following fifteen years before selling at its peak to the Chinese, had seen him head hunted for the position of chief executive at the British Horseracing Authority at the age of forty-eight.

I should have turned them down, he thought, giving himself a rueful smile. Four years of refereeing tiresome in-fighting among the factions in the racing industry had hardened his arteries and weakened his resolve. Never mind, he told himself, only six months more to endure of this poisoned chalice.

On the way out of the executive washroom, Tottering-Smythe bumped into his director of communications in the corridor. He didn't think much to Paul Jenkins. He was loquacious, yet uninspiring, and had something about him that made him easy to dislike. Asked to sum the man up in one word, Jeremy would have answered 'adequate'.

'I got your message and decided to pop into the office, rather than video call. I trust this is equitable?'

There's someone with no blasted home life, Tottering-Smythe decided, brusquely nodding his acceptance at his colleague and indicating the open door to his office.

'I'll call the others now. We're a few minutes early, but I want to get home before ten. I've been fielding calls regarding this woman since four o'clock. Where were you, I called and texted?'

'Sandown,' Jenkins responded, without elaborating.

'No phone reception at Sandown races?'

Jenkins caught the sarcasm in his boss's tone and tried to make his answer as conciliatory as possible.

'I was entertaining the chairman of the TBA,' he said in an

overly dramatic voice, 'It was difficult to find a moment between his interminable racing anecdotes…'

'Huh, breeders,' Tottering-Smythe agreed with a growl, sitting down heavily in one of the twelve high-backed chairs surrounding the oak meeting table that dominated one half of his office. He started to bash out commands on the controls to his videoconferencing system.

'Quite,' Jenkins noted. He got along with the chap from The Breeders Association pretty well, despite the fact the man was too fond of excessively loud, boozy lunches. In contrast, Jenkins was a light drinker, preferring to retain his sense of decorum and quick wittedness. Unlike his guest, he hadn't lost his faculties to a self-induced alcoholic haze by the second race. Instead, he'd sipped his champagne whilst concentrating his not inconsiderable guile on wooing the man's wife. Jenkins had already enjoyed a number of illicit liaisons with the lady, who was considerably younger than her rich, alcoholic husband. He'd not seen Tottering-Smythe's missed calls and text messages until after his erotic encounter with the lady in one of the unused private boxes during the fifth race.

Tottering-Smythe poked at the audiovisual handset and cursed under his breath when he made a mistake and had to start again. Taking greater care, a large screen leapt into life at the end of the table and he added three people to the call. Two minutes later, with perfunctory greetings behind them, Tottering-Smythe was inspecting three grainy faces on a variety of domestic backgrounds. Tarquin Wray, the director of corporate affairs was sat primly in what appeared to be a library, with his awards and trophies arranged in clear view behind him. Just what I'd expect from Tarquin, Jeremy thought grimly.

Conversely, his director of integrity appeared to have called in on a mobile phone from a deck chair in his garden. Leonard Horowitz looked glum, his hair was ruffled and he was wearing a chunky jumper that suggested he'd been gardening. The remaining face belonged to Sally Proctor, a non-executive director asked to join them because she ran the London branch of an international marketing and promotions agency. In the age of social media where the sound bite was king, Tottering-Smythe had found it invaluable to have a public relations expert to call upon for advice. Proctor was young, good looking, a talented spin doctor, and a breath of fresh air in what was otherwise a fusty, old-fashioned organisation.

'You'll all be aware of what happened at Ripon this afternoon?' Tottering-Smythe confirmed.

Jenkins listened to the expressions of understanding emanating from the screen but remained silent, hoping someone would explain. It seemed his lost afternoon at Sandown had him at a disadvantage.

'I've had the police, the clerk of the course at Ripon, and the Jockey Club on the phone this afternoon. Also, a deadly serious chap from CID in Yorkshire called me at home, asking a bunch of questions that necessitated me coming into the office to source the information he was after. This girl worked for the racing channel and has managed to damage the racing brand this afternoon by jumping off Ripon's grandstand. What's more, she was caught doing so by a bunch of race-goers on their mobile phones. So, I want a succinct, positive response to go out to the media in order to deal with this quickly. You know the sort of thing: our heart goes out to her family, internal investigation and review of security underway, unavoidable loss of a few races… that sort of thing. Any further ideas?'

'As you know, Jeremy, I've been monitoring the media for the last hour,' announced Proctor before anyone else could reply, 'This isn't just an attempted suicide, the girl was subject to a hit and run in Ripon after she was *forced* to climb across the roof by men pursuing her from inside. The police have named a racing commentator as the driver of the vehicle that ran her over. He's currently on the run with an accomplice and this Billie Davenport is in hospital. The incident is far more than just an attempted suicide.'

'Where the hell do you get your information from, Sally?' Tottering-Smythe asked incredulously, 'The CID officer didn't even know her name when I spoke with him!'

Proctor shook her blonde bob momentarily and stared disbelievingly into the camera on her laptop, 'It's all over the internet. There are theories already circulating that this was a professional hit gone wrong. I've already read articles on three of the press websites linking this to a blog Davenport wrote, and there are police warnings not to approach this commentator chap, Joe Lawlor.'

Jenkins cleared his throat, 'Perhaps this isn't something we need to concern ourselves with, given the police involvement. It sounds drugs related and the fact it happened on a racecourse is simply…' he curtailed his suggestion when groans of exasperation emanated from both Tottering-Smythe and Proctor simultaneously.

'Have her employers said anything about Ms Davenport?' asked Leonard Horowitz.

'I've spoken to their chief executive,' replied Proctor, 'Davenport was in a bad way when she arrived in hospital and has been placed in an induced coma while they work out what sort of head trauma she's sustained. There seems to be no indication of foul play on her part. She was a model employee by all accounts; intelligent, well liked, and destined for rapid advancement.'

'Well she's obviously hacked someone off pretty badly, Joe Lawlor for one,' remarked Tarquin Wray with a snigger.

Silence greeted Wray's remark. Presently, Tottering-Smythe ran a hand through his hair and sighed.

'That's not helpful, Tarquin.'

Once Wray's grin had fallen from his face, Tottering-Smythe continued.

'What do we know about Joe Lawlor? Could he have been having an affair with Davenport and it's just a crime of passion?'

Tarquin spoke up again, his words straight and stern this time, 'I doubt it. All the indications point to Davenport being gay.'

'What makes you say that?' demanded Sally.

The corporate director curled his lip and looked away from his screen. There was no love lost between Wray and Proctor, a rivalry that Tottering-Smythe enjoyed stoking.

After a pause Wray admitted, 'There's a report on the Sun website. They've spoken to one of her colleagues from the press room, Micky Goodham.'

Tottering-Smythe groaned again, 'Micky Goodham is bad news. I wouldn't believe anything that self-opinionated…'

'Given this is an active, ongoing situation, perhaps Tarquin could put out a holding press release tonight,' Leonard Horowitz's light tone suggested smoothly, cutting Tottering-Smythe's vitriol short.

Everyone on the call knew about Tottering-Smythe and Goodham. Their televised paddock-side spat six months ago had been big news at the time. The argument had centred on an issue that remained high profile in the sport: were the major bookmakers a bad influence on racing? It had been suggested that several changes pushed through by Tottering-Smythe concerning the racing programme book, prize-money, and alterations to how bookmakers contributed to racing, had the bookmakers' profits solely at their heart. Due to the way racing's finances operated it appeared the powerful bookmakers were holding the BHA, and therefore the racing industry, to ransom. Tottering-Smythe had lost his cool when the hectoring Goodham had suggested his tenure at the BHA had seen the bookies tighten their insidious grip on the industry as a result of his liberal approach and passive management style.

Leonard Horowitz continued, 'This matter falls squarely into my domain, as the integrity of people working in the industry has come into question…'

'Absolutely,' Tottering-Smythe agreed, cutting through his colleague's words, 'Thanks for that Leonard. I know it's Sunday tomorrow, but perhaps we should get some television coverage… I see Uttoxeter races is on tomorrow and…'

'Can I suggest the meeting at Pontefract, Jeremy?' Horowitz interrupted, 'I could do a press call in person and perhaps ask the clerk of the course from Ripon to join me. Pontefract is close to Wakefield, so it's easy to get to by rail plus a short taxi ride, and I can impress upon the public and the press that it's business as usual. Hopefully, the police will have caught up with Joe Lawlor and his accomplice by then, and Davenport may have recovered enough to give some evidence against him. It would provide us with the platform to display our compassion for one of our own, whilst ensuring we aren't criticized for playing down the seriousness of the situation.'

Tottering-Smythe placed his elbows on the table and steepled his hands as he contemplated this suggestion. Horowitz was reliable and often the broker of agreements across the board's table. Jeremy considered Horowitz a credible replacement for himself. And although that wasn't his decision to make, his recommendation would provide Horowitz with a substantial and possibly unassailable head start over any other candidate.

'I believe as I am the head of communications, I should be hosting the press call,' Jenkins suggested, trying hard not to come over as being petulant.

'Lawlor was supposed to be commentating at the Pontefract meeting as well,' Proctor commented, 'It's not such a bad idea, whoever speaks.'

'Well Lawlor won't be commentating now,' stated Tottering-Smythe, 'I tell you what. Paul and Leonard, I think you should both go… and I'll join you up there tomorrow. We can present a united front and make sure we nip this issue in the bud. What do you think, Sally?'

Tottering-Smythe watched Wray bristle as Proctor restated the plan and gave it her blessing. He enjoyed watching the man's face turn sour. Wray had made it known he wanted his job once he was gone and he'd already made representations to ensure that didn't happen.

'You get that press release out, Tarquin,' Tottering-Smythe said in assumptive fashion, and called the meeting closed. He watched Wray reach forward to close his laptop and smirked at the man's grimace before his portion of the screen went blank.

'Ok Paul, I'm heading home. I'll see you tomorrow,' Tottering-Smythe said, indicating his wish for Jenkins to leave so he could lock up his office.

'Shall we travel up to Pontefract together tomorrow?' Jenkins queried.

Tottering-Smythe paused, making a meal of pulling his notes together.

'I'm afraid not. I will have to see you there just after midday, I've er… promised my son I'd watch him play football in the morning.'

Jenkins bid his boss farewell in the knowledge that he had been stonewalled; Tottering-Smythe's only son had to be at least twenty-two and he was positive he worked abroad.

Jenkins slunk off to the office bathroom; this had been his primary reason for calling in at the office this evening. He needed to take a shower and wash away the smell of perfume before he went home to his wife.

Eight

'Pull over!' Joe demanded.

Sparky maintained her speed and direction, but seemed to crumple in her seat. He repeated his command and in return received a disgusted stare from the girl.

'Can't we talk and drive?' she complained.

Joe considered. The girl had an unhealthy passion for dangerous situations and driving far too quickly. He'd felt happiest in her company when he'd sat in the café, locking eyes with her over the table.

'No,' he replied firmly, 'We need to talk.'

Sparky gave him a belligerent stare which lasted so long he had to break eye contact with her.

'Billie made me promise to protect her and her partner, and it's why I started out on this crazy escapade. But now, it's spinning out of control. I want to speak with you without you running off the road.'

'Huh, escapade...' Sparky muttered. She was gripping the steering wheel with only two fingers at its base, a disgruntled hunch in her shoulders.

They pulled off the road half a mile later, locating a position in a deserted tree lined lay-by with a decent number of bushes to hide the mini from the main road. Sparky switched the engine off and the two of them remained stock still for a moment, neither wishing to catch their travelling companion's eye.

Finally, Joe broke the silence, trying to speak in a conciliatory tone.

'I assume that you're a little more involved in this, er... *situation* than you've been letting on?'

Sparky snorted and banged a weak fist against the steering wheel, 'Right, here it is. Billie had been posting stuff for a while, and when I took a look at it and noticed something in her data and well... I *may* have nudged Billie in the right direction.'

'Ah... so if I turn on her laptop am I going to find emails from you telling her to look at the possibility there is a time delay on Fairbet?'

'Pretty much,' she moaned.

'So what's your dad got to do with this?'

'Nothing. It's just his company,' she replied, suddenly

starchy, 'I took an interest in Billie's analysis because she was investigating my dad's company.'

'Do you work for him?'

'Good god. As if! Since he divorced mum I've had nothing to do with him. But I thought it was pretty cool that his company was being ripped off, that's all.'

'That would show the world he wasn't perfect, wouldn't it,' Joe ventured.

'That's blummin' right...' Sparky started before realising Joe had read between the lines all too accurately. She shot a petulant look at him for a second, crossed her arms, and switched her gaze to stare angrily out of the driver's door window.

'Listen, we're both in this mess for different reasons. I don't know about you, but I have no desire to be a wanted man for the rest of my life, and I assume you want to help Billie, otherwise you wouldn't have turned up at the cathedral.'

Sparky allowed her arms to untangle and she managed a snort and a small inclination of her head in agreement.

'And if you can embarrass your dad at the same time, all well and good!'

Sparky's face broke into an amused smirk but she quickly bit it back into something more serious. Joe had the feeling he'd just about managed to get the girl positive again and made a mental note not to go near her father, daughter relationship again unless he wanted to stoke her anger. Then again, there could come a time when he needed her anger...

Joe turned in his seat and sternly examined the girl. She looked into his face, but soon flicked her eyes away, producing a coy smile, as if embarrassed.

'What's up with you?' she asked with a sigh.

'Why do you call yourself Sparky and not Ruth?' he asked quietly.

The girl spun to face him, ending up much closer to him than she intended. Their noses almost touched and she could see the shades of green within his irises and a bloom of stubble on his chin. Joe maintained a steady gaze and in return Ruth produced a fierce stare.

'You took the time to google me then?' she blurted, staying only a few inches from Joe despite getting a rush of angst which told her she was invading his personal space. He inclined his head

54

slightly and half closed his eyes in a 'what did you expect?' shrug. Sparky's features softened and she pulled back, pleased to have an excuse to do so.

'Yes, alright. I'm *Ruth* Gray,' she admitted, slamming her back into her seat and visibly deflating as she spoke, 'And I guess you must know I was responsible for the 'Tree Planting' virus.'

'That's… interesting, but not important,' Joe told her. He had to admit to being slightly fascinated with this particular fact, uncovered by googling 'sparky247' during his visit to the café washrooms, although he'd not made the connection that she was Michael Gray's daughter.

A hacker called Sparky247 had managed to disrupt, and in one or two cases, disable the internal IT systems of a carefully targeted number of international companies. The virus had worked its way around the networks of these huge corporate structures, all of whom had questionable records when it came to the environment, and in particular, pollution.

Over the course of several months the virus inveigled its way into corporate email and messaging systems, sitting dormant until the fifth of June. On world environment day the then fifteen-year-old Ruth Gray had instructed her virus to begin email-bombing the internal networks of these oil companies, airlines, and one or two financial services companies. The way to disable the virus was to make a sizeable donation to one of several charitable tree planting websites. It emerged some time later that several companies had done just that.

The virus caused several of Ruth's targets to cease trading for a number of days, during which time huge sums were wiped off their share value. Ruth had been tracked down, although due to her age, she was given a non-custodial sentence. Sparky had been caught for one simple reason; she had signed every single email with an easily traceable username.

'Right now, I want to know whether I can trust you. That's all.'

'Of course you can!'

Joe paused, making a point of looking the teenager up and down.

'Okay, get the rucksack and let's see what's on that laptop. Billie must have been closer to the perpetrator than she realised. Are you able to get online?'

'Of course,' said Sparky, in a somewhat brighter tone, 'Just for the record, I'm a proper freelance software engineer, so I do know what I'm doing. I don't do the naughty stuff anymore.'

She leant over and grabbed the rucksack from the back seat, pulled it over and removed a thin, expensive looking computer and opened it up. There appeared to be no security and a familiar Windows interface appeared almost immediately.

'Huh, Billie must have left it logged in,' she explained. 'It'll take me a few minutes to look through everything,' Sparky warned, pushing her seat back, fingers already clicking across the keyboard.

'Okay, well whilst you're doing that can you confirm I have the Fairbet situation right?'

She nodded her ascent, her face lit by the glow of the laptop; outside it was getting darker by the minute.

Joe continued, 'If there's a delay, let's say, of five seconds in a race being marked as finished, would that be enough to allow an unscrupulous person to either back or lay the correct horse, because effectively they would already know the result?'

'Have you seen the film, 'The Sting'?' Sparky asked, her head buried in the laptop, 'You know, Robert Redford and Paul Newman run a delayed race results scam… Well, this is the same scam, only updated for the new millennium. Thing is, they don't need five seconds, half a second or less would be enough.'

Joe nodded, 'So an unscrupulous punter using this 'hacking' app, or code, could potentially win money on every single race in world, all day, every day?'

'No, no. They can't win in *every* race,' Sparky corrected, 'For this hack to work you need a race with a really close finish so that the betting continues right up to the finishing line. Then the hacking code takes the stake money away from those punters who still believe the race isn't finished. It's no good if a horse is many lengths clear and the result isn't in doubt from a long way out.'

'I get it, the extra couple of seconds allows the hacking code to know the result and snap up any outstanding bets on the loser. But surely they can't be making that much money, the odds will be miniscule?'

Sparky turned in her seat and her face lit up like a pinball machine, 'You really don't follow the exchanges do you!' she laughed, 'There are usually tens of thousands of pounds available to match at 1.01 at the end of most races. That's people staking thousands of pounds to win tiny amounts on what look like sure things. But if they get it wrong, they can literally lose a fortune in a split second. A finish to a race where a horse is three lengths clear with half a furlong to run might see it trade at 1.02 or 1.01, that means you have to stake a hundred pounds to win one or two pounds. But then a challenger comes out of the pack and runs the leader down in the last few strides and you'll see the odds change radically. That's when having a split second delay pays off big time.'

'So not only can you back the winner to all the stakes available, you can do the same by laying the loser,' Joe confirmed.

'Exactly, and that's how I, or rather… Billie, noticed what must be going on,' Sparky responded, now animated by the conversation, 'And what's even weirder is that it only happens in the first week of the month. They stop running the hacking code around the fifth or sixth day of each month.'

'But won't the punters losing the money notice the delay?'

Sparky shook her head, her pageboy haircut hardly moving, 'No, each market closes once the horses go past the post, but there is always a short delay before a punter's browser updates. As long as it's not done on every race they bet in, it would be almost impossible to pick it up.'

'Clever stuff,' Joe murmured. 'How much do you think they are making?'

'Tens, if not hundreds of thousands of pounds each month at the very least, perhaps more. And remember, it's all tax free.'

'From just a few days each month?'

'Yup… pretty cool, huh. So you can see why whoever is running this scam wanted to shut Billie up.'

This statement hung in the cab of the mini for longer than was comfortable. Joe caught Sparky rubbing the sides of her thighs out of the corner of his eye. It was as if she was cold, but he was sure it was an unconscious action, perhaps she was thinking about Billie.

'Surely Fairbet would pick up on someone screwing with their system?'

'You'd think so wouldn't you,' responded Sparky, 'But you don't find what you're not looking for. Besides, in my experience most coders are men, and most men are so arrogant they can't imagine a world where their crappy code will get exploited like this.'

Joe studied his companion as she continued to be absorbed by the contents of Billie's computer, impressed with her intensity.

Presently the laptop's fan started up, filling the dark interior of the car with its mechanical whirring and breaking Joe's train of thought. He determined that for the moment, he had to forget the fraud, his own threatening phone call, and the Mercedes men, and just concentrate on what was in front of him. He cleared his throat. In response, Sparky glanced up from the computer and rolled her eyes.

'I have to ensure Billie's boyfriend, Taz, is okay. I told Billie I'd do that. She said he'd been threatened too, at their house up in Durham, so we need to get up there. Once I know he's safe we can go to the police.'

'Really?' Sparky retorted scornfully, 'You really think the police will be capable of working out who's behind all of this?'

Joe was momentarily stumped for an answer.

'Just see whether you can find her address up in Durham, will you?'

While Sparky's attention was concentrated on the laptop Joe took the opportunity to check his national news app and a few local news services. There was still no mention of his car, although the Ripon races incident was being widely reported. A few of the reports stated a young woman had subsequently been taken to hospital, but with no mention of a road traffic accident, or her condition.

Joe checked the time and made a quick calculation. It was an hour since he'd left his car, and about forty-five minutes since they'd lost the Mercedes men. Would they follow Billie to the hospital? Or go to Billie's home? This boyfriend called Taz... perhaps he was holding further evidence of her analysis? Joe ruled this out straight away. Billie was careful and precise when it came to her work; she wouldn't knowingly leave anything that valuable lying around at home. No, she'd made it clear that everything was contained in her rucksack.

But now Billie was in hospital, badly injured... or worse, and he had no clue where she lived, other than it was somewhere in Durham. For all he knew, Billie's boyfriend had already been subjected to the same bone breaking treatment. Joe shuddered as he contemplated this, a thought that led him to accept a stark reality; the Mercedes men knew Sparky now possessed Billie's laptop, so he and Sparky were now their primary objective.

Joe buried his face in both hands, trying to consider the angles, the options, analysing the threat level for each scenario fizzing through his mind. It struck him that this was similar to

58

calling a horse race. As the complexion of a race constantly changed, a good caller kept an eye on *all* the runners, not just the front few. There was nothing worse than a commentary that missed those horses picking up speed from midfield or the back of the pack. A race caller could be left red-faced if a horse not mentioned throughout their commentary got up in the dying strides to win. Joe smiled inwardly; this situation *was* just like calling a horse race! The trouble was, at the moment he didn't even know who the players were in this race.

'We need to identify all the runners,' Joe blurted reactively to Sparky, feeling a shot of hot elation as he reached his solution. He caught himself; okay, it wasn't a solution, but it would help.

Sparky jumped a little and held a hand to her chest, for a moment allowing her eyes to leave the glowing laptop screen to inspect her suddenly animated passenger.

'You're full of surprises aren't you?'

'And you're not? Your dad runs Fairbet for crying out loud!'

Sparky snorted with laughter and watched as Joe's face reacted to his own sarcasm. It seemed he was initially shocked at his quick-fire response, and then a sort of guilty enjoyment crept onto his face. It's like he's a cat having its first tentative lick of cream, and then realising it tasted divine, she decided. Sparky winked at him and he returned a slightly embarrassed smile.

'Well, hold fire for a minute. You're going to love what I've got to show you on here,' Sparky told him, turning the laptop so Joe could share the contents of the screen. For the next few minutes she ran through the entire contents of the laptop, explaining the data she'd found, notes Billie had made, and even the local copies of the recent blogs she had posted.

Joe remained silent, listening intently. Finally, Sparky took him into Billie's email folders.

She explained: 'The data shows there is something funny going on with the last few seconds of certain races. Basically, someone is mopping up every last few pounds of outstanding odds on horses they know have already won or been beaten. Even Fairbet's own stats aren't reporting the matches, presumably because the system believes the race market is closed. Now look at these…'

It was dark outside now and Billie's laptop was the only source of light in the car, displaying line after line of email conversations. Sparky ran her finger down the screen.

'Look here,' she said indicating a group of emails with send dates from over the last fortnight, 'It's not just me she's been sharing her ideas with.'

Sparky's index finger indicated three email recipients who had conversations with Billie running to five or six emails both ways. She was about to open the first of them when a sharp metallic bang on the bonnet of the car made both of them jump.

Sparky slammed the laptop shut and without looking up turned the ignition key. The engine immediately sparked into life.

'No!' Joe warned, 'We'll run him over!'

Sparky peered through the windscreen. A dark figure was standing motionless in front of the car, blocking their exit. She flicked her headlights on and revealed a man of medium height dressed head to foot in black motorcycle leathers. He was wearing a crash helmet with a tinted visor and was standing with both hands on the bonnet of her car. The man appeared to be staring into the cabin.

Sparky nervously revved the mini's engine and Joe's hand immediately shot across and grabbed her knee.

'We can't hurt anyone,' he insisted. Sparky gripped the steering wheel with both hands, her knuckles turning white.

'So they're allowed to hurt us, but we can't hurt them?'

For the first time, the figure moved, perhaps considering the possibility the car could simply run him down.

'That sucks!' Sparky complained, revving the engine until the little car started to sway under the pressure.

The leathered figure held up a gloved hand to Sparky, and with the other, tore off the helmet in one slick motion, and tossed its head, sending black curls onto... *her* shoulders. A perfectly symmetrical female Indian face, wracked with angst yet endowed with powerful, soulful eyes, glared through the windscreen. The engine fell quiet.

'Wow,' Sparky exclaimed in astonishment, 'Got to admit it. Wasn't expecting that,'

The figure stepped back a pace, the headlight beams revealing the full extent of the woman's skin tight, head to toe leather outfit. Behind her, Joe now noticed an impossibly powerful looking motorbike which even leaning on its stand, gave the impression it wanted to accelerate noisily into the distance.

'Is that Joe?' shouted the woman, squinting against the glare of the headlights.

Joe and Sparky shared a bemused look and Joe swallowed hard.

'Cool biker chick,' Sparky offered with a shrug, 'Not exactly the type you would expect to be trying to trap us, steal from us, or kill us. But you never know. We can live in hope.'

Joe rolled his eyes, whispered a few words, opened his door, and got out.

'Yes, that's me. Could I just ask who...'

'Oh, thank goodness!' the woman exclaimed, the anxiety washing from her face in an instant. She strode over to Joe and he was sure her huge, brown eyes surrounded by perfectly white sclera were reflective. They shone when the beams from the headlights bounced off them.

'Tasmina Shaw,' she said, extending a hand awkwardly toward him over his open car door. He took it and watched as the woman, well, possibly girl, he corrected himself - she could have been aged anything between twenty and thirty in this light - blinked a pair of long lashes and locked eyes with him, displaying an expression full of hope.

'Billie said she might get you to help, and when I saw the news reports on the TV, I had to find you.'

There was the definite hint of an Indian accent in her speech, however, it was almost washed away by a northern accent. There was something else in there too; possibly a Yorkshire twang. Yet somehow, the combination seemed to meld harmoniously. Joe, still taken aback by the strangeness, but also the sheer beauty of the woman, took his time before answering. She had tiny creases around her eyes that might indicate she was older than he first thought. Eventually she stepped back, cocked her head to one side and asked, 'You *are* Joe Lawlor aren't you. I haven't got the wrong Joe have I?'

Joe heard a barely suppressed guffaw emanate from the other side of the car. Sparky was by her open door, leaning cross-armed on the car roof, watching with unabashed amusement.

'No. I mean... no, you haven't got it wrong. I'm Joe Lawlor.'

Relief flooded Tasmina's face, releasing worry lines from her forehead. She forced a smile whilst hugging her bike helmet to her chest, her eyes switching appraisingly between the two strangers and lingering on Sparky.

'Tasmina?' Joe queried, 'I don't suppose Billie calls you...'

'Taz,' the girl finished for him, '...Billie calls me Taz.'

Nine

'What the hell is going on?'

Antony Gerard's gruff voice provided an answer. It sounded as if he was making the call from the side of a busy road which resulted in half his words being garbled.

'Say that again and slower,' Michael Gray demanded.

'I was too late. Davenport was caught.'

'So they have her device?'

'No.'

'What? So you have it?'

'No,' Gerard repeated levelly.

'Gerard, I don't pay you to…'

'Your daughter has the device,' Gerard cut in.

Gray took a moment to steady himself, listening to the sound of vehicles passing close to his personal assistant somewhere in Yorkshire.

Presently Gray ran his tongue over his dry lips and asked, 'It was definitely her?'

'Yes, Sir. Her mini was caught on video. You can see it for yourself on YouTube.'

'What about this commentator?'

'Joe Lawlor.'

'Who?'

'The race caller is called Joe Lawlor,' Gerard repeated deliberately, 'He has Davenport's device and he's with your daughter, Ruth.'

Gray frowned. She was supposed to be with her mother. What on earth was she doing running around North Yorkshire…?

'What are your instructions?' Gerard queried, now shouting above the traffic noise.

Gray hesitated, 'They remain the same. Have you got eyes on those men?'

'Yes. At they are standing on a bridge over the A1. I assume they are watching out for a vintage red mini to go past. They…'

Gray glanced at the digital clock on his desk: six fifty-five in the evening. Hutchinson was right on time. He hung up on Gerard with his personal assistant still in mid-sentence.

William Hutchinson's profile was pulsing on one of the eight screens that were arranged in an array around his desk and Gray accepted the video call once he'd taken a deep, calming breath.

He offered his friend a perfunctory greeting, received the same in return, and then they were straight down to business. Both men knew the shareholders' meeting due in a few minutes would be troublesome. They might have to weather another round of demands to take this latest offer seriously, or rebuff demands to alter the company's weak credit position by consolidating shares, or even, god forbid, take the company public.

'How are we going to kill off these damn unsolicited bids for Fairbet, Bill?' Gray asked, 'They're coming thick and fast at the moment.'

Hutchinson didn't answer; he knew the question was rhetorical. He'd worked with Gray for the best part of twenty-five years. They'd built the company from scratch, Gray the technology man and Hutchinson managing the finances. Together they'd created a new type of betting business. More importantly, it was a business that created profits of around half a million pounds every week. Hutchinson waited for Gray to continue.

'We'll give them a resounding no, I don't care what the shareholders say. They're not getting their hands on our technology.'

'It's not the technology they want,' Hutchinson replied in his broad West Yorkshire drawl, closing his bloodshot eyes and rubbing the bridge of his nose, 'It may have been in the old days. Now they want us for our profit and growth. That's why these approaches are becoming more difficult to fend off.'

'We can see them off between us, can't we?'

Hutchinson gave a weak smile.

'It was a mistake to sell ten percent to that investment bank five years ago. Being left with only forty-eight percent between us was always going to make us vulnerable.'

'We needed the capital to grow fast enough to dominate the market. We'd only be half the company we are now if we hadn't taken that risk,' insisted Gray.

Hutchinson's long, flat face regarded his friend with fondness. They'd had this same discussion many times over the last five years, and up until now they had convinced the investors to maintain the status quo. But Hutchinson knew it wouldn't be long before the other shareholders had their heads turned by a big instant profit, rather than reaping their rewards each year in dividends.

'We could just get out... it's been twenty odd years now,

and…'

'Forget that, Bill,' Gray cut in reproachfully, 'We've got Asia and Eastern Europe to crack before I'll even consider selling.'

'Okay, Michael, it's always been your business, and your call. I'm still enjoying the ride. So how are we going to play this meeting?'

Gray considered this for a few seconds before replying, 'It will be Drew Cooper beating the drum for us to take this approach seriously. I get the impression he's always keen to make a quick buck. O'Neill might side with him if the profit is good enough for his corporate partners and might bring Peters with him. The rest will go with the flow I reckon. But together, our block of shares should defeat them, and of course, I always have my veto.'

Hutchinson smiled and slowly shook his head.

'That was the shrewdest thing you ever did, Michael,' he said warmly, 'If it wasn't for your veto on selling, we'd have been gobbled up by one of the international betting groups years ago. Sure, we'd have been rich, but not as filthy rich as we could be if we sold now.'

Gray flashed a quick smile back.

'I know you think I spend too much time with my head in the coding, Bill, but I was never going to allow anyone to sell my company from under me.'

The two men continued to discuss how they were going to manage the other shareholders until Gray had six more blinking profiles appearing across his screens, requesting to join the meeting. One by one, Gray accepted the other part-owners of the company to join him in his home office, which doubled as his lounge, now he was single again. He and Hutchinson spent the next thirty minutes defending their position.

'There's a reason we're having this discussion so regularly,' Drew Cooper stated once Gray had dropped his veto into the conversation, 'We are…'

'I know why we keep getting offers,' Gray interrupted abruptly, speaking over Cooper in a tone heavy with indignant irritation, 'But we're not selling. If you want to realise your investment, sell your shares and get out.'

'But the company needs…'

'I know what my company needs, Cooper,' Gray insisted, allowing his impatience to coalesce with his dislike for the man,

'This company needs investors with patience, foresight, and most of all, the fortitude to see our global expansion programme through to fruition.'

A disgruntled Cooper slowly shook his head, 'You'll need further investment to make that happen...'

'Perhaps we should vote and we'll see whether this confrontation is worthwhile or not,' Hutchinson suggested.

'It's pointless,' Gray pointed out, 'I can veto any sale. If you can't convince me, Fairbet isn't going to be sold. Even when I'm six foot under this company will remain be under my control.'

'Shareholders still have the right to a vote,' said Cooper, 'Or are you going to veto that too, Michael?'

Gray stared dully at Cooper's image on his monitor. Everything about the man was thin and sparse. From his drawn and creased facial features, to his paper thin comb-over, Cooper was insubstantial.

The vote completed, and the proposal to enter negotiations defeated, Cooper waited for any other business before dropping his bombshell on Gray.

'It's interesting that we're still getting approaches from these global companies, given reports are rife on the internet that your precious betting system is open to fraud.'

When Gray didn't reply, Cooper added, 'And I see that the woman concerned, a reporter with a media company specialising in horse racing, threw herself off the top of a racecourse grandstand this afternoon. Are you aware of these developments, Michael?'

Gray could sense his core temperature rising, and an involuntary tick made the muscle in his cheek twitch twice in rapid succession. He needed to move quickly.

'I'm aware of Ms Davenport's posting and the unfortunate incident involving her at Ripon today. But her work was all fanciful tittle-tattle. My systems have been proven to be robust. I'd like to add that the day I require technology advice from a manager of an investment bank... well, that day will never arrive.'

The meeting subsequently broke up quickly. Within a few minutes only Gray and Hutchinson remained on the video call.

'Are you okay, Michael? You look pale. Is your personal assistant with you... what's his name? Gerard?'

Gray didn't answer. Instead, he shrugged, asking, 'Will you be coming to Pontefract tomorrow, for the employee raceday?'

Hutchinson was used to Gray's penchant for answering a question with one of his own, often on an unrelated topic. It meant his line of questioning was off the table. Returning to his query again would see an escalation in Gray's attempts to shut him down, and darken his mood.

'Yeah, I couldn't miss it. I've attended every year. I'll be there mid-afternoon if that's okay.'

'Want me to send the helicopter for you, Bill?

'Sure, why not,' Hutchinson replied, still studying his business partner closely.

Having found an excuse to end the video call a few seconds later, Gray forced a smile as Bill's concerned image flicked off his monitor, then double checked to ensure all the participant connections to the video call had been terminated.

He picked up his mobile phone and called Gerard, issuing new instructions. The call took less than twenty seconds.

With a cursory check to ensure he'd rung off successfully, Michael Gray pushed back into his office chair. He remained in his seat for a few seconds then jumped to his feet and spent the next twenty minutes stalking erratically around his sparsely furnished open-plan house, periodically placing his head in hands and whimpering quietly, as he fought off the affects of a panic attack.

Ten

Joe scanned the lay-by, lit only by the two spears of light from the mini's headlights. His eyes were becoming accustomed to the gloom. He and Sparky peered at the stunning young woman who swung her crash helmet in a leather gloved hand and rested the other on her hip. A car rushed past beyond the line of bushes to their right, producing a sudden spray of strong light and engine growl that lit the scene for a second. Joe noticed her shiny black helmet was adorned with reflective flashes of lightning.

'Could I ask how you managed to find us?' he asked carefully, not wishing to upset the woman, but needing reassurance following her sudden arrival.

Taz's black eyelashes fluttered and she dropped her chin apologetically, allowing a curtain of dark hair to fall across her face. She flicked it away with a deft touch of her index finger and locked eyes with Joe.

'Billie called me a few hours ago. Have you seen her?'

Sparky had rounded the car and was leaning, cross-armed with her backside against the mini's grill. She stared intently at Joe, intimating that it was up to him to handle the girl's query. She carefully placed the laptop on the mini's bonnet.

'Yes, we saw her, but I'd be grateful if you could tell me how you...'

'Billie's laptop has a GPS tracker on it,' the girl cut in irritably, 'It doesn't need to be switched on or connected to the internet. I could track it on my phone each time you came into contact with an open broadband connection.'

'Nice! That's a proper bit of tech!' Sparky exclaimed, apparently impressed, 'So you've come from Carlisle... nice bike by the way...'

The young woman gave a faint smile, 'Yeah, we, er... I left when Billie...' she winced, but recovered quickly and gave Sparky a sharp look.

'I drove down from *Durham*. Why would you say Carlisle?'

Sparky didn't reply. She continued to size up the good looking Indian girl with an appraising stare.

'So where's Billie? Taz asked Joe, 'She's not with you?'

The young woman squinted through the car's windscreen, apparently trying to spot movement in the mini's back seat.

'You've been riding around following the laptop's signal for the last few hours then?' Joe asked.

'Yes, that's right. So where is she?'

There was an anxiety creeping into her voice and he noticed her bite her lip as she waited for his answer.

Joe remained silent, considering the best approach. Reporting Billie's accident needed tender handling, as Taz obviously wasn't aware of what had gone on at the cathedral. There was also a thought niggling him; if she had a phone capable of tracking the laptop, why had she not answered any of his calls?

Taz eyed him suspiciously; he must have somehow telegraphed his anxiety.

Sparky closed her eyes, shook her head and sighed. She sucked in a deep breath and pushed the laptop further onto the Mini's bonnet. In doing so, she managed to attract Taz's attention.

'Look, this isn't easy to tell, you being her girlfriend and all, but Billie was thrown into the path of Joe's car by some unsavoury men and the last we saw of her she was pretty badly hurt and was being loaded into an ambulance,' Sparky announced, 'We've got her laptop here and we were in the process of trying to find you. Now you're here, we can all go to the police together knowing you're safe and we have the evidence that someone is ripping off Fairbet punters.'

Sparky concluded by producing a thin-lipped smile for Taz, 'So, that's us all caught up.'

Joe was staring at Sparky open-mouthed. Disappointed with the lack of reaction from Taz, she cast a desultory look his way and shrugged, 'We'd have been here all day if we had to wait for your explanation. It strikes me you sometimes take a long time to say things, which is weird, given you're a commentator.'

Taz dropped her chin to her chest and remained silent. She allowed her helmet to bounce against her hip and began to swing it gently. Joe was watching the woman carefully, trying to judge her reaction. Even so, he didn't see the crash helmet arcing toward his head until it was almost too late. He cringed and waited for the impact as the helmet, still attached to Taz's hand, loomed large from out of the gloom. The shiny zig-zag of lightning bolts bounced off the top of his shoulder and cannoned into the side of his head, sending him staggering into the darkness.

Taz darted forward, once again swinging her helmet, this time threatening Sparky, who quickly backed away to the side of the mini. The woman grabbed the laptop off the bonnet of the car, shouted a few warnings, and sprinted back to her bike. Zipping the laptop into her biking suit and donning her helmet in one well-practised motion, she kicked the bike into life, gunned the throttle, and roared off into the inky blackness.

Sparky watched her go. She'd been shouting threats and expletives after the girl, but turning to Joe, immediately lost all signs of frustration at being the victim of a crime.

'You okay?' she asked, going over to where Joe was leaning against the side of the mini, rubbing his cheek. She placed a hand on his arm, pulled it down and squinted at him in the poor light.

'She just winged me,' he replied ruefully once Sparky had finished her inspection. He was rather more embarrassed than damaged. There had been a time when he'd have been quick enough to avoid such a telegraphed swing at him.

'And you?'

'A little bit hacked off that I had to give up my perfectly good laptop, but at least we've still got Billie's. Come on, we'd best get going. It's not going to take that biker bitch long to realise she swiped the wrong bit of kit.'

Joe jumped into the passenger seat and looked around.

'Where is it?' he asked, endeavouring not to hint at his consternation, now the buzz of being attacked was starting to wear off. Sparky didn't reply, preoccupied with starting the car.

'Under your seat. Get it out, we need to stop it from broadcasting that location signal. It can't be that accurate though, it took her a while to catch up with us. One thing for sure: the cool biker chick wasn't Taz, her reaction was all wrong when we told her about Billie going to hospital.'

A few minutes later they were tearing along a tree lined lane heading north, Joe gripping onto the door handle as Sparky plunged headlong into the darkness along country B roads. Joe had retrieved Billie's laptop and it was sitting unopened on his knees.

'Slow down and pull over when you get chance. I don't think we'll find Taz at home in Durham.'

Sparky swiveled her head toward him, her mouth already starting to shape a demand for an explanation. Catching Joe's stare, she took her foot off the accelerator and slowed, pulling off the road and onto a rough farm track. She brought the car to a halt when her headlights picked out a mature field of wheat a few yards ahead.

'Whoever it was, she thought we had Billie with us. She must not have seen the news; too busy tracking us, or as far as they were aware, tracking Billie. But she knew how to track the laptop, and surely only Taz, or one of Billie's really close friends would know how to do that...'

'...Or perhaps our cool biker chick, had already got to Taz and forced her to track Billie's laptop!' Sparky said, unable to keep the excitement of the chase from her voice, 'We need to catch up with her to find Taz.'

'Or... we get your biker chick to find us again,' Joe said quietly, his fingers drumming on the lid of Billie's laptop.

'Can you disable whatever is creating the signal from this laptop?'

'Shouldn't be a problem.'

'Only disable it. We may need to switch it back on again.'

Sparky grinned as she opened Billie's laptop and her fingers began touch-typing, 'You've got a plan.'

'I don't know what it is, but it's certainly not a plan. At least, not yet.'

Joe had been staring blindly through the windscreen as he spoke. He turned to Sparky and found her wide-eyed with anticipation.

'I think you need to put my SIM back into my phone. If I'm right, I have a feeling there could be one or two messages we need to hear.'

'You do know switching it on will give away our location?'

'Even if all I do is listen to my messages?'

''Fraid so. It'll track us to the local mast. If anyone is scanning your number, they'll know where you are to within about half a mile. Why, what messages are you expecting?'

'Billie said she'd spoken with Taz and warned her. If I was Taz, and I was scared, I'd try and keep in contact with Billie. If I couldn't get hold of her, then the next person I would call would be the man Billie hopes to escape with.'

'You're hoping Taz has called you and left a message to let you know where she is... so we can go and find her?'

'I have to know she's safe,' Joe said levelly, turning to face his companion, 'I promised Billie. Then we need to work out how we resolve this mess.'

'What happens if you get a message from her kidnappers?'

Joe gave a purposeful sigh and tapped the laptop, 'Then we trade this for her.'

The car returned to silence, both passengers staring out into the wheat field pierced by the mini's headlights, contemplating what state Billie was in, where her partner Taz might be, where the girl on the motorbike fitted in, and which direction they should go in next.

'She said to look for her ghost,' Joe said softly.

'What?'

'Billie. She said…'

'I heard!' shrieked Sparky, 'Why the hell didn't you tell me before?'

Joe frowned questioningly, but it had no effect on his companion. Sparky grabbed Billie's laptop back from him and whilst muttering a raft of complaints her fingertips rattled away.

'There!' she finally exclaimed and turned the laptop screen toward Joe, 'She's got a ghosted drive.'

Joe gave her a blank stare, uncertain what this meant. The laptop looked exactly as it had done previously.

'Billie had a ghosted…' Sparky looked up from the device and saw Joe was struggling to keep up.

'It's a hidden portion of the laptop's hard drive. By the look of it there's a bunch of spreadsheets, a zip file, and a…'

Joe turned to confirm his understanding, but Sparky's fingers became a blur once more as her attention was gripped by the constantly changing screen on her lap. It flickered as she worked, bathing the inside of the mini's cabin in a variety of shades and colours. Joe concentrated on the issue directly in front of them: it was getting late and they needed somewhere to stay. The idea of sleeping in Sparky's car didn't appeal, and they certainly couldn't stay on this farm track all night.

Sparky squealed, making Joe jump.

'Oh my…' she exclaimed, hitting a single button on the laptop and became engrossed once more.

'What is it?' Joe asked patiently. When no answer was forthcoming he added a stern, 'Sparky!' Shaken from her investigations the girl turned to face him with an open mouth. She blinked back into the present, and found her tongue.

'Billie has a copy of the software controlling the fraudulent hacking.'

'In English?' Joe responded blankly.

Sparky scrunched her face up in frustration, shook her balled fists and gave a suppressed cry of anguish.

'This is what makes this laptop so valuable,' she explained excitedly, 'It's a record of every Fairbet transaction, account and payout made using the hacking code.'

'So Billie found the smoking gun,' Joe declared.

She paused to stare out into the darkness, 'This is much more than a smoking gun. It's a forensic dissection of every crooked bet placed on Fairbet. In fact, it may even tell you the races they are planning to run the hacking code on in the future.'

'When you say 'they', can you tell who is controlling the software?'

'No, but it narrows the field considerably. I need to do some more work on the software to see if I can trace where the calls from the...'

Sparky stopped speaking abruptly, her irises expanding as her mind processed the ramifications of her discovery. She was staring through the windscreen again, but Joe doubted she was seeing anything. She was examining ideas, possibilities and outcomes within herself. He sat quietly, waiting.

'It's as if this is in-house software,' she finally whispered to herself, still inhabiting a world of her own creation.

Joe scratched his head, unimpressed. Whilst the discovery of this window into a hacker's playground was undoubtedly important, right now he was concerned with more rudimentary needs; like where they would sleep tonight.

As Sparky's fingers returned to play over the laptop's keyboard Joe made a phone call to an old friend. Then he removed the SIM and swapping his own back into the phone, spent the next ten minutes collecting his voicemail and text messages. It transpired he had suddenly become incredibly popular; there were dozens. He noted the time, content, and return number of each message of interest on the back of a fuel receipt he found among the crisp packets and sweet wrappers stuffed into the Mini's unused ashtray.

Taz had called. He tried her number once again, but it went straight to answer phone. He left a short message.

Changing the SIMs back, he swapped seats with Sparky and allowed the contents of his messages to filter through his mind as he drove at a sensible pace to York, carefully picking his way cross-country. Sparky's attention didn't leave the laptop's glowing screen for the entire hour, until they turned down the side of a terrace of Victorian houses, trundled down a narrow back street and pulled into an open garage. As he switched the ignition off Sparky slapped the laptop shut and turned to him, her eyes gleaming.

'You're going to absolutely *love* what I've found!'

'Really? he responded, trying to conjure up some enthusiasm. Sparky detected Joe's thinly masked concern and demanded an explanation.

'Taz left me a message,' he revealed gloomily, 'She managed to escape her Durham home this afternoon, just as a man she described as 'an ape' broke her front door down. He was demanding she handed over all Billie's computer stuff.'

'Isn't that good, you know, that she got away?'

'She left with her sister… on a motorbike.'

'Ah,' replied Sparky, wrinkling her nose. She began re-running their encounter with the laptop thief through her head, 'That explains…'

'…why our biker was confused and reacted badly when you told her about Billie being run down and left by us in the road. She was expecting me to be with Billie in my Volvo. She'd have no knowledge of what happened at Ripon races, or at the cathedral. The tracker on the laptop allowed her to locate us, but we weren't what she was expecting.'

'Cool biker chick was Taz's sister,' Sparky stated despondently, 'No wonder she nicked my laptop. She probably thought she was better off winging it, given the way I described what happened…'

She fell silent as she contemplated. Joe waited.

'Oh, crap.'

Joe nodded his agreement with a grimace.

'Activate the location app on Billie's laptop again,' he instructed.

Sparky bit the inside of her cheek.

'Huh, imagine that. I never turned it off,' she admitted, 'I got carried away with the ghosted drive…'

Eleven

Joe had never been too demonstrative. He would rather shake a hand than hug. But when it came to Sandie, all thoughts of avoiding physical contact had to be discarded. Once he and Sparky had stepped from the double garage at the bottom of his friend's narrow back garden in a quiet York suburb, a light went on in the house and the back door opened. Sandie's broad smile greeted them as she approached at a canter down the garden path. There was a hug for Joe and a kiss on the cheek for Sparky, punctuated by her exclamations of delight at their arrival, and a little scolding regarding the extended length of time since Joe's last visit.

Sparky watched in amusement as Joe coped with the advances of the deep-throated, good-looking middle-aged divorcee as she fussed around him. Joe had provided a short synopsis of his relationship with Sandie, warning Sparky to expect an upfront, gregarious, and most importantly, entirely trustworthy friend who would take them both in and expect nothing in return.

Joe and Sandie had met ten years previously during the most enjoyable acting job he'd ever landed. They had worked through the summer on a children's drama series for television, loosely based around the harbour of a village on the North East coast. Their roles had required them to share regular scenes together per episode, and it hadn't taken long for them to strike up a friendship based on Joe's dry sense of humour, and Sandie's sense of fun and lust for life. They enjoyed two summers of filming together and had become firm friends. Their friendship managed to endure and strengthen further once the drama series was cancelled and Sandie's subsequent need for his support during a messy divorce.

Sparky had guessed Sandie was the same age as Joe until she'd been the recipient of an unexpected kiss on both cheeks. As Sandie withdrew, Sparky noticed tell-tale wrinkles around her eyes, cleverly hidden under a thin veneer of expertly applied make-up. After this reassessment she guessed Sandie was in her late forties. Still, the woman's sparkling eyes and physical zest could easily see her mistaken for a thirty-year-old.

'Let's get you inside, you're both tired,' Sandie declared, slipping her hand around Joe's arm and marching him towards the house. As they crossed the small back lawn she whispered conspiratorially to them, 'Best be quick, Joe's a television star for all

74

the wrong reasons, and I have incredibly nosey neighbours.'

Sandie led them through an old-fashioned kitchen, down a hall and into her front room where they were introduced to Matt. Sparky nodded a silent hello to the lean, muscular twenty-two year old in jeans and t-shirt, lounging on one of three identical sofas. Joe had explained that Sandie worked at the Theatre Royal in the city, as a make-up and wardrobe artist and supplemented her income by running a guest house specifically for actors. They would stay anything from a few weeks to a number of months during the run of their play or musical. At present the house was devoid of thespians, so it was just Sandie and her son Matt, at home from university for the summer.

Matt gave Sparky an easy smile and sensing she was uncertain of him, asked whether he could get her a drink, or something to eat. She found herself surreptitiously watching him as he unfolded himself from the sofa, stretched, and loped lightly out of the room in search of a can of Pepsi Max for her.

'Come on Joey, tell Auntie Sandie. What on earth have you got yourself into? I told you horseracing wasn't a suitable area to concentrate your talents.'

Sparky grinned and raised an eyebrow at Joe; he rolled his eyes back at her. He looked tired, but was far more relaxed than during their drive to York. She'd noticed him tensing over the wheel, and couldn't help feeling it was because a route to Taz had slipped through their fingers and she felt a little responsible. He was clearly at ease in Sandie's company, and she could understand why. She too had been instantly beguiled by the older woman; there was a warmth and girlish fun about her that drew you in.

An old carriage clock caught Sparky's eye, sitting in the centre of the mantlepiece over an unlit open fire, its grate filled with large pine cones for the summer months. She was surprised to discover it was eleven o'clock. Time flies when you're on the run, she noted with tired amusement.

'Well, Auntie Sandie, you can ignore whatever you've seen on the television,' Joe insisted, 'I didn't hit anyone in my car, although I did run from the scene, but with good reason. Have they said anything further about Billie Davenport, the girl that was taken to hospital?'

'She's poorly, but in a stable condition according to the ten o'clock news,' Matt replied as he returned, handing Sparky a cold can of cola. He sat beside her on the sofa, aping her crossed legs and opened a can of his own.

Joe spent the next few minutes providing Sandie and her son with an abridged version of the events since he'd met Billie at Ripon, with Sparky interjecting to embellish his story here and there.

'We have to find Billie's partner, Taz. We think she could be in danger from whoever is trying to suppress this bookmaking fraud.'

'We don't think. We know,' stated Sparky dramatically, 'Tell them what I found on the ghosted portion of Billie's laptop.'

Joe's manner altered, as if the news he was about to impart was distasteful. He scratched the side of his head and screwed his face up before continuing.

'It seems Billie gained access to a piece of software that somehow allowed her to access the Fairbet systems and she uncovered a fraudulent hack that creates erroneous winnings.'

'I've been able to isolate the primary account,' Sparky added excitedly, 'You wouldn't believe how much…'

'Needless to say…' Joe broke in, aiming a stern stare at her, '…the owner of the account is innocent until proven guilty.'

Sparky yawned, tiredness suddenly weighing heavily on her eyelids. She blinked her eyes open, refusing to obey her body's need to rest. She was glad she did, as Matt had leaned forward and her interest piqued as his curly black hair flopped over his forehead, forcing him to brush it aside. Joe glanced over at Sandie and they shared a knowing smile that quickly dissolved. He wondered how much time Sparky had spent in front of a computer monitor as a teenager and therefore how little interaction she'd had with boys.

'So does that laptop have the ability to run this hacking code?' asked Sandie, nodding at the device on Sparky's lap.

Joe looked over at Sparky expectantly and found her biting her lip, seemingly oblivious to what was going on around her. He recognised the same faraway look she had adopted earlier in the night upon discovering the contents of the ghosted portion of Billie's laptop. This time, the teenage excitement on Sparky's face had been replaced with a far more serious undercurrent. He tried to identify it, and could only come up with fear. He dismissed this immediately, putting his clearly wrong reading of his co-conspirator's features down to his own tiredness. Fear wasn't something that computed where Sparky was concerned.

'I think a good night's sleep is in order,' Joe said, firing a hopeful glance Sandie's way.

'Absolutely. I've two beds made up for you and Sparky on the second floor. Separate rooms of course, unless you two...' Sandie suggested playfully.

'Good God, no!' Sparky shrieked, before glancing around the amused faces and realising she was being teased.

'That's quite enough of that, Sandie,' Joe remonstrated lightly, 'It's been a long day, and we're going to be busy again tomorrow.'

'On a Sunday?' queried Matt, following Sparky's lead and getting to his feet.

'We have no other option. We have to find Taz, and get Billie's laptop to her, or the authorities - whichever will ensure both of them will remain safe.'

'And we need to clear your name,' Sparky added, draining her cola and setting the empty can down beside Matt's.

Joe paused, looking thoughtful, 'Yes, I suppose you're right.'

Sandie joined the two youngsters, jumping to her feet and shooing them off to bed, instructing Matt to show Sparky to one of the guest rooms equipped with some night clothes and toiletries.

When the creaking sound of stairs being climbed could be heard, Sandie sat down beside Joe and put her hand on his knee.

'You're on another bloody mission, aren't you?'

Joe ruefully flicked an imaginary piece of fluff from his trousers before meeting his friend's accusatory stare.

'Thank you for pointing that out, but please remember, there's a young girl out there who could get hurt if I don't try and put this right.'

Sandie closed her eyes and shook her head.

'This isn't an episode of a kids' drama. You're a wanted man for crying out loud! A fugitive!' She rocked his knee back and forth insistently as she spoke, her eyes wide and imploring, 'You're in so much trouble...'

She fell silent. Recognising his steely expression, and the minute adjustment in the angle of his head, Sandie realised he was bracing himself against her argument. She concluded there was little point in continuing. God love him, he was going to save the girl, and if it didn't work out, he'd suffer the consequences.

Twelve

Joe woke in a cold sweat. A shallow sleep had come quickly, but consisted of a series of nonsensical dreams. The latest saw him as a passenger with Sparky at the wheel in a high speed car chase. Half awake, the sound of squealing wheels and a high-revving engine continued to swirl around his head before he realised the noise was coming from the street below. There was shouting, added to the engine noises. A tremor of fear ran through him, propelling him to the bedroom window, where he peered between the gap in the curtains at the scene in the street below. His pulse quickened as he looked for the tell-tale signs of a rotating blue light and armed men converging on the house. Instead, a powerful motorbike was touring up the street, loudly revving its engine, rider and pillion passenger staring up at each house through tinted visors. As they passed under a streetlight Joe picked out a flash of lightning on the rider's helmet.

His phone told him it was a few minutes after one in the morning. Pulling on his trousers and shirt Joe hurried down the stairs. Unlocking the dead-bolted front door he stepped onto an ancient concrete path riddled with cracks and crevices. He tried to tread lightly as the surface grit bit into the soles of his bare feet.

'Taz!'

He called the girl's name twice more, both times with a less positive, querying tone. Sandie and Sparky appeared at the doorway behind him and watched as Joe placated irate neighbours come to investigate the roar of a motorbike in the dead of the night. The bike's engine had dwindled to a faint rasp in the distance, but swelled in volume once more as Joe stepped out into the road, waving his arms above his head toward the shimmering headlight at the far end of the terrace.

The bike accelerated toward him, roaring intermittently as the rider accentuated each gear change with ear-splitting revving that bounced off the valley of houses and reverberated down the street. If she wanted to draw attention to herself, then Taz was succeeding in grand fashion, thought Joe, as the headlight momentarily blinded him. He continued to wave his arms frantically above his head. The bike suddenly decelerated and the beam of light ceased strafing the rest of the road and instead, settled on Joe.

The machine slowed as it approached and Joe ceased his waving, moving onto the pavement. The bike stopped opposite him and two black visors faced him. The rider's visor lifted and an impressive pair of dark brown eyes surveyed him pensively.

'Drive round the back. I'll meet you there,' he instructed in a businesslike manner, indicating their route with a hand gesture. In response, the bike's engine revved before moving off.

'Quietly!' he called after them.

After placating the remaining homeowners with gestures and apologetic shrugs, Joe scampered barefoot through the house and out the back. By the time he reached the garage at the bottom of the back garden Sandie was already there with Sparky, busy introducing the two young women. As he approached, Joe was struck by how small and vulnerable both of them appeared now they were separated from their bike. They were unmistakably sisters. They shared the same finely boned features and striking eyes, but it was the way they held themselves that struck Joe most. The older girl, and rider of the motorbike, was straight-backed, shoulders tensed, and feet firmly planted. She exuded defiance. However the smaller, younger girl in jeans, t-shirt and an ill-fitting leather jacket wore a hunted look. This had to be Taz.

'Vrinda, Taz… this is Joe,' Sparky advised as he sidled between cars down the dimly lit garage. As both the bikers turned their heads toward him Joe stood on something sharp, let out a muffled yelp and hopped sideways in order to maintain his balance while brushing away the painful object stuck to his foot.

'Race caller, actor, wanted man… and, er... aspiring dancer,' Sparky added sarcastically.

'I sense the latter still needs work,' Vrinda offered drily.

Joe leaned against the mini's roof as he massaged the sole of his foot. About to return a dancing quip, he caught the gaze of the smaller woman and his witty rejoinder was immediately forgotten. Unlike her relaxed, confident sister, Taz was on edge. Pale faced and unsmiling, she radiated a mixture of fear and suppressed rage. Joe sensed Taz was yearning for answers and if this initial impression of her was correct, she could easily explode if the comic banter continued.

'I only heard your voicemail message an hour ago, Taz.'

She eyed him warily for a few seconds before nodding a silent acknowledgment.

'When Vrinda met us we assumed you would know what had happened to Billie. It must have been strange when she wasn't with me.'

'That did kinda throw me,' Vrinda confirmed.

'And you did turn up in full leathers pretending to be Taz,' noted Sparky. She had intended to add that both she and Joe had expected a boyfriend, but never got the chance.

'Indy! You pretended to be me?' Taz cried, looking up at her leather-clad sister.

Vrinda shrugged, 'Billie wasn't there and they sort of assumed…'

'Never mind,' snapped Taz, returning her attention to Joe, 'Is Billie okay? Is she safe?'

'She was pretty badly hurt,' he admitted, concentrating on Taz, but also flicking a conciliatory glance at Vrinda, 'I can take you through everything that's happened…'

'Billie s-said you'd look a-after her!' blurted Taz, a rush of anger causing her to stutter, 'I've just read on the…' she paused to draw in breath, '…internet that she'd been taken to hospital… and why did you leave her behind and take her laptop?'

Joe didn't reply, as a raw, hollow feeling consumed him. Taz was right to be confused and angry. Despite his best efforts, Billie had suffered serious injury and he'd left her, unconscious in the road.

The developing silence was broken by Sparky, 'We checked with the hospital a few hours ago and Billie is out of intensive care.'

'Intensive care?' the girl echoed quietly.

'We did everything we could for her when she was thrown onto Joe's car…' Sparky continued, halting when shock, quickly followed by anguish, registered on Taz's face.

Taz made to reply, but her words stuck in her throat. Her eyes glistened and a blanket of tiredness engulfed her. She took a ragged, emotion fuelled breath and a second later found Sandie's arm supporting her around her waist.

'Okay, that's enough,' Sandie interjected, giving Joe a pointed stare, 'Let's get these ladies into the house.'

Thirteen

It took thirty minutes and two rounds of Sandie's marshmallow topped mugs of hot chocolate for everyone to swap their stories. Vrinda, or rather 'Indy' as she quickly insisted, recounted their day, with Taz confirming details via a few quietly offered words.

It was hardly surprising the nineteen-year-old Taz was showing signs of shock and fatigue. From being a carefree university student twelve hours ago, she and her twenty-nine year old sister had been forced to take flight, fleeing across two counties. Upon receiving Billie's phone call in the late afternoon, Taz had followed her partner's instructions by locking all the doors and had started to pull an overnight bag together with the objective of driving south to meet up with Billie and Joe. Before she was organised, a large man banged on the front door of their small, rented terrace house in Durham. He must have seen her in the house as he began shouting threats through her letterbox when she didn't answer the door. Taz had dropped everything apart from her phone, and fled out the back. The man had given chase, but was no match for the teenager, and once she had put a few streets between them she hid and called her sister for help.

Indy continued, 'That was about six o'clock in the evening. We've been on the road, following the position of Billie's laptop on Taz's phone ever since. We eventually tracked you to that lay-by at about eight-thirty, by which stage we'd found out more about what happened at the races, and also a report of something happening in Ripon. That's why I went to meet you alone; we didn't know what to expect and neither Billie, nor you, were answering.'

'Yeah, sorry about that, we were worried my phone would be traced,' said Joe apologetically, 'It would have been much easier on you, and the side of my face come to that, if we'd been able to speak.'

Indy became sanguine for a moment, her eyes firing inquisitively as she concentrated her stare on Joe. He couldn't help himself; he returned her look, holding her gaze for a few seconds longer than was necessary.

'So what's on the laptop? Why does Taz have intimidating men hammering on her door? And most importantly, why couldn't we have just gone to the police?'

Joe was still lost in Indy's features and the crackle of her leather as she leaned over the kitchen table. It was left to Sparky to provide an answer.

'Her laptop has evidence of fraud being committed on one of the biggest betting exchange platforms. I think Billie only just realised what she had, and was about to publish the details, but whoever is committing the fraud caught up with her.'

Joe found his voice, 'Billie didn't want the police involved. She was worried about the threatened violence against Taz. But now we've found each other, I see no reason why we can't take everything to them and explain what's going on.'

'In the morning,' Sandie said from the other side of the kitchen, 'This young lady needs to sleep,' she added, gesturing towards Taz, her head propped up on one hand, her eyes almost closed.

Joe knew not to complain. He followed as Sandie expertly bustled the three girls upstairs, setting aside all their worries and promising a detailed examination of every option in the morning, following a few hours of much needed sleep. Sandie took her new house guests up to the third floor, leaving Joe alone with Sparky. It struck him that she was fully clothed. She'd also been the first person downstairs when Indy's bike had announced its arrival, which meant...

'Haven't you been to bed yet?' he asked.

'Couldn't sleep, I was too wired.'

Joe mumbled an acceptance of her reply; it had been a rather eventful day. He was all set to wish her goodnight again and head to his bedroom but noticed a strange look on Sparky's face and a slight reticence from her to retire to her room.

'What is it?'

'I've been looking at the hacking code again. I think I've found some important clues as to who is running the fraud.'

'Great, you can give the police everything tomorrow.'

'It was definitely coded within Fairbet,' Sparky pressed, maintaining a steady gaze on Joe, trying to determine whether he understood the implication of her statement.

'How can you tell?' Joe queried, his thoughts of a soft, welcoming bed replaced with a thirst to reveal Billie's attackers and Taz's male aggressor.

'There is a Fairbet house coding style. You know, a way of

developing software internally within the company. I think this code was written by the original development team as a way of testing whether their exchange betting code could be hacked. I've seen the style plenty of times.'

'So it was written internally, but anyone could be running it,' Joe pointed out.

'It's got all the Fairbet indicators, Joe,' Sparky insisted, 'Which includes a way of displaying the authors…'

Sparky paused and Joe waited patiently as the teenager wrinkled her nose. She delivered her news as if announcing the winner of first prize in a raffle.

'And it was written by… my mum and dad.'

Wide-eyed, Joe rubbed his face with his palm as he tried to force the pieces of the jigsaw to fall into place.

'Your mother worked for Fairbet?' was all he could manage.

'It's how they met. She was on the team of five that did the initial development back in the late nineties. They were both still at university in Leeds when they began work on the core processing. My mum left five years later when I was born, and my dad went on to head up the company as it grew.'

'But my first point still applies,' Joe reasoned, 'Just because they wrote the code doesn't mean they've been running it. Someone must have stumbled upon it and decided to try their hand at fraud. Besides, your mum and dad can't be responsible for sending thugs to silence Billie and Taz, can they?'

'My mum abhors violence, but my dad... let's just say you don't build the biggest exchange in Europe without being tough on people. But you're missing the point!'

'Which is?' Joe asked with a resigned sigh.

'That it must be an inside job!' Sparky exclaimed, 'And someone, probably on the inside too, knows about it and has been drip feeding Billie information for the last month, finally sending her a copy of the hacking code with the means to follow exactly what the fraudster is doing.'

'You can tell all that from Billie's laptop?'

'That. And more.'

Joe straightened, crossed his arms, and raised an eyebrow in what he hoped represented incredulity, but was pretty sure, in retrospect, had come over as patronising. He hurriedly uncrossed his arms.

'What *more*?' he demanded in a hissed whisper, 'Will you stop pissing around and get to the point.'

A crazed grin and then a laugh burst from Sparky and she had to clamp a hand to her face to muffle her amusement. She continued to stifle giggles for another few seconds, during which Joe's eyes narrowed, only adding to her loss of control. Eventually Joe couldn't retain his straight face and broke into a self-deprecating smile.

'I've never heard you using language like that,' Sparky said from behind her hand, acting like a surprised schoolgirl.

Joe shrugged, 'Congratulations. You've known me for about fourteen hours and managed to make me into a criminal, scared me, got me bashed about the head, and finally, frustrated me. Why do I get the impression that for an encore you're going to shock me?'

Sparky giggled again, but her levity was tinged with a cold edge. Her whispers dropped in volume and increased in seriousness.

'The fraudster has targeted tens of thousands of Fairbet accounts to be defrauded with the hacking code tomorrow, all on the racing at Pontefract. This time the fraud is potentially so big it is bound to be noticed and it will expose the exchange as having been hacked...'

Sparky paused, and waited for her words to settle on Joe, wanting to be sure he'd grasped their gravity.

'So bettors' and layers' confidence will be lost,' Joe said quietly, his eyes drifting away and glazing over.

Sparky nodded, 'It's not about fraudulently lifting a set amount of money from certain races anymore. The fraudster is trying to kill the entire exchange.'

After a few seconds silence, Sparky scrunched her face up.

'And that's not all... before they hit the entire exchange they've targeting one account...'

Joe's gaze returned to Sparky, 'Who owns the account?'

'I don't know... I mean, I don't know... yet!'

Fourteen

Within seconds of Joe's head being reacquainted with his pillow, he fell asleep. The cut and thrust of an argument with Sparky still reverberating around his mind, but he had nevertheless drifted off feeling content. A trip to the local police station tomorrow with the evidence uncovered on Billie's laptop would hopefully ensure everyone remained safe and he would no longer be a wanted man.

Sitting on the edge of his bed at six-thirty the following morning, Joe reflected upon his argument with Sparky. It was probably the reason that after an initial hour of being dead to the world, the remainder of Joe's night was spent in fitful awakenings caused by his heated and unresolved debate with Sparky. She had argued that their quest for the truth, far from being over, now required them to not only trace the fraudster, but also uncover the true nature of what she believed to be a plot to force her father's company to its knees.

Sparky had advocated they attend Pontefract's Sunday race meeting, feeling sure the fraudster would not give up the opportunity to watch as his handiwork created a meltdown of one of the biggest betting companies. After all, her father, Michael Gray, would be there.

'Why on earth would Michael Gray, the head of the biggest betting exchange in Europe, attend a Sunday 'Funday' meeting at Pontefract?' Joe had demanded, his tiredness combining with the frustration he felt for Sparky's belligerent stance.

'Because he's sponsoring every race on the card and half his UK staff will be there,' Sparky had fired back, 'He started the company just up the road from Pontefract, in Leeds. Their head office is still there. Fairbet have sponsored this entire meeting for the last eighteen years. It's an annual staff outing.'

Stunned, Joe had tried to argue that his involvement in the matter was over, and it was time to pass the headache of locating the fraudster over to the authorities. He'd told her it was of no consequence to him whether an online bookmaker suffered a loss of customers as a result.

It was this comment that sent Sparky off the rails. Incensed, she had glared up at him with fire in her eyes and screamed a torrent of garbled reasons why he wasn't seeing the bigger picture, how he owed it to Billie to uncover the truth, and finally, that in her opinion he was 'spineless'. This comment, no doubt heard by the entire house, had drawn their day to a heated close. A red-faced Sparky had stomped off to bed, leaving him alone and nursing a headache.

There was still a pain behind his eyes. Joe rubbed at them but the insistent throbbing wouldn't abate. He pulled on the same clothes from the day before and made his way down to the kitchen in search of anything that might ease the prickling pain that had started to invade his forehead during his journey downstairs. The house was silent, so he was surprised when he heard a tap running as he opened the kitchen door. Indy was filling a glass with water.

'Have you seen the video of your car chase through Ripon?' she asked over her shoulder.

Joe was taken aback, firstly by the abruptness of her query, but also by the sight that greeted him when Indy turned to face him. Her leather bikers' outfit had been unzipped to her navel and peeled back to reveal a thin white cotton vest, delicate upper limbs and deep chestnut skin. Long, luxurious black hair curled downwards and fell just over her shoulder. Holding the glass between thumb and forefinger, she took a sip, leaned up against the sink and placing one bare foot on her other, but not quite crossing them, gazed expectantly his way.

'Erm… no,' he answered in a croaky voice and found himself self-consciously ensuring he didn't make eye contact.

'Watch it if you want,' she offered with a mildly amused smile, indicating her phone on the table, 'It was the last thing I viewed, so it should come straight up. It's a… worth a look. Oh, and your name is all over the internet this morning, too.'

'Great. Fame at last,' Joe grumbled as he pulled out a chair and picked up the phone. It immediately lit up to his touch, its artificial light creating a burning sensation behind his eyes once more. Gradually he focused on a title to the short video that claimed this was, 'Idiots play chicken in Ripon' and watched as first a vintage red mini dashed across the screen from left to right, causing a driver to swerve into a verge, followed by a large silver Mercedes that forced both lanes of traffic to come to a standstill as it weaved precariously across the junction.

'Try the BBC and any of the national dailies and you'll find yourself,' Indy suggested once the sound of shouted expletives and honked horns had ceased being broadcast from the video, 'You're in all of them as an 'On-the-run Race Caller', wanted in connection with a hit and run incident.'

Joe grimaced as his smiling promo shot appeared on the BBC News app alongside a headline that described him as an 'actor turned horseracing commentator'. He read the first two paragraphs of the report, shuddered, and switched the device off.

'How's Taz?' he asked, getting up and opening a random kitchen unit in the hope he would discover something to dull his headache. Cloths, cleaning products and brushes greeted him.

'Still asleep,' Indy replied, 'You looking for these?' she asked, holding out a yellow packet of aspirin.

'You too?' Joe inquired, gratefully taking the pills, popping a couple out of their foil prison and washing them down with a little cold water, also supplied by Indy.

'Yeah, didn't sleep so well,' she replied, flicking on the kettle and starting a search for instant coffee, 'So, today we're off to the local police station to report what went on?'

'It's the sensible option.'

'Sparky didn't think so.'

'Ah, you heard our little disagreement last night.'

'Couldn't help it,' Indy said, flashing a quick smile that lit up her face. Joe's immediately reaction was to smile back. He couldn't hold it for long and self-consciously looked away.

'She's young and impulsive,' he explained after a pause.

'And determined.'

'Oh, yes, she's certainly that.'

'Yes...' Indy stated positively, allowing her reply to linger for a few moments, '...she seems determined to discover who is sending people to hurt her friends, possibly ruin her father's business, and therefore her future economic wellbeing.'

Indy provided him with another bright, perfectly symmetrical smile. When Joe had finished picking her speech apart he leveled his astonished gaze on her.

'It would be madness to pursue those people.'

'So says the man who left an injured friend alone in the road in order to run off after a girl barely out of school.'

'I didn't... she wasn't...' The words left his mouth before he'd had chance to sense check them. Indy waited with an expectant smirk. Even when she's smirking she manages to make it look alluring, he decided. Pushing this distraction aside, he ploughed on.

'I didn't know what I was getting myself into. I'd promised

Billie to meet Taz and make sure she was safe, Sparky just popped up and...'

'Saved the day?'

Joe frowned indignantly, causing Indy to shake her head and turn away to finish making the coffee.

'I don't need it too strong,' he said, watching her haphazardly heap three spoonfuls of Maxwell House into a mug and add boiling water.

'Oh, I think you do.'

This is becoming exasperating, thought Joe. This woman may well be... good looking, but she's terribly hard work. He waited a few seconds before sighing and taking the bait.

'What makes you say that?'

'Because you're going to have to decide whether to run after Sparky again,' she replied curtly, placing the two steaming mugs on the table and taking a seat behind one of them.

'You mean...'

'She left in the mini about twenty minutes ago. Took Billie's laptop with her and told me she was going to Pontefract races. I assume the impulsive, reckless girl is going to try to save her dad's business.'

*****

A quick scout around Sparky's room revealed an unmade bed, a used towel on the floor but no sign of any personal belongings. A note on her bedside table read, 'You know where to find me if you want to help.' It was signed with a hand drawn image of a cartoon firework erupting a fountain of sparks. A mobile phone SIM card was sticky-taped to the bottom of the note.

'You have to admit, she has a style all of her own,' Indy commented as Joe fumbled with the tiny SIM.

'You could have stopped her,' he said in a low growl.

She ignored his tone, replying, 'No way. She was out the back door, down the garden, and pulling out of the garage before I could get to her. And by the look on her face, she would have quite happily run me over if I'd tried to stop her.'

SIM secured in place, Joe's phone sprang back to life. There was a single person added to the phone's contact list, entitled 'Sparks'. He tried to call the number but received a message saying his phone was now unable to make voice calls. Scrolling through the phone's options he noticed there was an unread text message. It was a message received from the contact 'Sparks' at a little after six in the morning that read, 'This is my number, it's a text-only SIM.'

He grumbled something unintelligible to Indy and she watched close by his side as he typed out 'Please come back,' and hit 'Send'. He waited a few seconds, his eyes not leaving the little screen in his palm. Presently the phone buzzed and a succinct reply popped into existence. Joe shared it with Indy, who produced her second annoyingly perfect smirk of the morning.

'I told you. That's one determined teenager.'

'You think I should go after her?'

Indy left his side, looking thoughtful. She sat down on the bed, pushed back and displaying a litheness that boggled Joe, folding her legs under each other as if she was about to start meditating.

'You can't go to the police, Sparky has your evidence on the laptop,' she began in a low voice, 'Taz is safe, therefore you've fulfilled your promise to Billie, so you're going to be at a bit of a loose end today.'

Joe began to speak but Indy held up a flat hand to silence him.

'What was that?' she asked, cocking her head to one side.

There was a knock, or rather a thumping noise, coming from downstairs.

By the time Indy and Joe reached the hallway, Sandie was already there in her dressing gown, peering through the front door's spy-hole. The banging of a fist on the ancient wooden door echoed around the hallway again and Sandie mimed a 'what shall I do?' at the two of them.

'It's a man. He's on his own. He's tallish, and has a really well-kept black beard,' whispered Sandie.

Joe gave her a sceptical frown and put his eye to the spyhole to take a look for himself. The man was indeed as described.

'I urgently need to speak with Ruth Gray,' called a smooth, confident voice through the letterbox.

Bowing his head close to the door, Joe replied, 'She's not here.'

'It's imperative I speak with her.'

'You can't, because she's not here. Who are you?'

'My name is Gerard, Antony Gerard. My employer, Mr

Michael Gray, wishes to speak with his daughter. We know she is on these premises.'

Joe thought for a moment, during which time Indy moved forward and silently indicated the phone in his trouser pocket. He handed it to her and she immediately started to compose a text message to Sparky.

Allowing a hint of disbelief to enter his tone, Joe asked, 'Michael Gray, the CEO of Fairbet, is with you?'

'No, he's on this phone.'

Gerard's reply was rippling with condescension. The letterbox cover immediately rattled and a thin mobile phone was promptly posted through. It landed on the hessian doormat, screen up, indicating a current live call was in progress to a mobile number. A tinny voice was calling Joe's surname.

Picking the phone up as if it might explode, Joe held the device tentatively to his ear.

'Mr Lawlor? If you're there, Mr Lawlor, please indicate by saying something.'

It was a man's voice. He sounded officious, impatience pervading his demand.

'This is Michael Gray,' stated the man after a short pause, 'If you are there, Mr Lawlor, at least respond so my words aren't wasted.'

Joe swallowed, prepared himself by blinking hard, and in a voice far more confident than he felt, asked, 'How do I know you are *the* Michael Gray?'

'Good. Thank you Mr Lawlor, could you please put my daughter on.'

'Not until I am satisfied you are her father.'

There was a two second silence, followed by an irritated sigh.

'Fine. I am Michael Joseph Gray, the CEO of Fairbet. My daughter is seventeen years old, is five feet four inches, often has weird strands of colour in her hair and is insufferably headstrong. She signs her name with a drawing instead of a signature, drives her car like a madman, chews American Glee gum because the mainstream brands are full of chemicals, and has a birthmark shaped like a crescent moon on her right hip, although as her father, I'm rather hoping you haven't seen that... but won't be at all surprised if you have.'

The line went silent for a few seconds during which Indy held up a text message reply from Sparky that read, 'Don't let Gerard in house. He is my dad's attack dog.'

'What else would you like to know about my daughter?' said Gray, in a tone dripping with condescension.

'Perhaps the fact she calls herself 'Sparky' instead of Ruth, simply to annoy me, will convince you. Maybe you and I can bond over the story of how I managed to keep her out of prison when she brought half the internet down with her pathetic tree virus...'

'No, Mr Gray, I think you've made your point,' Joe cut in hurriedly, 'But as I told Mr Gerard, Sparky.. er, *Ruth*, isn't here.'

'I beg to differ, Mr Lawlor. I pay for her phone. I'm looking at the tracking app now, which proves she is currently in... an area called Holgate, which is in York. Now put her on. There is a serious matter I need to discuss with her!'

Sandie and Indy had moved closer to Joe and were standing, heads sloped toward his, straining to listen in on the conversation.

Indy peeled away and looked thoughtful for a moment before whispering, 'Tell him to call Sparky's phone from a landline.'

Joe nodded and did so. Indy turned, and ran upstairs. Joe watched her ascend, leaping two and three steps at a time. When she'd bounced up the stairs and disappeared onto the first floor landing Sandie fixed him with a knowing look, and a raised eyebrow, which he did his best to ignore.

Thirty seconds later Indy's bare feet pattered back down to the bottom of the stairs. She was holding a ringing mobile phone and grinning broadly. Without prompting or discussion she strode to the front door, bobbed down and posted the phone through the letterbox.

'It was in her bedside table drawer. There were fifteen missed calls, all from the same number. I think she left it there knowing it would wind her father up.'

Still with Gerard's phone to his ear, Joe listened at the door and caught both ends of a stilted conversation between Gray and Gerard on the phone Sparky had left behind. It centred on the whereabouts of her mini.

Presently Gray asked, 'Mr Lawlor, can you tell me where Ruth is going? Please bear in mind I *am* her father and I'm acting in her best interests.'

'Can I ask why it's so imperative you track Sparky down?'

This was greeted with an excruciating silence that extended far longer than Joe was expecting. He had to force himself to maintain his silence and wait for Gray to answer. Finally, another long sigh of frustration travelled down the line.

'If I tell you, will you give me the information I need?' Gray demanded.

Joe pursed his lips in contemplation. Beside him, Indy was shaking her head and mouthing, 'No!'

'Yes, if I believe you have Sparky's best interests at heart.'

Indy angrily crossed her arms over her chest and glared at him in a manner that indicated he'd better not do what she thought he was about to do.

'For all I know you put her up to this, but if it allows me to stop my daughter ending up in prison, I will tell you...' said Gray, sucking in a deep breath, his supercilious manner melting into something more conciliatory.

'...she has demanded a ransom payment of one million pounds. Otherwise, she will initiate a systemic and systematic hacking of Fairbet accounts this afternoon.'

***

As he'd expected, Indy wasn't pleased.

'What on earth possessed you to tell him? We could have the police banging at the door in minutes!'

'Sparky's only seventeen, so he's still her official guardian, plus he sounded genuinely worried about her,' protested Joe, 'And he won't go to the police. He seems to think Sparky is responsible for everything; stirring things up on the blogs, sending the men to Ripon to get Billie's laptop. He even thought Billie and I were her accomplices! But it was clear he wants to keep the police as far away from Sparky as possible.'

'He wants to keep them away from his business, more like,' Sandie murmured, 'And keep your voices down, that chap is waiting for his phone back. He's still standing outside my front door!'

Joe took a breath and continued in a lower register.

'Gray told me that the Mercedes men at the cathedral were hired muscle. Mr Gerard tracked down all three of them last night and he discovered their contract had been terminated, so we don't need to worry about them hunting us down. Even so, Gray is convinced that Sparky is deeply involved.'

'There is no way Sparky is behind all this,' Indy stated in a defiant whisper, 'I saw her this morning and she was worried... really worried. She might tell everyone her father is scum, but I think she cares what happens to him and his business. Even though her dad did a real job on her mum during the divorce, there's more to her relationship with her father than she's willing to let on.'

'You got all that from her this morning?'

Indy exhibited the same scowl that had graced her face the moment Joe had acquiesced to Gray's demands and told him his daughter was heading to Pontefract races.

'She opened up to me, what can I say?'

Joe shrugged and pushed Gerard's mobile phone back through the letterbox. They moved into the front room to watch Gray's man stump off down the garden path and lift himself into a Land Rover. He drove off in a westerly direction, and Joe presumed he was on his way to Pontefract. Once the car had departed in a cloud of diesel fumes, Indy maintained her less than impressed manner by crossing her arms, glaring at Joe and adopting an expectant stance.

'I know it isn't Sparky,' he admitted sheepishly to her, 'Or at least... Sparky won't attack Fairbet. Although... I think she might be responsible for asking for the ransom money.'

Sandie adjusted her dressing gown, glanced conspiratorially at Indy and both women proceeded to lean forward and inspect Joe with narrowed eyes.

'Oh, Joey. You're such a hopeless liar, and an even worse keeper of secrets. So tell us what you know,' Sandie said sweetly.

Once Sandie had squeezed his hand once or twice and fluttered her eyelashes, Joe relented. They sat down on the sofas and it took him five minutes to brief them on the contents of Billie's laptop and abridge them of the plot the fraudster had in place for the afternoon's racing at Pontefract.

As he ran through the contents of the hidden portion of the laptop, and the effect wholesale fraud could have on customer accounts and therefore Fairbet, Joe reached a decision. If the epicentre of this plot was to be Pontefract races, and assuming Sparky was right and the person behind all this would be there to watch the unfolding chaos, then Sparky was in danger. If Gerard was wrong, then the Mercedes men could be there too. He winced as the image of Billie's unresponsive face tearing itself from his windscreen flitted across his mind, and tried not to imagine Sparky in her place.

'I have to go to Pontefract,' he stated.

Sandie made a low humming noise, a sign she wasn't in agreement. 'Are you the right person to be sorting this out? Surely going to the police would be a better option?'

Joe shook his head, 'We'd never convince them, we simply don't have the time, or the evidence. Besides, I doubt they'd be able to keep Sparky out of trouble.'

'And you can?'

'I don't know,' Joe admitted, 'I kept my promise to Billie, but couldn't have done it without Sparky. I'm loath to say it, but perhaps I was wrong last night, and I owe it to her to lend her a hand, or at least see she doesn't come to any harm.'

'I'm coming too,' Indy stated resolutely. She addressed Sandie first, 'If it's okay with you, can Taz stay here today? I'll pick her up once we're finished at Pontefract.'

Having gained an immediate yes from Sandie, she swiveled in her seat to lock eyes with Joe.

'No, no. Really, no!' Joe cried, trying to quash Indy's suggestion before she could continue pleading with him, 'I didn't go through all that yesterday just to place yet another person in danger, you'll have to...'

'How will you get to Pontefract?' Indy broke in. She was relaxed and confident. Joe found this troubling, and appealing at the same time, but didn't understand why.

He frowned at her, 'I... I can hire a car...'

'You *are* a wanted man, Joe,' Sandie pointed out.

'I am your only means of transport,' Indy declared with a triumphant smile.

Joe's frown deepened. He couldn't take Indy's motorbike on his own, he didn't have the first clue about driving such a powerful machine.

'I could borrow your car, Sandie!' he said hopefully. There was an old, sun-bleached Fiat Uno in the garage that Sandie used for trips around the York area.

She screwed her face into a weird shape, 'The exhaust fell off two months ago and I've not got around to fixing it,' she reported apologetically. Indy's smile grew larger, prompting Joe to slump in his seat.

'I actually enjoy taking the bus into York,' Sandie added

94

wistfully, 'You come across some really interesting people…'

'Well, we can't take the bus to Pontefract on a Sunday! You'll come with me on the back of the bike,' Indy insisted, getting to her feet, 'You're wanted, whereas I can move around the racecourse, find Sparky, and no one will recognise me.'

Joe didn't respond for a few seconds, his gaze off in the distance as he contemplated Indy's statement.

'That's not necessarily true,' he responded finally, returning to settle his gaze on Sandie.

Once again, Sandie recognised this look.

'Okay Joey, I'm on your side,' she said with a resigned sigh, 'What's the plan?'

Joe's features lifted themselves into a shiny smile.

'Are you still working for the city theatre doing the make-up, stage dressing, and props?'

'Yes?' Sandie queried.

'I wondered whether you would, um… place me into character, so I can move among people who know me without being recognised. I was thinking Mr Carpenter?'

As Joe continued to share the kernel of a plan with the women, and then expand upon it, the worry in Sandie's eyes gradually dissolved. Freshly accepted as a co-conspirator, Indy's face continued to be lit with a fiery excitement.

It was just after eight o'clock in the morning when Joe returned upstairs to shower and prepare himself for the day ahead. Checking his phone, it brought up the messages Sparky had sent him in reply to his plea for her to return to York. He read them again. There was one that struck a chord, 'Can't come back. Have to see the look on my dad's face when I save his precious company.'

He pondered the words for a few seconds. Gray thought his daughter was manufacturing an elaborate hoax in order to embarrass him. He didn't appear to know anything about the fraud that had already taken place.

Joe wondered if Sparky was capable of halting whoever was threatening one of the biggest betting company's in the world… or was Gray spot on, and Sparky had been playing him all along in order to acquire Billie's laptop? After all, it was the only available evidence that a fraud was being committed, and she certainly knew her way around technology, programming, and the internet.

But could the laptop be holding evidence of her *own*

wrongdoing? He found himself shaking his head. No. Despite knowing her for less than a day, he couldn't believe that. She wasn't that sort of girl... that said, he had no doubt she had her own agenda where her father was concerned.

He thumbed a text message reply, 'Coming to help. Your ransom demand had desired effect. Tell me where to meet,' and hit send.

Joe pocketed the phone and caught his reflection in a faded out mirror set into the door of an ancient wardrobe. He perused what he decided were his somewhat gaunt features. Moving closer, he ran a thumb and forefinger through his day old stubble and tried to flatten an unruly tuft of hair. He noticed his eyes. They looked tired, but the sharp flecks of dark green shone, and he was suddenly reminded of his mother. He had his mother's eyes.

For a few seconds he allowed his memories of her to emerge, but all too soon they turned sour. He turned away and concentrated his gaze out of the sash window and to the street below. Joe watched a car pass, and a young cyclist scoot by on the pavement. He watched the leaves shimmering on a birch tree as the morning sunlight caught them moving in the breeze. He watched as normal, everyday things happened, one after another. It was his own, well-practiced method of freeing his mind from unwanted thoughts.

Joe's concentration was broken by the vibration of his phone. He dug it out and read a reply from Sparky. It was to the point.

'What ransom demand?'

Using a borrowed phone capable of making voice calls, Joe spoke with Sparky a few minutes later. Their conversation had begun with his apology for spawning the argument, which she'd readily accepted. And Joe was pleased when she admitted leaving so abruptly this morning had been a shade reckless. Their relationship patched up, they soon moved on to address her father's breakfast visit. Sparky was adamant. She hadn't sent any ransom messages to her father.

'He thinks you're behind the hacking rumours online. He knew about Billie's blog, and thought the two of you were in league to try and damage Fairbet's reputation. He reckons Billie got cold feet and you decided to sort her out.'

'That's my dad all over,' marveled Sparky, 'He has little, if any, regard for me and my mum, and he's so arrogant he can't believe for one second his precious website has been infiltrated.'

96

Joe took a moment to choose his words before asking his next question.

'Sparky, why would your dad believe you were capable of hiring dangerous men to silence Billie?'

The line fell silent.

'Do *you* believe I'm trying to defraud Fairbet?'

'No,' Joe fired straight back, 'But, I know you have a score to settle with your dad, you've said as much. Still, I need you to tell me why he could even consider you capable of being involved with such violent men.'

Joe waited, but no reply was forthcoming.

'You need to tell me, or you're on your own, Sparky.'

This had the desired effect. There was a guttural grumbling sound followed by some heavy breathing. Joe read them as either sighs of discontent, or Sparky was swearing under her breath.

'Fine!' she announced finally, 'When the Tree Virus all blew up there was a bit of a confrontation when the police arrived at the door. I... got a bit too serious.'

'And did what?' Joe prompted.

Sparky growled down the phone at him, 'Alright, alright! I got a bit excited and a policeman tripped and fell... well tumbled really, down a flight of stairs. He was absolutely fine.'

It was Joe's turn to be silent.

'Joe? Are you still there? If it helps at all, I was only fifteen and terrified. It was all a bit of a laugh and then the whole thing turned serious very quickly,' Sparky added in a quiet voice.

Joe cleared his throat and replied in a businesslike manner.

'Okay, so tell me what you're aiming to achieve at Pontefract.'

Relieved to be leaving her past misdemeanours behind, Sparky ran through her plan for the day at the races. It was relatively simple. She would wander into the racecourse just before racing started. When the hacking of Fairbet accounts began to take effect after the first race she would approach her father and predict the downfall of his company, then stand back and delight in the ensuing firestorm as he panicked for the next thirty minutes before the next race. When all seemed lost and he was begging for his daughter's help, she would use Billie's laptop to reveal which Fairbet account had been affected, and leave the rest to her father and the police.

Joe was non-committal about her plan, but agreed he would

meet Sparky at a retail park close to the track later that morning.

In closing, he told her, 'I want to speak with you. Face to face - before we go into the racetrack.'

Sparky managed a slightly belligerent, 'Okay, if I have to,' and rang off.

Fifteen

It was only as Joe climbed off the back of Indy's motorbike and his on-loan brogues touched the tarmac of Pontefract's out-of-town retail park, that he became aware the soles of his feet were numb. He danced around for a moment, curling and unclenching his toes to eradicate the pain of pins and needles.

'First time on the back of a bike?' Indy asked, her words being piped directly to him via a two-way microphone in his crash helmet. She raised her visor, displaying an amused smile. The ability to hold a clear, personal conversation with Indy whilst on the back of the motorbike had been an intense experience. Clinging to her as she had sped into the first few corners at gravity defying angles, had been terrifying. The raw power of the bike had astounded him and his initial quandary over whether to hold on tight to Indy's perfectly sculpted waist had been answered quickly; he hung on for dear life and immediately dispensed with any worries about invading her personal space. But as the journey had progressed, his confidence and trust in Indy's handling skills had grown and Joe had begun to enjoy himself, anticipating and leaning into the corners with her.

'I rode on the back of a friend's moped once as a kid,' replied Joe, still bouncing on the balls of his feet, 'But I experienced nothing like the adrenaline rush your driving gave me.'

Indy's smile turned a little wry, 'I'll take that as a compliment. I thought you were going to crush me for the first mile.'

He was about to apologise when Sparky jumped out of her mini and hissed 'Get in!' at both of them. They had pulled up beside Sparky's mini, parked surreptitiously in the corner of the largely vacant kitchen retailer's car park, behind a group of trees.

'Welcome to Pontefract,' she whispered, slumping down in her seat. Her two passengers did the same.

'What's the matter?' asked Indy.

'I've just seen a silver Mercedes with a bent front-end go round the roundabout and pull into the McDonalds across the road. I think it's them.'

'Them?' echoed Indy.

'The two men who attacked Billie and threw her onto my car,' Joe explained, crouched low in the back seat.

A few seconds later he recognised the folly of hiding. It would be the car the Mercedes men would recognise, not the people within it. He sat upright and peered through the trees and over the road towards the fast food restaurant situated close to the entrance to the retail park. Unlike their car park, the drive through burger joint was busy with cars, even though it was only eleven o'clock on a Sunday morning.

'I'm going over to see if I can learn anything. We might not get another chance,' he said, removing his crash helmet.

Sparky wrenched her head around and before taking her first proper look at Joe, began to speak.

'Don't be so stupi…'

She stared open-mouthed at Joe for a few seconds, taking in the full effect.

'Oh, right. I see what you mean. That might work,' she admitted, taking a few more moments to fully appreciate this new version of Joe.

He was old. His thick brown hair and pliant, thirty-two year old skin was gone, replaced by receding, wispy silver hair and a set of facial features riven by the passage of time. The change was astonishing. Sparky thought about reaching out, fascinated enough to want to touch Joe's newly acquired crows' feet.

'Pretty good huh?' said Indy watching Sparky's reaction from low down in the passenger seat, 'Sandie managed to turn him into Mr Carpenter in about forty minutes.'

In response to Sparky's questioning expression, Joe explained, 'He was a character in that children's drama Sandie and I worked on together. I picked up a secondary role as Mr Carpenter accidentally when the original actor didn't turn up.'

Joe subtly altered the muscles in his face, and his voice took on a leathery quality. There were other small changes that helped transform him, such as drawing in his shoulders, crossing his legs and clasping his hands around one knee. He leaned forward and Sparky noticed an aroma coming off him, a sort of fustiness, mixed with aftershave. He even smells old, she decided, and was about to provide a flippant comment, but thought better of it.

'They needed an old man, and Sandie, being sharp to recognise an opportunity, did this to me,' Joe stated in character, 'The production team liked him so much Mr Carpenter ended up featuring regularly. They even re-wrote a couple of episodes in the second series to give him, or rather me, a leading role.'

He paused, and Sparky could have sworn the old man

managed to force his eyes to twinkle in the same watery way her grandmother's had done when she'd been alive.

'It was a good time,' Joe added wistfully, breaking eye contact with Sparky to peer out of the car window and toward the roundabout. As he turned his head Mr Carpenter moved his tongue inside his mouth and swallowed. A shiver started on the right-hand side of Sparky's neck, rippled down her spine and flowed across her back. A childhood memory had been awakened and she revelled in it for a few seconds before Indy's voice cut through the magic.

'Sandie reckons he was born to be an old man.'

Her comment was delivered with an element of reverence and Sparky could understand why. This was proper acting, the sort that beguiles. Joe's old man was totally believable. You sensed he had left the back seat of the mini, and instead here was... Mr Carpenter, a man with different views, values, and mannerisms, and a suggestion he had a strangely alluring back story to tell. Joe left the car, promising to be back soon, and yes, he would be careful.

'There's more to him than meets the eye, isn't there,' Indy commented as she and Sparky watched Joe pass below the huge yellow 'M' sign and head for the restaurant doors. Sandie had supplied him with a thin cotton suit, a flat cap and a walking stick which he used to great effect, placing weight on the hooked handle to support each swing of his left leg.

'Yes, I can see why Billie called him for help,' Sparky murmured.

'We talked all the way here, and yet when I think about it, he just said a few things and I spilled everything about myself. He knows pretty much my life story and I know practically nothing about him, well, apart from him being a race commentator and an actor.'

'Did you tell him the truth? About yourself, I mean,' asked Sparky.

Indy shot her a curious look, 'Yes, of course. Why?'

'I just... I guess he's a good guy. I haven't come across many of those.'

Quickly changing the subject, Sparky added, 'There were three men in the Mercedes today. Would you recognise the man that called on Taz yesterday?'

'No, she phoned me after she'd run out the back door. I got out of work, drove up from Darlington and picked her up. But Taz said he was huge. He was banging on the door with his fist and shouting stuff to intimidate her.'

'So you live in Darlington?'

'No, a village just outside. I travel in to work each day.'

'Any other sisters apart from Taz?'

'No, a younger brother. He's still at home with…. Hold on.'

Indy leaned forward in the passenger seat in order to examine Sparky's face in detail, and found her grinning.

'You were playing his trick! Pumping me for information and giving nothing back,' she complained.

'Only having a bit of fun,' Sparky replied soothingly, 'At least you're honest and willing to share, not everyone is. Besides, there is a difference between me and Joe, he was probably genuinely interested in what you had to say.'

Indy chuckled, 'So you can be honest too.'

They'd settled into another discussion when Sparky's driver's door was suddenly wrenched open. Before she could react, a man's fist clamped onto the back of her collar and dragged her from her seat, depositing her, kicking and screaming, onto the car park tarmac.

'Shut up, Ruth,' Gerard commanded, 'Stop behaving like a baby.'

He leaned into the car and tore the keys from the ignition, warning Indy not to move.

Sitting on the dusty, grit covered asphalt, Sparky didn't attempt to run. She knew it would be pointless. Her father had chosen well when he'd recruited Gerard; the man was a Rottweiler in human form - agile, strong, combat trained, and most annoyingly, incorruptible. They'd already had several run-ins and Sparky knew the drill. Gerard wouldn't stand for any nonsense from her, calmly dealing with all her protests, physical and verbal, before dispassionately returning the naughty offspring to his employer; the displeased parent. The fact she was almost eighteen and being taken against her will didn't matter to her father.

'Where's the device, Ruth?' Gerard demanded.

Sparky remained tight-lipped. He sighed, and gripping her collar once more, pulled her to her feet.

'Don't run,' he warned.

'Going to taser me again?' she asked sweetly, but with a face like thunder.

'Only if it's required,' he replied, flicking his slate coloured eyes up to meet hers; a warning in itself.

'It's in the boot,' she told him sourly. He ignored her, instead giving Indy a clipped warning to stay where she was or risk an unspecified injury. Accessing the shelf under the driver's seat with a bent arm, he pulled out the laptop. Turning it over, he gave a satisfied sniff, and tucked it under his arm.

'Seventy-five High Holborn. Tell Joe. It's where the hacking code is sending its commands from,' Sparky shouted through the open door toward Indy.

Gerard swung round, 'That's enough, save it for your father,' he warned, slamming the mini's door. He marched Sparky a few yards and bundled her into the back seat of his Land Rover, having somehow managed to park within twenty feet of them without either Sparky or Indy noticing.

Indy watched Gerard's car back up, a feeling of helplessness filling her. To her surprise the Land Rover pulled forward again and the driver's window wound down. A hand emerged and dropped the mini's keys onto the tarmac beside the passenger side door. The Land Rover reversed, toured to the car park exit and disappeared across the roundabout and into Pontefract Park, the home of Pontefract racecourse.

Sixteen

Joe returned to the car park ten minutes later, by which time Indy had discarded her biking leathers and changed into a knee-length grey and black flecked cotton dress, also supplied by Sandie's theatre props department. She turned to face him through the passenger side window of the mini and he tried not to gawk upon noticing her plunging neckline and bare legs when he bent down to try and hear what she was saying.

'Where's Sparky?' he queried once he realised she wasn't in the car.

'Gerard turned up and took Sparky and the laptop,' Indy started, quickly providing Joe with a rundown of events since he'd left and completing her synopsis with, 'And Sparky shouted something to me before she was... er, kidnapped.'

'I don't know if it's quite kidnapping,' Joe mused, 'From what you said, she's been taken to see her father without resorting to the use of force, and we know where she's gone. The racecourse is only four-hundred yards away.'

'Never mind the semantics for heaven's sake!' Indy remonstrated, 'Sparky thought this was important, so just *listen* will you!'

Joe read the warning signs and shut up.

'Are you listening now?'

'Yes. Yes, of course. Tell me what Sparky said, and I'll update you on the Mercedes men,' he said adopting a deeper, calming tone.

'What are you doing now?' she asked anxiously, cocking her head on one side like an inquisitive puppy, 'You don't sound right.'

Joe closed his eyes, breathed in and held it for a few seconds. In his normal voice, he told her 'I'm fine, just tell me what Sparky said.'

Her concern somewhat abated, Indy cleared her throat.

'Sparky shouted to me before she left, she said the app is sending commands from...' she paused, determined to ensure she got it correct, '...Seventy-five High Holborn.''

Indy watched as Joe's face contorted itself into a frown, his eyes focusing beyond her.

'What does it mean?' she pressed.

'Sparky said there was more to the app than just hacking,'

Joe stated. Staring into the middle distance, he paused before returning to focus on Indy, adding, 'She must have found... more.'

'What?' barked Indy, rolling her eyes, exasperated by his lack of clarity.

Joe ignored her, checking the time on his phone instead.

'It's eleven-fifteen. We need to be the first people into the racecourse. I have a feeling a lot might happen before the first race goes off at ten past two.'

'Tell me what Sparky meant!'

'I'll do it on the way. Come on, get everything you need,' he commanded, telegraphing his sense of urgency by waving his hands at her. He looked her up and down, and Indy watched his eyebrows rise as he reached her feet. She was still wearing her heavy duty bikers' boots. The incongruousness clash with the summer dress gave her a faintly ridiculous look.

'I know Sandie had to work quickly to kit you out for a day at the races, but didn't she think to give you some suitable shoes?'

Indy toyed with giving him a flippant reply, but Joe's whole demeanour had altered in the last minute. He seemed enthused and re-invigorated by her news regarding Sparky.

'Yes, don't worry!' she confirmed, 'There are some shoes with heels to go with this girly dress.'

'Good, get them on. You look great, by the way,' Joe remarked distractedly as he checked his jacket for his phone and wallet, then carefully pulled a flat cap over his silver hair, 'Come on, we need to get moving!'

Leaving Indy to ensure her bike and the mini were safely locked up, Joe sent several text messages to each of the mobile numbers he had for Sparky, and then the two of them crossed to the racecourse, Joe making use of his walking stick in character as an old man.

'If anyone asks, I'm your grandfather,' he whispered as they passed the rusting steel cutouts of horses and riders planted around the roundabout opposite the entrance to the racecourse.

'Do you think that's believable?' Indy challenged.

'Of course,' Joe countered without looking round. He was concentrating on their path across the acres of grassland leading to the inside of the racecourse and what he hoped would be an early entrance to the premier enclosure.

Indy was about to suggest that being a niece might be a better cover story, given their radically different skin colours, but stopped herself. It was rather refreshing to have a racially colour blind companion. Instead, she sidled closer to Joe and linked arms with him.

'I've never been racing before,' she told him as they approached the racecourse and were rewarded with their first sight of the cluster of grandstands, 'I don't know what to expect.'

Joe flashed Indy an uncertain smile, 'Nor do I.'

He took a few more steps before adding, 'I have the feeling today will be unlike any other day at the races.'

Seventeen

'Aren't we on the wrong side of the racecourse?'

Joe screwed his eyes up against the glare of the sun, peering over the white plastic rails and racetrack to examine the paddock side of Pontefract racecourse. Even with two and a half hours to go until the first race was due to run, and with the doors not open to the public yet, there were plenty of staff and horsemen moving around.

'We would be if we were normal race-goers. But today we are going to be owners,' he replied to Indy, directing her gaze about thirty yards away to where a portacabin nestled under the trees.

Indy took in the small green box with a ramp leading to a rickety looking door and curled her lip upwards on one side.

'Not exactly a grand entrance.'

Joe nodded his agreement, returning to the view across the track, 'I've always thought their arrangement for owners was a bit like asking your most important customers to enter through the stock room at the back of the shop.'

Joe stepped up to the trackside and leaned on the rails, still inspecting the paddock side of the track. Presently, Micky Goodham strode from the paddock entrance across in the direction of the winners' enclosure and Indy noticed Joe instinctively pull his cap down and turn his back.

'Know him?'

Joe didn't answer immediately, feeling a prickle of heat race across his forehead, 'Yes, he's a… colleague I guess. He must be the on-course presenter for the racing channel today.'

'There's no way he'll recognise you,' she told him. There was a hint of amusement around her eyes that, for some reason he couldn't fathom, shook his confidence.

'I forgot I was Mr Carpenter for a minute,' he said rather stiffly, 'I need to focus.'

He immediately regretted his words, realising they sounded a shade pompous. Meanwhile, Indy maintained a steady gaze.

'Sorry,' he blurted, removing his cap to carefully dab away the pinpricks of sweat with the back of his hand, 'I'm just coming to terms with the fact that I'm pretending to be a man fifty years older than myself in order to clear my name for a hit and run, save a young girl from a trio of thugs, whilst attempting to unmask a fraudster and save a major bookmaking business.'

Indy broke into a grin, 'That's okay. When you put it that way, I can see you have plenty on your plate.

'I'm not overly fond of Micky, and I guess spotting him made me nervous. He and I don't get on too well, and he'd love to expose me if he could.'

'I doubt anyone will even notice you,' Indy soothed.

'Well you'd better be right, otherwise we'll not get any farther than that owners entrance. The ladies who run it know me well.'

Indy waited through thirty seconds of silence before becoming impatient.

'So why are we waiting?'

'The racecourse isn't open yet.'

Indy checked her watch, 'It's twenty past eleven!'

'Ten more minutes then. Enough time to run you through what happened with the Mercedes men, and the plan for today again.'

Joe's visit to McDonalds had been mostly disappointing and uninformative. He'd sat as close as he dared to the Mercedes men and nursed a coffee whilst the three men worked their way through several muffins each. He hadn't overheard anything of interest, as the men hardly spoke. That was, until just before they got up to leave, and he'd caught the end of a conversation. The older, bald one told the blonde haired youth, 'Check it again. He'll be here today so no mistakes this time.'

'It was only something he said under his breath as they got up,' Joe told Indy as they walked under the trees on the inside of the course, 'Without knowing the context, it could mean anything. He said 'he'll', but I'm not sure there's any real significance of 'him' being here as it could refer to anyone.'

'So the Mercedes men must already be here?'

'Yes, they're over there,' Joe replied quietly, lifting his eyes in the direction of the owners' car park, 'I've been watching them for the last few minutes.'

'Why didn't you tell me?' Indy grumbled under her breath, 'Is that why we've been hanging around under these trees?'

Joe shrugged, 'I didn't want you to worry. It's not as if they're doing anything, they're just sat in their car. I imagine that like us, they're waiting for the doors to open.'

Indy shifted a little to her left to spy over Joe's shoulder and around the trunk of the tree they were loitering behind.

With his back to the Mercedes men, Joe watched as a mask of bewilderment washed across Indy's face.

'So they must be owners I guess, if they're using the owners' entrance?' she queried.

She switched her gaze back to Joe and found him staring at her with wide eyes and a toothy grin.

'Thank goodness you're here!' he cried, and was immediately shushed by Indy, who took another check of the Mercedes, just in case.

In a lower register he added, 'I was going to try and get into the racecourse before them to find and warn Sparky. I'm sure she'll be in a private box, probably her father's. But you're right! The Mercedes men must have been left badges by someone; another owner. I can't for one minute believe they actually have a runner at the meeting. Someone has organised for owners' badges to be left for them, and that someone could be our fraudster.'

Indy was staring at him blankly and Joe silently berated himself. She couldn't be expected to understand the idiosyncratic nature of how racecourses handled free badges for owners with runners.

'If we follow them in, we can find out which horse they've been left owners' badges under. Once we know the horse, the owner's name will be printed in the racecard. If we're really lucky we can find our fraudster's name even before we're in the racecourse!'

'I'm pleased I could help. Although I'm still not too sure how I've managed it,' Indy admitted with a tight smile, 'It means we're going to get pretty close to them in that owners' hut thingy over there.'

Joe thoughtfully rubbed the newly acquired bristles at the end of his chin, a mannerism he'd developed just for Mr Carpenter.

'We'll have no choice. It's tiny inside,' he confirmed, 'But that said, sometimes the closer you are to people, the less inclined they are to spend time looking at you.'

Indy considered this, and was about to question his logic, but her query was forgotten when the door to the owners' cabin was pushed open and a middle-aged lady in a floral print dress appeared momentarily. She bent to chock the door open before disappearing back inside the cabin. Movement in the car park caught Indy's attention and she watched over Joe's shoulder as two of the car's doors opened on the Mercedes.

'There's activity from the Mercedes men,' Indy whispered excitedly, 'Two of them have got out, the bald one and the big one. Another is just sitting in the back seat. Some people are getting out of another car as well. They're dressed for the races. God, this is like being in a Jason Bourne film!'

'We need to follow the Mercedes men in. Come on… and for heaven's sake try to stay calm. Just remember, these men almost killed your sister's partner. We're not in an action movie.'

Indy's excitement quickly faded from her face and she took on a more serious, determined expression.

They covered the short distance to the owners cabin at a leisurely stroll, Joe expertly swinging his walking stick, Indy on his arm once more, and managed to time their arrival in order to follow the two men in dark lounge suits up the ramp and into the cramped little office. Indy noticed the floor of the cabin rippled under their weight as they entered. An immaculately dressed man and women came up behind them, but with four people already filling the cabin, they were forced to wait outside.

Behind an ancient desk that took up half the cabin space, two ladies looked up and beamed at their first owners of the day, greeting them with a bright, 'Good morning!' The Mercedes men didn't reply, preferring to speak with their eyes.

Joe shuffled close up to the hulk of the large Mercedes man and with a quick flick of his walking stick, rapped the big man's heel. The collision made a woody noise and the Mercedes man swung round to find a slightly bent over old man with a smaller, black haired woman who was holding onto his arm and staring at the floor. He couldn't see their faces completely as they were so close and below him, invading his personal space.

'I'm so sorry young man,' Joe said, his chin two inches from the man's chest, 'It's a bit of a squeeze in here, isn't it?'

Grumbling, the big man tried to step back, but had to settle for only a few inches, before he bumped into his colleague. Joe immediately claimed the extra space as his own by shuffling his feet forward. The Mercedes man stared belligerently down at the old man's flat cap for a worrying few seconds before grumpily turning his back on Joe and Indy.

'Name of your horse?' one of the ladies asked the bald-headed man expectantly.

Clearing his throat, the man replied in a thick south London accent, 'Smart Missile in the four-forty,'

'And your name?'

'Smith.'

Very original, thought Joe.

The lady raised one eyebrow, 'We have you down for three owners' badges, Mr Smith.'

The Mercedes man eyed the lady, and she stared back at him with a hint of belligerence, awaiting his reply.

'He'll be along later.'

'Very good, I'll make a note,' she said, offering a little sigh after she'd spoken.

Two thick card badges were handed to the Mercedes men, plus racecards, and a lunch voucher each. The two ladies wished them a, 'Good day and good luck with your horse', which was entirely ignored by both men. They were directed to the end of the cabin where a second door led trackside. Just outside was a portly chap standing expectantly, a glum expression on his face and a hole punch in his hand. With their badges duly punched, the Mercedes men descended a ramp and set off across the uniform grass of the racetrack, toward the premier enclosure.

'Mr Carpenter with Glowing Rose in the second race,' Joe announced in his old man voice before either of the ladies could ask their questions, 'My trainer Dick South has left me two badges on the filly.'

Some checking of paperwork ensued, punctuated by heavy sighs. Joe had expected as much. Dick South was a cantankerous seventy-six year old trainer who was the bane of these ladies lives. There wasn't a race meeting in Yorkshire that passed by without Dick forgetting to inform the racecourse officials of how many of his owners would be attending with his runners.

'He said he would sort them out for me,' Joe pointed out, coughing and leaning a little more notably on his stick as the search for his name continued to flummox the two administrators.

After another twenty seconds Joe emitted a groan of pain. Holding his hip, he made a comment to Indy on how his back was playing up. The ladies relented and passed over two owners' badges, saying they would catch up with Dick and check the allocation when he arrived. Joe knew no such thing would happen. The no-nonsense

Yorkshire trainer would give the ladies short shrift if they challenged him. Dick was a training legend in these parts, known for his wily way with older handicappers and his blustering, self congratulatory interviews when his horses won. Most of all, and to the public's delight, he was politically incorrect and used foul language liberally. He was renowned for his lack of paperwork and as a result his owners were often waved through at owners entrances around the country, which is why Joe had been pleased when he saw Dick had three runners at the meeting.

Crossing the Pontefract racetrack into the premier enclosure was usually a fascinating experience for Joe. He always marveled at how steep and undulating the final few furlongs were up the straight. From the commentary box, positioned at the top of the main stand, it was easy to forget the severity of the incline facing the horses. It was worth taking a few seconds to appreciate the view from behind the winning post, as you crossed from the owners' cabin into the premier enclosure. However he and Indy didn't linger today; there were more pressing matters.

As they walked in front of the Dalby stand, Joe's phone beeped and vibrated in his jacket pocket.

'Keep an eye on those two while I check this. Hopefully, it's from Sparky,' Joe said, digging deep in his inside pocket. Indy watched as casually dressed race-goers entering through the silver and premier entrances started to filter into the course. A steady stream of families were now heading for the Funday attractions and the Mercedes men were becoming lost in the swathes of Yorkshire men, women and children intent on having a good time. Having never been racing before, Indy was surprised to see family groups spanning three generations carrying rugs, drinks, and picnic baskets.

'Is it normally like this at a race meeting?' she asked, trying to maintain a lock on the two Mercedes men, who had entered a small grassed area to the side of the main thoroughfare.

'No, this is one of their Funday Sunday meetings,' Joe explained without looking up, still absorbed in his phone, 'It's a family day and so the course puts on a host of attractions for the kids. They've become really popular in the last few years. Lots of the courses build them into their meetings during the summer holidays to attract larger crowds on days where the racing isn't particularly high quality. I've no doubt there will be bouncy castles, bands playing, face painting, and possibly Punch and Judy shows.

Commentating on a day like this can feel like being an announcer in a holiday camp.'

'Why's that?'

'You know,' Joe said, glancing up. He put on a Welsh accent and added, 'Announcing the best dressed lady competition starting in ten minutes in the parade ring, and for the children we have pony rides in the silver ring. And don't forget, the over sixty's knobbly knees competition begins at three o'clock prompt on the Belvedere Terrace...'

Indy gave a husky laugh and once again Joe was taken with how her dark eyes could sparkle with such brilliance.

'Our two Mercedes men stick out like a sore thumb amongst all these families,' noted Indy.

'At last,' Joe said, sounding relieved, 'Sparky has answered. I've sent her texts to every number I have for her.'

'What does she say?'

'She's texting from the... Oh, right.'

Indy frowned, 'From where?'

'It seems she's had to smuggle a phone into a toilet in the Dalby stand. She and Gerard are in a private room and he's insisting she stays there until her father arrives. Come on.'

Joe started to move off.

'What about those two?' Indy pointed out, indicating the Mercedes men by slanting a look their way, 'Surely we need to keep tabs on them in case they try anything.'

More people were making their way up the walkway after crossing the course from the owners and trainers cabin. Joe shuffled back and leant on his walking stick, very much in Mr Carpenter mode, to allow a large group of owners to pass. They thanked him as they came by and he replied with a gravelly, 'You're welcome!'

'Okay, you stay around and see what they do. But you must stay away from them. You've got my number, call me the minute anything untoward happens and I'll come running.'

'Alright, Grandad,' she replied sweetly, 'I'm a big girl now.'

For a moment he considered a politically incorrect answer, but instead stared at her with wide eyes and insisted she look after herself and to not try anything silly.

'You didn't see Billie's face after they'd finished with her. Keep tabs on them, but don't get close. Promise?'

Indy wiped the grin from her face and gave him a single,

positive nod.

Satisfied, Joe looked up and saw the Mercedes men were sitting down at one of the tables inside the owners' bar. He suggested Indy seated herself at a table on the grass outside the bar in order to monitor the streams of people passing, in-between perusing both her racecard and the two men.

'They've never met you, so you've no worries about being recognised. Just don't make it obvious you're watching them and keep your finger near to the instant redial button on your phone.'

Indy smiled and fixed him with a stare, 'I *will*.'

'Right,' he said, back in his Mr Carpenter persona, 'This old man is going to go and blag his way into the private rooms in the Dalby stand.'

Eighteen

Acting out the bumbling of an old man who only heard what he wanted to hear, made accessing the Dalby Stand relatively straightforward. The doorman was very accommodating once Joe had mentioned 'Michael Gray's private box' and dropped in words like 'personal invite.' Flashing his owners' badge had also helped.

He'd been directed to a private box on the third floor, at the top of the building. The door held a sign that simply read, 'Fairbet'. Inside, the suite was empty, save for a ring of chairs around the walls and a cold buffet table in the centre of the room groaning with all manner of seafood platters covered in cling film. However, an argument emanating from the box next door, right at the end of the corridor, helped him locate Sparky.

The raised voices had reached a pitch of such ferocity, he was able to enter the private box entitled 'Mr Michael Gray' without being noticed. Once he'd stepped inside and closed the door the ranting continued before Sparky, and then Gerard, turned to regard him curiously. Joe had seen plenty of private boxes in his time, but this room was more akin to a swanky hotel foyer, full of ancient high-backed leather armchairs with wooden arms, various small tables, and boasting a thick, deep blue paisley patterned carpet. Floor to ceiling windows covered the walls facing the racetrack and television monitors graced the remaining two sides of the room, placed between large prints of old-fashioned racing scenes. A small chandelier hung from the centre of the ceiling and two old oak cabinets almost filled the left-hand wall. Joe reassessed, and decided it was more like a gentleman's club from the nineteen fifties.

'This is a private box, please leave, Sir,' Gerard barked as he strode over to Joe. He swung the door open, and provided the old man with a cold stare.

'Stop it, Gerard!' interjected Sparky, allowing some of her anger to bubble up again. She took a few steps forward and addressed the old man face to face, 'I think you should be next door for the…'

Her words faded away as she scrutinized the uninvited guest.

'…for the Fairbet employee luncheon. You're a little early. Come on, I'll take you there and get you settled.'

Gerard glared at her and thought about protesting.

'I'm sure we could both do with a couple of minutes break

anyway,' Sparky said pointedly to her father's personal assistant.

'Ah! I do apologise to you both,' Joe stated in a weak, croaky tone, 'I'm Mr Carpenter, I do have my invite here...' and he started to tap and then dip into various pockets of his jacket with his free hand whilst leaning heavily on his walking stick with the other.

Gerard produced a frustrated sigh, indicating the corridor with a flick of his head, 'Go on, then.'

Sparky took the old man's arm and guided him out of the room. She started to pull the door closed behind her, but Gerard's foot intervened and he gave her another warning glare. She felt like shouting at him again, but swallowed it down and instead, gave him a sweet, sarcastic smile. Turning her back on Gerard, Sparky guided Mr Carpenter ten yards down the corridor and into the next room. It was still empty, and once inside, Sparky made sure the door was securely closed behind her.

'Crikey, Joe! I didn't recognise you at first look,' she spluttered in a breathy whisper, 'It's your eyes. That's how I knew, but up until then I was fooled with the way you spoke and held yourself. You're... pretty good at this aren't you.'

'I knew I should have worn contacts,' he moaned.

'Never mind that, I need to tell you something. I've only got a minute before lover boy will be in here.'

Joe nodded, allowing her slightly odd reference to Gerard to pass without comment.

'I think whoever is behind all of this will be here today.'

'I guessed as much.'

'No, I think they'll *have* to be here. But before we get to that there is something important...'

Sparky dropped a shoulder and rolled her eyes upwards, 'There's no easy way to say this.'

Joe's fake eyebrows inverted slightly. Sparky's playfulness had evaporated and she was now staring intently into Joe's perfectly wrinkled, grizzled features.

'...I've not been entirely honest with you.'

There was pain in her eyes. He allowed the moment to stretch, but couldn't hold it for too long before he broke into a broad grin.

'I know.'

Sparky gave Joe a look of confusion mixed with a smidgen of contempt.

116

'What? You mean…'

'Appearing out of the blue at the cathedral was a bit disconcerting. Discovering you're the daughter of Fairbet's founder was a revelation, but when I surreptitiously watched you login to Billie's laptop through at least three levels of security, and then fire up a Windows 95 emulator – I'm not quite as technically backward as you seem to think - I knew you were more than just an interested outsider.'

'In the café?' she questioned, feeling defeated, 'You didn't go to the…'

'Nope. I skirted around the counter and watched you check on what the fraudster had set up, then I visited the washroom and googled you.'

All the anger and bravado had gone from her. Sparky looked done in. Joe sat her down on the one of the chairs lined around the walls of the room and took a seat beside her.

'I assume you know Billie pretty well?' he asked softly.

Suddenly downcast, Sparky paused before replying.

'We've been online friends for a few years. She was helping me to try and flush out whoever got hold of my copy of the hacking code.'

'What, so you wrote it?'

'No, no. Not at all. It has all the hallmarks of my dad's work. I found the hacking code five years ago when I was working as an intern at Fairbet: my dad's idea to keep an eye on me during summer when I was thirteen. I was looking for some of the original versions of the exchange code to play with and I discovered this file buried in an old backup that had been forgotten about. I couldn't believe it when I ran it and it worked – it circumvents all their security protocols because it's an internally written piece of software.'

'So who did you give it to?' Joe asked quietly.

'I didn't!' she insisted, her colour and intensity returning, 'I've no idea how someone at the BHA got hold of it!'

'Oh, for…' Joe uttered, his eyes bulging.

Sparky gave him a faint smile, 'That's twice I've managed to almost make you swear in twenty-four hours.'

'That's what you meant by 75 High Holborn! Of course, it's the building the British Horseracing Authority work from,' Joe said, studiously ignoring her comment regarding his language, instead concentrating his thoughts on how, and why, an employee of the

BHA could be involved in this sort of fraud.

He became aware Sparky was glaring at him.

'Don't you want to hear the whole story?' she asked sarcastically.

Joe nodded and tried to concentrate and leave the BHA revelation for later.

'I made a copy of the hacking code and saved it to my private, secure server. Well… it was supposed to be secure. I thought I'd keep it for a rainy day, if you see what I mean. You know, with my dad being such a jerk.'

Sparky paused, as if waiting for some sort of acceptance or agreement from Joe. He just stared back.

'Anyway,' she continued grouchily, 'I've wracked my brains about how it could have been found and the only thing I can come up with is that the police stole a copy. I had to give them access to my server when they investigated me after my Tree Planting virus… blip.'

'One heck of a blip,' Joe commented with a single bushy eyebrow raised.

Sparky sighed and rolled her eyes.

'Have you considered that it might not be your copy the fraudster is using? Perhaps someone found the original on the Fairbet servers,' Joe suggested.

'I suppose, but they'd need to be a really serious hacker to break into Fairbet from the outside.'

Sparky paused to dig her fingers into one of the many buttoned pockets in her sleeveless jacket. Finding what she was looking for, she unwrapped a cube of chewing gum and popped it into her mouth.

'Look, whoever has got hold of this old, in-house hacking software has been running it almost invisibly on and off for the last fourteen months,' she said between chews, 'That's what Billie originally found. As soon as she wrote a blog about it, Billie was emailed a working copy that allowed her to confirm her suspicions beyond any doubt. The moment she told me about this weird software she'd received that had to be run on Windows 95 I knew what it was. I tried to convince her to leave it alone… but she was determined. Who on earth would send it to her?'

'And why,' Joe added, 'What would they hope to achieve…'

They traded a look that signalled neither of them had an

answer.

Presently, Sparky noted, 'Today is different as well.'

'How so?'

'Up to now the fraudster has been careful, I mean *really* careful. He's used the hacking code sparingly, spaced his races well apart and it was operated simply, sending the profits into a single user account each time. He also deleted the tracking, so you couldn't tell where he'd run it from. But today it's really complex. To set up what he's planned for this afternoon must have taken... well, *days*.'

Joe's confusion must have been obvious, as Sparky answered his next question before he could open his mouth.

'The software is *old school* Joe. It's not like modern apps. It's all run by typing commands, basically lines of text, into a virtually blank screen. You'd need to know the command structure, and understand what the code is capable of doing, which all takes time to create.'

'So why can't you just cancel it all from your copy, or run... I don't know, some sort of a cancel command and stop the hack happening?'

Sparky shook her head, 'Even if I had access to my laptop, it's not possible to control another copy of the hacking code. The copies synchronize, so I can see what's been planned. But only the fraudster can cancel his own setup.'

Sparky glanced up and their eyes met. Joe thought she looked tired, and for the first time since he'd met her, a little scared.

Seeking confirmation, Joe asked, 'And tell me why are you convinced the fraudster must work for the BHA?'

'Because he didn't delete the tracking this time,' Sparky answered, her eyes regaining some of their brightness, 'Whoever set up the fraud for today did so from that address in High Holborn.'

Joe didn't get a chance to follow this up with Sparky. The round doorknob squeaked as it turned and the door to the room was pushed open. A second later Gerard filled the doorframe.

'I'll be a few more minutes,' Sparky barked up at him, 'I'm looking after Mr Carpenter until his granddaughter arrives. You have a problem with that?'

Gerard gave each of them a disdainful stare and removed himself from the room without answering.

Once the clump of the personal assistant's footsteps had receded, Sparky explained, 'As long as Gerard knows I can't leave, we'll be okay in here. There's only one way out, and it's past him.'

'So, the Mercedes men?' prompted Sparky.

'They're here at the track. Gerard got duff information.'

Sparky nodded, but didn't comment. Joe noticed she was becoming more agitated with each passing moment, clearly wishing to voice her opinion on something, so he waited. When she next spoke the words burst from her, each one barbed with venom.

'I can't believe how angry Gerard was with me! He accused me of recruiting you into my own plot… as if! He said the only reason my dad hasn't got the police involved is because he's scared of what the bad publicity might do to his business. I don't know who's worse, Gerard or my dad.'

Sparky stared forlornly at the finger food piled up on fake silver platters in the centre of the room. Whether it was the thoughts of her father and Gerard, or the sheer abundance of food in front of her, she was feeling sick inside. Joe watched a sudden sadness wash over her and he suppressed a pang of sympathy for the young woman, aware that their time together was running out.

'Is there anything else about the fraudster, or the hacking code I should know about?'

Sparky blinked, and refocused on Joe, as if emerging from a daydream. She shrugged.

'That's why I came here. I don't know why, but the fraudster has recently taken to running the hacking code by hand. I'm guessing they are activating it on the in-play market.

It was Joe's turn to stare across the room, the cogs of his mind whirring through the possibilities.

'So the hacking code mops up every outstanding wager on the race, knowing it will win. I guess it could be thousands of pounds per race,' suggested Joe.

'In the right races, it could be tens of thousands,' Sparky agreed.

'So what's so special about today?'

'It's a bit weird to be honest,' admitted Sparky. They've set up the hacking code for the first two races, here at Pontefract. The first hack on the opening race will pay every single penny into a single Fairbet account, and the other, set for the second race, sprays smaller amounts of money into thousands of accounts at random.'

Joe produced a vexed frown as he tried to understand why the fraudster would do such a thing. The best explanation he could come up with was that the first hack would be used to show his threat was serious. The second was shaped to bring the entire Fairbet website to its knees.

'So how do we stop them?'

The lights in Sparky's eyes, which had been shining brightly when discussing the technical side of the fraud, now dimmed markedly upon hearing Joe's blunt question.

'*We* don't. It's down to you alone, Joe. There's no way Gerard will let me run around the racecourse trying to find an imaginary fraudster. He thinks he's already caught her!'

'So it'll just be Indy and myself... er, Vrinda who are here to help you.'

'Cool biker chick will be fine!' Sparky cried, 'That girl's got her head screwed on.'

'She's downstairs now, keeping an eye on the Mercedes men. Well, at least two of them.'

'Well you better get back and help her!' Sparky insisted, and was immediately being shushed by Joe.

He grabbed both her hands and squeezed them as he spoke, 'I need to know how I'm going to find, expose, and most importantly, stop the fraudster.'

He stared intently at the teenager. In response, Sparky took a moment to compose herself.

'I found a BHA employee list on their website,' she said in a whisper, 'If any of the people on the list pitch up here today with a laptop, they are our man... or woman. I've texted you the link.'

'So all I have to do is find a BHA employee who has a laptop and is using it, or rather, about to use it, when the opening race is entering the final furlong. And Indy and I have to locate this person among the five thousand race-goers... during a race.'

Sparky wrinkled her nose, 'When you put it like that... sorry.'

'Crikey, Sparky,' Joe spluttered, jumping to his feet, 'And we've got to do this whilst avoiding three thugs who have already framed me for a hit and run, and half-killed a good friend.'

Sparky turned her face up to him and in an angelic voice stated, 'That's about it, bucko!' She gave him a sad smile and dropped her gaze to the floor, unable to see her lame joke all the way through.

'I'll try and convince my dad of what's going on. But it's his big corporate bash today, so he'll be busy, and he's impatient at the best of times. Gerard told me he's arriving a few minutes before the first race, by helicopter.'

'Helicopter?' Joe echoed, shaking his head, 'Promise me you'll stay out of harm's way. Don't go out into the public enclosure or out onto the balcony of your private box. You must remember that the Mercedes men are looking for you.'

Sparky nodded her agreement. Then, as if remembering something, she scrabbled around in several of her jacket pockets, thrusting a handful of items into his hand, insisting he take them. Among the items were a book of matches, a padlock with a key, a marker pen, and a set of lock picks.

'I have no idea how to use these,' he complained, examining the lock picks with a frown.

'Just take them will you? They might come in handy. I've done the research. These are statistically the most useful things to carry with you.'

Joe didn't have time to argue, so did as he was told, ramming the lock picks and other items into his jacket pockets.

'Now come on, take my arm and guide Mr Carpenter out of here, he's got a lot to be getting on with.'

Sparky was leading Joe to the door when she squeezed his arm.

'By the way, Sandie's right,' she said in a whisper, 'You *were* born to play an old man.'

Nineteen

Paul Jenkins and Leonard Horowitz traded a quick glance and tried, unsuccessfully, to plaster a welcoming smile on their faces as Sally Proctor and Jeremy Tottering-Smythe approached them. They'd just spent an enjoyable ten minutes in the shade of a tree outside the racecourse gossiping about the BHA chairman and his non-executive acolyte, accusing them of all manner of heinous misdeeds. They were both struggling to rid themselves of the image of their colleagues being romantically involved, their latest assumption.

'Paul, Leonard. It's great to see you here on such a lovely day,' Tottering-Smythe said, greeting the men with an expansively plastic smile and an outstretched hand, 'I do appreciate you coming out to work on a Sunday,'

As if you gave us an option, Horowitz thought to himself whilst shaking his boss's limp and sweaty hand.

Sally Proctor remained silent, standing with arms crossed and heels together, a yard behind Tottering-Smythe. Horowitz caught her coolly looking him up and down with undisguised distaste. Upon reaching his face she broke into a prim smile that displayed no teeth. Each time they met she increasingly reminded him of a bird of prey. Horowitz imagined how a hawk would hang silently and unmoving on the breeze before folding its wings and diving down at terrific speed to sink its razor sharp talons into an unsuspecting small mammal. His analogy made him shudder. He glared dolefully at her, after all, she wasn't supposed to be here, and would only complicate matters.

'Sally has organized for us to do a few interviews before racing starts. The racing channel, the BBC, and also a local newspaper from Ripon is here and it will give us the chance to get our work done early,' Tottering-Smythe said breezily, but received nothing from the men in acknowledgement.

As they walked two by two toward the premier entrance, Jenkins cast an eye toward Proctor and noted her sensible business attire. She was attractive enough, in a working girl sort of way, but he wouldn't dare make a pass at her; she was far too dangerous. Jenkins told himself she was definitely off the menu.

'I'm feeling a little over-dressed,' Horowitz shared with Jenkins as they waited in line to enter the racecourse, 'It must be one of those dreadful Funday meetings.'

Jenkins took in the much longer queue for the standard entry to the Tattersalls area of the course and smirked at his colleague.

'You mean you haven't got tattoos down your legs and arms?' he whispered conspiratorially.

Proctor suddenly spun around from her position ahead of them in the queue. There was contempt burning in her eyes, causing both men to lean back in surprise.

'A racecourse like this is dependent on crowds of normal, everyday punters and their families attending. The reason you have a job with exorbitant wages is in no small way due to the general public supporting this sport. So I'd think twice about biting the hand that feeds you.'

Jenkins was about to fire a rebuke back. As far as he was concerned, it was this sort of lily-livered liberal ideology that was ruining racing's position as one of the last bastions of the class system. But Tottering-Smythe's grave expression behind the odious woman made him bite his tongue. Neither Jenkins', nor Horowitz apologised, preferring to roll their eyes at each other when Proctor huffily turned her back on them.

It was a shade after one o'clock in the afternoon when the BHA contingent emerged into the sun inside the premier enclosure and clustered together to receive instructions from their CEO. The four of them stood out like sore thumbs among Pontefract's Funday crowd. They looked around, trying to get their bearings at a racetrack not a single one of them had visited before, uncomfortably hot in their business attire, and all of them carrying briefcases or shouldering laptop satchels.

They didn't go unnoticed. From her position on the owners' lawn, Indy surreptitiously took several photos of the group on her phone before they moved off as one towards the parade ring. She compared her photos to the BHA website's list of employees and a triumphant, 'Got you!' fell quietly from her lips. Once she'd lost eye contact with the quartet, she sent Joe a short text message and checked the Mercedes men were still sipping at their drinks inside the Owners' bar.

Twenty

Joe felt his phone vibrate in his jacket pocket and upon reading Indy's message, his pulse quickened. Having reached the conclusion that his chances of tracking down the fraudster were impossibly low, the arrival of four potential BHA candidates gave him renewed hope. That was, until he realised he had the problem of tracking two different groups, and six individuals. If they split up, who did they follow?

After leaving Sparky in the Dalby Stand to wait for her father's arrival, Joe had settled in beside the parade ring. He'd worked out a position at the top left corner was the perfect pitch to watch as race-goers filtered in through the main entrance, or came from the silver enclosure. With the course enclosures built on a relatively steep hill, his elevated position at the back of the parade ring afforded him a view of the weighing room and winners' enclosure beneath him. He was currently keeping an eye on Micky Goodham. The course correspondent was standing in a little cordoned off area outside the winners' ring, accompanied by a cameraman, conducting preview interviews with jockeys to be broadcast later in the afternoon.

Despite the swelling crowd, the BHA employees stood out, much to Joe's relief. Thanks to Indy, he identified the three men and lone woman immediately from their online photos. The four of them looked a little lost for a moment. However, Tottering-Smythe seemed to get his bearings and approached Micky, had a perfunctory conversation with him, and then led his small team into the weighing room.

Joe couldn't help scowling. The one place in the entire racecourse into which he wouldn't be able to follow was the weighing room and associated stewards and judges quarters. If his four potential fraudsters stayed in there all afternoon, he'd never get close to them. He was pretty sure he could blag his way into the private areas of each stand, but the jockey and steward's rooms were off limits to all but a chosen few, with all access strictly monitored. Even owners and trainers weren't able to violate this inner sanctum, but Joe guessed members of racing's ruling body might be tolerated.

He waited, his nervousness growing with each passing minute until Jeremy Tottering-Smythe, Paul Jenkins, and Leonard Horowitz emerged from the weighing room. Fearing he might lose them in the swelling number of race-goers, Joe headed towards them at a pace commensurate with Mr Carpenter's age. He slowed once he realised their destination; they were about to be interviewed by Micky Goodham. There was a small group of race-goers standing behind the roped off area, watching the men prepare. Joe joined them.

Standing hunched over, his cap pulled down, he carefully positioned himself to overhear the interviews. Joe listened as Micky introduced the BHA CEO, communications director, and finally the integrity director. When questioned, each man made short statements regarding the events at Ripon. It was dry stuff, intended to placate the press by emphasising what security protocols and processes were already in place on Britain's racecourses. Joe recognised the clerk of the course for Ripon loitering on the steps of the weighing room, and sure enough, he was added to the lineup of men and produced his own half a minute explanation of the increased security they would be adopting following the 'sad, but extraordinary events' at his racecourse.

Joe had been evaluating each of the men intently as they spoke, trying to imagine each of them as a fraudster attempting to extort a huge sum of money by threatening to cause maximum disruption and embarrassment to one of the most important bookmaking businesses in the world. He considered this for a moment. Would most people be bothered about a bookmaker suffering at the hands of a blackmailer? Joe doubted it. Yet here he was, incognito, trying to determine who that blackmailer might be and in doing so, placing himself in danger. It wasn't until he reminded himself that it was likely one of the men in front of him paid three thugs to track Billie and Taz down, and in the process half kill the former and scare the latter senseless, that Joe's resolve hardened.

It was as Joe was feeling this renewed pulse of righteous indignation around his body that one of the race-goers in front of him, presumably bored with the interview, moved off, leaving a gap in the front row of observers. Something caught Joe's eye as he stared through the vacated space and his heart missed a beat. Pinpricks of sweat started to push their way through the make-up on his forehead as he studied the interviewee's laptop satchels, piled up on a small table only a yard in front of him.

It struck Joe that the interviews had been nothing more than a public relations exercise, well choreographed, but without substance.

Micky clearly shared the same sentiment. Once the clerk had finished his little pre-prepared speech, Micky didn't bother with any follow-up, instead swinging back to face Tottering-Smythe, his cameraman doing the same.

'Of course, what we have to remember is that as a result of the mistakes you have just outlined, a woman is lying ill in hospital and the perpetrator and his gang are on the run,' Micky pointed out, 'This episode comes on the back of continued pressure regarding the failures of your organisation to address reduced prize-money levels, bookmaker-led alterations to the programme book, and the questionable tactics - some say illegal activities - employed by bloodstock sales companies during your tenure as chief executive.'

Tottering-Smythe's face began to radiate heat, transforming him, from a pallid grey into a raging red. He started to splutter out an answer, but Micky hadn't flicked the microphone over to him.

'Is it not time to leave your post and allow a more effective team to run racing?' Micky asked, finally thrusting his microphone toward Tottering-Smythe.

For once, Joe was pleased with Micky's controversial line of questioning. With all eyes on the BHA chief executive, Joe moved forward through the onlookers, slowly skirted around the roped off area and to the small table upon which the men's laptop satchels were neatly stacked. He reached out a hand...

'I wouldn't if I were you... Mr Carpenter,' said a man's voice beside him, 'There's at least three people watching you, including that lady standing under the columns at the entrance to the weighing room.'

Retracting his hand, Joe glanced up toward the weighing room doors and sure enough, the blonde haired lady who had accompanied the three BHA executives was eyeing him curiously. Joe swung round and found not one, but two men gazing at him expectantly. In their late fifties, both wore suits and straw-coloured summer trilbies.

Joe had been holding his breath. He let out a relieved sigh when he recognised the duo that had prevented him from committing petty theft. His racecourse buddies, Neil Tuton and Simon Weller grinned back at him.

'Great to see you, old man. We told you we'd see you here today!' exclaimed Neil loudly, clapping a hand on Joe's shoulder and leaned in toward him. In a conspiratorial whisper he added,

'Best move away from here, Joe, you're attracting far too much attention.'

As Neil and Simon guided the old man away from the media area, behind them the interviews ended in acrimony. The three of them walked down a few steps, through a small tunnel, and past the Tote betting windows to where Indy was sitting alone at a table for two in the far corner of the owners' and trainers open-air grass terrace. Joe considered walking past, but came to the conclusion that bumping into Neil and Simon might be the first stroke of luck he'd encountered since leaving them at Newcastle races to embark on his mercy-mission south. He had to introduce them.

With an hour and a quarter to the first race, the course was starting to fill up, and the owners' bar was already busy. Joe planted himself beside Indy, quickly followed by his new accomplices who purloined chairs from another table.

Indy shot him a worried look, but was immediately pacified with a few words of explanation.

'They're good friends of mine. I've known these chaps for the best part of eight years,' he told Indy, who smiled nervously at the new additions to their inner circle. Neil raised his trilby as he was introduced, revealing thinning black hair. Simon sported a closely-cropped multi-coloured beard and was the bigger man of the two, but they shared two important attributes: they were extremely well turned out and both provided Indy with an extraordinarily warm smile. Pacified by their friendliness and good manners, Indy began to relax.

'They're professional northern race-goers,' Joe explained, a description that seemed to go down well with the two men, 'They go racing five times a week since they sold their business and took early retirement. We meet regularly, well, whenever I'm commentating, and what they don't know about racing isn't worth knowing.'

'Never mind all that!' Neil interrupted, 'I assume you have a good reason for being dressed as your alter-ego, Mr Carpenter?'

'Yes, you caught me out, calling me that name. How do you know about Mr Carpenter?' Joe queried.

Simon chuckled, 'We googled you a long time ago and found some of your acting work on YouTube. Mr Carpenter was our favourite. The combination of the old man rhetoric and physical comedy won us over. You were great in Smuggler's Cove!'

Joe inspected both men for a moment, saw they were serious,

and rolled his eyes dismissively, 'Well, regardless of your stalker-like knowledge of my acting career, my thanks are in order.'

'You'd make a hopeless thief,' remarked Neil, 'We'd been watching you for five minutes and you never noticed us, or that scary looking woman near the weighing room. Why did you want to steal those laptops and briefcases anyway?'

'Mr Carpenter was never meant to be a Fagin,' Joe replied defensively, 'To be honest, I was having a tough time deciding whether to pinch them or not.'

'It showed,' chuckled Simon.

'I think it's rather sweet that stealing is a step too far outside your comfort zone, despite the circumstances,' Indy said, 'But would you mind bringing me up to speed with what on earth has gone on? I've been sitting here watching the Mercedes men and trying to spot people arriving through the turnstiles with laptops for the last forty minutes.'

It only took Joe a few minutes of heavily abridged explanation to bring Indy, Neil, and Simon up to date.

'We knew you couldn't have run off and left that girl in the road without good reason,' Neil confirmed.

Simon nodded his agreement and added, 'And there was no way we would give you up, even though you are on the top ten most wanted list in Britain at the moment...'

Neil shook his head in mock admonishment, 'Everything is always a joke with you, isn't it?'

Simon beamed back at his friend.

'So how can we help?' asked Neil expectantly, returning his attention to Joe and Indy.

Joe locked eyes with Indy and quizzically raised both eyebrows. She returned a little nod of agreement.

'Well, we need to...'

Joe's words were cut short by a whirring noise that quickly grew in intensity. It soon developed into the clipped rotation of blades and a downdraft that sent racecards and napkins flying into the air. A helicopter passed over the main stand, crossed the racetrack and hovered above a football pitch in the centre of the racecourse, before slowly landing with a gentle bump.

'The Fairbet has landed,' Simon noted sarcastically once the engine noise began to fade.

Indy squeezed Joe's knee under the table, 'We have

movement from our Mercedes men,' she warned, directing his attention over at the entrance to the owners' area. The two men were making their way through the knots of race-goers. Pushing people aside to exit the owners and trainers bar, they walked single-file downhill towards the track. Halting upon reaching a small crest, the two men were standing side by side, looking out over the longest circular racetrack in Britain.

As they looked on, Joe realised the Mercedes men hadn't been searching for Sparky, they'd been waiting for Gray. Their vantage point would provide a view out over to the centre of the racecourse to where Michael Gray's helicopter was powering down.

'They know about Sparky,' Joe said to himself, not aware he'd said these words out loud.

He answered Indy's questioning look, saying, 'They must have traced the mini's plates. They know the girl they're after is Michael Gray's daughter.'

'Following the father to reach the daughter. It makes sense,' stated Neil.

'Shall I go after them?' asked Indy keenly, starting to get up from her seat.

Joe hesitated, allowing Neil time to push his chair back and answer for him, 'No, they might suspect something. Forgive me for saying this, but you are a striking young woman. Most men would notice if you started to follow them around a racecourse, whereas me...'

Joe shrugged, 'He's right, Indy. Besides, I think you and I can be more useful elsewhere.'

After issuing instructions, Joe insisted they all traded mobile phone numbers, and soon after, Neil headed into the increasingly thick crowd, his raffia trilby bobbing in and out of sight until it disappeared completely.

'I don't know what to make of you,' Indy commented as the three of them left the table, 'Everyone we meet wants to help you.'

'Apart from you,' Joe returned immediately, flashing his silver-tinted eyebrows at her and grinning, 'You attacked me at your first opportunity.'

Twenty-One

Lack of sleep was beginning to catch up with Michael Gray. But Fairbet had sponsored this race meeting for the last sixteen years, and when you added an employees' day out into the equation, his attendance wasn't just necessary, it was essential. It was just unfortunate it clashed with other, more pressing matters.

His problems had reached a critical stage over the weekend. As the helicopter descended the last few feet to the turf, Gray reflected on the fact that this day out in the north had become an unwelcome distraction. He could have done without the hassle, and certainly could have done without another of his daughter's childish pranks. That was downright annoying.

As he undid his seatbelt, he stifled another yawn and squeezed his eyes shut to rid himself of the feeling of nausea which always overwhelmed him at the end of a journey by air. Locating two small plastic bottles in the inside pocket of his suit he gobbled down a travel sickness pill, followed by two sleep suppressant tablets.

Sharing the flight with Charlotte, his ex-wife, had seemed a good idea at the time, but had proved to be a mistake. He'd expected to enjoy a power nap during the flight from London but instead he'd been harangued by Charlotte throughout the entire journey. It was apparently his fault that Ruth was such a handful. Gray consoled himself with the knowledge that his payoff for offering to provide Charlotte with transport to Pontefract would be in his ex-wife bringing their seventeen year old daughter to heel. This time Ruth had gone too far.

Before the rotor blades had stopped spinning, Gray was out of his seat, leaping from the helicopter door and striding over the short grass toward the owners cabin, leaving Charlotte to struggle down from the aircraft on her own. She watched the tall, almost gaunt figure of her ex-husband recede and made no attempt to catch up, or even match his pace.

Having jumped the queue of owners, Gray continued his power walk across the racetrack. He was met by a gaggle of Fairbet staff on the other side, including the three-man events team, responsible for ensuring the day was managed smoothly. He greeted his employees with a wan smile and a self deprecating wave. There would be up to two hundred Fairbet employees and their families enjoying this corporate day out at the races. This meant maintaining his cool, relaxed, nerd-turned-millionaire persona for the day.

Gray picked out the Fairbet events co-ordinator from the group, demanding a synopsis of his itinerary from her as they walked uphill from the track toward the centre of the premier enclosure.

'Seven races, the first in forty-five minutes. As usual, we've booked three private boxes on the top floor of the Dalby Stand, there's only one up there that isn't ours for the day. Your own private box in the top corner of the stand is available for your exclusive use. You have a staff 'meet and greet' buffet lunch starting in twenty minutes, and you're presenting the winning prize for the fourth race at two-thirty in the winners' enclosure. Finally, there is an invitation from the stewards to join them after the sixth race for a champagne reception in their private rooms, sir.'

Gray took in the event co-ordinator for the first time. She looked nervous and glanced away under his scrutiny, pushing her glasses up her nose the moment their eyes met.

'Where's Gerard and my daughter?'

'Waiting for you in your private box, sir.'

'I may miss the stewards' reception,' Gray advised curtly, 'It will depend on my daughter.'

'Very good, sir. But I do have some messages,' the young woman said quickly, recognizing Gray was keen to move on, 'I've received several messages from William Hutchinson asking for you to return his calls and you may wish to know that Mr Tottering-Smythe and a couple of his executive board are here conducting interviews with the press regarding the…'

'Yes, yes,' Gray cut in with a dismissive wave of his hand.

A woman in her early forties stomped up to Gray shouldering a rucksack. The event co-ordinator stepped back and the woman deposited her load on the ground with an agitated grunt. She radiated barely controlled anger.

'Problem, Charlotte?' Gray asked with a sigh.

She glowered at her ex-husband, her head shaking slightly. It made her curly, shoulder-length hair flop forward, masking her eyes.

Gray recognised the build up to a rant, and sought to nip it in the bud.

'Do something about your ridiculous haircut, Charlotte. I can't see your face. I refuse to hold a conversation with a hairy curtain.'

'You just left me,' she complained, bunching her hair and tying it back with a ribbon she'd liberated from her jeans pocket.

'Did you really expect me to walk in with you looking like that?' scoffed Gray, 'You're wearing ripped jeans and sandals for crying out loud.'

'And you're a pompous prig,' Charlotte fired back. She'd been suppressing several rebukes during their forty minute helicopter ride, and having released this phrase onto Michael in public, felt far better about herself.

Charlotte eyed the young girl beside Gray. His assistant was standing quietly, head down, inspecting the grass whilst playing unconsciously with her fringe. She's trying to look small, Charlotte decided. I don't blame her.

'Could you tell me where my daughter is being held against her will, pet?'

Gray winced and muttered something under his breath upon hearing Charlotte's north-eastern accent in full-on Geordie mode. He knew all too well she could turn it on and off at will. Charlotte smirked and raised an eyebrow at the girl.

'Remember that, pet,' she told the girl, 'A Geordie accent is guaranteed to wind your boss up.'

'She's in Mr Gray's private box up there, Mrs, er... Gray' replied the girl, pointing to the third floor of the stylish old building behind them, 'The room top left, with the balcony that wraps around the side of the building.'

'Thanks, pet,' Charlotte replied whilst looking up at the deserted balcony. Placing plenty of emphasis on her accent, she shouldered her rucksack and pushed past Gray, 'Ha'way, I know the way, hinny.'

The little knot of people around Gray held their collective breath as their employer's face contorted with a mixture of anger and frustration. Their relief was palpable when Gray's phone chirped his ringtone and they were able to melt away from their CEO and remain at a safe distance.

Gray checked the caller's name, and in doing so, noticed he had several missed calls. William Hutchinson's name was displayed, and he answered with a curt 'Yes?' and was met with his finance director's broad Yorkshire drawl, only slightly elevated. There was something wrong.

'Michael, are you aware of the reports circulating on the

internet regarding the members of the BHA and their Fairbet betting accounts?' Hutchinson asked.

'I've only just arrived at Pontefract, Bill. So these are new, not the crazy rumours about Fairbet being hacked?'

'No, these are completely different. They haven't hit the mainstream press yet, but it won't take long, they're already sniffing around for confirmation the rumours might be true.'

'Okay, but I can't discuss this at the moment, I'm not alone. Send me any details I might need. Oh, and I've been told Tottering-Smythe is here at the track today.'

'Then I advise you to see him straight away.'

Gray issued an irritated sigh. It seemed his problems were multiplying with every passing hour.

'What's so urgent that it can't wait? I've got one or two issues of my own to sort out!'

Hutchinson didn't answer for a few seconds, which told Gray his second-in-command was girding himself to deliver grave news.

'Even though it's Sunday, the phones have been ringing constantly, Michael. I've had half our board screaming at me because they couldn't reach you. Drew Cooper is apoplectic because the share price is bound to fall tomorrow when the markets open, and my public email account is being bombarded by questions from the press. It's just as well I'm joining you at the Pontefract later this afternoon, you're going to need my help.'

Hutchinson drew breath and added, 'They all want answers, Michael. Everyone wants to know whether the members of the executive board of the BHA have been receiving illicit payments into their Fairbet accounts.'

Twenty-Two

Micky Goodham was pleased with his morning's work. His handling of that stuck up double-barrelled twit from the BHA had received plenty of plaudits on his Twitter feed, even if his producer hadn't appreciated him re-visiting Tottering-Smythe's frankly appalling record in charge of the sport. It had been put out live to a small lunchtime audience, but was also recorded. He just hoped his ultra-conservative producer wasn't going to cut his last few questions when they re-ran it during the afternoon.

With thirty minutes to go before the first race, he and his cameraman were taking the opportunity to have their lunch. Micky bit down on his sandwich and chewed thoughtfully, watching the four BHA executives discuss something only a few yards away. They hadn't moved off after the interviews, and instead seemed to be agitated by something. He hoped it was as a result of his interview, but something told him there was other news afoot. The blonde haired woman and the director of integrity held phones clamped hard to their ears and were relaying news that had left Tottering-Smythe with his mouth open and eyes wide. Micky tilted his head their way, trying to catch the gist of what they were saying, but was interrupted by his producer's harsh voice demanding attention in his ear-piece.

'Alright, I'm here,' he answered irritably.

'Time to earn your money, Micky,' responded the disembodied voice, 'Get Tottering-Smythe back in front of the camera now and ask him about the reports that have just landed at every major newsdesk in the country!'

'Yeah, okay, that's fine, but...'

'Call yourself a reporter?' hollered the producer, 'He and the rest of his management team have been accused of fraud and race fixing linked to their Fairbet betting accounts. The whistle-blower is releasing evidence later this afternoon. Now do your job and go get a reaction interview.'

Micky dropped the remains of his sandwich, barked a command at his cameraman and grinning broadly, strode over to the BHA executives, the camera rolling as he thrust a microphone under Tottering-Smythe's nose.

Tottering-Smythe greeted the reporter with a look filled with pure loathing. This only served to delight Micky, and he allowed his grin to expand even further.

***

'Something's up,' Joe whispered urgently.

Having led his accomplices back to the winners' enclosure to spy on the people from the BHA during the first race, Joe was faced with all four of them now rushing towards him. Tottering-Smythe led the stampede of executives, with Micky Goodham and his cameraman in pursuit.

'Mr Tottering-Smythe!' called Micky several times as the Chief executive of the BHA pushed his way through the oncoming waves of race-goers heading to the parade ring to view the runners for the first race.

'Can you comment on the accusation that you and your team are corrupt? Have you been accepting illicit payments?' Micky persisted as the executives bustled past.

Joe allowed a few seconds for this revelation to sink in before coming to his senses. After despatching Indy and Simon to find out where Tottering-Smythe's little group were going in such a rush, he remained in the shadows of the small alley that led to the parade ring and winners' enclosure. Taking out his phone he spent a few seconds checking the news websites then started a text message conversation with Sparky.

Joe: 'There's more to this than blackmail for money. Someone is trying to damage the sport. See news on Racing Post and The Times websites.'

Sparky: 'Seen it. I agree. It must be a BHA account the hacker has targeted.'

Joe: 'Your dad in a position to stop it?'

Sparky: 'No. Thinks I'm responsible for the whole hoax. Idiot won't listen. Neither will mum. Where are Mercedes men?'

Joe: 'Don't worry. My spies have eyes on them. They are keeping low profile at the moment.'

Sparky: 'Let the first race run. Then my dad will have to start listening!'

'Joe: 'I'll be watching.'

Indy and Simon returned to Joe's side wearing subdued expressions.

'All four of them have gone into the Dalby Stand,' reported Indy.

'They scurried in there like rabbits bolting for their burrow,' Simon added, 'Then they took the lift up to the top floor. We tried to get in, but even Indy's owners' badge wouldn't get us past the chaps on the door.'

'Michael Gray's boxes,' Joe confirmed thoughtfully.

He looked around him, noticing for the first time that the narrow walkway was becoming thick with race-goers heading in both directions. The three of them were slowly being edged toward the wall of the tunnel which meant the first race couldn't be far away; he could hear horses whinnying in the parade ring and his inspection of a nearby Tote screen confirmed the betting was well underway. He checked his watch; twenty minutes to the first race.

'If Sparky is right, and the hacker is a BHA executive, we have to catch them in the act,' said Joe. Indy studied his sullen face, quickly realising Joe was focusing elsewhere. His eyes flitted between two points in the distance as his mind deconstructed their current situation.

Still staring vacantly, Joe stated, 'To catch our fraudster, we need to see which of them activates the hacking code from their laptop. If they're with Gray, they'll be in one of his boxes.'

'If they're with Gray, can't Sparky watch them?'

'We can't be sure she'll be in the right box, or they won't split up. No, we need to... look in on them, or more precisely, *over* them.'

'We can go up into the main public stand and look over towards the boxes,' suggested Simon.

Joe considered this for a moment, 'Actually, I need you to seek out a trainer for me instead,' said Joe, re-focusing on his two companions.

He spent a few seconds providing Simon with instructions that the retiree quickly repeated back to him perfectly.

'Good. Call me if you're successful.'

'Don't you mean *when*?'

Joe rolled his eyes, 'Of course, I forgot you're now a professional spy. Now get going!'

Simon tapped the brim of his trilby with his index finger, admitting, 'I haven't had this much fun in years,'

He turned to make off toward the parade ring and saddling boxes, calling back over his shoulder, 'So if I need you, where will you two be?'

After a short pause, Joe raised his eyes skyward, 'Indy and I are going to try and find somewhere with a little more…. height. But first, we're going to the men's toilets.'

Indy raised an eyebrow, 'That should be fun.'

***

Gerard didn't react well to being prodded. As a man who had served for eight years with the British Army and seen action in two wars, he'd had quite enough of being ordered around. So when Jeremy Tottering-Smythe's index finger jabbed at his chest for a third time and his clipped public school voice ascended an octave to demand he, 'Get out of the way, you annoying oik!' Gerard felt justified in reducing the man to tears.

Holding Tottering-Smythe's wrist in a vice-like grip he bent it backwards and pushed downwards. The chief executive of the BHA let out a yelp of pain, fell to his knees and began pleading for the pain to cease.

'Whatever your issue is with Mr Gray, it will wait until he is ready to see you. He is currently entertaining his staff and asked not to be disturbed,' Gerard stated firmly. He waited for a squeaky acceptance to be issued through Tottering-Smythe's gritted teeth before releasing him. The two men and woman who had rushed in after Tottering-Smythe gaped warily at Gerard. He regarded them with disinterest and remained steadfastly blocking the door to the Fairbet employees' private box.

'But it's imperative we see him immediately,' the blonde woman pleaded.

'As I've already pointed out, you may wait in Mr Gray's private box next door,' Gerard replied stoically.

Tottering-Smythe, tentatively holding his wrist, glared defiantly at Gerard, but then shuffled quietly down the corridor and into the next room, followed by his colleagues.

Charlotte and Sparky were sitting together on a distressed two-seater leather sofa and looked up without surprise at the four members of the BHA executive as they entered the room. Tottering-Smythe had already announced his arrival, having burst into their room a minute before demanding to know, 'Where the hell is Gray?'

In a rather subdued tone, and whilst flexing his wrist, Tottering-Smythe began introducing himself and his three executives, starting with Ms Sally Proctor. Charlotte interrupted his flow before he could get onto the first of the men.

'We've met,' she stated flatly as soon as Tottering-Smythe had pronounced the 'P' of Paul, 'Haven't we, Mr Jenkins?'

'Is this him?' Sparky said accusingly, standing up to get a better view of Paul Jenkins, currently partially hiding himself behind Sally Proctor. Proctor frowned, realised she was in the way, and moved aside.

'Yes, I'm afraid it is,' answered Charlotte unhappily.

Sparky stepped forward, looking Jenkins up and down as one side of her lip curled up in disgust. He remained silent, holding an uncertain expression but without embarrassment.

'You're kidding, mum?'

Charlotte sighed, 'No, that's him, pet.'

'*This* is the piece of garbage that ruined your marriage and means we have to live with grandma?'

At this, Jenkin's smirked. It was a facial reaction he immediately lived to regret.

***

Neil leaned against the red bricks on the side of the main stand and perused his racecard, periodically glancing up to ensure the Mercedes men were still standing quietly on the lawn beside the chute onto the racetrack.

It was becoming increasingly difficult to maintain eye contact with them, despite his elevated position higher up the hill, as the crowd had started to swell on the premier enclosure lawn ahead of the first race. However, they'd hardly moved for the last twenty minutes and the only exciting thing to report was that the smaller, fedora wearing man had taken a thirty second phone call. He'd discussed it briefly with his partner and since then they hadn't spoken, simply leaning side by side against the chute rails, facing the Dalby Stand.

Neil fired off a short text message.

***

Joe was doing his best not to lurk. It was proving difficult, situated as he was, outside the men's lavatory in the main stand.

He'd already received a number of disdainful looks from men entering the facilities and was starting to doubt his plan was going to come to fruition.

Checking his watch, Joe scowled. There were fifteen minutes to the first race and the horses would be leaving the paddock soon. He'd either missed him, or he'd used another set of facilities. His phone vibrated in his pocket, lifting his spirits, but it was only a message from Neil to confirm the Mercedes men were still on the premier enclosure lawn. He wondered how Indy was getting on, covering the second set of toilet facilities. It suddenly struck him that he'd asked a good looking twenty-nine year-old woman to hover outside a gents' public toilet, eyeing up each male user in order to identify, and then approach a chunky, almost bald, sixty-four year old man. Joe shuddered as the ramifications of this thought travelled through his mind, deciding he needed to go and rescue her.

George Meldrew had called races in the north for forty years. He'd witnessed some of the seminal moments in racing history and his voice would forever be associated with some of the most famous race commentaries. Now semi-retired, this titan of race commentating covered the odd meeting when it suited him, picking up an afternoon's work here and there, usually to cover for sickness or annual leave. Joe had been delighted to discover his own name had been replaced with 'G. Meldrew' in the racecard, as he not only counted George as a friend, he was a character that railed against the establishment. He was also a creature of habit.

Another minute ticked by, and Joe's hopes of catching up with George in the public area of the stand had all but faded away when the great man's ample outline filled the corridor. Joe could have cried out in joy.

Swallowing down his excitement, and a certain amount of relief, Joe waited until George was sidling past him and cleared his throat.

'Despite being beaten by Habibti three times, Soba was, without question, the better horse,' Joe declared in his normal voice.

George lumbered a further two steps toward the door of the urinals before coming to an abrupt halt. He swung around and eyed Joe uncertainly at first, but with a growing recognition once he noticed the stranger's vibrant green eyes.

'Why would you think that, old man?' George asked in his familiar low register, both eyebrows raised high on his forehead.

140

'Because you have to take into consideration their contributions as broodmares,' Joe replied. They had argued long into the night on more than one occasion about the relative merits of these two wonderful horses from what had turned out to be a halcyon period of racing.

George nodded sagely, allowing time for a couple of race-goers to pass by before he spoke again.

'Stay here, I'll be out in a minute or two... old man.'

He provided Joe with a surreptitious wink, turned, and pushed open the door to the gents' toilet.

Thank goodness for George's weak bladder, thought Joe as he tapped Indy's contact details on his phone and held it to his ear. Fifteen minutes before the first, third, and fifth races; you could set your watch by George's ablutions.

***

She hadn't expected his nose to explode with such devastating consequences, it being the first time Sparky had actually thrown a punch with proper venom. That said, it wasn't so much a punch, more of a flat palm thrust up with a straight arm, however the resulting crack of cartilage and splatter of blood were worthy of any boxer. Her initial delight at Jenkins' howl of pain and sight of blood coursing down his chin was quickly dimmed when he snarled, bunched a fist and lurched menacingly towards her. However, she was too quick, sidestepping his clumsy swing at her.

'Jenkins!' Tottering-Smythe barked, grabbing the man's collar and jerking him backwards. He caught him off-balance and Jenkins toppled and landed backside first between two antique armchairs. He sat on the floor of the private room holding the bridge of his nose, and glowering upwards at his seventeen-year-old aggressor.

'That's for being such a spineless, sex-starved pillock! Why did you have to say all those hateful things?' Sparky accused, her eyes beginning to fill with tears of rage.

Holding his nose, Jenkins sneered at the teen. He swiveled his eyes to catch Charlotte's reaction. She had an arm around her daughter and was gaping down at him.

'Ha! Your mother got everything she deserved,' he rasped.

Tottering-Smythe was still gripping Jenkins' collar firmly.

'Hold on, Paul, is this the woman who you accused of attempted blackmail and stealing from you?' he asked, pulling the smaller man to his feet, 'Michael Gray's wife?'

'She seduced me and then went all bunny boiler on me!'

'No I did not, you lying weasel!' Charlotte shot back.

Thin rivulets of blood were running between Jenkins' fingers, yet he was still incapable of masking how his expression altered once he'd found the perfect rebuttal.

'You're breaking the terms of your contract,' he told her with a sneer. Then to Tottering-Smythe he added in gasps, 'She's not allowed to come within two hundred yards of me, my office, or my family house. She signed an agreement. In return I didn't take her through the courts.'

Sparky, still seething, cut in, 'Instead, you sold your sordid lies to my father and robbed my mother of her marriage and the lion's share of the divorce settlement. You're the profiteering little snake here!'

The standoff was interrupted by the entrance of Michael Gray and Gerard. The door was thrown wide open and Gray entered first wearing a serious expression. He scanned the room, taking in the frozen tableau of his ex-wife and daughter with faces like thunder, a man he half recognised with a bloody nose, and three more individuals, apparently in shock. His stern gaze eventually alighted on Tottering-Smythe.

'I believe you have a problem that requires my input,' he stated in a commanding manner, casting his eyes appraisingly around the room for a second time.

Tottering-Smythe smiled thinly, 'I believe *you* are the one with the problem, Mr Gray.'

Twenty-Three

'Thanks for smuggling us up here, George,' Joe repeated as he and Indy settled into the corner of the commentator's booth.

George grinned, waved a dismissive hand at him and pulled on his headset.

'They're coming out for the first,' he warned, before holding his index finger to his lips. Joe and Indy nodded their understanding. The retiree opened a drawer and handed them each a set of binoculars.

Indy couldn't help but let loose a quiet exclamation of 'Wow!' when she took in the view from the commentator's box. Located at the very top of the main stand, the box was exactly that: a wooden built oblong box of about twenty feet long, perched on the roof of the highest public stand. After adjusting her sights, she allowed herself a few seconds to follow the entire left-handed circuit of the racecourse, running downhill from a sharp turn after the winning post, past a lake on the inside of the course, to where the track met the M62 motorway embankment. After a sharp left turn at its lowest point, the ribbon of green grass bordered by bright white rails climbed up its longest straight before taking in a sweeping turn and the final uphill stretch back to the finishing post.

Joe had spent many hours in this box, so the football pitches, children's playground, fields of grazing animals, lakes and trees in the centre of the racecourse held no fascination. What did interest him were the private boxes at the top of the Dalby Stand to their right. The commentary box was angled toward the racetrack, so he had to lean out a little awkwardly; however, the view was worth it. Even with the naked eye he could see all four boxes. He levelled his binoculars to his eyes, adjusted them and began checking each private box from right to left.

The far right-hand corner box contained only a few people, picking at a buffet. They were definitely Fairbet guests, as the company's livery had been mounted on the wall. Joe moved on to the next box to the left, but found its balcony doors closed and the curtains drawn. It appeared to be empty.

Joe moved left again to view the Fairbet box in which he'd spoken with Sparky. About a dozen or more people were milling around carrying small plates of food and champagne glasses. It seemed perfectly normal, with a further group of Fairbet employees standing on the balcony, looking down at the runners as they filed out of the chute below them. He left that box and transferred his attention to Michael Gray's private box in the top left-hand corner of the stand. Suddenly, a bloodied face came into stark focus.

'They're coming out onto the course for the first race of what should be an excellent card of competitive racing here at Pontefract this afternoon,' George said into his headset microphone.

'Who is that with the blood all over him?' Indy whispered into Joe's ear. Behind her, George started to reel off the runners and riders information for the opening race as the stable lads and lasses reached the end of the chute and released their charges onto the racetrack.

'I think that's Paul Jenkins, one of the BHA guys,' Joe answered under his breath, his binoculars never leaving his eyes, 'Is it just me, or are they having an argument?'

At the other end of the commentary box George continued to fulfil his duties, meanwhile Indy and Joe watched transfixed as Michael Gray's private box became the stage for a fascinating silent movie.

***

'This is all a teenage prank,' Gray insisted smoothly to the knot of BHA personnel, in an attempt to keep a lid on the shared anger around the room, 'My daughter has manufactured this scare story, sent it to the media, and because she's my daughter, and the press always love a scandal, they've taken it seriously. There is absolutely no way someone has hacked accounts on Fairbet. I can give you my cast iron guarantee.'

'I haven't, you're wrong, and I speak from personal experience when I say your guarantees aren't worth squat,' Sparky insisted petulantly from the sofa.

Ignoring the young girl behind him, an increasingly relieved Tottering-Smythe was after further clarification.

'So this is just a huge hoax, and the stories circulating on the internet about members of my team receiving illegitimate proceeds from your company via Fairbet betting accounts are fake?'

'Absolutely,' Gray confirmed.

'Ms Gray has a history of manipulating the media with scare stories,' Gerard stated.

144

This comment received a warning stare from Gray. Chastised, Gerard stepped back from the group.

'Fine!' shouted Sparky angrily. She crossed her arms and glaring up at the group on their feet added, 'We'll see how you feel about things once this first race has run.'

'Ruth! Will you please cease pursuing this insane vendetta you have against me. There is no hacking code, no plot to frame your mother with Mr…' he snapped his fingers, apparently searching for the man's name. His daughter muttered something sarcastic under her breath, but Gray chose to ignore it.

Jenkins removed the tissue he was holding to his nose and rasped a nasal version of his name.

'Thank you, Mr Jenkins,' Gray said graciously, 'And I might add that your mother received a fair settlement when we parted,' Gray paused to suck in a breath and steady himself, 'Now… Ruth, please apologise to Mr Jenkins.'

Sparky gave her father a look of pure loathing. Turning to regard her mother she silently willed her to say something supportive. Charlotte's response was to stare glumly at her daughter and eventually shrug her shoulders.

'I don't believe it. You too?'

'This isn't the way, love,' Charlotte said, laying a hand on her daughter's shoulder. Sparky immediately flicked the unwanted hand off and squirmed back in her seat.

'Well, we'll find out soon enough. The first race has just gone off,' she said huffily, pointing to the flat screen television on the wall. It showed a number of colourful runners jostling for position after leaving the starting stalls.

'The news reports quote a whistle blower who said he would provide evidence that members of the BHA executive were receiving fraudulent payments from the racing today at Pontefract,' a nervous Horowitz pointed out. He had said very little during the argument, preferring to listen, but now faced Sparky directly, 'What evidence have you got that this will happen?'

'I'll tell you after the race. Just watch.'

The room fell silent as the thirteen runners covered the first two furlongs in the race. As the field rounded the bend at the bottom of the hill and hit the rising ground, a group of five broke away from the pack. Three horses passed the furlong pole together, each of them with every chance. Sparky's heart thumped in her chest; it was a perfect race for the hacking code to be activated. As the jockey's urgings became desperate in order to squeeze an extra ounce of stamina from their equine partners, Sparky scrutinized the BHA personnel, all of whom were staring fixedly at the television monitor on the wall.

The volume of the crowd outside swelled to fill the room, competing with the words of the race commentator who called a tight finish that necessitated a photo to resolve the outcome. The three horses flashed past the winning post together.

'I have a copy of the hacking code on my laptop. I have records of when, where, and how the fraudster has set up today's races for a huge sting,' Sparky announced.

'So *you've* set up this... this electronic nonsense?' accused Tottering-Smythe.

'No, you imbecile,' Sparky replied patiently, 'Oh, for heaven's sake! Do you have a Fairbet account any of you?'

The four BHA executives looked at each other sheepishly.

'Okay, yes. Alright. I do,' stated Proctor.

'Me too,' admitted Horowitz quietly.

'Jenkins?' queried Tottering-Smythe, 'Am I the only one who isn't betting with Mr Gray?'

Jenkins didn't answer for a few seconds. Presently he dug a phone out of his inside pocket.

'I think so. I'll have a look,' he offered, despite knowing full well he was a regular user of the website.

The result of the photo finish was preceded by a hush throughout the racecourse, followed by cries of delight from those on the winner and groans from those punters who had narrowly missed out.

'Check your balances,' instructed Sparky, 'If I'm right, one of you is tens of thousands of pounds richer despite having never had a bet, and landed yourselves in a boat load of trouble.'

Sally Proctor's face was the first to lose the worry lines that had stacked up across her forehead.

'My account is exactly the same,' she reported in a relieved manner, 'I only had thirty pounds in there this morning and it's the same now.'

'Mine's fine too,' Horowitz confirmed, having booted up his laptop.

Jenkins was standing quietly, the fingers of one hand

tentatively touching his bloodied nose. Having powered on his phone, he was staring at the small screen with increasing anxiety. Aware that he was being watched intently by a number of people around the room, he tried to speak.

'Erm... Mr Gray?' he said, frowning, 'It seems...'

Michael Gray wasn't concentrating. He was standing facing the curtains and retractable windows that had been pushed fully open at the front of the box, his back to the people in the room, and his mind in another place.

'Gray!' demanded Tottering-Smythe.

Sparky leaned back on her sofa and twisted her neck so as to inspect her father's face. She'd seen this expression many times before, as a youngster; her dad was working through a problem.

The room waited for an answer and presently Gray gave a little snort. Sparky picked up a wry smile that flickered across his face before being replaced with an impenetrable stare when he wheeled around to face everyone.

'You know it wasn't me, don't you,' Sparky interjected.

Gray studied his daughter and telegraphed a mixture of pride and sadness to his child, an emotion only she and his ex-wife picked up on.

'Tell me, Mr Jenkins,' Gray asked gravely, 'Has your Fairbet account remained free of tampering?'

The bleeding had stopped, but Jenkins had a red stain on one cheek and his white shirt was dotted with blood spots. He looked up at Gray and shook his head.

'I had nothing in there. I'd run it to zero. But my balance is showing as one-hundred and thirty-five thousand, four hundred and twenty-two pounds.'

Gray remained grave-faced and sighed heavily.

A text message from Joe pinged onto Sparky's phone and she read it immediately: 'Was watching. Had eyes on everyone. No devices in use! Except your mum's phone. Did the hack run?'

Sparky typed a quick response and waited a few seconds for it to send. Then she opened her calling app, tapped a recently called icon, waited for a connection, and placed her phone face down on the coffee table in front of her, before returning her attention to what was happening around her.

A heated discussion was underway. Currently, Tottering-Smythe was blustering on about how his 'legacy as chief executive' was about to be ruined. It was left to Sparky to cut through the chatter.

'I'm sorry, everyone,' she stated in a clear, crisp voice that silenced the rumblings of discontent around the room, 'I'm really very, very sorry,' she added, and promptly burst into tears.

Once that wave of waterworks was done with, she stood, and checking she had the full attention of the BHA executives, told them how she had stumbled on the Fairbet hacking code and had put together today's prank in order to try and exact revenge against Paul Jenkins for being the catalyst that broke up her mother and father.

'I thought that by placing fraudulent winnings into his account, I could implicate Mr Jenkins as a fraudster. I also manufactured evidence to make it look like Mr Jenkins set up the hacking code and contacted the press to stir up more trouble for Mr Jenkins.'

The four executives looked stunned. Paul Jenkins had his mouth open and was clearly struggling to understand what the seventeen-year-old had just explained. Sparky renewed her tears, flopped back down on the sofa and curled up at one end, trying to look sorry for herself.

It took the next ten minutes for her father to step in, firstly issuing instructions via phone to his staff in his head office, then apologising profusely to the four executives on his daughter's behalf, and finally promising the whole sorry episode would be explained away as a case of miscommunication.

'The money has already been removed from Mr Jenkins' account, the hacking code traced and deleted, and Fairbet will immediately send out a press release calling the accusations on the various media platforms a case of misreporting,' he promised them.

'Fairbet will make a donation to the BHA's responsible gambling charity. Our press release will point out that we wished to announce a large donation to your charity this afternoon. However, internet chat being what it is, a wholly inaccurate and garbled version of the story began circulating before the official announcement was able to be made,' Gray assured the BHA contingent as he held the door to his private box open for them, 'After all, no one apart from myself can prove the money actually entered that account. A sizeable cheque will be in the post to you tomorrow Mr Tottering-Smythe for your charity, and I've arranged for you to have the use of one of my private boxes at the other end of this floor of the Dalby stand for the remainder of the afternoon where you may enjoy free food and drink. I assume it will suit all of us if my daughter's indiscretion can be forgotten.'

Tottering-Smythe had needed a little convincing, but when Proctor pointed out the complications that could arise should the press start probing their personal betting accounts, he soon fell into line.

'My publicity department are already putting out the necessary press releases,' Gray assured the CEO as he departed.

Gray shook their hands in turn, although he had to hold back a grimace when Paul Jenkins gripped him. He was the last to leave, and Gray held onto the man's hand and leaned his head forward.

'I trust we won't be hearing any more about your unfortunate accident when you ran into my daughter's hand?'

Jenkins hesitated for a moment. Gray sensed the beginnings of a smirk emanating from the man. He squeezed the director of communications' hand until his fingernails bit into the man's palms.

'No. No,' Jenkins insisted as he squirmed, 'We'll call it even.'

The executive yanked his hand back, a scowl playing on his lips. Gray watched Jenkins scurry away down the corridor after his colleagues.

Behind him, Charlotte called out, 'Paying Mr Jenkins the last of his thirty pieces of silver, eh Michael?'

Twenty-Four

Once the door had closed behind the BHA, Gray turned the key in the lock. He swung round and invited Gerard to take one of the two armchairs opposite Sparky and her mother.

'Nice acting, Ruth. You can stop it now,' Gray told her. He turned his attention to Charlotte and fixed her with a tired, appraising stare.

'Charlotte?'

He said her name and left it hanging like an accusation.

'Well? What have you got to say for yourself?'

Without asking, Sparky grabbed her mother's handbag from between them on the sofa and rifled through it until she found what she was looking for. Charlotte didn't attempt to stop her and instead started wringing her hands. Sparky lifted an ancient mobile phone, battered and scratched, from her mother's handbag and after a swift examination, pressed the power button.

'This old thing is running the Windows 95 operating system?' presumed Sparky.

'Of course it is,' said Gray, inspecting Charlotte's face for glimmers of guilt.

One by one, Charlotte flicked between the three solemn faces scrutinizing her. She stared vacantly at the wall of the room and poked her tongue thoughtfully into one cheek, finally locking eyes with her ex-husband.

'I wanted to hurt you, and that horrible man,' she said quietly, 'The hacking code allowed me to do both.'

'Where did you get it from?' Sparky demanded.

'It was sent to me,' she replied with a shrug, 'It arrived in my inbox one morning from someone saying they were a friend. I actually thought it might be you.'

Sparky snorted derisively but dropped her petulant expression when she caught a seriously dark look from her father. Nonetheless, she continued to pump her mother for answers.

'You sent the email to dad demanding a ransom, and to the press accusing a member of the BHA of fraud?'

Charlotte gave a taut sigh that wasn't so much an admission of guilt, rather it signalled her irritation at being discovered.

'The BHA put out a press release last night saying Jenkins would be here today, and I thought it was too good an opportunity to

150

miss, especially on Michael's big day.'

She turned to face her daughter, 'Your argument with your father gave me an excuse to be here, all I needed to do was run the hacking code and watch as Jenkins' life fell apart.'

Sparky looked thoughtful for a moment.

'Mum, have you been running the hacking code over the last few months, or is this the first time you've used it?' Sparky asked.

'Never mind that, we need to get rid of any evidence and cancel any further use of the hacking code,' Gray cut in, gesturing to Sparky to pass the old phone to him. She studied her father as she handed the phone over, slightly confused.

'Aren't you interested to know whether mum is the hacker who has been infiltrating Fairbet?

Ignoring the question, Gray took Charlotte's phone and began tapping at it with its old-fashioned plastic pointer. He paused momentarily to order Gerard to recover his daughter's laptop from the room next door. Without hesitation his personal assistant got up and left the room, locking the door behind him. As they waited for Gerard to return, Gray concentrated on Charlotte's phone, tossing it silently back into her bag when he was satisfied he'd cancelled her second, more dangerous attempt at fraud. It was Charlotte who broke the heavy silence.

'I could still remember some of my coding work from when we started Fairbet… once I worked out the basics, I saw the opportunity to kill two birds with one stone.'

'You felt so strongly, you worked out how to frame Paul Jenkins and *then* throw my company into chaos?'

Gray sounded a little impressed. He hadn't levelled his query as an accusation. If it was, the emphasis of his question was all wrong. There wasn't enough surprise or consternation. Sparky found herself frowning as she allowed this to sink in. Immediately, like a switch flicking, her father seemed to catch himself. He began acting disappointed and regretful that his ex-wife was capable of engineering such a diabolical plan.

On the verge of crying, Charlotte held her breath, willing her tears to dry up. She had no wish to allow Michael the pleasure of witnessing her crying on account of being found out. But if anything, she was confused by his show of concern, making it difficult to gather the courage to confront him. But it had to be done.

'I disovered Paul Jenkins' Fairbet account,' Charlotte told her ex-husband shakily. Now she was speaking again she felt better, and her confidence returned. Her despair slowly turning to anger, 'I know you've used the hacking code yourself, Michael. You ran ten thousand pounds into that awful man's account just before I met him, and added another twenty thousand once you'd got your divorce. You set me up that day at Newbury races. You paid Jenkins to flirt with me, and when I rejected his advances, he manufactured a reason to get me alone and grab hold of me just as you walked in. Then he spouted all those lies about me. It was entrapment.'

Gray had been on the edge of his seat. Now he leaned back, scrunched his face up, and wiped a palm over his hair.

Charlotte faced her daughter, 'Ruth, I want to thank you for digging me out of the hole I'd made for myself. But you have to know that I couldn't help myself. That hacking code held the means to make your father experience what you and I went through; having our lives turned upside down.'

Sparky's mind was still sorting through this new information. How had her mother worked out how to incriminate Jenkins? And how on earth had she gone about hiring people like the Mercedes men? However, the news that her father had some sort of financial arrangement with her mother's so-called lover proved enough to send her brain haring off at a tangent.

Sparky rounded on her father, fire in her eyes.

'You *paid* Jenkins? Why did...'

She halted mid-sentence, staring incredulously into her father's hooded, bloodshot eyes. Why did he look so...sad?

She cast her mind back to fourteen months previously when she'd entered the most emotionally confusing time of her life. Her father had been the catalyst. From being a work obsessed, rather selfish, but relatively easy-going father and husband, Michael Gray had altered, almost overnight, into a... he'd been horrible to her and her mother, it had been like living with a caged animal for a few weeks.Then his mood had pivoted, he'd become distant and even more work obsessed. He'd stayed like that ever since, even during their recovery from her mother's fall and her own car accident. This period had culminated in his demand for a divorce on the basis of her mother's infidelity. At the time Sparky had been supportive, yet baffled by her mother's resolute denial of her short, but sordid affair with Paul Jenkins, despite all the damning evidence. Given her father's behaviour, she hadn't blamed her mother, and in truth she'd been a little bit proud of her too.

'Mum wasn't lying…' Sparky murmured as her father closed his eyes and grimaced, '…you paid that weasel Jenkins to lie for you.'

Sparky's mobile phone, still face down on the table, rattled as a text message set off her vibrate alert.

Gray sat up. He silently rested his elbows on the arms of his chair, steepled his hands, and bounced his index fingers softly against his lips, as if in holy contemplation. A sudden crash of laughter coming from the employee's box next door broke the silence, but failed to relieve the tension.

'Yes I did,' Gray finally admitted.

Sparky's phone vibrated against the coffee table once more.

'Michael, did you send those men to Ripon to hurt that poor girl?' asked Charlotte.

Sparky frowned at her mother, 'What? No. *You* must have sent them, to make sure your plot wasn't uncovered before today.'

'You think I…' started Charlotte.

'None of us sent them,' Gray interrupted in a deeply disgruntled tone.

Sparky grimaced, whipping her phone off the coffee table as it rattled for a third, and then a fourth time. The phone was still connected to the call she'd made to Joe ten minutes earlier so he and Indy could listen in on the conversation in Gray's private box.

'So who are the men who hurt that poor girl then?' demanded Charlotte.

Rubbing his face with both hands in frustration, Gray didn't appear to be ready to answer his ex-wife's question any time soon.

Jabbing at her phone, Sparky discovered Joe had sent half a dozen text messages to her in the last minute. She read the last of Joe's four messages first. It read: 'Too late. The Mercedes men are on your floor,'

'I think we're about to find out exactly who those men are,' said Sparky darkly.

Twenty-Five

'Why is Sparky ignoring my texts?' Joe growled under his breath.

'She's quite the little actress, isn't she?' Indy noted quietly from their corner of the commentary box, speaking low enough to be sure the ongoing call Sparky had made to Joe's phone didn't pick up her voice.

'But I'm confused. Sparky can't have been the person behind all… this.'

Indy and Joe had their binoculars trained on the Gray private box, and were sharing a single set of earphones plugged into Joe's phone, with one ear-piece each. As a result, their heads were no more than a few inches apart. Joe lowered his binoculars and turned to say something, but suddenly found himself staring deep into Indy's incredibly dark brown eyes from no more than a few inches away.

He eventually pulled back, a little embarrassed with how long he'd spent lost in her gaze, and his ear-piece immediately popped out of his ear and was left dangling on its little wire, meaning he was no longer listening to what was happening over in the private box.

'Sorry, this is a bit awkward,' he whispered apologetically, reinserting the small ear-bud.

'No worries,' Indy replied with an impish grin.

It had been a little confusing, listening to a conversation that started with Sparky apparently admitting she was behind the whole episode, but it soon became apparent to Joe that she was staging this revelatory admission of guilt in order to protect her mother.

'To answer your question; no, Sparky wasn't responsible for running the hacking code, it was her mother. Sparky was protecting her.'

Indy considered this for a few moments. Joe noticed she was gently stroking her earlobe between finger and thumb as she tried to make sense of what had happened in the Gray's private box.

'Ahh! I get it now,' she declared, giving her lobe a final rub and refocusing on Joe, 'Crikey, she was quick off the blocks. She was way ahead of me. I suppose in the eyes of those racing people a teenager's prank is far more forgivable than an adult committing deception and fraud as a means of revenge.'

'Quite,' Joe agreed.

154

The two of them peered through their binoculars once more, bringing the top, left-hand box in the Dalby Stand back into focus. The Gray family remained in heated discussion but Joe was becoming increasingly anxious. He'd watched the Mercedes men move through the crowd in the premier enclosure and disappear into the walkway leading to the back of the Dalby Stand. Neil had texted him to say they had entered the stand and were entering the lift.

'Well, we've warned them about the Mercedes men. I can't for the life of me work out why they're still sitting around arguing with each other.'

'She's not read the messages,' Indy said, a touch agitated, 'I can see her phone. Look, it's on that small table in front of her.'

'It's also why we've been able to listen to them so clearly,' said Joe.

From behind them, George stirred and cleared his throat, getting ready to describe the runners and riders going down to the start for the second race. Neither Joe nor Indy looked George's way. They were glued to their binoculars. The door to the Gray private box had just burst open.

Twenty-Six

Gerard unlocked the door and stood, momentarily silhouetted in the door frame of the private box. He was holding Billie's laptop. Sparky jumped to her feet, intending to stride forward, pull Gerard into the room, and lock the door behind him. Instead, the personal assistant was immediately propelled forwards by a push from behind and two men strode into the room after him. One was small and stocky, the other tall and broad. Both wore lounge suits and loud shirts without ties.

Sparky stared into the faces of the two Mercedes men and hissed a rebuke at them when she was ordered to sit down. Angry at missing Joe's text message warnings, she remained standing, only to be ordered back to a sitting position on the sofa between her mother and father by the larger of the two men.

'My apologies, Mr Gray...'

Gerard was unable to continue, as he descended into a coughing fit. On closer inspection his hair was ruffled, his shirt untucked, and his trouser pocket was ripped, displaying the bare white flesh of his thigh beneath. He was holding his stomach as he fought to regain control of his breathing. Sparky was initially shocked, but the notion that Gerard had been thumped a few times by the Mercedes men before relaying the location of his boss's private box was unsurprising. After all, she recognised the older, hairless man as one of Billie's attackers at Ripon cathedral. He was standing motionless in front of them as his colleague worked, an impenetrable stare gracing a slate grey face.

Relieving Gerard of the laptop and door key, the larger man expertly threw an elbow at the personal assistant's temple. Gerard immediately went limp and his head lolled backwards. His attacker caught him and manhandled his body into an armchair. Sparky and Charlotte recoiled with shock at the suddenness of the violence, trading worried looks.

They large man locked the door, handed the laptop to his colleague and growled, 'Phones!' at the captives. Having liberated a device each from Gray and Charlotte, he found three on Sparky, as well as one lying face down on the coffee table. Sparky was relieved the bear of a man didn't appear to notice the latter had a live call in progress before he smashed it open and ripped the battery out.

Sparky noticed the smaller man's yellowing teeth. It was hard not to when he stepped forward, leaned over and sneered at the three of them close up. They were sitting in a line on the edge of their sofa, watching wide-eyed as the larger man systematically toured the room, tugging the curtains closed on all the windows. At the front of the box he pulled the retractable windows together, taking care to leave a two yard gap of window and curtain in the centre, allowing the incongruous sounds of the racecourse to continue to filter into the room.

'Any of you makes a noise or moves and the girl is dead,' the smaller man stated, reaching behind his back and producing a pistol that had been stuffed into his belt. He inspected it for a second, dipped his hand in his jacket pocket and screwed in what Sparky presumed was a silencer. He sat down opposite them and casually pointed the elongated metal instrument at her, resting it on his leg.

'Pop!' exclaimed the man suddenly. He smirked when the two women cringed.

'It's that easy. So, do as you're told,' he warned, leaning over toward them, so close Sparky could see the individual black bristles of day-old stubble on his chin, 'You don't want another scar to go with the one you've already got, do you, Mrs Gray?'

Charlotte couldn't help but brush her fingertips down the side of her face as she contemplated his statement, unconsciously tracing the line of her injury. The deep slice out of her cheek had healed well after her fall down the escalator ten months ago, and liberal use of foundation meant the scar was hardly visible. She was surprised he had picked it out.

Gray sat poker-faced, staring up at the man.

'What do you want, Ronnie?' Gray demanded, an undercurrent of anger lacing his question.

'You know him?' Sparky blurted, firing her father a confused frown.

'Unfortunately, I do. Meet my blackmailers, Ronnie and Reggie.'

'Come, come, Mr Gray. How many times must I remind you,' Ronnie scolded, 'We've been providing you with a valuable service. Besides, you've sampled the alternative, and it wasn't to your liking.'

Gray gritted his teeth. With Gerard incapacitated he wondered whether it was possible for him to overpower Ronnie and his henchman.

157

Gray eyed the pistol still levelled at his daughter and immediately thought better of making a move. Even though Ronnie was a similar age to himself, Reggie was in his late twenties; quicker, stronger. And he didn't doubt that either wouldn't hesitate to carry out their threats. He'd made the mistake of calling their bluff once before.

'All of this could have been avoided...' continued Ronnie airily, waving his pistol around the room like a wand, '...if you'd been honest with us, Mr Gray. Did you really think distributing the hacking code would force us to give up?'

This prompted Charlotte to forget her fear for a moment. She leaned forward until she could see her ex-husband's face at the other end of the sofa, 'Michael? *You* sent out the hacking code?'

Gray closed his eyes. After a short pause he answered, 'Yes. Meet Flutter#1... It was the only way I could see to force this to end.'

'Yes, you've been rather naughty, *Michael*,' Ronnie continued, 'So instead of our monthly stipend, we're going to take a final balloon payment right now.'

Ronnie started to chuckle in a way that reminded Sparky of someone with croup; his throat vibrated with a faint bark as he drew breath. This forced good humour, delivered with dead eyes made for an unnerving combination. Sparky felt a jolt of nervous electricity rip through her bones when Ronnie suddenly crossed his legs, ensuring his pistol remained pointed at her in the middle of the family group.

'It's been a confusing few days hasn't it?' Ronnie stated conversationally, 'First there was that reporter we had to deal with. Then your daughter steals a laptop capable of proving you've been defrauding your own company. I assume you thought that drip-feeding Billie Davenport with details of your hacking code and allowing your ex-wife and daughter to play around with it would bring our little arrangement to an end.'

Gray didn't reply, preferring to stare at the floor.

Ronnie continued, 'We know about the debacle with the BHA. Your wife might have ruined our investment if it wasn't for the fact that we already had our own little finale planned for today.'

Ronnie slowly passed a palm over the slick tight skin on his head, 'We're going to bring our relationship to a close, Mr Gray. Nice and neat, everything tied up.'

'And in the process, you almost killed an innocent girl,' Sparky growled indignantly.

Ronnie regarded her for a moment, tapping the barrel of his pistol against his knee. She noted with relief that his fingers were nowhere near the pistol's trigger.

'What happened to your pal, the commentator?' Ronnie asked.

Sparky shrugged, 'He wasn't my pal, and he's not here. He's gone to visit his friend, Billie, the girl you half killed.'

Ronnie chuckled again, 'Ah, I see why he was at Ripon now. Here I was, thinking you'd found yourself a sugar daddy!'

Sparky gawked at her captor, 'You are utterly disgusting.'

Ronnie smiled at her indulgently. He held the look of a benevolent uncle for a few seconds before his face soured once again.

'Stand up,' he ordered.

'You only need me. Let my wife and daughter go,' Gray insisted, pleading directly to Ronnie and making to stand up. Sparky and her mother traded a sidelong glance. Whilst this show of altruism was as sudden as it was unexpected, Ronnie ensured it was immediately forgotten by grabbing Gray by his throat, holding him and squeezing until Gray's eyes bulged, before forcing him back into his seat. With eyes watering and a rasping cough, the two women watched Gray cower in his seat.

Normal service is resumed, Sparky thought to herself as Reggie moved over and grasping her arm, pulled her up to her feet. He led her to the middle of the room and stood her there, commanding her to stay still. Choosing one of the high-backed leather chairs with carved wooden arms, he dragged it over and dumped Sparky into it.

Producing a handful of zip ties from his jacket pocket the big man tied her ankles to the chair legs. Both her wrists were similarly strapped to arms of the chair. With Sparky now virtually inert, Reggie spent time moving the chair around, apparently lining it up with the gap in the curtains facing the racetrack.

During this process, Gray felt his nerves becoming fraught as he began to contemplate what could befall himself, and his daughter. A feeling of helplessness washed over him; always the precursor to a panic attack. As his mind swirled, anxiety gripped him and he began to sweat under his arms. A need to be on his feet engulfed him, nervous energy forcing him to stand.

He'd experienced many panic attacks before, most when he was in his late teens. Each episode had been a scary reminder that he could slip across the paper-thin boundary from normality into mental anguish with worrying ease. The attacks had plagued him at times of upheaval in his life, but he'd forced himself forward and his life had improved, whilst the threat of them returning had receded. Until five months ago. Twenty years without the hint of a reccurrence, then the blackmailing increased, his divorce became finalised, he fell out with his daughter, and the panic returned with a vengeance, each episode far more debilitating than ever before.

Gray swallowed down a wave of nausea and tried to free his mind from his swirling, confused thoughts, swaying in an ungainly manner as he rose from the sofa. He was immediately ordered back down by Ronnie.

'Sit down. Sit quietly. Shut up. Or get shot.'

The words frightened him, but only enough to make Gray plant his backside back down on the sofa.

Sparky gaped at her father. A little frightened, and unable to comprehend what was happening.

'Dad...?'

Charlotte was ahead of her daughter, concentrating on her ex-husband, as she had done many times before. She'd recognised the same need in his fearful eyes, and the physical signs of his distress. It had been many years since he'd needed her like this, and although he'd hurt her, Charlotte wasn't so callous not to help her ex-husband when *he* was hurting. She may have wanted to bring Jenkins, and then Fairbet down, but staring at the pitiful sight beside her, she wondered whether she had *wanted* to be caught, simply to witness this moment.

Tentatively at first, then with greater confidence Charlotte held Gray's attention, looking directly into his eyes, warming his hands in hers, speaking to him in a low, tender voice. Sparky watched as her mother, stage by stage, managed to calm her father down and bring him back. Within another two minutes he was looking, and sounding like her father again.

Sparky gaped at her mother. She was impressed, even proud of her, but also confused; this was a complete reversal in their roles. She'd never seen her father so frail, so vulnerable, and her mother so... in control. She felt like she'd seen a side to their relationship she'd never even considered could exist.

'He can't cope with this,' Charlotte complained to Ronnie as Gray, head down on Charlotte's shoulder, completed his recovery.

From behind Sparky's chair, where he was checking Reggie's handiwork, Ronnie sniggered in response.

'You better pull yourself together, Mr Gray. You've got one last hacking job to do for us.'

Twenty-Seven

'Why can't we hear anything?' Indy queried quietly.

Joe checked his phone, then scanned the private box through his binoculars again. With the curtains being drawn, their view into the box had become restricted; limited to a gap of no more than six feet between the curtains.

'Blast,' he uttered in frustration, discarding the ear-piece, 'They must have switched Sparky's phone off. I can only just see a bit of her, sat in an armchair, and that's about it.'

'Do you think they know about us?'

'I doubt it,' replied Joe, trying to sound reassuring, 'The Mercedes men seemed to be concerned solely with Michael Gray before the curtains were closed.'

'Shouldn't we call the police?'

Joe allowed his binoculars to drop to his lap and considered this for a few seconds. These men were known to be violent, but quite apart from the fact that he was a wanted man, and might have difficulty convincing the police to take him seriously, there was something else bothering him. Something making him hesitate to run straight to the authorities.

'I think we need to wait.'

Indy curled her lip at him, 'Is that so? How do you work that out?'

On the other side of the commentary box, George started to call the runners and riders for the second race as one by one, they were released onto the track by their stable lads and lasses. As his voice boomed around the stand, drowning out conversation, it provided Joe with the opportunity to ignore Indy's sarcasm and afforded him some time to try and explain himself.

'It was something Michael Gray told me on the phone at Sandie's this morning,' he told Indy in hushed, earnest tones once the last of the thirteen runners had jogged past the stands toward the five furlongs start.

'When I told him I thought his company could be under attack from a hacker, Gray said he was going to *sort this, once and for all.*'

Joe paused, 'Once and for all,' he repeated.

'It was the way he said it,' he continued, wearing a quizzical expression, as if he couldn't quite verbalise his thoughts, 'It... it struck me he wasn't speaking about his daughter or some family feud. Just for a moment he sounded beaten, you know, resigned to some sort of... fate.'

His shoulders dropped and he shook his head slowly in frustration, unhappy with his muddy thinking. He eventually refocused on Indy.

'Does that make any sense?'

'Not one bit.'

'I thought so,' he moaned.

George flicked the switch on his microphone and announced that the runners had all reached the start for the nursery handicap over five furlongs, and there were four minutes to post time, so it was time for the race-goers to get their bets on. He turned back to his two guests who had returned to staring glumly at the Dalby Stand. The veteran race caller switched his microphone off and asked them to put their binoculars down.

'In my experience, bookmaking attracts a certain type of person. They are natural risk takers. But every bookmaker needs the odds to be in their favour, and that's a constant battle. Michael Gray had two major competitors when he started Fairbet over twenty years ago, and in the late nineties there was a power struggle which he eventually won because Fairbet had better technology, but more importantly, deeper pockets. He bought the competitors out and Michael Gray's company became *the* betting exchange.'

George paused, reading the faces of his small audience to ensure they were following him. Satisfied, he continued.

'There were many accusations flying around at the time that there was false liquidity in the Fairbet markets, timings were wrong and in-play bets were being matched when the race had finished, that sort of thing. But it was a new technology and by the time the regulators caught up with them, the exchanges had got their act together.'

George checked his monitor; the runners were milling around in front of the stalls at the five furlong start.

'All I'm saying is that in those days, Michael Gray had a reputation for being a tough boss, and an even tougher businessman. He was willing to take big risks for big rewards. Of course he's probably mellowed since then... but by all accounts in those days he wasn't too fussed at bending the rules if it gave him an advantage over his opposition. The stakes were high in those early days of the exchanges, and he won the race to be the biggest…'

He smiled benignly at Indy. She returned his smile, but something told him she hadn't completely followed everything he'd said. In contrast, Joe had that faraway look that meant he understood, and was busy processing the information.

'There is something else I've only just noticed,' George said as he swiveled back to his monitor and clamped a set of professional headphones onto his ears, 'I think there is someone else watching the Dalby Stand.'

He pointed over the track to where a disused race information building stood. Built over a hundred years ago, it was an archaic remnant of the days when thousands of race-goers would flood the inside of the Pontefract track on race-days. Managed by men from within, the forty foot high square building with a flat roof and a castle-like turret in one corner would provide information on the going, runners, riders, and results, all powered by hooking hand-painted wooden boards on a rotating mechanism.

'There he is!' George noted, binoculars held to his eyes, 'He's lying down on the roof with what looks like a telescope pointed at the Dalby Stand. Can you see him?'

Joe trained his binoculars onto the isolated building set back at an angle from the inside of the track, about sixty yards away. From this elevated position, he still didn't have a perfect view, but the angle was good enough to pick out the object George was referring to on the old race director's tower. Sure enough, there was the figure of a perfectly still, prone man dressed in grey coveralls, hood up, lying close to the near edge of the roof. His telescope was resting just over the edge of the building.

'What's that beside him?' whispered Indy.

Joe had been asking himself that same question. He tracked his binoculars from the flat roof of the race information building, over to the Grays private box in the top corner of the Dalby Stand, a distance of about eighty yards. Lingering there for a few seconds and noting the gap in the curtains onto the balcony, he tracked back to the figure lying motionless on the roof and focused on the long, bulky instrument he was holding. He wasn't so much holding it, he seemed to be… hunched over and gripping it. When recognition dawned his mouth became dry and a shiver of utter horror rippled through him.

Twenty-Eight

'Don't move,' insisted Ronnie, balancing a bottle of champagne on a small occasional table he'd placed to the right of Sparky's armchair. Reggie dragged Gerard's armchair over, complete with its unconscious occupant, and positioned him at the other side of the small table.

Sparky turned her nose up, 'I don't drink champagne.'

'I'm not asking you to drink it,' Ronnie assured her.

The atmosphere in the box had become increasingly tense since Reggie had smashed a fist into her father's ribs because of his initial refusal to leave the sofa. When the request was repeated, her father had stumbled crablike over to an armchair Reggie had lifted into position beside Gerard, gingerly seating himself. Billie's laptop was placed on his knees and his ankles zip tied, but not his wrists; Sparky realised they still wanted him to have the ability to type. Ronnie played with a phone he produced from his suit pocket for a few seconds, said a few words into it, then placed it on the coffee table and ordered Gray to use the data connection to link the laptop to the internet.

Sparky was worried about her father, but even more so her mother. The abruptness with which these men inflicted violence had sent Charlotte into shock. She was now curled up in the corner of the sofa, staring wildly around as the two men went about their business. The mask of confidence she had exhibited earlier in the day had quickly dissolved and Sparky was reminded of how much of a crutch she'd been for her mother during the upheaval of her parent's divorce.

After placing another armchair directly to Sparky's left, Reggie pulled Charlotte to her feet and guided her into it, zip tying each ankle and wrist separately to the chair legs and arms.

Charlotte, Sparky, Gerard, and Gray sat in a straight row, rigid in their identical armchairs, unable to move more than an inch or two. They were facing the balcony and the gap in the curtains. Reggie stood behind them for a few seconds, appraising his work. Seemingly dissatisfied with the arrangement, he headed to the balcony and pulled the bi-folding glass windows open a touch and widened the gap in the curtains by a foot either side. Both men retreated to the back of the room, standing together behind the line of armchairs.

Sparky twisted her head round and found Ronnie gripping the top of her father's armchair. He was staring at the gap in the curtains and the view beyond. She tried to follow his gaze and was treated to an uninterrupted view of the last furlong of the Pontefract racetrack.

Ronnie thumped Gray's armchair with both fists, then rounded the row and pulled up a chair in front of Fairbet's CEO. He silently crossed his arms and regarded the self-made man for a good twenty seconds before he spoke.

'I don't care how you do it, Gray. But you're going to place ten million pounds into our Fairbet account over the course of this afternoon.'

Despite his ribs singing with pain, Gray gave a contemptuous laugh, grimacing at the discomfort which increased in intensity with each rise and fall of his chest.

'It can't be done,' he confirmed after a few steadying breaths, 'I've been paying you thirty to forty thousand pounds each month. That's been built up over several days of careful management of the hacking code. I can't just find ten million all in one go!'

'You don't seem to understand,' Ronnie replied sweetly, continuing to adopt a patient, measured approach, 'How long have we known each other?'

Gray studied Ronnie's expectant face and didn't answer, it was pointless. If there was one thing he'd learned about this man in the half dozen times he'd been bullied by him, Ronnie loved a rhetorical question.

'We've worked together for …' Ronnie began.

Gray found himself examining Ronnie's eyes; they were hard and lifeless. He wondered whether he had any sort of life outside of his rotten job. He imagined not. Harming people with impunity, and probably without remorse, had to have consequences in your private life. Ronnie continued to speak but Gray didn't register his words, it would be more of the same self-satisfied twaddle the man had spouted for the last year and a half. Instead he began to reflect on what brought Ronnie and his colleagues into his life; a brace of tough decisions… decisions he had come to bitterly regret.

The first was to commit fraud.

Twenty years ago he'd written the hacking code as a set of in-house fraud testing routines to ensure his Fairbet systems could be made impregnable. The exercise had been worthwhile, improving the website's resilience. In fact, the hacking code had proved extremely powerful, and virtually invisible when used sparingly. It was code he'd been proud of, so he'd neglected to delete it.

In the early 2000's, when Fairbet was desperately short of cash, he'd resurrected the hacking code to illegally siphon off funds. He'd had no other option; it was clean, quick, and invisible - if run conservatively. At the time, it had been touch and go whether Fairbet was going to be crushed by a competitor, and Fairbet was at the limit of its private funding. So he'd quietly and invisibly defrauded his customers of a hundred and twenty thousand pounds over the course of six weeks, laundering the money through several company accounts to eventually cover the wage bill. He hadn't slept soundly for months afterwards, fearing customers would notice, but they never did; his hacking code was too good.

His second poor decision was made almost fourteen months ago when he'd employed the services of a shady corporate hacker to provide advice on where Fairbet could be subject to potential future data breaches. The man specialised in advising large online companies where they may be vulnerable to attacks from professional, malicious hackers. Gray had never met this man, he'd come recommended, and like many people in the world of internet fraud detection, he worked under a pseudonym. The hacker only communicated via a disposable email address and was paid in Bitcoin.

This professional hacker had proved to be worthy of his recommendation, and then some. He had found a way into the Fairbet corporate network and then started digging around in their archives. Discovering the hacking code on an ancient back-up, the hacker had immediately realised the gravity of his discovery and with a little more investigative work, uncovered that Gray had used it to defraud his customers. The hacker then revealed his true colours by sending an email demanding five million pounds, or he would sell this knowledge on the dark web. When Gray refused, the hacker had been true to his word, and Ronnie, Reggie, and Jack (surely false names, the similarity to the Krays was not lost on him), had arrived at his office door a week later to blackmail him. They were always quite clear that they were the hired muscle. Their orders came from someone else.

He'd been paying out tens of thousands of pounds a month to them for the last fourteen months. He would run the hacking code on a few races early in the month, the money would be credited to their

Fairbet account and they would withdraw it as winnings, thus neatly sidestepping any question of money laundering, as their account showed them winning legitimately.

Gray straightened enough in his chair to eyeball Ronnie. His blackmailer was still pontificating on how the proceeds from the fraud would be transferred into their Fairbet account. One way or another, it would end this weekend, Gray decided. The worry, the stress… the reoccurrence of his panic attacks… He'd planned for this eventuality. He typed a few commands into the laptop, ensured the connection had been made, and looking up at Ronnie with narrowed eyes.

'This is the man who pushed you down the escalators at Ascot racecourse last year, Charlotte,' Gray interjected above Ronnie's monotonous rambling, 'I refused to believe his threats so I didn't pay him, and as a result, he almost killed you.'

Ronnie clammed up and glared at Gray, his face like thunder. But Gray hadn't finished.

'Ruth,' he called out, 'Your car accident. Ronnie was the hit and run driver who ran over you as you waited to cross by the side of the road outside our house…'

Gray's revelatory speech was cut short. Reggie slammed a fist into his ribs once again, eliciting a breathy, guttural groan from his victim. Reggie rubbed the knuckles on his right hand and scowled down at the Gray. He was on his knees in front of his armchair, doubled up in pain, having slipped off his armchair. His ankles screamed too, where the zip ties were biting into his skin.

Her father's statement had caused Sparky to experience an introverted numbness. She was examining her memory of the day she'd been hospitalized over a year ago; her hip broken by the wing of a silver car that had mounted the verge and driven into her. She'd been sure the driver was *aiming* for her. Her father had held her hand at her bedside, exhibiting a strange aura of fear, and he'd promised her something: he'd told her *this will never happen again*. It had taken months for her to process that day and realise how odd her father's words had been. When she'd eventually confronted him, he'd laughed it off, claiming he couldn't remember the conversation and blamed shock for his strange bedside manner. That's when he became more than just a workaholic father, thought Sparky, that's when things fell apart.

Sparky emerged from her introspection and became aware of

her mother trembling beside her, tears streaming, her cheeks an angry red. Calling a few soft words of support to her had the desired effect; Charlotte nodded back, trying to recover her composure.

In the armchair beside her, Gerard stirred. He groggily raised his head and forlornly watched Gray being man-handled back into his seat by the Mercedes men. Sparky eyed the personal assistant cum bodyguard with unconcealed contempt; he had failed her father. She'd never understood why her father had employed a man to trail around after him, it wasn't his style. He liked silence, solitude, and a computer in front of him. It was now painfully obvious he'd had good reason.

Ronnie was starting to lose patience. His fist thumped the coffee table, making her father jump.

'You've been holding back on us, Mr Gray. We know that hacking software of yours is capable of delivering much more than twenty or thirty thousand a month. We've learned it's capable of inflicting serious damage to your precious betting exchange,' Ronnie barked. He grabbed a handful of Gray's hair and squeezing his fist, pulled Gray's head back so he could eyeball his victim.

'*We* can also inflict serious damage,' he whispered maliciously into Gray's ear.

Propelling Gray back into his armchair, Ronnie glanced around at Sparky and Gerard, then typed a short message into his phone and punched the send button. He nodded at Reggie, who backed away.

'Time for your daughter to take a drink,' Ronnie told the room, 'She's almost eighteen, I think it's allowed.'

Sparky eyed the unopened bottle of Moet suspiciously. It was perched on the small table between her and Gerard, no more than two feet to her right, slightly behind her, at chest height. Was he going to force her to drink it all? The thought repulsed her; she hated champagne.

'I recommend you close your eyes when you take a sip,' suggested Ronnie.

Sparky narrowed her eyes, expecting him to get up and start uncorking the green bottle topped with gold foil. Instead, Ronnie crossed to the side wall, joining Reggie. He stared fixedly at her whilst a devilish smile played on his lips.

There was a faintest zipping sound before the world exploded around Sparky. A loud pop signalled the impact and a deadly cloud of champagne laced with tiny shards of glass was propelled to the back of the room. Sparky had spotted Ronnie covering his eyes with an arm, and had thankfully slammed her own eyes shut a split second before the bullet shattered the Moet bottle. Even so, the pricks of pain as slivers of glass simultaneously dug their way into her flesh, was excruciating.

She didn't scream. She couldn't. The shock was too much. With hearing dulled by the pop, the pain came a few seconds later when her brain eventually realised the right-hand side of her neck, ear, and part of her face had been lacerated with glass and champagne bubbles. Her natural reaction was to try and touch the injured area, but no amount of struggling with her bonds allowed her to release herself, and she gave up when her wrists started to hurt more than her neck.

Ronnie waited a few seconds, enjoying the aftermath.

'We'll be off now,' he said with unashamed amusement, 'It's up to Mr Gray now. There's hundreds of thousands of pounds, sometimes millions, traded on every single betting event on Fairbet. The betting events are all over Europe, every few minutes. We know there is more to that hacking code than simply fooling the in-play punters. Mr Gray can decide to start placing serious cash into our account now, or not. If I'm not mistaken, the next race here is due off soon, and we'll expect to see the first healthy deposit once the bets have been settled. If Mr Gray decides not to accept our terms, the next bullet into this room won't be striking a cheap bottle of fizz.'

Despite Gray's ankles being tethered to his chair, he moved to get to his feet, desperate to come to the aid of his daughter. Ronnie shook his head, warning him he would be shot if he attempted to leave his seat. This was followed up by a number of other do's and don'ts, all of which would bring about a similar result if they went unheeded.

'You could email the police. You could call for help,' Ronnie droned, 'Doing so will see your family picked off... one by one. Besides, I think your business is more important to you than your family, Mr Gray. If we don't get our ten million, at the touch of a button we will report the details of all your fraudulent activity to date over every single communication channel, and watch as Fairbet dies.'

Sparky had been listening, but not really following what

Ronnie was saying. She was staring out of the gap between the curtains at the front of the box. She started at the top sill, filled with an azure sky, then tree tops, white balcony railings, and finally down to lush green grass. However, in the middle distance a strange, partially flat topped building stood in splendid isolation. There appeared to be horizontal white boards and a clock on a sort of turret, and at the left-hand corner of the flattened roof, there was the glint of a spyglass.

'That weird building... tower out there...' Sparky mumbled, '...someone is on the roof, watching us.'

Ronnie produced a half laugh, 'You're not being watched,' he announced in a patronizing tone, 'You're being targeted.'

Gray spat out a torrent of expletives in Ronnie's direction, his eyes blazing, again struggling to get to his feet.

'Ah, good! I think I'm starting to get through to you, Mr Gray,' Ronnie returned, striding around the line of chairs and slapping the side of Gray's head with a flat hand, 'We will be monitoring our Fairbet account. Should we be... *disappointed* with your performance, we will send you a reminder, via your daughter or your ex-wife. Our sniper is quite the surgeon when it comes to putting a bullet through people. I imagine he'll start with the arms and legs and work inwards from there.'

Still feeling the effects of Reggie battering his ribcage, Gray held an arm around himself while he tried desperately to find a good reason for not carrying out Ronnie's command.

'I've told you, I can't just conjure up hundreds of thousands of pounds from each race,' he spluttered.

Ronnie leaned on the arms of the chair and studied Gray's face, appraising him. Presently he shook his head and rounded the chair. Standing behind him, Ronnie placed his hands onto Gray's shoulders and began to rhythmically massage them. Gray flinched away at his first touch and was rewarded with another swift slap around his head and two rough hands straightening him up. Gray's face immediately turned red.

'While you were paying our monthly fee, we didn't mind too much how you generated the payment,' Ronnie stated, wrinkling the fabric of Gray's jacket as he rubbed more vigorously, 'But releasing the hacking code was a mistake, Mr Gray. It reduced our opportunity to blackmail you, which meant we had to act quickly to... realise our investment. We went back to the hacker who introduced you to us, and guess what?'

Gray was grimacing as Ronnie's grip moved to his neck and started to squeeze. Thick, strong fingers pushed into his windpipe and he started to choke.

'We now know that you have half a dozen different ways to commit fraud using that hacking code,' continued Ronnie, his words strained and becoming tinged with anger as he pushed his thumbs harder into Gray's windpipe.'

'Perhaps you need a small reminder of who holds the power in this situation,' he added, releasing Gray's neck with a final push forward. He tapped at his phone while Gray coughed hoarsely, tentatively touching his throat. Sparky again railed against her bonds to little effect. Ronnie nodded to Reggie, who backed away to the wall of the box and ordered Gray, who was still bent forward, trying to recover his breath, to take a look at his daughter.

The same zipping sound cut through the air and there was a twang and a small puff of sawdust from the back of Sparky's armchair. Gray watched through watery eyes and with growing dread as his daughter looked down, checking for an injury.

'Your arm, Ruth?' he called hoarsely.

Sparky examined her right arm, but all was well. Two inches to the left was a different matter. The armchair leather was deformed, residue from the puncture wound surrounding an inch wide, symmetrical hole. She winced. It was as if inspecting the bullet hole forced her brain to flip, and once it did, her whole body started to shake. Sparky felt a chill wash over her and nothing she tried seemed to have an effect on the trembling.

'We will forensically pick off pieces of your wife and daughter every few minutes until ten million pounds has been deposited into our Fairbet account. That's an average of five hundred thousand pounds every ten minutes. Miss that target, and a chunk of flesh will be removed by the next bullet. If you shout, scream, move, or try to leave the room before we've been able to transfer the money from our Fairbet account, we will stop targeting their extremities, and take out all of you one by one.'

Ronnie glared at Gray, ensuring he had his full attention.

'Believe me, Mr Gray, the person behind that rifle would *love* you not to pay. He's trigger happy at the best of times, and slowly picking all four of you off from eighty yards away would make his day.'

172

Gray responded with a sullen nod and returned his attention to the laptop, trying to ignore the pain in his throat by chewing nervously on the inside of his mouth.

'Goodbye, Mr Gray. It's been a pleasure working with you and your family. I really do hope you do the right thing, after all, it's only other people's money.'

Ronnie flashed a mirthless smile at Gray before he and Reggie exited the room.

Twenty-Nine

Once the door had clicked shut and the key turned in the lock Gray immediately began to fumble with the zip ties attached to his ankles. In response, a bullet zipped past Sparky's left ear and slammed into the back wall.

'What the heck?' Sparky stammered, the shock from the previous bullet punching a hole a few inches from her shoulder blade having receded enough to allow her to shape her words.

'It was worth trying,' Gray responded, his fingers now moving over the laptop, 'He could hardly shoot holes in me before I'd started giving them money.'

'You are so selfish!' Sparky hissed reproachfully.

Gray ignored her. With something important to occupy his mind, all thoughts of his recent panic attack were forgotten. Gray was concentrating on what was in front of him; on what mattered.

'But he did shoot. Not at you, at me!' Sparky complained.

Gray glanced up at his daughter, 'It was just a warning. As long as I give them what they want, we'll be fine.'

'He could have shot *any* of us,' Sparky persisted.

'But he didn't,' Gray replied drily.

'Are you hurt, love?' Charlotte asked, fearing the answer.

'I'm okay,' Sparky assured her, 'Most of the glass missed me, it just stings a bit.'

In truth, Sparky couldn't tell if the fluid congealing on the side of her neck was blood or champagne. She simply chose to imagine it was the contents of the bottle, rather than the contents of her circulatory system. She turned her head to regard Gerard next to her, smarting at the resulting ripple of pain from her ear down to her shoulder. Her father's personal assistant was still struggling to stay conscious. His head was currently lolling forward and although there were shards of glass and evidence of champagne splatter on his shirt and jacket, he'd been spared any lacerations to his neck and face.

'Three to go,' said a voice which reverberated around the course outside, indicating the second race was about to start.

'Dad, you have to deposit something in that account. Do something, even if it's something to buy us time.'

Gray glanced at his daughter and took in the jumble of glass and blood across the side of her neck. Trying to hide any negative reaction he might accidentally telegraph to her, he silently nodded

174

his agreement. Switching his gaze to Charlotte he wasn't surprised to find her shivering, almost certainly with shock. Their eyes met and he offered her a weak smile. He'd hoped it would give her strength, instead, her eyes refilled with tears and she looked away, hiding her face from him.

Gray began to run the hacking code across every open betting market in every sport around the world. Five race meetings, twenty football matches, five rugby games, basketball, ice-hockey, tennis and handball matches. He infiltrated his own exchange and directed the fraudulently earned winnings into a Fairbet account with an ID he knew off by heart, an account he regularly lost sleep over.

Outside the private box, the race-day crowd's hum of excitement had risen in volume ahead of the second race. The race caller announced they were off, and Gray watched a grid of numbers on his screen start to automatically update.

Ronnie had been correct. Only a small percentage of the hacking code's capability had been realised by Billie Davenport, and as it turned out, his wife. It could defraud on multiple levels. One of its most potent abilities was to redirect some of the exchanges own commission around the system and pay fractions of percentages into a specified account. And those fractions added up.

That's why he'd written it. He'd aimed to create the ultimate hacking code for his own betting system. The intention had been to learn how it could be done, to keep malicious hackers out. And here he was, running his own code to defraud his own company, as he had done, every month for the last fourteen months.

Gray was glued to the small laptop screen. As the numbers increased, a sense of hollowness grew within him. He was witnessing the death of his creation; a business to which he'd dedicated more than twenty years of his life. There was no way removing ten million pounds from the exchange markets in the space of a few hours would go unnoticed, no matter how clever your hacking techniques.

Thirty

Neil Tuton hadn't felt this invigorated since he and Simon had sold their company. That now seemed such a long time ago. Since then, they'd both got their kicks from their horse racing. But the excitement gained in running around a racecourse on a mission for a wanted man was managing to beat the rush he received from betting on horses.

Joe's task had seemed simple: locate the trainer of the horse under which the Mercedes men had been left owners' badges, and pump him for information. After twenty-five minutes of fruitless searching, he'd almost given up, having trawled all the bars the trainer usually frequented. However, his pulse quickened when on his third visit to the owners' and trainer' bar he caught sight of a squat man huddled over a paper cup filled with weak tea. Neil approached the trainer, raised his trilby in greeting, and received a cursory twitch of an eyebrow from the horseman in return.

Keith Citron wasn't the sort of horseman who attracted well-heeled owners with perfect diction; he made his living from a wholly different set of racing enthusiasts. Training moderate horses to win low class races, he had a reputation for setting horses up for big punts that were invariably successful. As a result, he was the go-to trainer for owners who were in the sport for nothing more than gambling purposes.

Five minutes later and with his wallet a hundred and fifty pounds lighter, Neil left the bar, his opinion of the trainer having been initially confirmed, and subsequently hardened. Feeling faintly tainted by his grubby conversation with Citron, he waited until he was well out of sight of the bar before he composed and sent a text message to Joe.

Thirty-One

Joe read Neil's message and frowned.

'What?' Indy mouthed silently.

The second race was well under way. A few yards away George was absorbed in his race commentary. Joe would have to wait the sixty-five seconds it would take the two-year-old's to complete their five furlong trip before he could explain Neil's message to Indy. Instead, he passed her his phone. A few seconds later the eight lines of text elicited a similar reaction in her.

They had watched the Mercedes men rearranging the room and once the glass doors had been folded back to reveal the row of four armchairs, the role of the man on the information tower roof had become all too clear. Before they could decide what to do, in quick succession the Mercedes men left the room in the Dalby Stand and the second race of the day had gone off.

Joe was currently suppressing the urge to rush over to the Dalby Stand, break the door down and somehow safely extract all three Grays and Gerard. The phrase 'sitting ducks' had been whirling around his mind and the thought of them being shot during his attempt to untie them was successfully flattening his enthusiasm for such a blunt approach. There was every possibility he could get shot too, in fact, if Sparky's appearance was anything to go by, the man on the roof had already been toying with his targets.

He checked the room again through his binoculars, taking solace from the fact that Sparky seemed to be speaking with her father, while he was consumed with the laptop rested on his knees. On closer inspection, the laptop appeared to be Billie's. He was relieved to find Gerard awake and looking around the room wearing a glazed expression; he had a minor bruise on his face but was otherwise in good shape. Despite the lack of any blood or injury, Charlotte Gray's mental anguish was telegraphed so strongly via her body language that Joe found it difficult to concentrate on her for any length of time without being filled with a mixture of empathy and anger.

Joe switched his focus to the centre of the racecourse and the man on the roof of the information tower, oblivious to a surge in noise from the crowd as the race entered its final stages. The sniper remained absolutely still. George completed his commentary, removed his headphones, and fixed the two people he was shielding with a concerned gaze.

'It could be time for the police.'

Joe shook his head.

'No. He's already let off one, perhaps two shots. It would take too long. Mr Gray has Billie's computer on his lap, which means he must be running the hacking code. I'm guessing the man on the tower is there to make sure he keeps paying the Mercedes men. We have to do something now.'

'But this place is crawling with police!' Indy pointed out.

'Yes, unarmed bobbies,' Joe fired back, 'They're not equipped to deal with a sniper on a roof.'

Joe checked out the tower again, 'There's a hundred yards of rolling grass right around that tower, the gunman could pick off everyone in that private box as soon as a few policemen start to converge on him, not to mention the policemen themselves. No, the only way to get the Grays out of that room is to stop him getting his shots on target.'

Indy had been concentrating hard, biting the end of her thumbnail. Suddenly her face brightened.

'If we could distract him long enough, we could get everyone out of that room.'

'That's the idea.'

George looked dubious, 'So then he starts shooting at the police... or the public?'

Joe visibly deflated, his shoulders dropping. Indy was holding her hand to her mouth and staring blindly at the floor. An awkward silence descended within the commentator's box. George glumly examining the two of them whilst his body language seemed to scream, 'This is a fine mess, and no mistake!'

Joe leaned on the thin bench below the viewing window, staring sullenly down at the betting area below him. It was a seething mass of people queuing to cash in winning betting tickets after the favourite had prevailed in the second race. He lifted his head, taking in the virtually empty track, save for a few groundsmen replacing divots, and then the expansive grassland at its centre. There were a smattering of people about a hundred yards away from the tower, beside the children's playground where a small race-day fair was giving rides to toddlers and several garishly coloured inflatables were being bounced on by shoeless youngsters.

Joe was suddenly reminded of the photos that hung on the

walls of the main stand. In the glory days of horseracing at Pontefract the centre of the racecourse would have been teeming with people, all around the director's tower and down to the two furlong pole. If they were there now, the hustle and bustle would have provided the perfect cover. He'd be able to simply pick his way through the crowd and walk right up to the tower... but where would he get a few thousand people from?

From the recesses of Joe's memory he dredged up the scene of a grandstand being evacuated and the race-goers streaming across a racetrack.

'Aintree... The Grand National,' he said quietly. It had been 1997 and he'd been ten years old when the IRA's bomb scare had emptied the racecourse grandstands and forced the race to be run the following Monday. He and his mother had settled down in their small front room that afternoon to watch the spectacle of forty chasers complete the marathon journey around Aintree, to be met with confusion which saw a mass exodus of race-goers from every enclosure as the course was evacuated. The following month had seen copy-cat calls to several racecourses, delaying, rather than disrupting the entire race meeting.

Joe inspected the tower once again, and the unmoving figure hunched over a rifle pointed at the Dalby Stand. He spun round to face George.

'Isn't it time you made a visit to the men's room again?'

Thirty-Two

'How much did you send to their account?' Sparky demanded.

Gray didn't answer, preferring to remain transfixed by the screen of the laptop and the sound of his fingers thumping the keyboard.

Next to him Gerard repeated the question. It was a long way removed from the deferential tone he was used to hearing from his personal assistant. Gray raised one side of his upper lip in disgruntled disappointment. A fat lot of use Gerard had been when he really needed him. He ignored the question again.

'Are we going to get shot, Michael?'

Charlotte asked her question in a tearful, frightened voice and Gray couldn't help himself. He broke away from the rows of numbers dancing across the screen and quickly assessed her. With head bowed, the streaks of blue in Charlotte's hair hung vertically, masking her face. She'd spoken, but hadn't bothered looking at him. An unexpected rush of guilt rippled through him. He swallowed it down, having decided upon the answer he believed his ex-wife needed to hear. He aimed to reassure, to ease her pain...

Without the sound of the commentary or the crowd, an audible pop came from the other side of the track this time. It was an insignificant sound, easily dismissed, but a warning nonetheless. The bullet zipped through the front of the private box and slammed into the leather just above Charlotte's shoulder. Gray froze, unable to take his eyes off her, filled with a mixture of fascination and horror.

'What happened?' Charlotte asked, suddenly wide-eyed and looking around her. She'd been aware of the jolt to her torso, but not its cause.

Gray was mesmerized, unable to tear himself from her, or shape a reply. Charlotte followed her ex-husband's gaze and found the marble sized wound to her chair a few inches from her head. When the panic reached her Charlotte instinctively struggled with her bonds, attempting to lift her hands and push herself away from the bullet hole, whimpering when the plastic ties bit deep into her wrists. Instead, she looked down, and watched her chest heave with sharp, frightened breaths.

Gray blinked away the tears of frustration that had welled in his eyes and returned his concentration to the device on his lap.

Huge figures representing life-changing amounts of money blinked at him. But it wasn't enough. They'd demanded a million every fifteen minutes. He'd got nowhere near that with the in-play hacking... and he'd received his warning.

'Like the man said,' offered Gerard in a hoarse whisper from beside him, 'It's only money.'

Gray shot him a filthy look.

'It's my business. My life,' he hissed contemptuously.

'Maybe,' Gerard countered, 'But I'm guessing the two people who actually give your life meaning are sat at the other end of this line of armchairs, close to having heart attacks.'

'They'll be fine,' Gray insisted after tilting his head to look down the line of armchairs at Sparky and Charlotte.

'Perhaps. But the next bullet might be two inches to the left and go through her jugular. Are you willing to take that chance?'

Gray stopped typing, screwed his eyes shut and let out a sigh.

Gerard continued in a conspiratorial tone, 'They won't aim at you or me. They need you fit and well, and I'm not important. Ruth will be next.'

Sparky had been listening to this exchange whilst attempting to calm her mother. She leaned forward to make it clear she was about to enter the conversation, but found herself silenced by Gerard's grave expression and a warning shake of his head.

'You forget I helped you to push your wife and daughter away, Mr Gray,' Gerard continued as his boss's fingers rattled the keys once more, 'I thought you were just another callous, self-obsessed businessman... but I was wrong. You were trying to distance them from the threat. You were protecting your family.'

'That's enough, Gerard,' Gray growled without leaving the sanctuary of his laptop. His irritation increased just as a cold sweat broke out on his forehead.

'Mum's fall. My accident...' Sparky began. She strained against her bonds, leaning forward and twisting her neck to catch a glimpse of her father's face, wincing at the ripple of stinging pain the movement caused her. Her mother's sobs had ceased, she too was looking down the line of chairs, biting her bottom lip to mitigate her fear.

'Oh God, dad! Did you divorce mum simply to stop those men from hurting us?'

Sparky's mind bounced this possibility around and when,

after a pause, her father hadn't answered, she reached her own conclusion.

'You manufactured mum's affair by paying that weasel, Jenkins. I thought you'd done it to force a better divorce settlement, but that wasn't the reason, was it? We both had our accidents and a month later you'd filed for divorce...'

'They could have killed you with that car,' Gray said, staring blankly out of the open doors, 'I couldn't see any other way of distancing you from my blackmailers. I'd told them I'd had enough and I was going to the authorities. Within a few weeks you'd both been targeted.'

For a moment Gray saw himself beside his daughter's hospital bed after she had been struck by the hit and run driver. She'd looked frail, even vulnerable, nothing like his daughter. Her swagger, determination, and youthful exuberance had been blunted. They had diminished her. Beside him, Charlotte had been seated in a wheelchair, trying to put on a brave face, still unable to stand unaided after her own 'accident' a week before. He'd decided there and then. Even if his secret came out and ruined him, he had to bring this nightmare to an end. But first, he had to take the people he loved out of the firing line.

He'd not touched the laptop for thirty seconds. Worried this could prompt another bullet, Gray feigned interest in the device by rattling the hard plastic rim with his fingers. Whoever was shooting at them must be watching, and he also expected they were listening via the mobile phone Ronnie had left for him to connect to the internet. As he drummed on the casing of the laptop more rather unsavoury memories came to mind.

The divorce had needed to look real, suggesting there was good reason to rid himself of his wife and child... a reason that told his blackmailers they were less important, insignificant targets. Being physically distanced from them and not encouraging visiting had helped. Inventing his wife's lover had been relatively straightforward. He'd been introduced to Jenkins at the races and it hadn't taken long to work out the BHA man was an insatiable lothario and easily bribed.

Once his family was out of the picture, he'd released the hacking code to someone who wouldn't use it for their own gain, but instead publicise it enough to scare his blackmailers away for good. He rationalized that the fear of being caught might be enough for

Ronnie and his two side-kicks to drop their intimidation.

He'd started rumours on message boards, posted cryptic blogs on Fairbet forums and eventually discovered Billie Davenport. She had been perfect: principled, young, with direct access to the press. He'd become desperate for things to end once his panic attacks started again, but Billie had done well. He'd thought his plan was working, until he'd watched her jump from the roof of the grandstand and concluded all he'd done was place an innocent girl in peril and anger his blackmailers.

'This is my fault.'

Charlotte had broken the silence before Gray could say anything.

'Mum! That's not true,' Sparky reassured her.

'No it is. You father was trying to protect us and I selfishly brought both of us back into... well, this nightmare!'

Gray turned his head slowly to the left and locked eyes with his ex-wife. She held his gaze for several seconds, unspoken truths passing between them. But he understood Charlotte needed more.

'I want you and Ruth in my life, as it was before all of this,' stated Gray levelly.

Even before he'd fully explained what forces and actions had brought the four of them to be lined up in front of a firing squad, Gray knew his wife had got there ahead of him. Her smile was enough to confirm she'd worked it out.

'Jesus, dad,' Sparky exclaimed, 'With mum and her revenge plot and you and your weird strategy for extracting yourself from a protection racket, it's no wonder I'm screwed up!'

Her father laughed at that. Actually, it was no more than a half-laugh and a shake of his head, but for the first time in months he felt he'd connected with his daughter.

It took Gerard's husky voice to bring the three Grays back into the moment.

'I hate to break up this little family reunion, but shouldn't you be paying your blackmailers?'

Gray glanced out of the open doors to the tower in the distance and caught a glint of what he assumed was a telescopic lens.

'Why are *you* so interested in paying those thugs off?' said Sparky, shooting Gerard a sharp look.

'It's just money.'

'Aren't you the one who should be getting us out of this?

Isn't that what *you're for?*'

Gerard seemed to be considering this possibility, frowning in contemplation. Sparky watched his face adopt a strangely serene expression before his mouth opened to shape a reply.

Whatever he said was drowned out by the public address system. It buzzed with three loud chimes, louder than any commentary, then a voice she recognised blasted through speakers in the ceiling of the room.

'This is a staff announcement. Status is Indigo. I repeat, status is Indigo. Please adopt your starting positions.'

Within a few seconds the voice was back with a new message. It boomed around the racecourse, giving clear and concise instructions, this time his words were intended for race-goers.

Halfway through his speech, Charlotte turned to her daughter, her face wracked with shock. To her astonishment, Sparky was smiling as she listened. How could she be enjoying such a deeply disturbing announcement? Sparky met her mother's worried countenance with a huge grin.

Thirty-Three

Before George left the commentators' box he wished Indy and Joe the best of luck. He set off down the stand at a measured pace, knowing that whatever happened, the third race of the day was sure to be delayed. Joe's message to staff came over the public address system as George was ordering a coffee. Once Joe's follow-up announcement to race-goers had been given, George ambled back into the grandstand, sipping his coffee and mulling over the instructions Joe had given him, should the right circumstances occur.

George had to hand it to the two youngsters; they were quick-witted, and fearless. He reckoned they had ten minutes before the racecourse directors realised that Joe's instruction to all staff and race-goers to leave the enclosures and assemble on the inside of the racecourse was a hoax.

Behind him he could hear the voice of a female member of staff echoing around the inside of the grandstand as she called to the crowd to leave the stand in a steady, calm fashion and congregate on the inside of the racecourse. He found a smile working its way onto his face and allowed it to develop. This was the most fun he'd had at work for years.

When Joe and Indy reached ground level at the back of the grandstand, they walked out into a thick flow of race-goers being shepherded by racecourse staff. A wave of guilt engulfed Joe as he watched families hurry past, the adults wearing serious expressions, their children uncomprehending. He had caused this mass exodus by invoking the emergency protocol, but easily shrugged the guilt off when an image of the blood on Sparky's neck came to mind.

Joe spotted Simon and Neil's straw coloured trilbies loitering beside the winner's enclosure and grabbing Indy by the hand, and, careful to move in character as Mr Carpenter, led her through the crowd toward them. They wasted no time, immediately delivering their updates, but were soon moved on by an officious woman with a clipboard, so Joe had to settle for briefing his friends as they shuffled down the steps that led to the front of the grandstand.

'I need one of you to help me, the other to act as lookout for Indy,' Joe said under his breath, his eyes searching the middle distance for policemen or other threats to avoid.

'I'll go with Indy,' Neil offered. Simon nodded his agreement to accompany Joe.

'Don't take any chances,' Joe instructed Indy, 'You send me a text, distract him, and run. Understand?'

Indy silent acknowledged this with a nod.

'Oh, and take these,' he added, digging into his pocket and passing her the items Sparky had given him.

'What am I supposed to do with this little lot?' she asked, 'I've no pockets.'

'Sparky thought they might help.'

The four of them quickly inspected the handful of items.

'I'll take them,' Neil affirmed, stuffing them into his jacket pockets, merely as a means of moving the conversation along.

Addressing Neil, Joe asked, 'Where are the Mercedes men?'

'I never saw them leave the Dalby Stand,' he admitted, 'I'm guessing I missed them and they are in their car, as it hasn't left the centre of the racecourse.'

'Waiting for their man up on the tower?' Indy suggested.

'Mmm... that makes your job harder.'

'She'll have me watching out for her,' Neil said warmly.

Indy gave him a tight smile, 'Come on then, my faithful watchdog.'

Neil and Indy joined the river of race-goers snaking down the hill and crossing over the racetrack. Joe was relieved to see a significant group of people was now growing in the centre of the track, spreading over the grass beneath the trees and starting to spill toward the tower. He quickly counted between thirty to forty people actually milling around the base of the tower, probably drawn to the strange structure out of sheer curiosity.

He lost sight of Indy quickly, but was still watching Neil's trilby bobbing among the crowd when Simon tugged on his sleeve.

'Heads up, Joe!'

Spinning around to face uphill, Joe was met with the sight of three members of the BHA, two policemen, the clerk of the course, and the judge huddled together in conference. He allowed Simon to pull him to one side, placing the moving column of race-goers between them and the knot of racecourse executives. The group were set apart from the rest of the crowd, their backs to the grandstand and seemed oblivious to what was going on around them. Their body language spoke volumes, something wasn't right. There was a mixture of anger and frustration about the group, not the fear and barking of commands you would associate with an evacuation.

If they'd already tumbled that the bomb protocol announcements had been a hoax, he and Indy only had a minute or two before the order for the crowd to retake their places in the grandstand would be given over the public address system. They had to move into position now.

Indicating the entrance to the Dalby Stand via a flick of his eyes, he and Simon set off, striding with purpose against the flow of Funday families, leaping up the steps. He'd covered fifteen yards when Simon caught his arm.

'Slow down!' he insisted through gritted teeth, 'You're an old man, remember!'

Joe broke into a sweat. How could he have been so stupid? He'd forgotten he was Mr Carpenter. Chancing a quick look around, he was relieved to find there were no querying looks or policemen bearing down on him. He took a steadying breath; it appeared no-one had noticed his mistake. Directing a tight smile Simon's way as a sign of thanks, the two of them set off again, Joe leaning heavily on his walking stick.

They'd not met anyone on their way into the building, and it was quiet and felt empty. The lift doors slid back and Joe stuck his head out. He peered down the corridor in the direction of the Grays private box. There was no one there, his route was clear.

An accusatory London accent asked, 'What you doing here, old man?' making Joe jump. He swung around to take his first look the opposite way down the corridor and froze as he alighted on a face he recognised.

Thirty-Four

Indy and Neil had little trouble crossing onto the centre of the racecourse, and to their relief, there was no sign of the Mercedes men in their car.

'It could mean all three of them are inside the tower or on its roof,' Neil pointed out as the two of them hurried between the bemused race-goers. After watching Indy's face age ten years, he hopefully added, 'But I doubt it.'

'If so, you'd better be on the ball as my lookout,' Indy pointed out, her words coming out stronger and more certain than she was feeling inside.

Telling Joe she enjoyed rock climbing had been one of those comments she would drop into conversation to add spice to her hum-drum life story. People tended to glaze over when they learned that although she had a degree in applied mathematics, the stop-gap position she'd taken in a travel shop through necessity after university, had become her long term career. In reality, she spent most of her time helping people book their annual fortnight in Benidorm. To be fair, she had become quite adept at scaling the climbing wall at her local leisure centre, and attempted a couple of small rocky outcrops in the Dales, but that was the extent of her climbing experience. When Joe had asked whether she could climb the tower, it had been easy to give him a confident yes. He was the sort of person that you wanted to say yes to.

Standing in the shadow of the information tower, Indy tried to push her white lie and lack of foresight to the back of her mind. People's lives might depend on her, and she wanted these men out of her sister's life. Looking up, only the last inch of what she believed was the barrel of a rifle poked out over the top lip of the tower. She estimated it was thirty to forty feet to the roof, and a molded cornice running around the top edge and projecting out a foot or more, meant negotiating the last few feet would be problematic. However, there were potential footholds, unintentionally created by the grips that held the wooden boards for the runners and riders.

They walked around the back of the tower and found a black, steel re-enforced door. Neil pointed out a broken padlock lying in the grass a few feet away. He gave Indy a sidelong glance filled with hope, and pushed at the door. To his astonishment, it swung open to reveal a dark interior dominated by a skeleton of wooden stages.

Until now, they'd attracted little attention from the other race-goers around the tower, but a quick check confirmed one or two people in the vicinity had been witness to the tower's door opening.

'Text me if you see anything,' said Indy, before slipping inside the tower and pushing the door closed behind her. Neil examined the locking mechanism then moved away to watch for anyone approaching the tower.

Once inside, Indy took out her mobile phone and switched its flashlight on, relieved when the harsh beam of unnaturally blue light allowed her to know where she was placing her feet. The basement of the tower was dank and when she breathed in, a musty smell of rotten wood coated the inside of her nose. A stone staircase invited her to climb higher and in an attempt to cast her fears aside she stopped to compose herself and straightened her back, before tip-toeing up the steps to the first landing.

Flashing her phone around the insides of the first floor, Indy realised it was a perfect square, brick built for the first fifteen feet, the rest was worked in wood by a skilled carpenter. The 'turret' was almost independent, and resembled a pentagon rising in the far corner. She crossed the boarded platform toward another staircase against the far wall, halting and biting her lip when one of the floorboards squeaked noisily under her weight. She listened intently over the drumming of her heartbeat, but nothing stirred above.

Ignoring the now obsolete rows of boards covered in hand painted numbers, jockey, racehorse, and trainer names, Indy ascended a set of slatted wooden steps and tentatively crossed another boarded platform. This part of the building had cracks between some of the wooden sidings where sunlight was able to seep through, creating a patchwork of perpendicular lines that lit up motes of dust in the stale air. There were two doors, one set into the side of the building and the other into the pentagonal turret. Her confidence rocketed; the first was a door out onto the flat roof where the gunman lay.

Crossing the wooden boards carefully, Indy tested each new plank with her toe, managing to reach the door without any major squeaks that might alert anyone on the roof outside. After discovering a crack big enough, she knelt down and with one eye closed, peeped through and onto the roof. To her annoyance, she realised the roof was slightly L-shaped to accommodate the results turret, and the shooter was lying just out of sight. She could pick out a tiny patch of camouflage, presumably belonging to his trousers, or a discarded jacket, but she'd have to venture outside to get a proper look at him.

Joe had told her he only needed forty-five seconds. If she could somehow distract this man on the roof for a minute it would be enough time for Joe to get into the Grays' private box, free all four of them and get them to safety. As he had pointed out, timing this was critical. Once she'd told Joe to make his move, she had to immediately attract the shooter's attention and ensure he couldn't fire for about a minute.

No pressure, then, Indy said to herself. If I get it wrong, four people, plus Joe, could die. This thought caused a strange itching to start at the back of her neck and travel down her spine, causing her to shudder.

Truth be told, I'd quite like to get to know Joe a bit better, her inner monologue continued, allowing him to get shot would rather take the shine off our fledgling friendship.

Standing with her back to the boarded wall, she frowned into the darkness, telling herself there would be time to examine this last thought in more detail once she'd carried out what was definitely the most dangerous act of her life. She sidled towards the door to the roof and tried the circular doorknob, noticing for the first time that the locking mechanism had been forced and was almost hanging out of its recess. Of course, they must have forced the locks, which was why all the doors were open. It was also the sniper's way out.

Indy turned the door knob and it opened outwards an inch.

'Thank God. There'll be no climbing,' she told herself.

She cancelled her phone's flashlight, typed a short text to Joe and waited impatiently for a reply. It was through nervous boredom that she pushed at the door again and to her dismay found it wouldn't open any further than that first inch. It cracked open enough to allow a thin ribbon of light to cut into the darkness, but no more. Bending down to examine the door in more detail, Indy grimaced when a foot below the broken lock she found a padlock hanging off a heavy duty bolt. It had to be the work of the man on the roof, both the bolt and padlock were brand new.

Indy bit her lip. It struck her as strange that the man on the roof was effectively locked out of his only exit, but it didn't alter the fact that she needed to get out there. Accessing the roof via this exit would be impossible. She needed to find an alternative, and quickly.

Thirty-Five

Joe stepped out of the lift and into the corridor on the third floor of the Dalby stand. He leaned heavily on his walking stick, hunching his back so as to look small and frail. Simon remained hidden inside the lift, pressed up against the wall, one hand on the door hold button.

'Are you the chap who is supposed to be helping me to leave the racecourse?' Joe demanded as Mr Carpenter, piercing the Mercedes man with an expectant stare.

Faced with a flustered octogenarian, the Mercedes man relaxed and approached him. Seizing the opportunity, Joe took a faltering, but deliberate step forward, brandished his stick vertically in a pose he hoped was reminiscent of Gandalf, and shook it as he spoke.

'Well then? Speak up, I can't hear so well. I've been up and down in this blasted lift five times looking for you!'

Initially surprised at the old man's demand, Ronnie found his voice.

'I 'ain't no home help, old man. Turn around and get back in that lift.'

Ronnie wasn't tall, but he made up for that with a formidable presence. Placing himself in the centre of the corridor, he made it clear he wasn't for moving.

Joe didn't trouble himself with analysing his next move. He was playing a role, and cantankerous old Mr Carpenter wouldn't have stood for some petty posturing by someone much younger. Waving his stick, and muttering an unintelligible complaint, Joe surprised the Mercedes man by pushing past. A conversation reached him, becoming heated, in the nearest box, one from the end of the corridor. It was the box that had looked unused, always with its curtains closed. He headed straight for it.

'Don't you go in there! Come here you old goat,' Ronnie growled under his breath, turning to follow the old man.

Interesting, Joe thought as he maintained his jaunty walk down the corridor. He was expecting a hand on his shoulder any moment, as the Mercedes man was sure to catch up with him. He was still wondering how he might blag his passage closer to the door of the occupied box when a dull bell sound rang out. He spun back, expecting to find the Mercedes man ready to haul him back to the

191

lift. Instead, the man was lying unconscious on the corridor floor. Simon was standing over the collapsed body, breathing heavily, a fire extinguisher swinging from one hand.

For a second the two of them fixed each other with a stare filled with shock and relief, overlaid with excitement.

'It was on the wall... I thought... I hope I haven't...,' Simon whispered, peering down at his handiwork and giving a shrug.

'He's one of the Mercedes men, Ronnie I think. Feet,' Joe instructed after finding a strong pulse in the man's neck, 'We'll put him in there.' He indicated the door to the gentleman's toilets a few yards away on the opposite side of the corridor.

Half lifting, half dragging the Mercedes man, they bundled him into the bathroom, having first checked it was empty.

'You leave. I'll sort him out. You need to get to the Grays' room,' Simon insisted.

Back out in the corridor, raised voices still emanated from the room Ronnie had been protecting. The first was a heavily London accented and low, the second softer and well spoken. A door squeaking behind him announced Simon's arrival back in the corridor.

'The other Mercedes men,' he told him in a low voice, pointing to the room.

Simon frowned, 'So they didn't leave the racecourse?'

'Looks that way,' Joe whispered. Although who knows what they are doing in a private box along the corridor from the Grays, he thought. It had to be the other two Mercedes men in there. But if that was the case...

Joe nervously checked his phone, the device sliding in his sweaty hand as he pulled it from his pocket; still nothing from Indy. The voices from the room rose once more. Holding a flat hand up to Simon to instruct him to stay put, Joe ventured nearer to the box door, sliding closer with his back pushed against the corridor wall. He was desperate to hear anything that would aid his rescue of the Grays, or mean Indy wouldn't need to make her dangerous climb up the outside of the tower.

Unbidden, a shiver of cold intensity ran through him and sweat seemed to bubble up from every pore on his forehead. He froze, staring wide-eyed at the blank white wall of the corridor opposite. What was he doing? Whether it was some sort of delayed reaction to how Simon had dealt with the Mercedes man, or simply a consequence of worrying about Indy, his progress to the room door had halted. This was crazy. He was dealing with professional criminals. They'd been lucky to deck Ronnie, but they had guns, and they'd already proved weren't shy about using them…

Joe blinked, drew in a deep breath and swallowed hard, trying desperately to regain some sense of scale, forcing this unreal situation to make sense. It was the wrong time to suffer a crisis of conscience or lose belief in himself and his plan. He slammed his eyes shut, desperate to push away thoughts of Indy, Sparky, Neil, Simon… any of them being hurt. Strangely, he found solace in picturing Sparky bound to her armchair, looking aghast at the hole in the leather two inches from her. For all he knew, she was being lined up to be shot while he was faffing around in this corridor… Sparky needed him to fulfil his promise to her. Warmth radiated around his body.

He snapped back, helped by the sound of two, or could it be three men? They were having a fast-paced argument peppered with swearing, but Joe picked up that the main protagonist was worried, repeating the phrase 'It's time to leave,' several times. The second, softer voice was becoming terse, bordering on condescending, with an indistinct accent.

Had the larger man spoken when he was in the Gray's room? Joe couldn't remember, he just wished he could see who was behind this door. There had only ever been three Mercedes men, and he was convinced the man Simon had incapacitated was the leader. He'd assumed Jack, the missing third man, was in the tower. A few more moments in the corridor, listening to the two men argue might…

Joe's attention was drawn to his mobile vibrating in his trouser pocket. The room was suddenly silent. A sharp tap with his finger through his trouser material killed the buzzing from the device and he froze, listening a moment, ready to run, not breathing. After what seemed to be an age, their discussion restarted and Joe silently blew air out through rounded lips. In doing so, he noticed his false beard had moved slightly, his exhalation now caused a hissing through an area of stray moustache hair. The glue must have been affected by his perspiration, which made him wonder what state his make-up was in, but rejected the impulse to tear the disguise from his face.

Twenty seconds later his cheeks and forehead were itching and his fingers sticky from pressing the false hair back onto his chin and upper lip. Ignoring his heart's persistently loud thumping, he read the text message from Indy. It told him she was, 'In position. Tell me when to start diversion.'

Joe listened at the door for a few seconds, desperate to learn more, when without warning the tone of the conversation within the room altered. Once he caught the exclamation, '… the proximity alarm! There's someone on the tower,' passing through the door, Joe fled.

Thirty-Six

Stepping out into fresh air and sunshine should have been liberating compared to the darkness inside the tower, but Indy wasn't enjoying the experience. She'd just swung out onto the outside of the information tower and was currently fighting to find a foothold.

She'd calculated there were only three yards of horizontal climbing required before she could descend onto the flat roof. Removing five of the horizontal black boards from the side of the tower that faced the grandstand had been easy enough, after all, that's how the information boards were updated, but swinging out and pushing her fingertips between the boards had demanded cock-sure recklessness.

Hanging there, the muscles in her fingers screaming to be relaxed, Indy risked a look down whilst scrabbling with her feet to detect the ledge she'd been sure she was tall enough to reach. One of her bare toes caught on the edge of the black steel gutter. At the second attempt, her toes dipped into wet sludge, so she allowed some of her weight to transfer onto the guttering. It bent a little, but held.

As Indy took a few breaths, she became aware of the interest she was causing. Thirty-five feet below her a ring of people had gathered and were calling up to her.

'Great. So much for me thinking I could sneak up on this guy unawares,' she complained to herself.

She wasn't surprised she'd garnered some attention. Having dispensed with her heels so she could climb properly, her other issue had been how to deal with the lovely light summer dress Sandie had found for her. She couldn't risk it limiting her movement so it was currently hitched up and tied in a knot. No wonder she was hearing a few cat calls among the shouts of concern. And they were sure to attract others to the spectacle.

Gritting her teeth, she edged along the guttering, one foot then the other, hand over hand, until she reached the corner of the tower. The guttering squeaked and dropped an inch as she placed all her weight onto it in order to find new hand holds and pull herself up onto the flat roof. As she disappeared from sight, there was a little cheer from the knot of race-goers below.

She didn't have time to catch her breath. Indy had been on the clock ever since she'd made that first move out onto the face of the tower. Joe was about to enter the Grays' room, so her distraction had to start *now*. Scanning the roof she was shocked to find no sign of an angry, violent Mercedes man. Where she was expecting the shooter to be lying there was something, but she could now tell it wasn't human, it had been made to *look* human.

It was too angular, like a lump of covered machinery. Perplexed, she ran lightly over to where the rifle should have been and pulled at a camouflaged sheet covering a long tubular shape. Casting the heavy canvas sheet aside confirmed she was indeed alone on the roof. Alone with a metal tube. Beside it was a poor version of a manikin, yet it had fooled all three of them in the commentators box. From the right angle it did take on the appearance of a prone man, but Indy berated herself for falling for such basic fakery. The brand new padlock on the inside of the roof door now made perfect sense.

She knelt down and pulled the manikin away, then leaned out over the edge of the roof to inspect the end of the tube from which the barrel of a rifle protruded. Spying down the end of the tube confirmed her suspicions. Entombed within the metal tube, in some sort of waxy substance, was a high powered rifle with telescopic sights attached to an electronic mechanism that she assumed gave someone, somewhere, control.

Indy pulled back onto the roof and tried to push the tube with both hands. It remained rock solid and appeared to be securely bolted to the roof. She tried sitting, bracing herself with her arms, and kicking. The tube juddered, encouraging her to try again.

It was as she was about to aim a third barefooted kick at the end of the tube that Indy's eyes narrowed and she frantically began thumping the box with her feet and tearing at it with her hands. Up until now there had been silence up there on the roof. But something had changed. From within the thick metal casing she had heard the sound of whirring and metallic clicking.

The balls of her feet pounded into the tube again and again, each strike sending pain rocketing through her legs and up to her hips, yet the tube remained solid, an immovable object. The whirring reached a new pitch. She dug her hand into the inside pocket of her dress and drew out her phone. Holding her breath, Indy punched at Joe's name on her caller list.

196

Thirty-Seven

The proximity alarm had been tripped as soon as someone came within fifteen feet of the weapon. His immediate reaction to the warning on his laptop was to run, just as it was for the others, but he'd come too far and risked too much not to finish the job. Lord knows how or where they'd found a lethal, remotely operated snipers rifle... And now whoever it was up there on that flat roof, was close to the equipment. Equipment placed in the perfect position to scare the life out of the CEO of Europe's biggest betting exchange and make him pay up.

A wire hung from his ear, plugged into the phone in his pocket. He was listening to what was happening in the Grays' box thanks to the mobile phone Ronnie had left on the table, but was distracted by the small figure in the distance, removing some of the display boards from the side of the tower.

They looked small. It was probably just a child who had climbed up the outside of the tower and stumbled across one of the sensors Jack had set up inside the tower. Yes, that must be it, the course was stuffed full of snotty-nosed brats. He grimaced at the sea of rag-tag families over in the centre of the racecourse and the toddler's fair beyond. He possessed a deep personal loathing for these Sunday Funday race meetings. To his mind they destroyed the ambiance of a day at the races and ruined the image of racing when bands of kids, and their obese parents, slouched around the enclosures dressed in jeans and t-shirts. He sneered down at the passing proletariat beneath him, thanking God that in the upper echelons of the sport, racing remained one of the last bastions of the class system. Being the son of an Earl still counted for something in this sport.

The hoax bomb scare had filled the centre of the course with families, but through a crack in the curtain he could see they were starting to return into the enclosures in numbers. To his left, a trio of runners for the delayed third race had been led into the parade ring. Meanwhile, race-day staff welcomed people back through the emergency exits across the racetrack. That meant the rooms around him would soon be filling with his colleagues once more. The hoax hadn't ruined his plan, but it had certainly delayed it.

Ronnie was already out in the corridor on lookout, so Jack and Reggie had gone to deal with the tower. Once they'd left, he sat

197

down at his laptop and checked on the gun. He moved the crosshairs with a click of his touchpad and waited for the telescopic sights to react, frowning when they juddered slightly, relaxing his shoulders when the targeting system seemed to recover. The crosshairs continued inexorably onto the chest of Michael Gray, and then moved smoothly upwards to sit just over his shoulder. Not for the first time, he marveled at the accuracy this gun could achieve. It really was impressive.

He returned to the curtains, careful to only open them with two fingers and peep through. He checked the tower once again before switching to pick out Jack and Reggie as they approached the monument to a bygone time. The two men were easy identified as they crossed the racetrack and entered the inside of the racecourse. Their lounge suits stood out as they jogging against the flow of casually dressed race-goers returning to the enclosures.

Checking his phone, he submitted another transfer request on his banking app, whilst listening to what was going on in the Gray's private box. It was a monumental moment. A decade of hopelessness, then another trying to forget, but the last fourteen months of careful execution had led him here; to this racecourse on a Sunday afternoon in late summer. Everything and everybody was in place. He was finally about to reclaim everything his family was owed and allow the Earl of Stretford to regain his rightful place in society.

He allowed a wan smile to spread slowly across his lips. The words he'd been waiting to hear had just broken the silence in the Grays' room. He listened as the personal assistant began to speak.

As he listened to Gerard, he returned to his laptop and toyed with the controls of the gun, idly tracing the outline of Michael Gray's head with the crosshairs. The shooting was over now, Jack and Reggie were on a retrieval mission. He'd reached his goal.

Gerard kept talking, and so did Gray.

Leonard Horowitz, head of integrity at the British Horseracing Authority, graduate of Eton, son of the eighth Earl of Stretford, went red in the face and began to sweat. Still toying with the gun's controls he minutely adjusted the crosshairs to sit on Michael Gray's right ear. Another thirty seconds of listening saw the crosshairs move to lie on the man's chest.

He listened in disgust to the conversation in the Grays' room. Michael Gray began to rant, causing Horowitz's cheeks to burn with hot, uncontrollable indignation. Fired by Gray's words, tempered by his newfound love, and cooled by an unquenchable revenge, his resolve hardened. Horowitz guided the targeting system to sit directly between Michael Gray's eyes. Just above the laptop's trackpad, his finger trembled. Within seconds, his whole hand was twitching.

When he could stand no more, Horowitz clicked the fire button on his sniper software.

Thirty-Eight

Joe and Simon bounded down the corridor and threw themselves into the lift. Simon immediately slammed the ground floor button.

Joe had heard the words, 'We'll scare that kid off the tower and bring the gun back,' being delivered and they'd had to react immediately. Joe had no wish to risk an encounter with the remaining Mercedes men with nothing more than Simon's fire extinguisher as a weapon. He'd considered running to the end of the corridor in order to burst in on the Grays, but immediately ruled it out. The door was undoubtedly locked and because this grandstand had been built in an age where quality counted, there was no way he and Simon would have been able to break the door down with any sort of alacrity.

'Push the second floor button,' Joe panted as the lift doors began to slide shut.

He'd heard steps outside and waited for a hand to insert itself between the doors before they met, but thankfully it never came.

'Why the second floor?'

'I've got to get into the Grays' room.'

'From the wrong floor?' Simon queried.

'I think… I can climb. With a little help.'

The lift doors opened with a bright ding and they reached the room directly below the Gray's a few seconds later. Joe closed his eyes in silent prayer and turned the door knob, hugely relieved when the door, emblazoned with a name tag that read 'Lewis Marketing Ltd.' swung inwards. They were met with a young man and a woman in a passionate embrace. The couple stepped away from each other in embarrassed fashion as Joe and Simon dashed in.

'Can't stop, racecourse business,' said Simon authoritatively, 'We need use of your balcony.'

Clearly shocked at having been caught alone together, the couple stood back, wide-eyed. The fact two unknown men, one of them spritely for his age, with a wonky moustache and smudged make-up, went scuttling past them at speed seemed to be the lesser of two evils. The woman actually waved them through.

'Give me a leg up,' said Joe once they'd rounded the corner of the L-shaped balcony and stood at the white railings that surrounded it, looking up at the room above. Seconds later, Joe was tottering on the top of the railings, reaching up to the identical vertical white steel railings of the room above.

'For heaven's sake, don't look down,' Simon warned, his hands holding onto Joe's ankles.

Joe didn't reply immediately, instead he tested the strength of the railings on the balcony above.

'Let go of me,' he demanded, glancing down at Simon and immediately wishing he hadn't. It was a forty foot drop to the turf below. One slip and he'd...

'Really? For crying out loud, Joe, there has to be another way up there.'

'Let go!'

Simon released his friend's ankles, stepped backwards and watched aghast as Joe bent his knees and jumped upwards.

Thirty-Nine

'How much have you transferred into that account?'

Gray shot Gerard a disdainful look and ground his teeth, forcing the muscles in his cheeks to bulge.

He'd been working hard, and it didn't help that his Gerard wouldn't shut up. There had been no further shots and no one had spoken for the last two minutes, apart from Gerard repeating the same question over and over.

'Why are you so obsessed with the money?' demanded Sparky. Gerard didn't answer, his attention wholly focused on her father's tapping fingers.

Gray closed his eyes and tilted his head back, frustrated by Gerard's interruption. He'd been in the zone; creating code as if he was back in the late 1990's. He'd forgotten how it felt – to be completely engrossed in nothing but the lines of a programming language. So much of his time these days was spent dealing with bank managers, board directors, employees, marketing people... all sorts of *people*, and in general he didn't get on with people. They were difficult to read, and that irritated him. Writing code was different, he was in control – the code did what it was told. Even though he was writing and running code to help ruin his business, there was a kind of exhilaration attached to it, in getting it right, to make it deliver the correct output...Gerard had just asked his question again. God, he was annoying. It didn't help that he was prevented from shouting, phoning someone or emailing for help. There was no one to contact, the only person in the world he had ever really trusted was tied up in this room with him, besides, he had defrauded his own company... no one else would help him. He wished he could stand up. He always thought best on his feet. He'd written most of the original code for Fairbet standing at Charlotte's breakfast bar in that small flat she rented at university up in Newcastle...

'How much?' Gerard repeated.

'Six point two million,' Gray replied irritably.

'Then I think you can stop.'

Sparky and Gray eyed the personal assistant, both confused. Charlotte had her eyes shut; blocking the outside world out.

'I can stop?'

'What the...' Sparky's voice trailed away when she noticed a steel blade glinting in Gerard's hand. The zip ties on his wrists seemed to have slackened considerably.

'I put this small penknife into my closed fist before they tied me up,' Gerard explained, 'They thought I was unconscious after they caught me in the corridor outside, but I was faking it.'

He pursed his lips as he concentrated on his right hand, before continuing, 'I think you're safe now, Mr Gray.'

'You've paid your debt,' he added, expertly turning the penknife in his palm and flicking the blade upwards so it slowly began slicing through the thin plastic restraints on his right wrist.

'What do you mean?' Gray asked suspiciously, watching with growing incredulity as Gerard freed his right hand and proceeded to cut through the rest of his zip ties.

Gerard produced a sad smile.

'I imagine he's feeling elated, now he's reached his goal,' Gerard said, stretching his legs out straight and pumping his arms a few times.

'The man controlling all of this,' Gerard continued, speaking in a clear voice and gesturing around the room with open palms, 'Perhaps, it's just a powerful sense of relief he's feeling. It would be fascinating to know.'

He stood, and passing Sparky, began to strip Charlotte's bonds with his penknife. She twitched at the touch of his hand and her eyes flicked open, filled with fear for a moment, but quickly softened when she realised what was happening.

'I caught up with our friends, Ronnie, Reggie, and Jack last night. They were trying to track Ruth and that race caller down. I got quite a bit of information. Unfortunately, they lied about their plans for today, but did tell me how much money their boss was determined to take you for,' he stated in easy fashion as he released Charlotte's wrists.

Moving onto her ankles he continued, 'They spun me a line that they'd only been employed for the odd day to threaten you and sent at short notice to retrieve Davenport's laptop. I now realise they were building up to today.'

'Nice speech,' Gray noted with distaste, trying to keep his impatience in check, 'Now tell me what the hell is going on.'

'Six million, seven-hundred and ten thousand pounds,' Gerard enunciated slowly, before raising his head from Charlotte's feet, 'Give or take a few quid either way.'

He smiled again, which Sparky found disconcerting, coming from a man whose default facial setting for the last fourteen months had either been a hollow stare or a steel-like grimace.

'That's the amount of money the person responsible for today wanted paying, according to Ronnie. That's what your blackmailer's father lost on your betting exchange in a matter of months,' Gerard continued, 'It was a range of established businesses. Built up over two generations and lost in three months because he believed your marketing. He thought it would be easy money because he could *become the bookie*. Isn't that what you used to tell prospective gamblers, Mr Gray?'

Gray was staring wide-eyed and uncomprehendingly at his personal assistant, unable to find an immediate response. Standing with hands on hips, relaxed, Gerard returned Gray's stare, only his expression was more akin to an indulgent parent waiting for a child to provide excuses for why they'd not done their chores. The employer, employee code was forgotten.

'So, someone's father lost some money betting on my exchange. Boo hoo!' Gray growled indignantly, 'That's no reason to shoot holes in my family.'

'The last time I looked, no one has actually been shot,' Gerard remarked calmly.

Gray shuffled uncomfortably in his seat, railing against his tethered ankles. He curled a lip at his personal assistant but Gerard didn't offer any response. There was no doubt in Gray's mind who held the stronger hand here, and he was guessing there had to be more to come from his, now rogue, personal assistant.

'Your betting exchange ran his father dry. He believes his father became fodder for the statisticians, the city analysts that were the first to create their own fiefdoms on what was a new, exciting, and ultimately dangerous, betting platform. When his father had gambled his businesses and home away, as well as running up serious debt, your blackmailer came home from school at the end of term and found his father in a bath of his own blood.'

Gerard wasn't looking at Gray, instead, he'd moved to Sparky and was starting to free her ankles.

'He was fifteen years old, so I'm told. He buried his father, and wouldn't you know it, two months later his mother walked off a Northern Line platform and into an oncoming train. She simply couldn't live without her husband.'

'I still don't see how any of this is my problem, Gerard,' Gray said after a short pause. This was greeted with gasps of disbelief from Sparky and Charlotte.

He blundered on, 'I can't be held responsible for every punter who thinks gambling is the easy way to get rich! And I'm certainly not responsible for people committing suicide.'

Ignoring her father, Sparky asked, 'So this is just about some chap getting even with dad?'

Gerard nodded, moving to release her wrists.

'How much did that hacker charge him for the ability to blackmail me?' Gray interjected angrily.

Gerard laughed. It was a strange, whistling sort of chortle. Sparky studied him as he worked on her bonds and found herself wondering how long he went between laughs.

'My information is that the hacker charged him nothing,' Gerard replied, his amusement giving his words a sing-song quality, 'You wound him up to such an extent, that once the hacker heard the story I've just told you, he handed the hacking code, and the instructions, over to your blackmailer for free.'

Gray swore viciously under his breath.

Bent down on his haunches in front of Sparky, Gerard slipped his penknife between the zip ties around her wrist. He paused before slicing through the last loop of plastic, cocking his head side-ways to regard Gray in the next chair.

'Don't you have any empathy for your blackmailer? Perhaps just a single shred of understanding for what you and your company have done to him? How you've ruined his life?'

The questions hung in the air for a few seconds. Gray locked eyes with his personal assistant, wearing an expression of pure disgust.

'If you don't,' Gerard warned, 'He might not stop at taking your money…'

'You actually believe for one second I'd give a flying toss for my blackmailer and his sob story? The money he's taken from me is piffling…'

Gray sucked in a ragged breath. In his compulsion to rage at Gerard he'd forgotten to breathe. He swore again, filling his lungs once more before continuing.

'There are people making and losing thousands of pounds on my betting exchange every day,' he raged, spittle flying from his lips, 'I don't care where the money comes from, or what they do to themselves if they lose, just so long as they do it on my betting platform...'

Gray never got to complete his rant. A frenzied shout of 'Get down!' from out on the balcony cut through his words. Startled, Gray flicked his eyes up from his armchair, trying to make sense of the sudden commotion. A figure tore into the room with raised hands, momentarily being silhouetted against the cloudless sky between the gap in the curtains. Before Gray could draw breath, the hurtling blur of silver and black cannoned into him.

Forty

Joe hung from the balcony railings on the side of the Gray's private box. His hands were slowly slipping down the rails. His feet kicked at nothing but air and he was desperately suppressing the urge to shout for help.

The wave of relief he experienced when he felt Simon's hands grab his right leg and force his body upwards, was intoxicating. Simon's push enabled him to insert a knee between the railings and Joe levered himself onto the base of the balcony. As he pulled himself up and over the railings of the Gray's box he glanced down and gave Simon a grateful look.

Quickly checking the curtains on this side of the box were closed, Joe crawled over to crouch with his back up against one of the windows. With the balcony wrapping around this end of the stand he was facing the section of the racecourse after the finishing line. From behind him the sound of an animated conversation was making its way through the glass. Taking a few seconds to catch his breath, he listened as Gray and his personal assistant engaged in an exchange that was both confusing and illuminating in equal measure.

His phone vibrated in his trouser pocket and this time it was a voice call from Indy. He didn't speak, he just listened.

Five seconds later he stood up, breathed in, held his breath, and strode around the corner of the balcony, shouting a warning as he went. Entering the room through the open curtains at the front of the balcony, he ignored the shock on every face, although a split second glance allowed him to register Sparky's surprise, which instantly transformed into delight.

Locating his target, Joe surged forward. Using a coffee table as a springboard, he launched himself at the incredulous middle-aged man. He was sitting bolt upright, a computer on his lap and his feet tethered to the front legs of his armchair.

Forty-One

It was an anticlimax when the rifle discharged itself, just a dull thump emanated from within its steel tomb and then the whining from inside fizzled away to nothing. Indy stopped kicking, unaware of the tears of frustration cascading down her cheeks, or the heat from bruising to the soles of her feet. Filled with dread, she followed what she imagined to be the trajectory of the bullet, as it travelled into the top left-hand corner room of the Dalby Stand.

Sitting beside the rifle's metal tube, Indy could feel the heat in the black rubber matting that covered the entire flat roof of the tower. It permeated the thin material of her dress and warmed the palms of her hands as she leaned back. She was staring fixedly at the six foot metal pipe and forcing herself to think. It had fired as she had still been screaming into her phone at Joe to get into the room.

The sounds of the mechanism restarted. Indy shouted a loud curse at the metal tube, and kicked a foot at it once more. The whirring intensified; it was definitely preparing to fire again. She had twenty seconds, if that. Scrambling to the end of the pipe, she tried to shake the end of the gun's barrel but it remained solid, just like its partner tube. Again she tried the steel bolts that held the tube in place, quickly realising she would get nowhere without an industrial sized spanner.

Jumping to her feet, she tore at the bottom of her dress, intending to tear a length of cotton off and use it to lasso the end of the rifle and lever it away from its target. It was no good, after one attempt at ripping the hem she discarded the idea; it would take too long, the cotton was too tightly woven.

From the grass below she heard her name being called, but ignored it. Instead, she stalked around the roof, desperately searching for anything that might spark an idea. Behind her the pipe was clicking and the whirring sound intensified.

Again she toured the roof, panic rising in her. She returned to the pipe empty-handed, angrily kicking it in frustration with her bare feet, swearing at the pain that flowered up her leg from her heel as a result. Indy fell to her knees and tried rocking the tube, but even with all her weight behind her, it refused to budge. She looked around for her phone, frightening herself when she couldn't locate it on the roof.

The whirr had become a whine and she fell to the floor, her

head bouncing softly off the rubber matting, desperate to locate her lost phone. She had to warn Joe a second shot was on its way.

She wouldn't have noticed it normally, no one would. After all, it was a black bolt against a black rubber surface. But from this angle, eyes on the floor, searching for her phone under the deadly tube, it stood out as a tiny turret against the steel plates that held the pipe in place.

Reaching out, Indy picked up a black, six-inch bolt. It was lying right beside her phone. Whoever installed the pipe had left this bolt behind. It had been lost, almost invisible against the blackness of the roof, perhaps kicked under, into the shadow of the metal tube. Using her thumb and forefinger she turned it over, hoping against hope.

Scrabbling to the end of the tube she got down on her stomach and pinching the bolt, she placed it delicately into the end of the gun's barrel, feeling a rush of joy when it fitted. Indy left an inch of the bolt still showing, then with a flat hand, rammed it down the barrel. The whining from the tube suddenly ceased. Indy pushed herself to her feet and ran to the other side of the roof.

She wasn't sure whether she threw herself to the floor, or the explosion from the rifle was responsible. Either way, she ended up slamming her face into the rubber at the same time the other end of the roof erupted with an ear-splitting crack.

Forty-Two

Joe's chest landed squarely in Michael Gray's face, the momentum of his leap sending the armchair, and its occupant, crashing over backwards. The now familiar zipping sound fizzed through the air and there was a sharp ping and a puff of plasterboard as the bullet cracked into the back wall. It was followed by a moment of silence, soon interrupted by a barrage of complaints from Gray.

'What the hell are you doing?' yelled Gray into Joe's armpit as the two men tried to untangle themselves. The armchair had tipped over, launching the two of them into the foot of the wall, but with Gray's ankles still being zip tied, he was lying on his back, legs in the air. For a number of seconds they struggled with each other, trying to extract limbs from chair, cushion and clothes. From the open window there was a sharp crack. Joe froze, waiting for another impact, but this time there was no zipping of bullets.

Gray glowered at him, 'I'll ask again. What the h...'

'Saving your blummin' life, Mr Gray,' Joe barked at him, adding in a more conciliatory tone, 'I'm a friend of your daughter.'

This didn't appear to help Joe's cause. Gray let out a string of expletives and didn't stop muttering his discontent until Gerard had cut his ankles free and all five of them had crawled over and were lined up, standing with their backs against the side wall. Gerard assured them the gun on the tower wouldn't have a line of sight to this wall.

'I knew you'd come,' Sparky told Joe happily.

'Really?' he gasped.

'Oh yes. I was sure. Sandie told me about you.'

'Oh,' Joe responded uncertainly, his chest heaving.

'Screw the reunion,' barked Gray, 'Who the hell are you?'

'He's Joe Lawlor,' Sparky responded brightly, 'He's the race caller everyone is looking for.'

'He's also just saved you from being killed by your blackmailer,' Gerard added grimly.

'That was supposed to be your job,' Gray replied darkly, peering over to the back wall, where a fresh bullet hole had been punched into the plaster. A couple of feet below, his armchair lay on its back. Gerard inspected his feet and remained silent.

'I'm certain your blackmailer is down the corridor, ' Joe

breathed, still catching his breath. 'I heard the Mercedes men in there.'

Gray looked down the line and frowned.

'The thugs who came after us,' Sparky explained sourly, 'The ones that hurt Billie Davenport. They're the Mercedes men,'

Beside him, Charlotte jumped when Joe's phone vibrated.

'He apologised as he brought the phone out. It was Indy on a voice call again. She sounded out of breath, but elated. He listened for thirty seconds then rang off after promising to get back to her.

'We're safe. Indy er... *broke* the gun.'

The five of them pushed themselves tentatively off the wall, Gerard and Joe first, looking out toward the tower through the gap in the curtains, followed by Sparky, Gray, and finally Charlotte. Joe was sure Charlotte was in shock. Her face was pale and she flinched as he crunched champagne bottle shards under his shoes.

'Let's get down the corridor and collar this blackmailer,' Gerard suggested.

'Not before we agree that what happened here today goes no further.'

Everyone spun round to eyeball Gray. He was standing in the middle of the room, taking in each of them one by one, deadly serious.

'I've no doubt I will need to buy your silence, but the future of my company is at stake. I can explain away the errors on the website and refund those who have lost out, but I can't afford for the police to get involved or my...'

'Fraud, dad?' Sparky offered.

Gray paused to consider his response. Finally, he met his daughter's gaze.

'Indeed,' Gray agreed ruefully, 'My fraudulent activity must not be discovered.'

Forty-Three

'Indy,' he called in a stage whisper, then again, in a louder, questioning tone, 'Indy?'

Neil had been calling to her from the foot of the tower for some time now. It felt like minutes, but probably wasn't. The two Mercedes men had been crossing the track when he first spotted them, and they were still about a hundred yards away now, jogging down the hill on the inside of the course, heading straight for the tower. But he only had a couple more shouts left before they came into earshot.

'Indy!' he shouted up toward the edge of the roof for a third time since the building had been shaken by a sound akin to a thunderclap.

When a good looking young Indian girl in a thin, floral print dress appeared at the edge of the roof and shouted a slightly frustrated, 'What?' back at him, his relief was short-lived.

'Mercedes men!' he called, surreptitiously pointing to the two approaching figures making a beeline for the tower through the odd race-goer still enjoying the inside of the racecourse.

Indy looked over the far edge of the roof and immediately understood she had been caught. They were just too close. The larger one, Reggie, she thought, was shading his eyes and squinting at her. His younger colleague loped along beside his companion. Her options were limited, climbing down would see her drop straight into these men's arms. Jumping would result in at least two broken legs and possibly much worse. She was now castigating herself for spending half a minute inspecting what was left of the rifle and its metal tubing after it exploded in spectacular fashion, leaving bits of itself scattered all over the roof.

'I can't get down in time,' Indy called down the forty feet to Neil.

'Wait there,' he called back after a short pause, turned and walked away from the tower, heading toward the childrens' playground and fair fifty yards away.

What else can I do, Indy thought miserably as she watched Neil go from a walk to a run away from the tower.

The Mercedes men were now only twenty yards from the tower. Reggie grinned up at her as they rounded the square structure. They disappeared from view and Indy heard the tower door creak open and the men's voices beneath her.

Crossing to the roof door, she leaned against it, wondering how long she could hold it shut once the two men had unlocked it. Probably not too long. She spent the next half a minute scavenging some of the metal tube and what was left of the rifle, forcing both pieces up against the door handle. She stood back and inspected her handiwork and decided she might have bought herself fifteen seconds. She could hear the men's feet on the other side of the roof door and a rattling of keys.

'Indy!'

Indy took three steps to the edge of the roof and took in Neil, his new-found friend, and... their bouncy castle.

'I've locked them in!' he shouted, holding up a small key, 'Come on, jump!'

Neil didn't believe the small padlock he'd found among Sparky's items Joe had given him would hold the Mercedes men too long, so continued to urge Indy to jump. He glanced over at the showman he'd paid to drag a children's inflatable and its air pump fifty yards down the hill and place them beside the tower.

'That'll be okay, won't it?'

The young lad shrugged, 'Whatever you say, boss. It's your call. It's got a roof, so it should break her fall... I guess.'

Indy inspected the large yellow inflatable and swallowed hard. To her left the door to the roof was being soundly shaken. Muttering a short prayer, she strode into the middle of the roof, spun around, gritted her teeth and set off at a run.

The roof door burst open and Reggie staggered through, with Jack following. Both men froze in wonderment as Indy completed her run up and launched herself off the edge of the tower roof.

Forty-Four

Once the door to the Gray's box had been forced open, Gerard was the first out. He had been promised a large bonus by Gray if he could identify the blackmailer. He was also to ensure the Mercedes men were escorted off the racecourse, along with any evidence of their involvement.

Joe and Sparky dashed after the personal assistant. Dodging through returning race-goers they reached the third private room down the corridor as one.

'What if the Mercedes men are in there?' Sparky queried.

'We'll have to take that chance. We have to confront whoever is in there,' Joe replied.

Gerard led, pushing the door to the private room open. He waited a second, a frown developing, and finally his shoulders slumped. Joe and Sparky peered around the door jam and immediately understood why the personal assistant hadn't moved into the room. It was empty.

'Damn it,' Gerard growled.

'We're too late,' moaned Sparky.

'We took too long,' admitted Joe, 'While your dad was busy issuing instructions, the blackmailer has made good his escape.'

The three of them remained standing in the doorway, inspecting the large, square room in silence.

'Come on, let's take a look around, just in case,' Joe suggested. An assortment of furniture had been pushed to the walls, but a single table and chair had been left in the centre of the room. Gerard flung the curtains apart, revealing an empty balcony. Sparky searched the carpet, but it was bereft of clues to who had been there earlier that afternoon.

'Nothing,' Gerard complained, kicking the leg of one of the chairs in frustration.

The three of them trailed out of the room feeling defeated. Joe was the last out, clicking the door closed. The corridor was now bustling with people and to his right, the sounds of eating, drinking and loud conversation came in bursts as door the last private room on the corridor opened and closed.

From across the corridor, someone called 'Joe? Joe Lawlor!' and a number of heads turned.

Joe caught the eye of the person calling his name and winced.

Micky Goodham was pushing past people to get to him. Having lost most of his false beard in the tussle with Gray, Joe had decided to tear the rest off. He imagined there was make-up and glue smeared all over his face, not to mention his clothes. Even so, despite his silver hair, he'd still been recognised.

Micky made it to within a couple of yards of Joe before Gerard stepped in.

'I'll deal with this. You two get going,' he advised.

Joe followed Sparky down the corridor, fighting the urge to look back. Micky was being barred from making any further process down the corridor by an insistent Gerard. Joe could hear the presenter's indignant protests as he and Sparky headed for the lift. There was a steady flow of race-goers milling around the corridor and he was aware he needed to get out of his compromised disguise. If Micky could recognise him, then the chances were plenty of others would too. Besides, he needed to make sure Indy, Simon and Neil were okay and then head to a police station to explain why he'd left his car at the scene of an accident.

They met up with Neil and Simon outside the back of the Dalby stand. The two men were standing with their backs to them, and Joe was soon hunting for his phone, concerned Indy wasn't with them. He pushed redial and the call connected after only one ring, just as Neil and Simon turned around, and the diminutive Indy stepped out from behind them, her phone pressed to her ear.

'Oh, so you're still alive?' she scolded lightly, looking up to meet his gaze, still speaking into the phone.

From ten yards away, she watched as Joe's shoulders relaxed and the beginnings of a smile creased his lips.

'Just about. What happened to you?'

'Well...' she replied, rolling her eyes in a mildly suggestive manner, 'Buy me a drink... and I might tell all!'

'Okay...' he agreed, taking in all of her once Simon and Neil had moved aside, '...and perhaps you could explain why you're barefoot?'

Forty-Five

Joe followed the finishers of the delayed third race as they walked past him, up the chute alongside the owners and trainers lawn, on their way to be unsaddled. As the last of the eight runners filed past, he let out a sigh, realising he wasn't really concentrating on the horses. He turned his attention to the people sat around the oval table on the owners' lawn.

'Is it just me who has the feeling there is unfinished business here?' Joe asked, looking from face to face.

Since sitting down he'd been feeling increasingly despondent and had been unable to pinpoint a reason. Even Indy and Neil's animated rendering of their scrape at the tower wasn't enough to lift him from his funk. Possibly the sudden dip in adrenaline streaming around his body was partly to blame, but he doubted it was the only explanation. This was more a sense of unease, of a fear that he had left a task half-done. That was it. The last forty-eight hours felt incomplete. Something was missing.

Indy's descent into quiet reflection signalled she might agree, but the others didn't appear to share his nervousness. Perhaps they couldn't. He'd been attempting to make sense of the changing situation since Saturday afternoon at Ripon. He'd lived with it longer and travelled further down the rabbit hole. However, the blank looks he was receiving from around the table were hardly inspiring.

Charlotte said in a quiet voice, 'Nothing my ex-husband does is ever cut and dried. You never get to know the full story.'

The table contemplated this in silence for a few seconds.

Joe's eyes landed on Sparky. Her neck was now looking much better. She'd emerged from the washroom with a number of small cuts to her neck, but nothing requiring medical attention. She was examining his features closely and in response, he raised an expectant eyebrow.

'You without your beard,' she stated in perfunctory fashion, 'I was getting to like it.'

After the introductions had been made, Joe had spent a few minutes in the owner's restroom painstakingly removing his make-up and fake whiskers, emerging clean shaven and walking normally. He'd thrown his walking stick aside in the third-floor corridor when he'd bolted for the lift and never recovered it. Besides, he saw no reason to hide from anyone now. Being spotted and escorted to the

216

nearest police station by the authorities would be totally acceptable, as that would be his next port of call anyway.

He had joined his three accomplices, plus Sparky and her mother, at a table in the open air on the owner's lawn. Charlotte seemed to have bounced back somewhat, although Joe noticed her hand still trembled a little when she lifted a large glass of Merlot to her lips.

'The Mercedes men walking away without facing justice isn't right,' he moaned. The double whisky Neil had bought for him was starting to give him a warm edge, but he pushed it away now, placing elbows on the table and planting his face in both hands.

'What makes you think that?' queried Indy.

'Gerard the personal assistant. He's getting them to take their gun and leave the racecourse. Gray wants everything hushed up and thinks he has the money to make that happen.'

'He'll have a job.'

Suddenly Indy had the attention of the table.

'What?' Indy complained, 'After I jumped off the tower onto that bouncy castle - which I wouldn't recommend by the way, it blummin' hurt - Neil locked those two men in the tower and I called the police. They'll probably be there by now.'

There was a short silence as this information sunk in around the table. Sparky began to laugh. It started as a giggle and then grew into a full blown, uncontrollable laughing fit. As it continued Charlotte began laughing too, making the others smile.

Unable to comprehend why her comment was so funny, Indy added, 'I told the police there were two nasty men and a big gun up there!'

This was received with an expression laden with gloom from Joe and further laughter from Charlotte and Sparky.

'The police getting involved will be bound to ruin dad's cover up story!' Sparky enthused.

Joe couldn't participate in the celebration of Gray's potential downfall, staring glumly at his whisky. This feeling of incompleteness was beginning to irritate him and he pushed his drink further away, no longer in the mood for alcohol.

Noticing his gloom, Indy reached over and patted Joe's arm. She began to say something, but was drowned out by the sound of helicopter rotor blades chopping their way through the air above them.

Joe didn't join the rest of the table, and virtually every race-goer in the vicinity, in lifting their chins to stare skyward at the huge metal beast that seemed to defy gravity only a hundred yards above. He remained eyes shut, head in hands, trying to piece together his thoughts. He furiously arranged and rearranged the last two days, trying to make the people, their actions, and the facts make sense. At first it had all been about money; the extortion of millions of pounds with threat, but it had altered and coalesced around Gray's attempt at keeping his own fraud from becoming public. Then it had become personal. That last shot. Gerard had told the blackmailer's story, and warned Gray the blackmailer might decide to kill him anyway. Or had he…? Joe's thoughts converged and he was suddenly thinking about the phone that had been on the coffee table in the Gray's box, providing the laptop Gray has used with its internet connection.

Joe lost focus as the downdraft from the helicopter blades momentarily caused a forceful breeze to send losing betting slips and race cards fluttering. He covered his eyes with his fingers, trying to force his thoughts to coalesce by pressing progressively harder, until the blackness was broken by intricate white clouds that swirled around his vision.

'That will be Bill Hutchinson,' he heard Sparky remark in a half-shout, 'I wonder if he knows about the fraud.'

It's been a two horse race, and Pontefract was the winning line, Joe thought. Yes, that was better, he could understand how a race would unfold. The blackmailer had jumped from the gates, jostled for early position, then settled into a rhythm, taking his monthly protection money. He'd been challenged along the way by Gray, moving upsides him, threatening not to pay, but a swift move by the blackmailer had seen Gray lose ground when his family was threatened. Finally, Gray had switched to the outside, onto fresh ground, making progress by releasing his hacking code into the hands of a person he knew would eventually make the code public, thus casting a shadow over the longevity of their blackmail. Once in the public domain, there would be no way Gray could continue using the hacking code. The blackmailer would be treading used, worn ground and Gray could move past and stretch out to the finishing line. But the blackmailer had fought back with violence, moving out to block Gray's move, bumping and boring as they entered the final furlong. The blackmailer had reached across and torn the reigns from Gray's hands and demanded he weaken and pay all the prize-money at once, right now. Unable to steer his horse to victory, Gray had crumpled and weakened, allowing the blackmailer to…

Once again, Gerard's speech about the blackmailer forced its way into Joe's mind, and a new possibility was revealed. What if this had been a three horse race all along? An unregarded outsider, a runner virtually ignored, who had used the ongoing fight between the two horses disputing the lead as a distraction in order to land the spoils undetected, with the help of the running rail to guide him…

'Neil, I know you sent that message telling me it was a military man who booked the owners badges for the Mercedes men, but what did Keith Citron actually say?'

Neil considered this for a few moments, playing with the brim of his trilby, casting his mind back to the few minutes he'd spent in the company of the rather unsavoury trainer.

'The horse ran under Citron's name, but is actually owned by a retired army chap. He'd insisted the horse ran today and asked for three owners badges to be left in the name of Smith. He didn't know who they were for. I think he said this army chap had spent time in the Far East. Citron reckoned his owner couldn't use his own name because he'd been involved in counter-terrorism in the past and couldn't risk putting his name against the horse in case it was targeted.'

'I don't suppose Citron gave you his real name?'

'Not for any price,' Neil confirmed with a shake of his head.

'Has anyone got a racecard?' Joe asked.

Simon produced one from inside his jacket and handed it over. Joe flicked through the pages until he reached Citron's runner in the last race. It wasn't a surprise to find the five-year-old gelding was a sprinter, but running in a ten furlong race. It was the rank outsider with virtually no chance.

'It's been declared for the owners' badges,' said Joe.

'And it's a non-runner now, it's just been announced,' added Simon.

'After the Mercedes men had claimed their free passes to virtually anywhere around the racecourse,' Joe stated thoughtfully.

The noise from the helicopter was ebbing away in the distance as it powered down after landing in the centre of the racecourse, allowing Joe to speak in a lower register. He peered over the track and realised there was only one helicopter sitting on the football pitches.

'Did Gray's helicopter leave and then come back?' he asked.

'Yeah, it left about an hour ago,' replied Neil.

'It's the same helicopter?'

'Yes, of course. Fairbet always use the same company,' said Charlotte.

The whole table was now giving Joe the same confused look.

'So does Bill Hutchinson work for Fairbet?'

Sparky answered, 'Yes, he's been with Fairbet as long as dad. They started the company together. Bill does the financial stuff and owns a percentage too.'

'And he's Ruth's godfather,' Charlotte added, pointing her three-quarter empty wine glass toward her daughter.

'I've seen that look before, Joe. It's the same look you gave me at Sandie's house,' challenged Indy, 'What have you worked out?'

Desperate to maintain his concentration, Joe said, 'The best jockey's are those who understand pace. They time their challenge at exactly the right moment, for the greatest effect.'

This received another blank stare.

'Bear with me,' Joe insisted, turning to Sparky and peering over her shoulder. She craned her neck around to discover what had piqued Joe's interest.

Down the hill at the owners and trainers entrance Bill Hutchinson and another man were crossing the racetrack together. Waiting in the premier enclosure, Gerard was there to meet them. He was smiling.

Joe switched his attention to Sparky.

'Is it normal for Gerard to be escorting your dad's guests?'

'I don't think so. I get the impression he's hardly left his side for the last year and a half.'

Joe nodded, watching as the three men walked up the chute and through the gate that led to the Dalby Stand. He asked which was Hutchinson and Sparky indicated the larger, heavier man with a weather-beaten face and the thick thatch of finely combed silver hair. She couldn't identify the second man. Joe watched the three men disappear into the shadows of the Dalby Stand.

Joe leaned over and put his hand on Sparky's arm.

'You heard Gerard speaking to his... his lover, I think you said. Earlier today.'

'I called him loverboy. It was great, he hated it. So what?'

'Tell me exactly what you overheard.'

Sparky hesitated, trying to recall the few seconds she had witnessed after walking into the Gray's private room unannounced.

'He was talking to a girl called Alex. He told her he loved her and everything would work out. He rang off as soon as he clocked me.'

'Are you sure? What did he say *exactly*. It's important.'

Adopting an expression of mild condescension, Sparky replied, 'He said - Look Alex, I love you. It's all going to work out.'

Joe dug deep into his pocket for his phone and started tapping the screen. Every person around the table was leaning forward, hanging on what he would do or say next.

'Fool me once... fool me twice..' muttered Joe.

'These multi gender first names do nothing but cause confusion... my kids aren't going to... I've found him!' he gasped, 'Come on, if he's still here, we've got to speak with him.'

'Who?' Indy demanded as Joe rose from the table.

'Michael Gray's blackmailer, Alexander L. Horowitz, the director of integrity at the BHA.'

Forty-Six

Michael Gray was engrossed in monitoring the melt-down currently occurring on the Fairbet betting forums. As a result, he was only dimly aware of the helicopter arriving. His private room had been rearranged, the two armchairs with bullet holes pushed into the back corner and the zip ties and other debris removed. He was alone, already shifting what little money he could find in reserves, crediting accounts; trying to put things right.

It was useless. He couldn't do it. He was robbing Peter to pay Paul, just shifting the problems, all ten million of them.

The blackmailer's Fairbet account balance stood at zero. The fraudulent funds had been transferred to a variety of bank accounts almost the second it had began arriving, and was lost. He also didn't have enough personal assets to plug the shortfall, not by a long chalk. The best way forward for the company was to recredit all the affected customers, over three hundred thousand of them, claim a minor technical issue, now remedied, had caused the problem, and worry about the huge hole in the company accounts later. But that was just it; the ten million pounds wasn't there.

Stability was paramount in his business. Once punters, and more importantly, the premier customers upon whom the liquidity of markets was reliant, lost confidence in the platform, it could start a chain of events that could kill an exchange; a run on the bank. He knew this, because he'd watched it happen to one of his competitors in the early days, in fact, once the rumours had started, he'd made sure he'd contributed to it in order to quicken the demise of his rival. Fairbet had eventually bought out their remaining customer base at a fraction of their worth only a few weeks later. He wasn't going to allow that to happen to Fairbet.

Gray stopped typing. Despite the warm summer's day and only the mere breath of a breeze, a shroud of icy air engulfed him, making him shiver. Gray's fingers left his keyboard. Here it came, back again... unbidden, the cold touch of his sleeping foe. As his breathing became shallow he sensed his arms, shoulders, and chest beginning to tense. Then the horrible feeling of hollowness struck, as the panic attack took control of both his mind and body. He fought it for a few seconds, using the breathing exercises his doctor had given him, but soon succumbed, elbows on the table, head in hands riding out the assault on his brain and body with short, panting breaths. It helped to think of Charlotte, so he tried to fill his mind with her. Their university days were always the best, the memories somehow brighter, clearer.

A minute later, sweat dripping from his chin and drenching the armpits of his cotton shirt, Gray's brain relented and slowly returned him use of his faculties.

Groggily, he crossed to the back of the room, opened a chestnut cabinet and ignoring the rows of beer and spirits, grabbed a bottle of water, drinking the tepid contents in gulps. His thirst sated, Gray grasped the cabinet with both hands, leaning against it with arms locked straight, head bowed. As he looked down, his eye was drawn to a small spherical hole in one of the polished panelled doors. It was perfectly round; about the size of a...

Michael Gray decided enough, really was enough.

Forty-Seven

With the fourth race of the day running, the corridor at the top of the Dalby Stand was virtually empty when Joe and his party of five burst out of the lift on the third floor. They turned left and headed straight to the Fairbet room given over to corporate entertaining at the end of the corridor.

Joe reached for the door knob, but froze before his fingers began to rotate its brass beveling.

'I can't go in there,' Joe told his friends, 'I'm bound to be recognised. If he's still in here, someone will need to bring him out so I can speak with him.'

Thirty seconds later Indy and Simon entered the Fairbet private room and began mingling with the thirty or so guests from Fairbet, the BHA, and the racing press. Scanning the room, Simon spotted the familiar face of the BHA Chairman, Tottering-Smythe. He was accompanied by the director of communications, Paul Jenkins. With Indy on his arm, they toured over to them.

'You've still got bare feet!' he hissed through the side of his mouth as they approached.

'Bet they don't notice,' she responded, plastering an endearing smile on her face and adjusting the neckline of her dress downwards in order to display another inch of cleavage.

Three minutes later Indy gave an involuntary shudder as they left the two BHA men.

'There is no way Charlotte Gray fell for Jenkins. The man is vile,' Indy whispered.

'I couldn't get you away from him fast enough,' agreed Simon. He looked back over his shoulder and found Jenkins, sporting a reddened nose, still following them with his eyes. More precisely, he was watching Indy's backside. Simon caught Jenkins's attention, raised an unimpressed eyebrow and the BHA man got the message and looked away.

Indy's spirits were raised when a moment later they stepped out of the room and into the sunshine on the balcony. It was filled with a dozen people, most of whom were leaning on the railings and watching the horses file out of the paddock and walk down the chute beneath them. However, she noticed an increasing number were having their attention drawn to the centre of the racecourse where a trio of policemen appeared to be gesticulating to a man on the roof of the information tower.

Simon looked around and located his mark after a second scan of the balcony. The small, neatly dressed man was standing alone in the corner, in the only available piece of shade.

Simon forced himself to swallow down his initial disappointment. Horowitz certainly wasn't brimming with charisma; in fact, he had been easy to overlook. He had delicate, almost feminine features and was preoccupied with feigning interest in his race card. In reality his attention was actually taken up with his mobile phone that lay within its folded pages. Simon took a moment to adjust his thinking. This man wasn't even close to his preconceived idea of a cold blooded killer, and hardly the sort you would associate with the Mercedes men. Simon also doubted Indy's good looks would have the same effect they'd had on Jenkins.

At six foot four, Simon towered over Horowitz by a good ten inches and managed to catch a glimpse of his phone over Horowitz's shoulder before the smaller man flinched and snapped his race card shut. He'd been using a banking app.

'I'm sorry to interrupt, are you Mr Horowitz?' Simon asked, proffering his hand.

Horowitz took it and produced a weak shake whilst eyeing the two of them suspiciously. His gaze darted down to Indy's feet and stayed there for a split second longer than was necessary.

'High heels,' she said with an embarrassed shrug, 'They're no good for standing around in all day.'

Horowitz sniffed, 'I suppose so, madam.'

'We actually sought you out in order to give you a message,' Simon ventured, keen to move the conversation along.

'There's a young, fit looking chap out there in the corridor. Very nice man. Lovely baritone speaking voice. He asked us to give you a message. Poor chap said he couldn't come in here as he wasn't a guest.'

Simon watched as Horowitz's eyes hardened. He noticed the lids were sagging, and they were underlined with dark crescents. Pinpricks of sweat began to appear on his forehead.

'He asked us to give you a message,' Simon continued airly, 'Now then, what was it again, Indy?'

'Erm… I think his name was Gerard and he asked if we could tell you…' she looked up at Simon, as if inspiration would arrive from peering at him. She paused, fingers rubbing her chin.

'Alex!' she blurted loudly.

Horowitz cringed and his mouth dropped open.

'That's right my dear,' Simon agreed, snapping his fingers in delight, 'He was asking for Alex. And the chap asked if you could possibly pop outside to have a word. Seemed quite important by all accounts. He was in a bit of an anxious state.'

The name had managed to drain all remaining colour from Horowitz's face. Offering a quick thank you to Indy and Simon he shoved his race card into his suit pocket and pushed past them, into the room, making a beeline for the door.

Simon grinned at Indy, 'Lovely job! Come on, whatever Joe has in store for him, I don't want to miss it.'

Joe's spirits were lifted significantly when he spied Horowitz. The little man darted out of the private room and began dodging around race-goers as he hurried down the corridor, searching for Gerard.

'I was right,' he said under his breath.

Assuming the blackmailer was linked to the BHA had been a bit of a leap, but not a massive one. The voice he'd heard speaking with the Mercedes men had been soft and with perfect diction. He'd been reminded of a similar softness when listening on the phone when the four members of the BHA had come into Michale Gray's private room. However, finding an 'Alex' had been a longshot. Horowitz must use his middle name for business, as he'd been introduced as 'Leonard' earlier in the day, so discovering on the BHA's website that his first name was actually Alexander, had been pure luck.

Horowitz almost ran into Joe in his desperation to find Gerard. Joe had been bending over to retrieve a walking stick, *his* walking stick, which he'd dropped in the corridor when running for the lift an hour previously. With Neil and Sparky standing to block Horowitz's progress Joe joined them and managed to pin the small, nervous man up against the wall.

'Please remain calm Mr Horowitz. What I have to say could save your life,' Joe stated in a businesslike manner, 'We know about your blackmail plot, and the extortion of several million pounds from Mr Michael Gray. I also know you shot at him using remote controlled sniper software.'

This last accusation had been a bit of a stab in the dark, Joe was sure it had to be either one of the Mercedes men or Horowitz who had controlled the rifle, but his money was on Horowitz. Gerard's story about the gambling father and the eventual death of his parents must have been about Horowitz. When the small man's eyes suddenly flicked nervously away, Joe knew he'd guessed right.

'There is still a way out for you, but you have to answer my questions quickly and correctly. Do you understand?' Joe continued.

Horowitz used the back of a hand to rub his eyes. When he'd finished, they were reddened and the small, delicate man appeared bewildered. Presently, Horowitz composed himself enough to manage a strangled, 'I understand.'

A steady stream of people were moving up and down the corridor now the fourth race had run. Sparky, Indy, Neil, and Simon created a huddle around Horowitz and Joe went to work.

'I need to know about your relationship with Gerard,' Joe began, and Horowitz's lips snapped together and his eyes gained ferocity. Joe paused. Clearly, a different tack was required.

'Look, I know about the hacking code and your involvement in blackmailing Michael Gray. I heard you talking to the thugs who threw Billie Davenport onto…'

'I didn't have anything to do with that, or what happened to Gray's wife and…'

Horowitz fell silent and his mouth hung open as the ramifications of his hasty words hit him. For a moment, Joe marveled at how a man so obviously compromised by his childhood trauma and thirst for revenge could have held down his job. Then he considered the sort of falsehoods and dirty deals Horowitz must have encountered daily in his role as director of integrity for racing, and felt a pang of sympathy for him.

'That awful story Gerard told, that was your story, wasn't it? You lost your father to a gambling addiction, and then your mother to suicide,' Joe said softly.

Horowitz screwed his eyes up and nodded.

'I don't think you meant to hurt anyone,' Joe continued, 'I think you just wanted some justice for your father.'

'I don't… know what came over me.'

'I listened to Gerard's speech,' Joe said, allowing little wistfulness to play in his words. He slowly placed a hand on the wall behind Horowitz and leaned in so he could whisper in the man's ear, 'It was such a powerful, emotional speech. I'd go so far as to say it was heart-wrenching… even inspiring. I'm not surprised it had such a strong effect on you… the person who lived that agony.'

He paused, studying Horowitz closely to see if his words were working. The small man blinked rapidly for a second, then stared hard at the floor.

'In fact, I wouldn't be surprised if Gerard hadn't learnt those lines, he delivered them so wonderfully.'

Joe allowed this to settle on Horowitz for a few seconds. He pushed back off the wall and regarded him sadly.

'Why now? Why today?' he asked, crossing his arms.

Horowitz took a while to respond. Joe didn't move.

'The monthly money was going to stop because Gray had made the hacking code public. Gerard said we needed to get the rest of the money out of him in one go, while we could,' Horowitz admitted miserably.

Joe slowly nodded his understanding, but before long was frowning once more.

'How did you two meet?'

Horowitz brightened somewhat, the memory making his eyes glisten.

'We met at my…' he searched for an appropriate word, '…counselor's office. We were introduced so we could be each other's emotional support.'

Joe smiled warmly, putting the man further at his ease.

'So what does Gerard get from all of this?' he ventured quietly, 'Does he get any of your money?'

'No,' Horowitz shot straight back, 'His own family suffered from Fairbet's promises too, he just wanted to help me get even.'

'So he got a job as Gray's personal assistant, found you three thugs to help you threaten Gray, gave you a military grade gun and software and…'

'He loves me!' Horowitz cut in, his words suddenly vicious.

Joe's arms dropped to his sides. He understood. Horowitz stared up at him, certainty pouring from his furrowed brow and upturned chin.

He'd thought love was the missing link, but needed to hear it from the man himself. It was time to be blunt.

'I think Gerard tried to manipulate you into killing Michael Gray,' Joe stated softly, 'I hope Gerard does love you, but I doubt it. I'm wondering if he's been using you.'

Horowitz shook his head violently, casting this possibility

228

away.

'No. No. We're going away. Far away. We're going together.'

'Think about it, Leonard,' Joe said tenderly, 'If you had shot and killed Michael Gray, the police would track the bullets, the gun, and then the software to your laptop. They may already be tracking the money from your Fairbet account to all those bank accounts I'm sure you have used. Everything points to you... and no one else.'

Horowitz was becoming increasingly agitated, obsessively chewing his lip, eyes darting around the floor. Joe evaluated his options; time was slipping by and with it, the opportunity to expose Gerard. As Horowitz stubbornly remained silent, Joe decided he needed to take another, bigger gamble.

'Leonard, Gerard is young, fit and good-looking. He's twenty years younger than you... tell me,' he whispered, '...could he be lying to you?'

Horowitz stopped scouring the floor in search of answers and raised his head to stare into Joe's pitying, but hopeful green eyes. He slowly took in each of the people standing in a semicircle around him, before returning to Joe.

'Leonard, could I be right?' Joe pressed.

The small group watched a pained expression begin to form across Horowitz's finely sculpted features.

'I could have... shot him,' he croaked, 'I had the sights right between Gray's eyes... but I...'

'But you didn't.'

'No. I couldn't bring myself to *kill* him,' Horowitz moaned.

'Are you *sure* Gerard did all this just for you?

Horowitz didn't reply.

'Why don't we go and ask him?' Joe suggested gently.

Horowitz contemplated this nervously, regarding Joe, and then checking the other faces surrounding him.

'Like I said, there could still be a way out of this for you.'

'How?'

This time there was no microphone, no audience of thousands hanging on every word of Joe's commentary. He called this race quietly to a crowd of one. Joe told Horowitz of the many ways the final furlong could play out, and how the ultimate winner might alter, according to the tactics of the primary players.

Forty-Eight

Michael Gray had just about got his breathing under control by the time the door to the box had been rapped hard several times in quick succession, making him jump. Gerard called his name through the locked door. Taking a moment to steady himself, Gray unlocked the door and threw it open with a fixed smile.

'Come on in Bill, it's great to see...'

Gray's eyes travelled past his friend and to the smaller man almost obscured by Hutchinson's bulk. He was smirking at Gray when their eyes met.

'Drew Cooper.'

'Michael,' Cooper responded tartly, barely opening his lips.

The two members of the Fairbet board stepped into the room, Hutchinson empty handed and Cooper with a slim briefcase. Gerard followed, choosing to stand with his back to the windows on the right-hand side of the room. Hutchinson flopped into an armchair but Cooper remained on his feet, casting a disdainful eye around the room.

'I must apologise for making Mr Hutchinson late,' Cooper remarked, 'However, given the serious issues that have arisen today I insisted he picked me up on his way here.'

'You're referring to the minor problems we've had with a few accounts this afternoon?' Gray enquired lightly.

Cooper smirked again, 'Yes, I thought you'd find it difficult to accept that your precious website might be at fault. That's why I've been in contact with your head of operations. He tells me there is around ten million pounds unaccounted for following a widespread and systematic fraud.'

'It's a mess, Michael,' growled Hutchinson, 'The blogs and message boards are full of irate punters and the press have got hold of it. The website is in meltdown due to there being no fluidity in the markets as our key punters go elsewhere. And get this, there's some cock and bull story about the BHA being targeted for fraud through their personal Fairbet accounts. You must have caught some of this? I've been trying everything to get hold of you but your phone went straight to voicemail and none of your staff here at the course could reach you.'

'I've been busy.'

'So it seems,' Cooper said sarcastically, cocking his head

toward Hutchinson, who sighed, and began rubbing his temples.

'Here's the thing, Michael,' Cooper added, placing his briefcase on the coffee table and clicking it open, 'I have received information from a very reliable source that tells me you are directly responsible for this hole in the Fairbet accounts.'

He spun round, stepped forward and stared accusingly up at Gray.

'Will you admit it, or do I need to provide evidence?'

Gray tried hard to suppress the urge to throw a punch in Cooper's direction, and found himself balling his fists. Just one swipe would wipe that smug look off his face. Drew Cooper had been a constant thorn in his side from the moment he'd joined the board, and here he was, casting aspersions about his ability to lead the company.

'No matter!' Cooper cut in before Gray could respond, 'As I see it, you have two options. You may pay the money back immediately, and subsequently face a vote of no confidence and be forced to leave the company, or don't pay the money back and face prosecution for fraud.'

Gray stared down at Cooper with unbridled loathing. He considered beginning a war of words with him. Whether it was the fact that this reptile's accusations were, to a point, true… or that his current state of mind was shaky at best, …or simply tiredness, Michael Gray decided it wasn't worth it.

He replied, 'Both of those options would decimate the company, and you know it. Stop playing games and give me your third option.'

Cooper paused and regarded Gray, trying to evaluate whether his foe was serious or not. When Gray's grim gaze didn't waver, Cooper licked his lips and began his rehearsed speech.

'My company will fill the hole in the accounts. Immediately. Today. We will put out a press release saying there was a coding error which manifested itself early this afternoon and a cascade effect caused errors which have now been rectified. We'll say the money was never lost, accounts are back to normal, and systems have been put in place to ensure it will never happen again.'

Cooper took a breath, and Gray waited.

'In return, you will sign an agreement that removes your veto, allowing a sale of the company… should a suitable opportunity present itself.'

Forty-Nine

Joe and Horowitz stood side by side, the door to Gray's private room looming large in front of them. Joe checked his watch; another thirty seconds. He swiveled his eyes to examine the director of integrity. Still emotional, Horowitz was sniffing every few seconds, although Joe noticed his chin was sticking out with a hint of resolution. Now he'd had time to allow the facts to sink in, Horowitz had become stronger rather than weaker. Joe no longer feared the man could break down at any moment, he'd seen through the lies, and understood. Joe was more worried about keeping a lid on the man's anger.

It also flashed through Joe's mind that he was standing beside a man who had almost murdered someone only an hour ago. He shivered, fought the urge to turn and run, and told himself it was too late to go back.

The corridor was busy; the room next to Gray's, full of his employees, was bubbling with conversation, a constant flow of people going in and out. A sudden crackle of laughter floated out of the open door but did nothing to assuage Joe's nervousness. He checked his watch; the girls should be in place.

Fairly sure Gray's door would be locked, he tried it anyway. When the door knob wouldn't move, he took a breath and knocked.

'It's Joe Lawlor, I need to speak with you, Mr Gray,' called Joe between banging the door with his fist, 'I need to speak with you urgently.'

It was as he was thumping on the door a second time that a key turned and it opened a crack. Joe had been tensed, waiting for this opportunity and he and Horowitz immediately pushed forward, the two of them bundling haphazardly into the room.

Gerard took a few steps back, a scowl playing on his lips. Joe pushed the door shut and turned the key.

'Mr Lawlor, and…' queried Gray, giving Joe an expectant stare.

'Leonard Horowitz,' Joe answered.

'Ah, yes, from the BHA?'

Horowitz didn't reply. His attention was wholly ascribed to Gerard, who had backed off further to position himself behind one of the armchairs. Joe quickly scanned the room and spotted a briefcase open on the coffee table, papers neatly lined up alongside. The folding windows had been pulled across and curtains drawn, but a two foot gap still remained onto the balcony, allowing a faint breeze to cool the air in the room. Otherwise, the private box had become cut off from the outside world. He discovered Bill Hutchinson sitting unmoving, deeply ensconced in an armchair, facing the standing men. It was his expression that confused Joe. Hutchinson had the air of an aged king, relaxed, in control, and possibly amused by the actions of his courtiers.

The owner of the briefcase had been sitting on the edge of his seat but he now stood, said his name was 'Cooper,' and held out his hand.

'Those documents over there,' said Joe, ignoring the man's hand and waving two fingers at the table, 'What are they for?'

Gray frowned, 'Whilst I remain in your debt for what you did for me earlier today, I can't see what business...'

'Tell me!'

'No, really...'

'Leonard Horowitz is the ninth earl of Stretford...' Joe broke in, '...he blackmailed you and almost killed you this afternoon.'

Gray's mouth dropped open. Behind him Cooper and Hutchinson traded a mystified look.

'So, those documents...' said Joe.

'I've just signed an agreement to remove my veto of the sale of Fairbet. It will potentially allow Mr Cooper and the other members of the board to place my company for sale on the open market,' said Gray shakily.

His eyes widened as he renewed his inspection of Horowitz, momentarily spellbound by the seemingly benign little man. Meanwhile, Joe's gaze was elsewhere. His attention was on Gerard.

'You...' started Gray.

'Yes, I blackmailed you. For what you did to my family,' said Horowitz resentfully, steadily holding Gray's stare, 'That story Gerard told you... is my story. I never meant anyone to get hurt, it was just about getting my father's money back. It was only fair I took back every single penny you stole from him.'

'It was you firing that gun at myself and my family?'

Horowitz swallowed, 'Yes.'

The small man seemed to crumble a little as he answered, his face contorting from stable contrition into a hot, turbulent mixture of emotions. His focus switched from Gray to Gerard and he quickly covered the few steps toward the personal assistant so only the armchair was between them.

'Tell me you love me.'

The room fell silent.

Gerard stared back at Horowitz, horror etched into his face

'Tell me… please tell me, that it wasn't a lie.'

His plea was made with such tenderness, and with so much honesty, the entire room held its breath.

All eyes were on Gerard, willing him to speak. The silence extended, slowly sucking the air from the room.

Horowitz finally broke eye contact with Gerard, sniffing and smiling wryly at his own foolishness.

'It was a lie, wasn't it?' he admitted despondently, glancing at Joe for a moment, 'The race caller is right. You lied. I even allowed you to call me Alex. Only my mother called me by that name. You don't love me… you wanted me to kill Gray.'

Gerard remained silent for a few seconds before clearing his throat. But before he could form an answer, Horowitz had leaned toward him, his eyes gleaming with renewed purpose.

'You lied. Just like everyone else in this rotten industry.'

Gerard hadn't moved, determined not to be intimidated. He placed a relaxed hand on the back of the armchair and smirked at Horowitz. It was only then that Joe realised his mistake. He'd been watching Gerard, believing that if he was correct, it would be the personal assistant who would be the danger in the room.

Horowitz bowed his head, whipped out what looked like a steak knife from his trouser pocket, and lifted it above his head.

Gerard's smirk became a frown, yet he remained rooted to the spot, bewildered by the little man's actions.

In a single whirling movement, Horowitz hacked downwards, aiming to embed the serrated blade in Gerard's chest. Leaping forward, Joe caught hold of Horowitz's suit jacket and dragged the little man back just enough that instead of the knife plunging into Gerard's chest its new trajectory saw it come down into the top of the armchair. The steak knife made a popping noise as it pierced the leather, continuing deep into the padding and embedding itself into the wooden frame.

Gerard was standing frozen, transfixed by the knife as it wobbled to and fro on the top of the chair.

Joe man-handled Horowitz into a chair on the opposite side of the room and warned him to stay put.

'Lawlor, for Christ's sake, what is going on?' Gray demanded.

Before Joe could answer, Gerard interjected, 'Isn't it obvious? These men are trying to kill you. I'll deal with them,' and strode toward Joe, grasped his arm and expertly twisted it behind his back and grinning when Joe yelped in pain.

'Your bodyguard has set you up, Gray,' Joe said through gritted teeth, 'That's why you recruited him, isn't it? He's not your assistant, he's your bodyguard… to protect you from Ronnie's crew. Gerard may have wanted your money, but I've a suspicion he also wanted you to sign those papers too.'

Gerard twisted Joe's arm further up his back, forcing him to let out another howl of pain.

'The Mercedes men… the thugs,' he quickly modified, 'Gerard must know then from his army days. Horowitz was recruited to be his patsy, to take the blame. Gerard is part of the plot to hurt your family by maintaining relentless pressure on you. He's put this day together in the hope that it would push you over the edge. Gambling on Fairbet cost his brother's life. Gerard wants revenge.'

'Shut the hell up,' Gerard hissed, twisting Joe's arm further up his back. A white hot pain seared its way from his shoulder and down Joe's spine and he fell to his knees, blobs of white clouding his retinas.

Gerard flashed Gray a black look, 'He's lying. The two of them are working together.'

'Tell… them Leonard,' Joe managed between further surges of pain in his shoulder.

Gray glanced at Cooper, who had taken his seat. He returned a bemused stare. Beside him, Hutchinson hadn't moved from his armchair and Gray also traded a questioning look with him.

'Get your man to ease off. Listen to what this Horowitz chap has got to say. What have you got to lose?' Hutchinson suggested.

Gray sniffed, 'Gerard, let Lawlor go.'

Gerard started to argue, but eventually loosened his grip. Joe shrugged the man off, limply holding his arm, willing the pain to subside, but focusing on Horowitz, who looked as if he wanted his armchair to swallow him whole. Joe bobbed down beside him.

'Tell Gray how you came to be like this,' Joe urged.

Horowitz sighed, seeming to shrink even further into the

chair. Joe thought for a moment the emotional drain had been too much, but Horowitz gathered himself, cleared his throat and began to tell the room his story.

It was the same one he'd taken Joe through, out in the corridor. Only this version was tainted by the sure knowledge that he had been groomed by the man he loved.

Horowitz explained how he'd been introduced to Gerard eighteen months previously whilst undergoing therapy. He'd attended weekly sessions by a lauded psychologist in the field of gambling addiction. The therapy wasn't to deal with his own addiction, Horowitz didn't gamble. He had sought professional help to deal with the mental scars caused by his father's gambling problem during his childhood.

Horowitz told of how he and Gerard bonded over their grief, sense of betrayal, and thirst for revenge. Gerard's brother had racked up huge debts on credit cards trying to lay horses to lose on Gray's exchange, eventually committing suicide when the pressure of repayment became too much for him. Horowitz and Gerard had dreamed of how sweet it would be to rectify the pain and hardship Fairbet had brought into their lives. For Horowitz, that repayment amounted to almost ten million pounds.

'Antony… that is to say, Mr Gerard became a trusted friend and confidante. We quickly became close friends and about fourteen months ago he announced he'd found a way to get my money back. Not only had he secured a job with Michael Gray, he'd discovered someone online who had damning evidence they could use against him. He introduced me to three men and said they would work with me to do what was necessary – they would do the dirty work,' explained Horowitz.

Joe slowly moved to the door as Horowitz continued his story. Gerard had become a statue in the centre of the room, listening to the story with arms crossed, and a contemptuous glare. Joe was keen to ensure the personal assistant couldn't make a run for it, but was bemused by Gerard's lack of emotion. He didn't seem to be phased at all by the revelations Horowitz was making.

'At first it was fine, I was getting money every month from Fairbet. I was so, so happy,' Horowitz continued, addressing himself to Gray, 'Fairbet's betrayal was being repaid. Then Gerard said you had refused to pay and they needed to hurt your family, just as you had done to mine. I don't know what Gerard did, he wouldn't tell me, but the payments started again.'

Gray found himself up on his feet again, bearing down on Horowitz, close to striking the man.

'Your thugs hospitalized my wife for two weeks! Then they broke my daughter's hip in a hit and run that could have killed her if they'd been an inch closer,' Gray intoned darkly, 'It forced me to distance them both from my life.'

Horowitz cowered lower in his armchair before muttering, 'I didn't know. They just did those things. I only heard about what went on at Ripon after it had happened. I had nothing to do with that girl being hurt.'

'You were there, overseeing that, weren't you Gerard?' Joe said, 'I can prove it.'

He dug out his phone and poked at it a few times. A phone started to ring in the room. Everyone looked at Gerard; the ringing was coming from his pocket.

'Don't bother answering it,' Joe told him. Then to Gray he said, 'That's the number that contacted me when I was at Ripon Cathedral. He called to scare me into handing over Billie's version of the hacking code.'

Gray stared at his personal assistant, 'I sent you there to look out for Davenport and protect her,' he said accusingly.

'Tell them how today came about,' Joe suggested to Horowitz, sensing there was a change of allegiances happening in the room.

'It was Gerard's idea. He said the fraud was going to be exposed. If it became public knowledge, Gray would be able to stop paying. He said there was no time, and we'd have to shake the rest of the money from Gray in one go. Gerard came up with this idea to come to Pontefract because Gray always attended this meeting.'

Horowitz took a breath whilst eyeing his audience. Everyone in the room was focused on him.

'When I got here, Gerard said I'd have to operate something to help them convince Gray to pay up. I really didn't know it was a gun until I got here. When I saw the software I got really nervous and called Gerard, but he said he had no one else to do it. He would set things up and be in here with Gray making sure everything went well in the room.'

'It went okay, but...' Horowitz looked up at Gray, 'You said those horrible, disgusting things and I... snapped.'

'You set him up,' Joe called over to Gerard, 'All the way along…'

'Be quiet,' Gerard spat.

'You were playing on his emotional frailties, hoping…'

'I'm warning you…'

'Hoping Horowitz would do your dirty job for you…'

'Enough!' Gerard insisted, holding a hand up to Joe. He spun round and stared at Hutchinson, still watching on from his armchair.

'Tell them. Go on…'

Hutchinson frowned back, momentarily confused.

'Go on, tell them!'

There was an icy pause. Gray was staring questioningly at his friend too. He broke the silence.

'What does he mean, Bill?'

Hutchinson remained glued to his chair, raised his bushy eyebrows and replied, 'I have no idea,' then after a pause, slowly lifted his head to examine Gerard, 'But it's nonetheless fascinating. What *do* you mean, young man?'

'Don't mess with me,' Gerard countered.

'I assure you…'

'You're the one who recruited me, got me this job and made me convince Leonard to take the fall, just so you could get that precious veto from Gray! Well, you're going to rescue me now.'

Hutchinson didn't move a muscle. He didn't move, preferring to stare up at Gerard and examining him as if he was something he could work out, if only he concentrated hard enough.

Gerard waited, but finally gave up.

'Fine! Two can play at the race caller's game.'

He pulled his own phone from the pocket and tapped it a few times.

'I've been speaking with you for over two years. Don't you think I worked out who was behind all of this?'

Gerard held his phone out at arm's length toward Gray.

'Now you'll find out whether he's a friend or not!'

Gerard had placed his phone on loudspeaker, so the call tone reverberated around the room. Hutchinson reached inside his waistcoat and perused his phone expectantly. However Gerard's brow wrinkled when Hutchinson's phone didn't come to life.

'He must have used a burner phone. He hasn't got it on him.'

Hutchinson placed an index finger to his lips and a hush

descended. Almost immediately, a faint digital ringing could be heard. Its insistent jangling continued, slowly becoming louder.

Hutchinson angled his head to his right and with eyes wide declared, 'I think it's for you, Mr Cooper.'

Hutchinson stood up and he and Gray traded a long, knowing glance.

Cooper pulled a slim mobile phone from his inside pocket and inspected the caller information, answering the call with a single jab of a thin index finger. The buzzing of Gerard's phone ceased.

'You sort this. Right now,' Gerard growled, 'You've got your precious veto, now sort it out.'

Cooper blinked back, his mouth open, unable to give a response.

'You are going to burn,' Gray said in a tone barbed with poison, 'I'm going to tear your tin pot investment bank apart.'

Gray didn't have to wait long for a reply. Standing chin to chin with his fellow director, Cooper found his voice and the room was treated to an expletive ridden response where he denied all knowledge of the plot to secure the sale of Fairbet. In return, Gray lashed the smaller man with his own colourful language. They went at each other, screaming obscenities, toe to toe. Gerard, positioned behind Gray, eventually cut across the two bickering men, shouldering Gray aside in order to address Cooper.

'Are you going to fix this for me?'

Cooper cast a disdainful glance Gerard's way.

'You can go screw yourself,' he spat, lingering to watch the personal assistant's shocked reaction before returning his attention to Gray. Joe noted Cooper was gripping his briefcase, the papers having been tucked safely away during the telling of Horowitz's story. The banker breathed heavily and for a moment the shaft of sun coming into the room made the perspiration standing on his forehead sparkle like tiny diamonds.

The room appeared to take a breath itself, everyone using the few moments of calm to assess. Joe's mind was racing, he didn't know who Cooper was, apart from Gray and Hutchinson's business associate, but they seemed only too aware of him. It was as Hutchinson waded into the argument that he noticed Gerard's hands were bunched into fists by his side. Joe's first thought was to warn Gray to expect a thump, but the personal assistant surprised him by suddenly side-stepping Gray and moving behind Cooper. The investment banker was too busy remonstrating with a wagging finger in Gray's face to notice Gerard.

Joe glanced to his right and opened his mouth, but by the time he had realised the steak knife had disappeared from the top of the armchair, Gerard had already plunged it deep into Cooper's back and was busy twisting it, withdrawing, then burying it again, silently and professionally. Joe leapt forward, both hands clasping Gerard's knife hand. The struggle was short-lived, with Gerard being the far stronger. He wrenched his hand free from Joe's grip, slashing the knife downwards.

Cooper's tirade of abuse faltered, and he frowned at Gray, as if he wished to ask a question he somehow couldn't bring himself to broach. Gray, unaware Cooper had been stabbed, stared at his nemesis with contempt. His expression was soon transformed into disgust when Cooper's eyes bulged and he coughed up a stream of blood. The investment banker examined the front of his shirt in astonishment, his eyelids fluttered, and he toppled forward, crashing to the floor with an inhuman thump.

Gerard reached the entrance to the balcony without Hutchinson or Gray fully realising what had happened. It was Horowitz who set off after the personal assistant, having witnessed the stabbing from behind Cooper.

Gerard had started to angle his stride to his left, intending to use the balcony as a method of escape onto the balcony of the room next door. As he thrust the curtains aside, his stride was caught by the hook of a walking stick poking out from the left-hand side of the window, about a foot from the floor. It had a mobile phone attached to it with adhesive tape. Holding it was Sparky, Indy crouching down beside her.

Hitting the walking stick at pace, Gerard lurched forward, his hands wind-milling through the air in a vain attempt to correct his loss of balance. Such was his momentum it carried him forward at pace as he fell. The top of Gerard's head struck the balcony railings with such force the clanging sound reverberated right across the third floor of the Dalby stand, prompting race-goers below to stare upwards.

Horowitz dived through the gap in the curtains and onto the balcony, careful not to step on Gerard's legs. For a split second he took in Indy and Sparky crouched to his left, their concerned faces turned toward the railings. As one, they inched over to surround

Gerard's unmoving body, uncertain how to proceed.

A few second later Gerard stirred, emitted a weak groan and tried to push himself up. Sparky and Indy's faces flushed with relief.

Fifty

'He's dead,' Hutchinson reported with a grimace, his fingers pressed into Cooper's neck.

They had rolled the banker over and he now lay on his back, staring blankly up at the three of them. An involuntary shudder went through Joe. This was the second time he'd seen a dead body, and memories of the first now filled him. He could see his mother, lying perfectly still on the cold yellow linoleum of the kitchen floor, congealed blood matting her long auburn hair. It was an accident, just a stupid accident

He remembered the sound of the back door, almost closed but banging relentlessly in the breeze, and there was a smell of firelighters, where the backroom fire had been set for his arrival back home, but never lit. Small patches of blood were smeared on the floor where she'd dragged herself inside after slipping on the wet stone steps and cracking her head open. A trail of damp washing led to a plastic wash basket lying on its side out in the back yard.

He'd been late. He'd *promised* to be home at five o'clock, but stayed in the arcade with his friends an extra half an hour. He'd broken his promise. If he'd come home at five o'clock, as he had promised her when she'd kissed him on his cheek that morning before he set off to school, he might have been able to... So he kept his promises. Whatever happened, he would keep...

'You need to get that arm sorted out.'

It was a woman's voice. Still crouched at Cooper's side, Joe shook the memories of his mother from his mind and concentrated on the voice. Focus returned. He was warm, sweating under his arms, and there was a dryness in his throat. Indy was beside him, her finely boned hand pressing gently on his shoulder.

'Joe,' she said in the same soft tone, 'You zoned out for a minute. Your arm. It's bleeding. I think Gerard must have...'

She gently lifted his right arm. He looked at his hand, only then realising blood was trickling between his fingers. It didn't feel part of him. Indy pulled his jacket off him and rolled up his shirt sleeve revealing a deep, three inch slice, just below the crook of his arm. Joe followed a rivulet of blood as it pulsed from the wound, rushed down to his knuckles and finally dripped off his little finger, adding to the small red puddles already formed beside him. Only then did he feel the throb of pain.

With Indy still holding his arm, Joe got to his feet. The pain had somehow cleared his mind, and he took in Gray, standing beside Hutchinson, who was barking commands into his phone, Charlotte standing behind them looking on. Hutchinson glanced up at him momentarily, saw his wound and grimaced. The room door was open and a number of faces, including Simon's, were observing the scene, displaying a mixture of shock and curiosity.

'Gerard?' Joe asked Indy.

'A bad cut across his forehead and he looks awful, but there's an ambulance crew on their way. Sparky and Neil are with him. We got pretty much everything on video though. Come on, you need to get that cut seen to.'

'Wait, where's…'

Joe swung his eyes around the room again and found the object of his query sitting, hardly moving, head in his hands. Joe crossed over to Horowitz, Indy following. Sensing the approach, he lifted his head to reveal features contorted in mental anguish. He gave them a pitiful stare. Despite having only met him today, Joe could read the signs of distress, the imploring eyes that signalled a breakdown.

'Dear me…' Indy said out of the side of her mouth.

'He needs someone with him,' said Joe, glancing back over his shoulder toward the other side of the room, momentarily distracted, 'You stay here and see to him. I'll find someone to sew me back together again, and then come back.'

Indy nodded her agreement, bobbed down in front of Horowitz, placed a hand in his and began speaking with him.

Joe turned and saw Hutchinson was on his way to the door. Joe stared at him for a moment, trying to rid himself of a fuzziness of thinking, before he managed to focus properly on the Fairbet executive. Their eyes met and Hutchinson stared back warily.

'I'm going to offer the company helicopter to the ambulance crew on their way up here to treat that Gerard chap,' he offered in way of explanation.

Hutchinson paused, waiting for a reaction. When all he received was the same troubling expression from the race caller, he dropped his gaze to Joe's arm and added, 'You're injured. You should come with me and we'll find them together.'

'I don't think it's too bad,' Joe said, shaking himself from his stupor and forcing a half smile.

243

'Still, I think you should get that looked at. I've seen a few injuries like that in my time, and it looks like a bad cut.'

'Perhaps you're right. Give me a moment and I'll be with you,' Joe replied, turning back to where Indy was comforting Horowitz. They shared a quick word, he made a phone call of only a few seconds, and finally crossed the room to shake Gray's hand before leaving.

Joe was soon following Hutchinson through the small huddle of concerned people hanging around in the corridor and the two of them walked together to the lift.

Hutchinson sighed as they stood facing the lift doors, waiting for them to open, 'This is a dark day for Fairbet.'

Joe didn't pass comment beyond a muttered agreement. The pain in his arm was pulsing with every beat of his heart and the haunted look Horowitz had given him kept returning, as if the image was burned onto his retinas. He'd been mentally broken, first by the loss of his parents, his thirst for revenge, and then by Gerard, and the promise of love. Gray had exhibited a similarly forlorn look… This was more than just a dark day for Fairbet.

The lift doors opened and they walked forward, both men automatically turning around to face the corridor. Hutchinson put down his briefcase and stretched out a finger to press the ground floor button.

'Hold the doors!'

There was no one there, but Hutchinson's finger hovered over the green ground floor button on the small console to the right of the door then moved to press the hold button.

A man lurched into view. He looked a little worse for wear, possibly drunk, and Joe recognised him immediately. Ronnie, still feeling the effects of having being struck with the extinguisher, placed an unsteady hand against one of the lift doors and glared uncomprehendingly into the metal box.

Hutchinson and Joe stared back. They remained locked in a three-way staring match for a few seconds, Ronnie eventually rubbing his eyes and squinting, a confused frown slowly being replaced with a faint smile of recognition.

Hutchinson let go of the hold button and pushed the ground floor option and the doors started to close.

'Never mind, Sergeant. I'll get the next one,' Ronnie slurred, removing his hand from the other door and stepping back. Joe managed to catch the Mercedes man flicking a quick salute into the lift before the sliding doors met.

As the lift began its descent Hutchinson sighed and took a sidelong glance at his travelling partner. Joe studiously examined the lift doors, praying his face wouldn't reveal the confirmation of truth he now possessed.

'Oh dear me,' Hutchinson complained, reaching out and hitting the hold button. The lift came to a stuttering halt between floors.

'The question is... what sort of man are you?'

'I don't...'

Hutchinson scowled, 'No use denying it Lawlor, I know you've worked it out. But now I need to know what sort of man you are. What makes you tick, what motivates you...'

Joe's mind was racing, busy working through scenarios, making connections. But he forced these thoughts aside. Hutchinson was the architect of what happened here today, that's all he needed to know. Joe regarded Hutchinson anew. Late fifties, moderately overweight and possibly out of condition, but ex-army, maybe special forces; he'd know how to kill. Yet he didn't appear to be a physical threat, standing in the corner of the lift in his grey lounge suit, white shirt and deep purple tie, thin black belt and slip on leather shoes.

Eyeing Joe pensively, Hutchinson's gaze alighted on his blood soaked arm. His hands went to his midriff and he began to unbuckle his belt. Joe tried not to react, but Hutchinson must have read something in his eye or body language.

'Relax, you need a tourniquet on that arm. It looks like Gerard has sliced into your radial artery.'

'Keep your belt.'

'Fine,' Hutchinson replied, swinging his eyes to the ceiling contemptuously and crossing his arms, 'If it was a severed artery you'd have been unconscious within a minute and dead in another couple. That would solve my problem. The fact the blood is pulsing from the cut means an artery has been nicked, or worse. Either way, you'll need medical attention in the next ten minutes or you'll die here, in this metal cell.'

Whipping the belt out of his trousers, he handed it over to Joe and instructed him to wrap it further up his arm. Joe did his best, but the leather wasn't supple and he had difficulty pulling it tight.

Hutchinson watched Joe struggle without offering any assistance.

'I'm more interested in you,' he continued, casually leaning on the brown painted steel panel wall of the lift, speaking slowly, watching every micro movement in Joe's face, 'I could let you die, but I think you could be a valuable asset. You've managed to give my men the run around for two days, protected the people around you, and discovered my part in this game. Faking the bomb scare was a particularly innovative move. I could use a man like you...'

Hutchinson grinned, leaving that thought hanging.

'...but it comes back to my original question. What sort of man are you? Can I rely on your silence, your loyalty... or is there *something else* that would motivate you to work with me?'

Joe didn't answer straight away, instead he watched Hutchinson balance the tip of his tongue on his lower lip and rhythmically roll it from one side of his mouth to the other. It made him feel faintly sick.

Summoning strength, Joe took a step toward Hutchinson, who remained in the corner of the lift, his index finger pressed onto the hold button, 'You're asking whether I'd accept a bribe. To ensure you get away with murder?'

'Stay there,' Hutchinson warned gruffly, holding out a flat palm. Joe halted at the centre of the lift, only two feet from the Fairbet man. He wondered about taking a swing or a kick at his foe, but pushed the thought away, he was too weak.

Hutchinson continued, 'It's more of an agreement... an *understanding* between two associates.'

A sudden spasm from Joe's wound was followed by an aching that seemed to travel up the bones in his arm and into his shoulder. He winced, any remaining thought of trying to physically dominate Hutchinson cast away.

Cocking his head to one side, Hutchinson inspected Joe's arm.

'You better be quick. You've got less than five minutes before you lose the ability to think straight, and that pool on the floor is growing by the minute. You'll pass out and die in a puddle of your own blood at this rate.'

'What guarantee have I got that you won't sacrifice me like you did Horowitz, Gerard, and Cooper?'

Hutchinson scratched his head, 'You really want to talk about them as you're bleeding out in front of me?'

Joe nodded, 'I feel fine. I want to know you'll keep your end of any bargain.'

Hutchinson tilted his head slightly, assessing the injured man in front of him. He'd seen enough dead and dying men to know this one didn't have much time. It was just a case of waiting.

'Gerard hadn't met you had he? You were maintaining two degrees of separation I guess. Gerard was your man on the inside, you recommended him to Gray after his wife and daughter had their accidents.'

This was met with an impressed smile from Hutchinson.

'Go on, Mr Lawlor. Let's see how clever you really are,' he cajoled, his eyes dropping to Joe's hand and the slick of blood amassing on the stainless steel plates of the lift floor.

'Ronnie was with you in the forces. A strong bond of trust formed there, and he recruited the other two younger ones, again army trained; used to following orders. I'm guessing Horowitz and Gerard were more difficult, well chosen and placed though, as they were already emotionally compromised. It was easy for you to manipulate them. You just pushed their buttons of revenge and greed. Gerard realised it wasn't about the few million pounds Horowitz got today… you were playing the long game, slowly forcing Michael Gray into a sale of Fairbet. How am I doing?'

Hutchinson's smile had faded, becoming crooked and warped around the edges of his mouth.

'Cooper was an easy set-up,' continued Joe, pausing to wince when another bolt of pain pushed up his arm, 'You brought him along with the promise of… profit of some kind. I guess he would benefit from a sale of Fairbet. But he was here expressly to take the blame. I'm interested, how did you make his phone ring?'

Hutchinson had dropped any semblance of a smile now. He inspected the belt around Joe's arm and gave him a knowing nod.

'Three minutes,' he said, 'Before you're unconscious. But to answer your question, one of my areas of responsibility as finance director is to control all communication devices company wide. Forwarding the mobile number I'd given to Gerard was child's play and worked even better than I'd hoped.'

'I saw you covering your tracks,' Joe said levelly, 'You deleted something, probably the call register, on Cooper's phone after he went down. I imagine the call forwarding will be removed as soon as you're back in front of an internet enabled device.'

'Oh, please!' Hutchinson said through a half laugh, 'That loose end was tied up before I left the room. Seriously, Mr Lawlor, you have a minute and a half left to live. Why not take your hush money and come work for me? I like you. You're different. You combine intelligence and a relentless need to fulfil...'

'My promises?'

Hutchinson smirked, 'Yes, I suppose so.'

'What about Gray?'

'Ah, yes. Michael,' Hutchinson mused, 'Truly, a man for whom control of his business is paramount. A man with few friends. He was willing to divorce his wife and snub his daughter to save his company, and his skin... in that order. I admire that single-mindedness; it's what drew me to Michael when we started Fairbet. He'd do anything to keep his precious company from being sold or taken over. But... he's small minded. I realised many years ago that he'd rather die than give up control of his company, and even then, he wouldn't go quietly.'

'So you decided to kill him?'

Hutchinson's graying eyebrows dived into a frown.

'Absolutely not! You appear to have missed the point of my little plot,' he said reproachfully, 'Killing Michael solves nothing. Even in death he ensured his veto would remain in place. Michael delights in reminding me that on the event of his death, all his Fairbet shares pass onto his daughter, but only if she maintains his veto of a sale of Fairbet for a minimum of five years. Can you imagine if that little firebrand held the reins at Fairbet!'

The big man gave a snort of derision and glanced at the lift control pad. He renewed the pressure of his finger on the hold button before returning to inspect Joe.

'Two and a half minutes, Mr Lawlor. Are you going to work for me?'

'Your plan almost failed,' Joe replied, ignoring Hutchinson's question, 'Gerard tried to goad Horowitz into shooting Gray.'

'Really?' Hutchinson said with a smirk, 'Let me guess, Horowitz couldn't go through with it... in his hands the gun wouldn't hurt anyone, and despite your heroics, his playacting with the steak knife was just a cry for help, he aimed for the armchair... you see, I chose the players in my team *extremely* carefully.'

'Not carefully enough,' Joe noted, 'What about Gerard?'

'Mmm...Gerard began displaying volatility in the last few

days when the pressure was real on. I admit I may have underestimated his slyness, and the depth of his hatred for Michael. But even then, Mr Lawlor, I had planned for such an eventually. That's why I never met face to face with any of my people, except for Ronnie.'

'So what's your plan now?' Joe asked, keen to move on. Hutchinson's arrogance was beginning to grate.

'I'm going to release the *real value* in what I've built at Fairbet Mr Lawlor, which means pitching several bidders against each other. And that's what I have been manufacturing for the last four years. Selling Fairbet will net me hundreds of millions.'

'You've been planning this for *four years*?'

Hutchinson renewed his smirk.

'Michael fails to remember how long I've been with the company. I knew about his hacking code, I even covered up his first effort to use it, twenty years ago. After all, I am the finance director. I saw money appear from nowhere all those years ago and soon uncovered what he'd done, but I caressed the figures and filed his misdemeanor away, ready for when it would become useful.'

Hutchinson leaned against the opposite wall of the lift. He seemed to be enjoying himself.

'I also knew how fragile Michael's mind would become when he lost the primary anchor in his life, his wife Charlotte. He's a classic case of obsessive compulsive disorder – never diagnosed of course – and she was the only one who could keep him balanced. I recruited my men, recommended an imaginary hacker to Michael and started to apply the pressure.'

'I had hoped Michael would simply burst under the stress of being blackmailed and take the easy route of running with the money from a sale of Fairbet. I watched him spiral downwards at work, but realised I needed someone like Gerard to help turn the screw, especially after he divorced Charlotte.'

Hutchinson grinned, 'I believe Michael actually managed to convince himself Charlotte *did* cheat on him! I guess it was the only way he could bring himself to do it. That was precious!'

'Yet he hung on, and even tried to fight back by giving the hacking code to that girl we had to deal with at Ripon cathedral,' Hutchinson added, 'Eventually, I had to force the issue and place Michael in a position where he had to choose between Fairbet failing, or relinquishing his veto... given that sort of choice, Michael would never allow his company to fail.'

Hutchinson paused to inspect Joe's arm again, 'I think Michael was genuinely relieved when he signed over his veto.'

He suddenly thrust out his free hand, gripping Joe's injured arm near the cut and squeezed, making the blood bubble up.

'You have a minute at most, probably seconds' he grinned, 'Your pupils are dilated, you've gone pale and your lips have turned blue…'

Hutchinson pushed Joe in the chest, and he stumbled backwards into the opposite corner of the lift. His mobile phone slipped from the top pocket of his old man jacket and tumbled into the slick of blood on the lift floor. His vision was starting to fail, the lift and Hutchinson beginning to slowly spin, his head suddenly becoming incredibly heavy. Joe slumped, sliding down until he was sitting, legs outstretched and experiencing an ever increasing sense of claustrophobia.

'I can be honest with you now,' hissed Hutchinson, leaning as far forward as he could whilst maintaining his finger on the hold button, 'I won't be giving you any of my money. You will not be my accomplice. You've called your last race, Mr Lawlor. I'm going to enjoy watching you die here in front of me, then I'll step out of this lift, and with tears streaming down my cheeks, I'll tell these gullible race-goers how I tried to save your life when the lift jammed. It will be another sad death marked down to Mr Gerard.'

Joe hadn't heard anything Hutchinson was saying since he started his slide to the floor. Sensing movement, he wondered whether Hutchinson was touching him and mentally shuddered at the thought, his body being incapable.

He realised Hutchinson, still holding the lift on hold, was kicking his foot, presumably to determine whether he was still alive. Despite the huge effort and excruciating pain, Joe managed to lift his chin and squint up at the fuzzy image of his tormentor.

'You know the difference… between us?' Joe slurred, 'You have associates and accomplices… and I… have friends.'

He was trying desperately to keep his eyes open, to stay awake, but the blackness was rushing in, warm, painless, and inviting.

Fifty-One

The lift control panel complained with a metallic wrenching noise as Sparky levered it open using the two screwdrivers she always kept in her jacket. She inspected the jumble of switches her three minutes of nail splitting work had revealed and located the over-ride. The lift mechanism started to hum.

Screaming in a mixture of joy and relief, she joined Neil at the lift doors on the ground floor of the Dalby Stand. Indy and Simon rushed over to join them, out of breath after a helter-skelter descent of the stairs. The lift doors opened with an incongruously bright ding and several policemen rushed forward, dragging a complaining Hutchinson out, pinning him to the ground and handcuffing him.

The ambulance crew entered the lift and crowded around a lifeless form slumped on the floor.

'Such a lot of blood,' Neil muttered.

Indy, hand clasped to her mouth, stared into the small recess, willing a foot or a finger to move.

From behind her, Sparky heard Hutchinson begin another tirade of demands as he was forced to remain face down, flat on the carpet of the grandstand foyer, a policeman with a knee in his back, baton ready. Chin set, head down, she strode over to Hutchinson and landed a hard kick to his ribs. His squeal of pain was joy to her ears.

The policeman held out a hand and in a stern voice insisted she back off. However, Sparky was quickly onto her knees, crawling up to whisper to Hutchinson. The policeman had heard. He knew what this man had done, and to whom. He allowed her to speak.

'Want to know why you're on your fat stomach with a policeman's knee in your back?' she hissed.

Hutchinson grunted from the effort of turning his head to face his goddaughter.

'Because Joe Lawlor knew it was you. Even before he got in that lift. He saw you meddle with Cooper's phone and pick up that briefcase, the one you didn't arrive with. The one that wasn't yours. The one containing the signed veto.'

Hutchinson grinned and Sparky had to grit her teeth and fight the urge to jump up and kick the man again. Inexplicably, her expression suddenly brightened and she dropped her voice to a whisper, drawing herself up close to the man's face.

'We all heard,' she said, pulling away and nodding at him condescendingly, 'The whole racecourse heard you. Joe made you confess to an audience of five thousand people.'

Hutchinson's grin began to fade.

'His phone was on a live call. He'd called his friend in the commentator's box before you both left the room,' Sparky continued, her tone conversational but with a cruel edge.

'The race caller broadcast your whole conversation across the entire racecourse through the public address system.'

She bent down low, so low she could count the hairs protruding from the man's ear.

'Joe *got* you. He got you *good*. He promised us he'd get you, and Joe Lawlor is a man who doesn't break his promises.'

Hutchinson's eyes trained upwards to follow his goddaughter as she got to her feet. She scowled at him one last time, disappearing into the growing crowd of people surrounding him.

'She's right. You're for the chop, mate,' the policeman told his prisoner happily.

Fifty-Two

'But my sister and Billie are here. Please can you to pick us up from McGruders bar?'

'Seriously Indy, I'm working! I can't discuss this now, the race goes off in a few minutes.'

'Who on earth is at Newcastle races at eight o'clock on a Friday evening in the middle of winter?'

Joe paused to look out of his viewing window, down at the parade ring and betting concourse, completely lacking in race-goers. It was close to zero degrees, dark, with the floodlights shining down on the straight course, and this class six handicap was the last on an eight race card. She had a point.

'That's not the point,' he told her, cringing as soon as the words left his mouth, 'I can't leave before I've finished... er, hold on a minute.'

He checked his monitor, cleared his throat and switched his microphone on.

'The runners are at the start and going behind the stalls for this seven furlong nursery handicap, due off in four minutes time.'

'So you're in town and you want me to drive in and...'

'Yes, pick us up.'

'Can't you...'

'Listen, Joe Lawlor. Who visited you every single day you spent in hospital, who drove you home from hospital, and who looked after you when you...'

'It's been six months!' Joe protested, 'Do you really need to bring it up every single time you want me to do something for you?'

'I can't help it,' Indy giggled into his ear.

'Hold up!' he said, a smile spreading across his face. He loved it when she giggled. It was so full of joy. He switched his microphone on again.

'Two to load. Jungle Call is moving forward and Sleeping Sarah is out of line. She will be the last in.'

'Yes, alright, I'll be there. But they'd better not be as drunk as last time...'

'Can't promise that,' Indy interrupted, 'It's girls' night. See you in half an hour.'

Joe cast the phone to one side, clamped his headset back over his head and clicked his microphone on once more.

'And they're off. It's a clean break, although Roaring Rory has missed the kick, and...'

***

As Joe drove into the centre of Newcastle from Gosforth Park, he reflected that even Simon and Neil hadn't stayed for the last few races tonight. Night meetings on the All-Weather in February tended to be quite soulless affairs. Even the more hardy race-goers rarely stayed for the full card, especially when the temperature dipped below zero.

He parked his car up beside St James's football ground and set off to walk downhill towards the city centre, and Indy's favourite Irish pub. She insisted the journey into the city was worth it; stout tasted better there.

Passing a virtually empty restaurant, he caught his reflection in the window and was forced to stop, retrace his steps and stare for a moment. He'd been right, he *was* smiling. And he hadn't been aware he was doing it. Joe tried to straighten his face out as he walked on. It didn't work, his smile quickly reappeared.

He and Indy had been together for six months. The longest relationship of his life, and things were going well. And it was true, Indy had supported him throughout his recovery. He'd been incredibly lucky. Another minute in the lift would have seen him dead. Along with everyone at the racetrack, the ambulance crew had been listening to his conversation with Hutchinson over the racecourse's public address system. They had been prepared to act as soon as the lift doors opened. Hutchinson's belt, although poorly twisted around his arm, had been the major reason he'd remained alive for that extra, all important minute. It was somewhat ironic given Hutchinson had only offered it as a means to falsely prove he'd attempted to help his lift companion.

A number of days in hospital to repair his partially severed artery had been followed by a proper grilling from the police. They'd taken a dim view of him failing to get them involved until he was laying half-dead on the floor of a lift, but hadn't charged him with anything. He surmised that this case had given them enough villains to be going on with.

Gerard had been taken to the same hospital suffering from

severe concussion and a nasty cut to his head. Joe had wondered how the personal assistant had taken the news he murdered the wrong man, reflecting that the luckless Cooper had never lived long enough to realise he'd been set up. His foul mouth had unfortunately sealed his fate; he'd been abusive to the wrong man, at the wrong time.

Horowitz and Hutchinson had both been charged with fraud and attempted murder. Joe had tried to impress upon the police that Horowitz's mental health should be examined, but he wasn't too sure they would follow through on his request, given the money he'd stolen still hadn't been traced. It had been spirited away and apparently Horowitz was unable, or unwilling, to provide details of the bank accounts he had washed the millions through, once the money left Fairbet.

As expected, Horowitz's colleagues at the BHA had condemned his involvement and immediately attempted to distance themselves from any wrongdoing. Fairbet suffered weeks of negative coverage in the press, and plenty of criticism from their customers. Gray had initially attempted to stem the flood of customers leaving the betting exchange, but eventually called in help to repair the hole in the company's finances. It was no surprise to Joe when three months later it was announced that Fairbet had been put up for sale.

He hadn't cared too much what happened to Gray, but was hugely relieved when he learned Sparky and Charlotte had been released with nothing more than warnings, due in main to Gray and the BHA offering no evidence. As for Charlotte and Gray, Sparky had intimated that they were on speaking terms, but not much else.

Billie Davenport had also made a recovery, although hers wasn't as speedy as his own. She had needed three weeks of hospital treatment before being allowed home. A further period of recuperation had seen her return to work three months after her attack, where her heightened public image had meant she walked straight into a presenting job on the racing channel.

A further relief had been to learn that Ronnie had recovered from being beaten around the head by Simon's extinguisher. Thankfully, it appeared Ronnie had no recollection of how he'd sustained the head injury. All three Mercedes men were in custody, awaiting trial for a number of offences, including grievous bodily harm.

Joe rounded the corner of Leazes Park Road, bracing himself against the chill breeze. The sound of music overlaid with the crackle of conversation, laughter, and the clink of glasses, reached him before the door to McGruder's was in sight. Entering the Irish pub, he pulled off his hat and gloves and was shocked to find Neil standing at the bar with a pint in his hand and an expectant smile. He started to make his way toward him, only to find Sparky and Simon popping up with cheesy grins and wishing him well.

Joe found his girlfriend in her favourite booth, a red leather ellipse large enough to seat eight people. She was being propped up by Taz and Billie on one side and to his surprise and delight, Sandie on the other. She flashed him a big grin when he appeared at the table.

'Here's our favourite race caller!' screamed Sparky from behind him, sporting a new piercing through her tongue and waving a shot glass around. Despite only turning eighteen a few weeks earlier, Sparky had previously proven herself more than capable of drinking Joe under the table on a visit to his house at Seaton Delaval a few weeks earlier.

'What's going on?' he asked, a little confused, 'Why are you all here?'

'We're celebrating!' Indy cheered, raising her pint of stout. It was immediately clinked by everyone with a glass in their hands. Joe watched on, vaguely amused, waiting patiently for an explanation.

Sandie said, 'When Indy called with her news I decided it was a good excuse to meet up… and I fancied a day shopping in Newcastle too!'

Joe narrowed his eyes and examined Sandie closely, suddenly switching his gaze to Indy.

'You're not…?'

Indy, her eyes sparkling, shook her head, enjoying Joe's few seconds of uncertainly.

'No, not that! How would that be even possible,' she exclaimed reproachfully.

She shared a giggling fit with Sandie and then announced, 'Come on, everyone, drink up. There's something Sparky and I want to show you all.'

Indy's request was initially greeted with groans, but once they realised she was serious, everyone grabbed their coats. Ten minutes later all eight of them were standing outside an empty shop on the

Great North Road following a short walk towards the east of the city. Joe had realised where they were going once they got within a hundred yards of the road, famous for the string of motorbike showrooms and various other bike related shops clustered at the bottom of the hill.

It was Joe's turn to have a big grin on his face.

'I think it's perfect,' he told Indy.

She wrapped her arms around him and planted a warm kiss on his chilled cheek.

'Sparky and I have become business partners.'

'And the money came from?'

Indy gave him a sheepish grin, 'A loan from a businessman.'

'You mean Michael Gray?'

'Well, he's got all that money... and we still had to get it past him. But Sparky and I were quite persuasive.'

'She threatened to go and move in with him again, didn't she?' Joe joked.

Sparky appeared, placing her arms around both of them and sticking her head between their shoulders.

'Naa! Indy took Dad out for a ride on the back of her bike and he gave her the investment on the spot. That was with a proviso that he never had to ride a bike with her again!'

Indy opened the shop up, switched on the lights so they lit up the road and invited everyone to tour their currently empty, retail empire. While Sparky took the small group into the shop and started to share their plans for the space, Indy remained outside on the pavement and held onto Joe, pulling him back when he made to go in.

'Am I doing the right thing?' she whispered, staring up at the shop's blank façade.

'Absolutely. It's a great idea. Electric bikes, motorbikes, and scooters are the way forward. More importantly, you'll be working with something you love.'

'Thanks,' she replied, 'That means a lot.'

'So what about a name?'

Indy grinned, 'I haven't decided. Sparky likes the sound of e-Biker Chicks.'

'Hmm… catchy but perhaps it could do with some refinement,' Joe suggested with a touch of alarm, 'How about Indy's e-Bikes?'

'That's just as bad,' she replied with a shake of her head.

Joe rubbed his chin and joined her, looking up at the blank façade.

Twenty seconds later Indy was still gazing upwards, transfixed by the backlit fascia. She seemed distracted, and Joe remained silent, only moving to take her gloved hand in his as the pause in their conversation lengthened.

'You know I'm going to have to find somewhere to live locally,' she said quietly, squeezing Joe's hand, 'It's been nice spending the odd night with you, but… I need something more permanent.'

Joe allowed a few seconds to tick by while he pretended to ruminate, blowing his cheeks out a couple of times.

'Well, I know this little place up in Seaton Delaval. It's got all the mod cons and breakfast is thrown in for free. I believe the landlord is very accommodating and the rent is incredibly cheap.'

Finding his other hand Indy lifted her finely sculpted chin upwards and faced him. Joe looked into her immense brown eyes, and they leaned against each other, their breath condensing between them in a cloudy dance.

'So, has this des-res got a spare room for a lodger?' Indy enquired, her eyes attaining a new, playful twinkle.

'Oh yes. And I believe the landlord lives on site.'

'And will the landlord *promise* to keep to his own room?'

'Ahh...'

'Ahh?'

'Yes, Ahh…' Joe answered with a smile on his lips, 'This landlord takes his promises extremely seriously.'

Indy glanced away for a moment, as if in thought. A car swished past, sending the chill air swirling around them. She pulled Joe closer.

'That's okay,' she said, close enough to feel Joe's breath on her cheeks, 'I'm not sure it's a promise I'd want you to keep.'

Fifty-Three

With an index finger hovering over the button on his mouse, Michael Gray hesitated, once again considering the ramifications of deleting the last remaining copy of his hacking code.

He had underestimated the sense of loss he would experience, having sold Fairbet to a huge American gaming conglomerate. Despite their lucrative offers, he'd also decided not to work for them. He knew it would have ended in acrimony; he wasn't a corporate player. But there were already benefits. He tried to remember when his last panic attack had struck and realised it had been two months since his last episode.

And then there were Charlotte and Ruth. His relationship with his daughter remained lukewarm, but was slowly improving. Agreeing to release a significant investment into a retail venture with her biker friend had been against his better judgment, but worthwhile in terms of increasing his contact with his daughter. It meant Ruth had to report to him on a bi-monthly basis, and he'd already noticed that when she aimed sarcastic remarks at him, they were loaded with far less vitriol. Charlotte had approved of this involvement in his daughter's life, and the rebuilding of their own relationship was progressing, slowly but surely. Letting go of Fairbet had helped enormously. Now the sale was complete he was hoping she would agree to join him on holiday. He couldn't remember taking a holiday that hadn't been linked to his business interests since... to be honest, he couldn't remember *any*.

Even the authorities appeared to be on his side at present. They had recently confirmed that the fraud he'd committed twenty years ago was unlikely to result in any court proceedings. Despite Hutchinson's efforts to reduce his jail sentence by squealing to the police about a catalogue of his CEO's alleged misdeeds at Fairbet, the CPS had recommended no further action against him. It proved somewhat ironic that Hutchinson's skills as a financial controller at Fairbet had led the authorities to accept there were no charges to bring against Gray... due to lack of evidence. Hutchinson's obsessive attention to detail and ability to cover up any dubious activities had created a situation where he was effectively unable to incriminate his CEO.

So, here he was, on day one of the rest of his life, alone in a largely bare house, sitting at his impressive arrangement of desk, keyboards, monitors, powerful computers, and industrial sized internet pipe, about to expunge from existence the last remaining evidence linking him to his hacking code. He'd seen to it that every other copy of the twenty-year-old version was now inoperable. All that was left was his own, updated, personal version which he had used on that day in Pontefract, by linking remotely to his server, here, at his home.

Gray couldn't help but smile with satisfaction. He'd perfected the new version of the hacking code only a few days before Davenport had started to publish her blogs. It ran from his own, personal server, accessing the exchange betting system through an invisible backdoor; an electronic route he had written into the core processing of Fairbet. The old code had been clunky, and would never have amassed the million pounds every fifteen minutes Ronnie had demanded. He'd responded by using his new, updated hacking code. By connecting Billie's laptop to his own server and running the new code, he'd been able to send the eight million pounds to Horowitz's Fairbet account. He was proud of the new code and that made erasing it… troublesome.

Gray left his chair and stalked around the house, trying to weigh up the pros and cons of leaving the code on his private server… just in case. After five minutes of aimless wandering, he found himself staring at a photograph of his daughter, the only one Charlotte had left in the house when she'd moved out. Ruth was three-years-old, sitting on his shoulders, and he was holding tightly onto her tiny red wellingtons. It was autumn, and he was standing under a huge maple tree in Roundhay Park in Leeds. The little girl was looking up, her arms raised and tiny fingers clawing at the air, trying to catch one of the huge flat leaves as they cascaded down upon them on a light breeze. Ruth looked insanely happy.

He had all the money he could ever spend. He had his health. Why would he need some hacking code for a business he no longer owned? He had far more important things to occupy his time.

Back at his desk, Gray brought up the folder that contained the hacking code. He was about to activate the erase command when something caught his eye. A text file had appeared from nowhere. It had just popped into existence, as if the act of opening the folder had summoned its creation.

Gray took in the title of the file: youve-been-hacked.txt.

He froze, gawping at his monitor in disbelief. He hadn't

created that file, there could only be one explanation. He clicked on the file, a sick feeling in his stomach. It opened immediately and displayed a few lines of text.

Hi Dad,
I watched you using this version of the hacking code in that room at Pontefract races. If I can hack into your server, so can plenty of other hackers. Erase the code. NOW!
Love,
Sparky247

P.S. I'll know if you haven't.

Gray allowed himself a minute to calm down, another minute to marvel at his daughter's ingenuity, and a further ten seconds to watch as all traces of his hacking code were being erased.

Enjoyed this story?

I do hope you have enjoyed reading this horseracing story. If you have, I'd *really* appreciate it if you would visit the Amazon website and leave a rating and perhaps a short review. Your ratings and reviews help readers find my books, which in turn means I can dedicate more time to writing.

Simply visit **www.amazon.co.uk** and search for 'Richard Laws'.

You can also register for my book alert emails and news on upcoming books at **www.thesyndicatemanager.co.uk**

Many thanks,

Richard Laws
January 2021

Printed in Great Britain
by Amazon

62924261R00149